The Husky & His White Cat Shizun

ERHA HE TA DE BAI MAO SHIZUN

2

The Husky & His White Cat Shizun

ERHA HE TA DE BAI MAO SHIZUN

2

WRITTEN BY

Rou Bao Bu Chi Rou

ILLUSTRATED BY

St

TRANSLATED BY

Rynn & Jun

Seven Seas Entertainment

THE HUSKY & HIS WHITE CAT SHIZUN:
ERHA HE TA DE BAI MAO SHIZUN VOL. 2

Cover and Interior Illustrations by St

Seven Seas press and purchase enquiries can be sent to Marketing Manager Lianne Sentar at press@gomanga.com. Information regarding the distribution and purchase of digital editions is available from Digital Manager CK Russell at digital@gomanga.com.

Follow Seven Seas Entertainment online at sevenseasentertainment.com.

TRANSLATION: Rynn, Jun
SPECIAL THANKS: Suika, Peri, Fim
COVER DESIGN: M. A. Lewife
INTERIOR DESIGN: Clay Gardner
INTERIOR LAYOUT: Karis Page
PROOFREADER: Jehanne Bell, Hnä
COPY EDITOR: Stephanie Cohen
EDITOR: E.M. Candon
BRAND MANAGER: Lissa Pattillo
PREPRESS TECHNICIAN: Melanie Ujimori, Jules Valera
EDITOR-IN-CHIEF: Julie Davis
ASSOCIATE PUBLISHER: Adam Arnold
PUBLISHER: Jason DeAngelis

ISBN: 978-1-63858-933-4
Printed in Canada
First Printing: January 2023
10 9 8 7 6 5 4 3 2 1

TABLE OF CONTENTS

46 This Venerable One Awakens

When Mo Ran came to, he discovered that he was still inside the holy weapon arsenal. It seemed he had been asleep for a long while, but when he opened his eyes, he found that not much time had passed. In fact, everything he had just endured might have passed in the blink of an eye.

He didn't know if it was because the spell had been successfully broken, but when he woke, he found he was lying on the ground without a single injury. That savage wound, that blood and gore—they were nothing more than a nightmare. They had left not a trace on his body.

Despite himself, Mo Ran was both surprised and delighted. Then he looked over to Shi Mei. He didn't know when Shi Mei had lost consciousness, but he was also free from harm.

Was it possible that, after Shi Mei passed the Exalted Gouchen's trial, Gouchen had not only broken the illusion, but had healed the wounds they had received within it?

Hm... Although when Mo Ran thought about it, it wasn't like Gouchen the Exalted wanted to *hurt* them, just test them. So this made sense. All the same, it didn't feel real to Mo Ran, and he still felt like he'd barely escaped with his life.

Among the four of them, he was the first to wake. The next to rise was Shi Mei. At the sight of Shi Mei's lashes slowly fluttering open,

Mo Ran was overjoyed. "Shi Mei!" he exclaimed eagerly. "We're all right! Quite all right! Quick, look at me!"

Within Shi Mei's gaze there was, at first, a flash of confusion. Then he gradually became more lucid, and his eyes abruptly widened. "A-Ran?! You—"

Before he could finish, Mo Ran wrapped him in a tight embrace.

Shi Mei couldn't help but be taken aback, but he gently patted Mo Ran's shoulder and said hesitantly, "What's with you?"

"I'm sorry that I made you suffer so."

Shi Mei was perplexed. "Well, it wasn't really anything. I just had a dream, that's all."

"But the pain was real!" Mo Ran protested.

"What pain?" Shi Mei asked.

Just then, Xue Meng also woke. There was no telling what dreams he'd had, but as he shot up, he yelled, "Insolent ruffian! How dare you feel me up!"

At the sight of him rising, Shi Mei walked over. "Young master."

"Huh... You? Why are *you* here?" Xue Meng apparently thought he was still dreaming.

Mo Ran was in a great mood, and consequently his attitude toward Xue Meng was rather soft. He smiled as he gave an account of the events that had just unfolded. Only then did reality dawn on Xue Meng.

"So it was a dream... And here I thought..." In order to hide his awkwardness, Xue Meng cleared his throat. At that moment, he discovered that Chu Wanning, typically the most powerful among them, was still asleep, not yet roused. He was astonished in spite of himself. "How come Shizun hasn't woken up?"

The trio approached to examine Chu Wanning's wounds. Chu Wanning had been injured before the illusion activated, and

Gouchen the Exalted's trial only healed those injuries suffered within the illusion. Thus his shoulder was still soaked in a great deal of blood, making it a shocking sight.

Mo Ran sighed. "Let's wait a bit longer."

It took about half an hour before Chu Wanning finally came to. He slowly opened his phoenix eyes, and when he woke, his gaze was empty and cold, as if veiled by the thick blanket of white left by a heavy snow. It was a long time before his eyes moved, and they fell upon Mo Ran.

However, like Xue Meng, it seemed that for the time being, he hadn't completely freed himself of his dream. Chu Wanning gazed at Mo Ran, then slowly reached out, his voice cracking. "You..."

"Shizun," Mo Ran said.

Upon hearing Mo Ran call him thus, Chu Wanning's hand paused in midair. A trace of warmth finally seemed to appear on his pale face, and his eyes also suddenly brightened. "Mn..."

"Shizun!" Xue Meng shoved Mo Ran aside and threw himself at Chu Wanning to clutch his hand. "Are you all right? Are you feeling better? Shizun, it took you so long to wake up—I was going to die from worry!"

When Chu Wanning saw Xue Meng, he was slightly bemused. Then the thin layer of fog in his eyes gradually faded. Now that he could take a closer look at Mo Ran, he saw that while Mo Ran was looking back at him, he was holding Shi Mei's hand tightly. He had never let go, not for a second.

The sight gave Chu Wanning pause, and as he more fully woke, his expression cooled. Then, like a fish in a dried-up pond, it utterly died.

"Shizun, are you all right?" Shi Mei asked, concerned. "Does your shoulder hurt?"

"I'm fine," Chu Wanning replied tranquilly. "It doesn't hurt."

With Xue Meng's assistance, he slowly stood. Mo Ran was a little puzzled. Chu Wanning had hurt his shoulder, so why was he stepping so gingerly as he rose, like it was his feet that had been injured?

Mo Ran, assuming that Chu Wanning didn't know what had happened in the illusion, once again offered a brief account.

When Shi Mei had first heard the tale, he'd thought that something about it wasn't right. Now that he heard it again, he felt even more perplexed. Unable to hold back, he said, "A-Ran, you say I was the one who saved you?"

"Yeah."

Shi Mei was quiet for a moment, then said slowly, "But I...I was dreaming the whole time. I never woke up."

Mo Ran was taken aback, but he immediately laughed. "Stop joking around."

"I'm not joking," Shi Mei said. "I dreamed... I dreamed about my mom and dad. They were still alive. That dream was so real, I didn't think... I didn't think I could leave them behind. I really—"

He didn't finish before Chu Wanning said mildly, "That's not so strange. Gouchen probably wiped your memory of rescuing him. Either way, neither myself nor Xue Meng did it, and since he said it was you who did, then it must be so."

Shi Mei fell silent.

"Otherwise, what? Do you think Gouchen has a means by which to swap people's souls?" Chu Wanning asked coldly.

Chu Wanning hadn't wanted to suffer all that for nothing, and he had originally intended to tell Mo Ran the truth. He'd furthermore hoped that Mo Ran would realize that the person within the illusion hadn't been Shi Mei, but Chu Wanning, with whom his heart had been switched. However, when Mo Ran confessed his feelings to Shi Mei at the end, it had become too embarrassing for Chu Wanning to bear.

When Chu Wanning woke, he had gazed into Mo Ran's bright black eyes. For a moment, Chu Wanning had thought that perhaps, deep in his heart, Mo Ran did care for him, even if just a little.

It was such a modest and unassuming hope, a vulnerable thought that only dared to surface quietly, and after a long, long stretch of time.

As it turned out, it had all been in his head. The blood Chu Wanning had bled, the injuries he'd suffered, Mo Ran knew nothing of them—and neither was there a need for him to know.

Chu Wanning wasn't stupid. Even if Mo Ran didn't say anything, it was easy to see just how much he treasured the gentle and beautiful person beside him. Why would Mo Ran ever turn his gaze toward Chu Wanning, who stood in the corner like a puppet covered in dust?

Yet even when he'd heard the words, "I've always liked you," pass Mo Ran's lips, Chu Wanning had still felt like he'd conclusively lost. That he had suffered an unmistakably miserable defeat.

To Mo Ran, that embrace within an illusion had been charity that Shi Mei bestowed upon him. Mo Ran would never, ever know that this embrace had instead been charity that he bestowed upon another pitiful soul.

Chu Wanning had never believed that Mo Ran would ever like him in that way, so he had done his best to suppress his own feelings. He never acted on them, never disturbed them, never went near them.

Reckless affection and passionate, obsessive entanglements, these things only grew in the soil of youth. When Chu Wanning was young, he'd also hoped there might be someone who would stay by his side, with whom he might share wine beneath the moon, but he'd waited and waited, and still this person had never arrived. Later, as time passed day by day, his reputation within the cultivation world had climbed higher and higher, and everyone had placed him on a pedestal. While they greatly admired him, they'd kept their distance and called him cold-hearted. Eventually, he'd come to accept the pedestal as well as the cold heart.

It was as if he was hiding in a cocoon, and time was continuously spinning silk around him. At first, he had still seen some light from the outside seeping through the walls, but year after year, there was more and more silk, and the cocoon grew thicker and thicker, so much so that he could no longer see the light. Within the cocoon there was only himself, and the darkness.

Chu Wanning didn't believe in love, nor in chance encounters, and he certainly didn't want to go chasing after any such thing. If he were to arduously gnaw through the cocoon, getting cut and scraped all over in the process, and come crawling clumsily out only to find no one waiting for him on the other side—what would he do?

Perhaps he did like Mo Ran, but this boy was too young, too far out of reach, and too fiery. Chu Wanning didn't want to get close, lest one day that flame burn him to ashes.

Thus, any time he could take a step back, he did.

He didn't know where he had gone wrong. What had he done, for even such a small daydream to be drowned by storming, frigid rain?

"Shizun, look over there, quick!"

Xue Meng's sudden startled cry brought Chu Wanning's mind back to the present, and his gaze followed the call only to see that roaring molten metal was again rolling in the crucible. The ancient tree spirit broke through the waters once more, wreathed with flames. However, the tree spirit's eyes were rolled back; it was obviously not in its right mind. In its hands, it held that shimmering silver sword, the sacred blade of Gouchen the Exalted.

"Run! Quickly!" Chu Wanning barked.

There was no need to repeat himself. His disciples dashed toward the exit.

The controlled tree spirit raised its head toward the sky and shrieked. The iron chains that hung across his body rattled violently, clinking and clanking. No one had spoken, but all four of them simultaneously heard a voice in their ears:

Stop them. Not a single one shall escape.

"Someone's talking in my head!" Xue Meng cried out in dismay.

"Don't pay him any mind," Chu Wanning said. "It's the Heart-Pluck Willow's technique: Temptation of the Heart! Just focus on escaping!"

Now that he said it, the rest remembered. The Heart-Pluck Willow had warned them while he retained consciousness. Temptation of the Heart used the greed and desire in people's hearts as bait to compel them to slaughter one another.

Sure enough, the voice in Chu Wanning's ears hissed, *Chu Wanning, aren't you tired? Esteemed Zongshi, Yuheng of the Night Sky. Such a distinguished individual, yet you're reduced to pining for your own disciple in secret. You have given him much, and he's taken it all for granted. He never had eyes for you—he only likes that gentle and beautiful little shige. How pitiful.*

Chu Wanning's face turned ashen. He furiously ignored the noise in his ears and continued to run for the exit.

Come to my side and take up this Ancestral Sword, then kill Shi Mei and no one will stand between you. Come to my side—I can help you achieve your wish for your beloved to love only you. Come to my side...

"What a reprobate—get the hell out!" Chu Wanning snarled angrily.

The disciples were obviously also hearing the various enticements that voice proposed. While their pace slowed, they fought the temptation. The closer they got to the exit, the more the Heart-Pluck Willow seemed to thrash in his madness. The hissing howls in their ears became practically gnarled.

Think it through! Once you're past that door, you'll never get another chance!

The voices within their ears differed, but all shrieked sharply.

Chu Wanning, Chu Wanning, do you truly wish to be alone for the rest of your days?

Mo Weiyu, I'm the only person in this world who knows where to find the resurrection pill. Come to me, let me tell you—

Shi Mingjing, I know the desire that lies in the deepest recesses of your heart—only I can help you!

Xue Ziming, the holy weapon you chose was a counterfeit! There is only one weapon left in Jincheng Lake that was forged by Gouchen the Exalted. Return and it's yours! Don't you desire a magnificent holy weapon? Don't you wish to be the darling of the heavens? Without a holy weapon, you'll never measure up to the rest! Come to me...

"Xue Meng!" Mo Ran suddenly realized that his cousin, who had been running by his side, had disappeared. He whipped his head around only to see Xue Meng's steps slowing until, eventually, they came to a stop. Xue Meng was looking back to gaze at a silvery blue sacred sword, floating up and down in the crucible.

Mo Ran's heart lurched. He knew how Xue Meng obsessed over holy weapons. When the kid first realized that the weapon he'd received was a forgery, he must've been crushed. The Heart-Pluck Willow really knew how to hit below the belt, tempting him with the Ancestral Sword.

"Xue Meng, don't believe him. Don't go!"

"Young master, let's go," Shi Mei chimed in. "We're almost at the exit!"

Looking lost, Xue Meng turned his head back and glanced at them. All the while, the voice echoing in his head grew even more hypnotizing.

They're jealous of you. They don't want you to have a holy weapon. Think about Mo Weiyu—he's already won his weapon, so of course he'd rather you have nothing. You two are brothers, but if you fail to be his better, then the position of honored leader of Sisheng Peak will naturally fall to him.

"Shut up," Xue Meng muttered. In front of him, Mo Ran seemed to be anxiously yelling something, but he couldn't hear anything distinctly. He could only hug his head and cry out repeatedly, "You shut your mouth! Shut up!"

Xue Ziming, no weapons suitable for you remain in the holy weapon arsenal. If you give up the Ancestral Sword, in the future, you will have no choice but to submit yourself in servitude to Mo Weiyu. When that time comes, he will be your master. You will be obliged to kneel before him, to obey his every command! Just think, if you kill him, none of that will come to pass! Fratricide has recurred time and time again throughout history, and he's only your cousin! Why should you hesitate? Come, allow me to give you the sword...

"Xue Meng!"

"Young master!"

Xue Meng suddenly ceased his struggling, and his eyes shot open, his pupils red.

Come to my side... You are the darling of the heavens... You are worthy to lead an army of millions...

"Xue Meng!" Chu Wanning shouted sharply.

Come here... Only when you've become the leader of Sisheng Peak will the lower cultivation world know peace... Think of those who suffer; think of the injustices you have all *suffered... Xue Ziming, let me help you...*

Unwittingly, Xue Meng had already approached the bubbling crucible. The spirit of the Heart-Pluck Willow presented him with the Ancestral Sword of Gouchen the Exalted. Bloody veins crawled across the whites of its rolled eyes.

Very good. Take this sword and go. Stop them!

Xue Meng slowly raised his trembling hand and took that silvery blue sacred blade.

Kill them. Kill Mo Weiyu. Quickly... Augghh!

Xue Meng abruptly unsheathed the longsword, the weapon a splendid steel blossom in his hand. Then he swung, striking swiftly with a backhand swing. The handsome visage of the darling of the heavens was brilliantly reflected in the spiritual aura of the Ancestral Sword. Illuminated by the shine of the blade, his eyes were clearer and brighter than ever before, and not the least bit drunk on bloodlust.

This strike was directed not at Mo Ran. Rather, Xue Meng lunged straight for the body of the Heart-Pluck Willow and pierced through its abdomen.

Instantly, the earth juddered, and the ancient willow shook. The spell was broken, and the interior of the holy weapon arsenal began to crack and collapse.

Xue Meng panted harshly; he had used everything he had to break free from the enchantment. He glared at the Heart-Pluck Willow, his young face filled with youthful innocence and determination. In those shining eyes gleamed both naivete and pride. There was more to the son of the phoenix than mere martial prowess, after all.

"Don't you bewitch me—and don't even think about harming anyone else." Xue Meng gasped as he finished and swiftly wrenched out the longsword.

The astringent stench of blood erupted from the Heart-Pluck Willow. As he slumped over in his dying moments, his consciousness returned to his body, and the resentful energy within him was thoroughly dispersed.

The Heart-Pluck Willow clutched his chest and arduously steadied his drooping body as he lifted his face. He opened then closed his mouth, and while no voice escaped him, the movement of his lips was easily interpreted.

Thank...you...for...stopping...me...

The Heart-Pluck Willow's original body was a spirit of ancient times, equal in power to the Ancestral Sword. Pitted against each other, both sword and spirit had been damaged irrevocably. The spiritual aura of the Ancestral Sword in Xue Meng's hand dimmed and wilted.

All at once, the form of this millennia-old tree spirit dissipated.

In an instant, millions of sparkles scattered into the crucible. They danced and circled overhead like flowing and fluttering fireflies, their golden shimmer bright, until finally they faded one by one, never to be seen again.

"Young master, come here, quickly!" Shi Mei called. "The arsenal is going to collapse!"

The earth was still shaking. They couldn't stay for long.

Xue Meng looked back and gave the holy weapon arsenal a final glance. Then he threw aside the destroyed Ancestral Sword with a clang and left. Behind him, bricks and shingles cascaded down like a crashing avalanche.

47 This Venerable One Feels Like Something Is Off

CHU WANNING WAS INJURED, and the three disciples were exhausted, so once they reached the corridor outside the arsenal, Chu Wanning ordered them to rest a while. No one spoke for a bit, either standing or sitting as they inspected the injuries on themselves or one another and recovered their strength.

That is, except for Xue Meng, who was staring at nothing with his head drooping, seemingly lost in thought.

"Xue Meng..." Mo Ran murmured.

Xue Meng paid no heed to anyone else. He only walked stiffly over to stand before Chu Wanning and look up. When he opened his mouth, his voice was like shattered glass. "Shizun."

When Chu Wanning looked at him, he felt an urge to pet his tousled hair, but in the end, he managed to push it down.

"The holy weapon I picked before, was it a fake?"

Chu Wanning was silent.

The rims of Xue Meng's eyes became even redder, and his eyes themselves grew bloodshot. If not for the pride and stubbornness that kept him upright, his tears would likely have fallen on the spot. "Does this mean I'll never be able to claim a holy weapon?"

Chu Wanning closed his eyes with a sigh. The corridor was silent save for his clear voice: "Silly child."

A single, "silly child," said with a helpless sigh, and the last of Xue Meng's rationality crumbled. Unable to endure it any longer, he threw himself into Chu Wanning's arms and, clinging to his waist, began to bawl.

"Shizun... Shizun..."

Failing to obtain a holy weapon from Jincheng Lake was tantamount to forfeiting one's potential to rise in the cultivation world; it meant surrendering one's chance to ever stand at the top. Everyone was well aware of this. A mortal's powers were finite, and without a holy weapon, however strong, a person was limited by their body of flesh and blood.

The young masters of the sects in the upper cultivation realm more or less all possessed holy weapons that had been passed down to them by their predecessors. Even though these weapons weren't perfectly compatible with their spiritual energies, they were still considerably powerful. Among the sects' young masters, Xue Meng alone had not received a holy weapon from Jincheng Lake, as Xue Zhengyong and his brother had started from scratch.

And so, when Xue Meng had chosen to wield the Ancestral Sword against the Heart-Pluck Willow and thereby destroyed them both, he had essentially chosen to sacrifice his spirited ambitions to rise above everyone else.

Chu Wanning didn't ask him anything and didn't say any more. He only held Xue Meng and stroked his hair as the boy cried it out.

Xue Meng had grown up pampered, never really suffering any injustice. He spent all his days arrogantly strutting about, and ever since he was old enough to remember, he had never once cried. But at this moment, tears streaked down his youthful face, and his every word came out broken like the holy weapon he would never have—like the lionhearted aspirations that he had once thought were a sure thing. All of them lay shattered.

"Xue Meng." Chu Wanning held his disciple in his arms, consoling him.

The waves at the bottom of the lake rippled past Chu Wanning's white cloak and his long, inky hair. In that instant, Mo Ran could see aught but for his fine curtain of lashes lowering over the fragments of gentle light beneath them. Then the waves picked up, ruffling hair and garment, and he could no longer see Chu Wanning's face clearly in the dim light. He could only hear him say, "Don't cry. You're already great."

His voice wasn't quite gentle, but when those words came from Chu Wanning's mouth, they were indescribably soft.

In the corridor, they had all fallen silent as they each dwelt on their own thoughts.

Mo Ran leaned against the ice-cold wall, watching Chu Wanning hold Xue Meng and pat his shoulder, and his own heart felt heavy.

On this journey to Jincheng Lake, they'd come all fresh and energized. Now they were leaving laden with wounds.

Xue Meng had been the darling of the heavens for fifteen years, well-regarded and high-spirited. In the span of a single day, his future had collapsed upon itself.

From here on out, he would have to spend the rest of his lengthy life striving to forget these fifteen years of blazing glory.

As they escaped from the arsenal, they saw the Heart-Pluck Willow buckling slowly into the crucible like an ancient colossus finally exhausted. Like the death of a gentle giant, or the demise of the sun itself. The remaining merfolk scattered in fright.

The holy weapon arsenal that had stood for millions of years was destroyed in an instant. The celestial tree fell with a deafening rumble and set off a surging tide throughout Jincheng Lake. Faced with the enormous whirlpool that resulted from it, the merfolk assumed their larger original forms in an attempt to weather the storm. Jincheng Lake was instantly filled with glimmering scales, with little room left for mere mortals.

"We can't get out this way!" Mo Ran shouted.

As he spoke, a thick sea dragon's tail smashed toward him. Mo Ran swiftly moved aside, barely managing to dodge.

A black dragon suddenly swooped forward, larger than all the others, its blue-black scales shimmering with a golden sheen.

"Wangyue?!" Mo Ran yelled, startled.

Wangyue let out a mighty roar, and the mute dragon spoke with a voice low like the chime of a great clock, "Climb on my back. With the destruction of the Heart-Pluck Willow, Jincheng Lake is soon to follow. Quickly! I will ferry you away!"

They didn't know if Wangyue was friend or foe, but having no other options, they could only do as instructed. Wangyue carried the four of them and surged through the perilous waves that were filled with thousands of dragons, the waters parting in his wake.

"Hold on tight!"

This was the ancient dragon's only warning before he lunged out of the lake and soared into the skies. The pressure hit his passengers like a ton of bricks, the flow of water like a thousand galloping horses against their bodies. They couldn't open their eyes, could hardly breathe, as they desperately clung with all their might to the dragon's back in order to not be flung into the lake.

By the time they could open their eyes again, they were high above Jincheng Lake and soaring through the clouds at the summit of Dawning Peak. Droplets of water flew off of the dragon's large, mirrored scales, and the spray turned into countless sparkles of light that manifested a rainbow in the sky. Wangyue raised his head in a roar as color washed over the land.

Mo Ran heard Xue Meng's voice from behind him against the fierce gale, full of excitement. He was indeed young, after all, and easily distracted from his worries. "Oh my god! I'm flying! On a dragon!"

Wangyue circled above Dawning Peak, gradually shrinking in size while descending. He landed on the bank of Jincheng Lake at less than half his original magnitude—so as to not crush the surrounding rocks and vegetation. The dragon stayed quietly in place while they dismounted.

When they turned to look toward Jincheng Lake, they saw that the thick frozen surface had melted. Waves churned and scattered fragments of ice. The first light of dawn lent the eastern skies a pure-white hue, and sunlight spilled into Jincheng Lake with a brilliant glimmer.

"Look at the dragons in the lake!" Shi Mei cried.

The dragons twisted and coiled in the waters, rising and falling with the waves, until they gradually stopped moving, at which point they crumbled one after another and turned into so many specks of dust. Black chess pieces floated up from the surface and gathered in midair.

"The Zhenlong Chess Formation..." Mo Ran muttered.

Everything in the lake, from the sea dragons to the Heart-Pluck Willow, had been under the control of the Zhenlong Chess Formation. All that had transpired below had been a match devised by someone hiding in the shadows.

Mo Ran shuddered. Something was off about this reborn era.

Certain events were occurring earlier than they should have, and for no apparent reason.

In his previous life, he was certain that no one had been able to command the Zhenlong Chess Formation with such mastery at the time when he had been sixteen. Just who was this fake Gouchen?

"Wangyue!" Xue Meng cried out.

Mo Ran turned only to see Wangyue crouching on the ground, unmoving. While no black chess piece emerged from his body, he appeared extremely weak, his eyes half-closed.

"You lot...did well... It's far preferable to see our Exalted God Gouchen's Jincheng Lake destroyed, than to...to see it fall into the hands of a villain..."

When Wangyue finished speaking, his body began to glow with golden light, and when the light subsided, he had assumed human form.

"It was you?!" Mo Ran and Xue Meng exclaimed simultaneously.

The Wangyue before them was the very same elderly, white-haired merman who had led them to the holy weapon arsenal. Wangyue lifted his head, a hint of guilt in his eyes. "It was me."

Xue Meng was shocked. "Y-you—why did you lead us to the arsenal? Do you mean us help or harm? If you mean harm, then why have you brought us ashore? But if you mean to help—if we hadn't passed the Heart-Pluck Willow's trial, wouldn't we have..."

Wangyue looked down, and his voice was hoarse as he said, "Please accept my apologies. Circumstances being what they were, there was naught else I could do. The false Gouchen's own cultivation is insufficient, and he relied wholly on the Heart-Pluck Willow's spiritual power to wield the forbidden technique. The only way to dispel his magic was to overcome the Heart-Pluck Willow. I had no choice but to vest my hope in the four of you."

Chu Wanning shook his head slightly, then walked over to Wangyue and began channeling spiritual energy to heal his injuries.

Wangyue let out a long sigh. "Daozhang is kind, but there is no need. It is my time. I am no different from the other creatures of the lake; I subsisted on the Heart-Pluck Willow's spiritual energy. Now that it has fallen, I am not long for this world."

Chu Wanning remained silent.

Wangyue continued, "The order of life and death cannot be altered. I have lived to see the nightmare of Jincheng Lake broken, so my wish is fulfilled. But I am full of remorse for having involved you in these perils."

"It's no matter," Chu Wanning said. After a pause, he asked, "Do you know the identity of the pretender, and what he wants?"

"I do not know his identity," Wangyue replied. "However, his goal was most likely to obtain the Heart-Pluck Willow's power in order to command the three forbidden techniques."

"The forbidden techniques require an incredible amount of spiritual energy," Chu Wanning muttered. "They would indeed be much easier to master with the help of an ancient tree spirit."

"Yes, that man said as much. He also said that while ancient spirits are immensely powerful, they are extremely difficult to find. The only one whose location can be traced from the ancient records was the Heart-Pluck Willow.

"The intruder appeared only recently, and after taking control of Jincheng Lake, he spent all his time at the bottom of its depths, using the Heart-Pluck Willow's power to practice the forbidden techniques of 'Rebirth' and the 'Zhenlong Chess Formation.'"

Wangyue sighed, his eyes somewhat empty and dull.

Mo Ran felt his heart drop. Sure enough, this trip to Jincheng Lake had been entirely different from the one in his past life, and everything that had caused the changes had taken place not long ago. Just what was going wrong to make these events change course?

"He lacked the strength to control living beings, so he killed innumerable creatures in the lake and attempted to control the dead instead. He managed this, and in a mere few weeks' time, he had slaughtered practically all who lived in the lake and turned them into chess pieces. He left only a few alive to experiment on, myself included."

"When you came out of the water to meet me, were you being controlled by the fake Gouchen?" Mo Ran asked.

"No." Wangyue slowly closed his eyes. "He may be able to control the others, like the fox spirit or even the Heart-Pluck Willow, but he cannot control me. I am a spirit beast who was tamed by Gouchen the Exalted at the creation of the world, millennia ago. When I submitted to being his steed, I was branded with his seal on my inverted scale,[1] and thus I shall be loyal to one master only in life and in death."

"Then why did you..."

"It was an act; I had no choice." Wangyue sighed. "The intruder may not have been able to totally control me, but the brand of Gouchen the Exalted is millions of years old, its effectiveness a mere fraction of its original potency. A portion of my body fell under the fake Gouchen's influence—the reason I was mute at our first meeting was because the pretender had control of my throat. Only when his magic was dispelled was I able to speak again."

"Did that fake Gouchen know you were pretending?" asked Mo Ran.

---

1 *In Chinese mythology, dragons possess an inverted scale on their throats. The scale must not be touched, lest the dragon kill the offender. The inverted scale is also used as a metaphor for a sore spot or weakness that can provoke strong negative reactions.*

"I doubt it." Wangyue looked to Mo Ran. "He planned to take your spiritual core today, in order to extend the Heart-Pluck Willow's life. He didn't anticipate that I would bring you back to the holy weapon arsenal to destroy the ancient willow, and he took no precautions against my interference."

"Perhaps it's not that he did not take precautions against you," Chu Wanning suddenly suggested, "but rather that he didn't have the strength to spare for any such thing."

"What does Daozhang mean?"

"There's another odd thing about this pretender."

48

This Venerable One's Old Dragon

NOW THAT CHU WANNING mentioned it, Mo Ran couldn't help but agree. His shizun was right.

A faint odor had followed the fake Gouchen. Mo Ran had thought he was imagining it, but if Chu Wanning had also noticed it, then there could be no mistake. The smell of death.

So not only was this Gouchen not the true god himself—he wasn't even a living person! In other words, the one behind this mess had just pulled the strings attached to a corpse dressed as the God of Weaponry. The real puppeteer wasn't even here.

Mo Ran's thoughts were interrupted by a low, sorrowful chuckle from the direction of Jincheng Lake. Immediately after, a deathly pale body shot out from the water like an arrow as the fake Gouchen leapt into the air. But both his appearance and behavior had become terrible to behold, his skin wrinkled all over like a snake in the midst of molting, or a silkworm writhing to break through its cocoon.

"Yuheng of the Night Sky, the Beidou Immortal. Chu-zongshi, you really do live up to your name." The fake Gouchen levitated above the crystalline water of the lake, face twisting into a semblance of a gnarled smirk even as pieces peeled off. "How did Rufeng Sect let someone like you slip through their fingers?"

Chu Wanning's voice was frosty as he asked, "Just who exactly are you?"

"You don't need to know who I am," said the fake Gouchen. "I won't let you know who I am either. You can just think of me as someone who should have died long ago—but who crawled out of hell solely to take the lives of you, the righteous and honorable!"

"Shameless!" Wangyue rumbled. "The Heart-Pluck Willow has been destroyed! With your strength alone, without the help of the holy tree, you neither have a way to use the forbidden techniques, nor a means to carry out further transgressions!"

The fake Gouchen sneered. "You old eel, on your last breath and still trying to get in my way. What makes you think you have the right to speak here? Get lost!"

"And do you think that you, as a white chess piece, have any right to speak?" Chu Wanning interrupted.

A "white chess piece," as implied by the name, was a special game piece in the Zhenlong Chess Formation. The individual using the technique could place a portion of their soul into a newly deceased body and fuse the two to form a chess piece as white as pure jade.

This white chess piece differed from the common black variety, which merely obeyed commands. In short, a white chess piece was a stand-in for the spellcaster. Though their spiritual power was weaker than that of their original form, they could think and act independently, and the things they saw and heard were conveyed to the person controlling them.

The fake Gouchen's identity was exposed, but his only reaction was to laugh and clap. "Very good! Good, good!"

After these three cries, the fake Gouchen's face had become even more broken and contorted. It seemed that the spell was nearing its end and was unable to support the white chess piece for much longer. Thus, the original form of the corpse was emerging.

"Chu Wanning, don't get too full of yourself now. Do you really think this will stop me? Even if the Heart-Pluck Willow was destroyed, my true self can always find other sources of spiritual energy. You, on the other hand..."

As the false god spoke, his eyes, which grew dimmer and less focused by the second, suddenly swept past Chu Wanning to land on Mo Ran, filled with malicious intent. Mo Ran was struck by a sudden wave of apprehension.

"If you think that I'm the only one in this world who knows the three forbidden techniques," the fake Gouchen said languidly, mockingly, "then I'm afraid you won't have much longer to live."

"What do you mean by that?" Chu Wanning demanded sternly, his eyebrows lowered in a frown.

However, the fake Gouchen ceased to speak. He froze, then exploded into foul-smelling chunks as a jade-white chess piece shot out from his body and whirled into the air, backlit by the rising sun—before it fell into Jincheng Lake with a plop.

It seemed that the puppeteer in the shadows, having lost the assistance of the Heart-Pluck Willow, had exhausted his spiritual energy.

Simultaneously, Wangyue, who had also relied on the Heart-Pluck Willow's spiritual energy to survive, staggered and fell to the ground with a thud. "Ah..."

Xue Meng let out a startled cry, "Wangyue!"

"Wangyue!" Mo Ran also exclaimed.

All four of them gathered around the old dragon. Wangyue was barely hanging on, his lips colorless. He looked to them and spoke with a voice that faltered like the setting sun. "Don't... Don't believe that man's nonsense. In his words, there was more...more falsehood than truth..."

Shi Mei's face brimmed with worry and sorrow. "Qianbei, please don't speak any further," he said softly. "Let me heal you."

"No, there's no need. If even your master couldn't do it...then... you..." Wangyue coughed roughly several times, then said, panting, "All these years, many came seeking weapons. But...when that villain arrived, the Heart-Pluck Willow was loath to let him claim the holy weapons left behind by our master, and so destroyed them all. The only ones remaining...were...were a willow vine equal to it in power, and the—the sword of the Exalted God..."

At the mention of this blade, Xue Meng's expression grew darker, his mouth set in a thin and wordless line.

"The willow vine...went to this young daozhang." Wangyue glanced at Mo Ran. "That day, by the lakeside, I said to you that even if you were evil in the past, I would not stop you, and that I could only hope that you would pursue virtue in the future... But in actuality...in actuality, in accordance with my master's wishes, holy weapons should belong only to the virtuous. That's why, I hope that you...that you will..."

Mo Ran understood that it was already difficult for him to speak, and so interrupted. "Don't worry, Qianbei. I understand."

"That's good... That's good..." Wangyue murmured. "Then I can... rest easy..."

He gazed skyward, lips trembling slightly.

"It is said that when one goes to Jincheng Lake seeking a weapon, a creature from the lake will...will make a request. Most of those requests...were to gauge the seeker's moral character, but there were the occasional exceptions..."

Wangyue's voice grew quieter and quieter, tens of thousands of years flitting past his eyes like a carousel lantern.

"I had an agreement with my master. When he departed, I was to stay and guard Jincheng Lake, without leaving... Who could have known that I would be standing guard for millennia upon millennia? The sights I beheld in my youth, the mountains and rivers... I never got to...to...see...them again..."

He turned his head slowly to gaze beseechingly at Mo Ran, his eyes flickering with a warm wetness. In that instant, Mo Ran suddenly knew what he was about to say.

Sure enough, Wangyue said softly, "Young Daozhang, the plum blossoms at the waist of the mountain bloom splendidly throughout the year. I was very fond of them when I was young. Even though you have already received your holy weapon, would you still...still be willing to..."

Mo Ran was about to say, Yes, I'll go get you a branch.

However, before he could even start, the light in Wangyue's golden eyes abruptly went out.

Jiangnan has little but for a gift of spring in the form of a blossoming branch.[2]

Snow-tipped peaks towered majestically in the distance, and gleaming gold danced resplendent on the lake surface as the rising sun bathed the waters in its red-hued light. The waves and spray shattered the rays into glimmering crimson.

Wangyue had passed.

He had been among the first dragons at the creation of the world, had once been earth-shakingly powerful, and had once bowed in servitude and carried his master to all corners of the land. Everyone had said that the brand compelled his submission, but it had been his respect for Gouchen that bound him to his millennia-long promise.

---

2 *An excerpt from "Poems for Fanye," by Lu Kai; Jiangnan is a region of China, south of the Yangtze River, known for its beautiful spring scenery.*

In this vast land, few remained who remembered the founding of the world. Wangyue knew. He knew that although the real Gouchen the Exalted's veins coursed with demonic blood, his mother had been taken against her will. Gouchen had abhorred demons, and so stood with Fuxi against their invasion. He had used that very powerful demonic blood of his to forge the first true sword for Fuxi's hand, and had aided him in eradicating the demon race from the mortal realm.

But after the unification of heaven and earth, Fuxi had harbored misgivings and resentment toward Gouchen the Exalted, due to that half-demon blood. Gouchen the Exalted was no fool; a hundred years later, he excused himself from the realm of the gods of his own volition and descended to the realm of man.

During his journey, he saw endless suffering and slaughter. He concluded that he shouldn't have brought the very notion of "sword" into existence, and he was filled with remorse. So, he gathered many of the weapons he had left in the mortal realm, sealed them in the arsenal in Jincheng Lake, planted the Heart-Pluck Willow as guardian, and instructed the creatures of the lake that of those who came seeking, only the virtuous were befitting.

Now Gouchen was no more and Wangyue had passed. Henceforth there would be no more holy weapons within Jincheng Lake, and no more merfolk. With the thunderous fall of the Heart-Pluck Willow, all of these sins and acts of repentance, the distortion and dedication, had scattered like smoke and ash.

For a moment, no one spoke. In the ferocious snowstorm, the scarlet words written on the stone tablet by the side of Jincheng Lake—"The Path Forward is Difficult"—were the same as when they had first seen them. Meanwhile, the surface of the lake, now serene, hid all the calamity and suffering that had transpired beneath it.

It looked just like it had when they first climbed up Dawning Peak, when they were as yet unaware of the bloody story hidden behind "The Path Forward is Difficult."

Mo Ran looked up at the sky. Above the precipice of the peak, a lone eagle soared against the snowdrift.

He suddenly thought of how, in his past life, Wangyue had given him a powerful long blade. In this life, the blade he'd seen was a mere fake, and the original that had once belonged to him had likely already been destroyed by the Heart-Pluck Willow before he could so much as glimpse it.

A short while passed and, unbidden, Mo Ran's mind conjured up old memories.

It was the year he had come to Jincheng Lake seeking a weapon. Wangyue emerged from the water, studied him with golden eyes that were gentle and friendly, and said:

"The plum blossoms at the waist of the mountain are blooming beautifully. Could you go retrieve a branch for me?"

Mo Ran closed his eyes and raised an arm to cover them. He didn't know what events had transpired below the lake in his past life. At the time, he had taken Wangyue's request for pointless pretentiousness...

It took many days before they returned to Sisheng Peak. Chu Wanning's shoulder was seriously injured, and the three youths were exhausted, so they rested at Dai City for several days before returning.

Xue Meng said nothing of what had happened to Xue Zhengyong and Madam Wang. Proud as he was, regardless of whether his parents reacted with disappointment or sympathy, either would be salt in the wound. Chu Wanning noticed this, and his heart ached. So, he buried himself in ancient tomes and scrolls all day, searching for some other way of obtaining a holy weapon for Xue Meng, or else some means of allowing a mortal to rival a holy weapon in strength.

Apart from this, just who had that fake Gouchen been, and where was his true self? And what was the meaning behind the last thing that white chess piece had said before it disintegrated?

There were many and more things to worry about, and so the candle in the library of the Red Lotus Pavilion burned all night as the water clock dripped away. Scrolls scrawled with complicated passages littered the floor, and buried in the depths of the files was Chu Wanning's exhausted face.

"Yuheng, look at the state of your shoulder. Don't be so reckless." Xue Zhengyong sat next to him and chattered fussily, holding a warm cup of tea. "The Tanlang Elder is a master of the healing arts; make some time and go have him take a look."

"No need. It's already started to heal."

Xue Zhengyong clicked his tongue. "That won't do. Look at yourself—you've looked terrible ever since you got back. Nine out of ten people who've seen you say you seem like you're about to pass out. If you ask me, there's something strange about that wound. Might be some kind of poison or whatever. It's better to be careful."

Chu Wanning glanced up. "I seem like I'm about to pass out?" He paused and smiled coldly. "Who said that?"

Xue Zhengyong paused for a long moment before eventually saying, "Aiya, Yuheng, can you not always act like you're made of metal and everyone else is made of paper?"

"I know my own limits."

Xue Zhengyong mumbled something inaudibly. From the

movement of his lips, it was very possibly, "Know your limits, my ass." Luckily, Chu Wanning was too absorbed in his book to see.

They chatted for a while longer, until Xue Zhengyong saw that it was getting late and got up to head back and keep his wifey company. Before leaving, he made sure to fuss some more. "Yuheng, don't stay up too late. Meng-er will die of guilt if he sees you like this."

Chu Wanning ignored him with gusto.

Having been met with such a frosty reception, Xue Zhengyong could only scratch his head awkwardly and leave.

Chu Wanning drank some medicine, then returned to the table to continue his research until he started feeling a bit light-headed. He propped his forehead in one hand, nauseous. The nausea faded in short order, so he chalked it up to being tired and paid it no heed.

The night grew late, and finally too woozy to continue, Chu Wanning fell asleep with his brows drawn tightly together and his head pillowed on a sweeping sleeve next to the small mountain of tomes. An unfinished scroll still lay across his knees while the hem of his robes drooped to the floor like a water wave.

That night, he dreamt. This dream, unlike most, was clear and distinct, nearly real.

Chu Wanning was standing within Loyalty Hall of Sisheng Peak, but this Loyalty Hall was somewhat different from the one he knew; many furnishings and details had been altered. Before he had a chance to take a closer look, the gates swung open, setting crimson curtains adrift.

A person walked in.

"Shizun."

This individual had a handsome face and deep-black eyes tinted purple. He was a young man, but when he curled the corners of his lips, he looked almost childlike.

"Mo Ran?" Chu Wanning stood and was about to walk over, but he found that his wrists and ankles were shackled by four lengths of metal chains that flowed with spiritual power. They fettered him in place and rendered him unable to move.

Shock was followed by overflowing rage. Chu Wanning glared at the chains with disbelief, anger twisting his expression and stoppering his words. It was a good while before he lifted his head to say harshly, "Mo Weiyu, what do you think you're doing? Unbind me at once!"

But this man acted like he hadn't heard a word of Chu Wanning's furious bellows. A lazy smile and a pair of dimples appeared on his face as he strode over and gripped Chu Wanning by the jaw.

49 This Venerable One's Shizun is Always So Mad

CHU WANNING'S INCREDULITY could no longer be captured in words. His eyes opened wide, and he stared at the Mo Ran in his dream as if he were staring at a ghost.

The grown-up Mo Weiyu was gallant, with broad shoulders and long legs, and half a head taller than himself. When he looked down at Chu Wanning, amusement and mockery could both be found in the corners of his eyes.

"This venerable one's dear shizun really ought to take a look in the mirror." Mo Ran's finger slid along Chu Wanning's cheek to rest by his ear, his eyes dark and threatening.

A moment passed in silence, then he let out a cold hmph and abruptly leaned over. This lean was accompanied by a soft, searing-hot sensation as he captured Chu Wanning's lips with his own.

Caught completely off guard, Chu Wanning's head hummed with white noise. Something in his mind seemed to...snap...

Mo Ran was kissing him, and Mo Ran's breath invaded him, moist, agitated, full of filthy, sinful desire.

Lips met roughly with the scraping of teeth as stormy waves surged in Chu Wanning's chest. He was nearly shivering with fright, his phoenix eyes wide open and his mind equal parts furious and stupefied. In this dream, it was as if he had lost his spiritual powers.

He could hardly even gather his physical strength. Instead he was held tightly against Mo Ran's chest and couldn't remotely struggle free of his grip.

For some reason, the Mo Ran in this dream was wholly different from the one Chu Wanning knew. That deferential ingratiation had vanished, replaced by a domineering presence.

He could distinctly feel Mo Ran's heated breaths as he exhaled, low and rapid, animalistic desire searing like lava and threatening to melt him down, flesh and bone alike.

Chu Wanning's face was pale with anger, nearly about to spit blood. He never could have imagined that he would be held down by Mo Ran without the strength to resist. Even harder to accept was the heat gathering in his abdomen and the weakness in his fingers from the wet, frantic friction of these kisses. He trembled in Mo Ran's embrace; Mo Ran's chest was furiously hot, so hot that it was like Chu Wanning would be burned and drowned even through the layers of fabric. He wanted desperately to struggle, but he couldn't summon the strength.

By the time they parted, Chu Wanning's legs were boneless. Mo Ran, still holding him, turned to press his face against the back of his ear. Chu Wanning felt the caress of warm, damp breaths at the base of his neck as Mo Ran panted. Then he heard Mo Ran say, "Didn't you want to discuss conditions with this venerable one?"

His voice was hoarse, so much so that it sounded nearly unfamiliar to Chu Wanning.

Chu Wanning looked down only to see the jut of Mo Ran's throat bobbing, a swallowing motion as he fought a losing battle to maintain control.

"But you own little of value to this venerable one, so you'll have to bargain with the last remaining thing in your possession."

Chu Wanning's voice grew hoarse as well, but he didn't know if it was from anger or desire. Quietly, he asked, "What do you mean?"

Mo Ran backed him into a wall, then abruptly raised a hand to strike the hard surface. The other hand closed tightly around Chu Wanning's shackled wrist. Not without malicious spite, but also not without timid desire, he bent down to capture the lobe of an ear between his lips.

Chu Wanning shuddered violently, a frightening numbness shooting up his spine and spreading over his scalp.

Mo Ran's voice was husky, his breaths heavy and oppressive. "Let me screw you, and I'll let you have what you demand."

Chu Wanning's eyes shot wide open, the wetness in his gaze colored with arousal, but even more with disbelief.

Mo Ran's hand had already felt its way to Chu Wanning's waist, and his lips moved against the side of his neck. He spoke venomous words in the tenderest tone. "However, this venerable one loathes Shizun so very much, so it'll probably be hard to summon any interest in Shizun's body. You'll have to work a little to make it worth my while."

Mo Ran paused before pulling him in even closer, still stroking his waist.

"So really, think it over. If you're willing, then get on your knees like a good boy and put your mouth to work. Serve me well. Then go spread yourself on the bed and beg me to fuck you."

Chu Wanning was about to lose it.

The virtuous, proud, pure, austere Yuheng Elder kept his distance from men and women alike and indulged in neither erotic art nor amorous song, ever incorruptibly chaste and aloof. Or, in simpler words, he knew practically nothing of matters of love and lust.

And so, very unfortunately for him, in spite of his anger, all of his defenses fell apart in the face of this intense, unfamiliar feeling. He was utterly defeated.

Mo Ran waited for a short while but received no reaction. He cursed under his breath and started kissing Chu Wanning again, unable to hold back. He pulled back after having had his fill of his shizun's lips, trailing a translucent thread—before biting down none too gently on Chu Wanning's neck, licking and kissing along it to his shoulder, his ear.

Chu Wanning's scalp grew even more numb when Mo Ran began to roughly pull and tear at his robes, muttering, "What're you pretending to be so virtuous and saintly for?!" as he ripped.

When Chu Wanning lifted his eyes to look at him, Mo Ran's gaze was heated, crazed, a strange light in the corners of his eyes like long-accumulated hatred finally spilling forth.

But also like, after long years of restraint, the screaming-hot lava of desire that had been trapped under layers of rocks was finally overflowing.

Chu Wanning wanted to look away, as if burned by the intensity of Mo Ran's predatory gaze, but Mo Ran saw through his intentions and gripped his face before he could.

"Look at me." Mo Ran's voice was rough and heated, shaking faintly from arousal—or perhaps something else—and filled with the craving of a beast about to devour its prey. "I said, *look at me*!"

Chu Wanning shakily closed his eyes.

This dream was far too absurd...

"Shizun." The voice by his ear suddenly became soft and warm, more akin to the tone with which Chu Wanning was familiar. "Shizun, wake up."

Chu Wanning blearily made out Mo Ran's face hovering mere inches from his own. He instantly reacted with a fierce and well-aimed slap that landed soundly on the boy's cheek.

Mo Ran, caught off guard, ate the slap head-on. He let out an, "ah," and opened his eyes wide. "Shizun! What was that for?"

Chu Wanning didn't reply as he sat up, his phoenix eyes flickering with anger and alarm. His body was still shaking slightly, dream and reality blending together and driving him mad.

"Shizun..."

"Stay away!" Chu Wanning shouted harshly, brows lowered in a scowl.

Mo Ran was startled by this extreme reaction, and a while passed before he asked cautiously, "Did you have a nightmare?"

Nightmare... That's right, it was a dream...It was just a dream. Chu Wanning stared blankly at the person in front of him for quite a while before he was able to slowly collect the pieces of his composure.

He was lying in the library at the Red Lotus Pavilion. Loyalty Hall and the grown-up Mo Ran were nowhere to be seen. The only thing in front of him was a face that was as yet young and childlike.

Finally fully awake, Chu Wanning paused for a moment to school his expression into one of propriety as he made a show of rearranging his clothes. His slender fingers still shook slightly as he suppressed the agitation and unease that yet remained, and it was only after a pause that he said, "Mn. I was dreaming and...hitting someone."

Mo Ran rubbed the redness on his cheek and let out a little hiss of pain. "What was Shizun dreaming about? What a forceful hit..."

Embarrassment flashed across Chu Wanning's features. He pressed his lips together and, turning a bit away, loftily said nothing.

His face was as calm waters, but his heart was full of wildly crashing waves. He could practically feel his own pride on the verge of shattering into a million tiny pieces. He couldn't believe that he would dream of something so unspeakably preposterous, of such filthy words. How absolutely shameless! How could he even call himself a teacher anymore?

Even worse, his useless body had reacted to that humiliating dream. He felt like he was about to have a breakdown...

Thankfully, his robes were wide and loose-fitting, hiding his shame from the eyes of others.

Chu Wanning's face still darkened gloomily as he propped his forehead in one hand. He couldn't grab the dream Mo Ran to vent his anger, but there *was* an available alternative right in front of his eyes, who had conveniently delivered himself to Chu Wanning's door. So, glowering, he asked sullenly, "What are you doing, barging into my private quarters in the middle of the night like you own the Red Lotus Pavilion? Since when were you the Yuheng Elder?"

Mo Ran could not immediately reply. First a slap for no reason, then a thorough tongue-lashing. He felt a little wronged and mumbled in a tiny voice, "What's got you so mad this time?"

Chu Wanning scowled. "I'm not mad. I'm going back to sleep—get out!"

"But Shizun, it's already morning."

Chu Wanning paused.

"I only dared to enter the Red Lotus Pavilion without permission to look for you because we've been waiting at the Platform of Sin and Virtue for quite a while, but Shizun never came."

After a long, long moment of silence, Chu Wanning opened a shuttered window. Sure enough, the sun had already risen a ways into the sky, the birds were singing, and the bugs were buzzing.

Chu Wanning's scowl grew even darker. He looked like he might summon Tianwen and start whipping it about at any second.

To think he had actually been immersed in an erotic dream all the way through to early morning. On top of that, if Mo Ran hadn't come looking for him, the dream might have even continued—

The thought made the vein at Chu Wanning's temple throb, and where his grip tightened on the window frame, the joints of his fingers turned pale like jade.

Chu Wanning practiced mental cultivation, which involved cultivating his mind with restraint and discipline, and made him proficient in suppressing desires. Before this, he'd never even had an unbecoming thought, much less an erotic dream.

His principles being what they were, Chu Wanning was like a wooden man: stupid, clumsy, and on top of that, stiff. His mental cultivation was so advanced that he had entirely severed himself from all desire, and when he had nothing else to do, he often looked down in contempt on pairs of lovers and dual cultivation partners, feeling quite self-satisfied that he was virtuous and incorruptible.

Who could've anticipated that in the end, he would fall like this? At the hands of his own disciple.

The wise, strong, noble, and aloof Chu-zongshi dared not even look at Mo Ran as he furiously spat out, "Hurry and come with me to the Platform of Sin and Virtue for morning practice!" before abruptly turning and leaving, vanishing in an instant.

Xue Meng and Shi Mei had been waiting for a long while and were sitting in the shade of a tree chatting when Chu Wanning arrived.

Shi Mei was distraught. "Shizun is never tardy. Did something happen? It's so late, and he's still nowhere to be seen."

Xue Meng was even more distressed. "Didn't Mo Ran go looking for Shizun? It's been a while and he's still not back. If I'd known this was gonna happen, I would've gone with him. I hope Shizun's not sick!"

"Shizun's shoulder wound was quite severe, even after proper care," said Shi Mei. "And he's prone to falling ill, so that's not unlikely..."

At this, Xue Meng grew even more restless until he abruptly stood. "I can't wait anymore. We can't count on that unreliable mutt Mo Ran—I'm gonna go check on Shizun myself!"

But when he turned around, there was Chu Wanning, pristine robes fluttering as he strode over.

"Shizun!" the pair beneath the tree called out simultaneously.

"I got held up by some business," Chu Wanning said. "We're doing martial practice today. Let's go."

When Chu Wanning wasn't paying attention, Shi Mei turned to Mo Ran, who was following behind him. "Is Shizun all right?" he asked in a low voice. "What was the holdup?"

Mo Ran rolled his eyes. "He just overslept."

"Eh?"

"Shh, act like you don't know." Mo Ran rubbed his cheek, still sore from the slap. He definitely didn't want an encore.

Shi Mei blinked. "Why's your left cheek so red?"

"If you keep asking, my right cheek's gonna join it," Mo Ran said quietly. "Let it be. Let's just hurry and follow."

When they arrived at the practice field, Chu Wanning instructed Mo Ran and Shi Mei to have a practice match first, keeping Xue Meng behind.

"Sit," said Chu Wanning.

Although Xue Meng didn't know the reason for the command,

he always treated his shizun's every word like law. He promptly complied, sitting down on the spot.

Chu Wanning sat down across from him. "The Spiritual Mountain Competition is in three years. What are your plans?"

Xue Meng looked down, and a moment passed before he said through gritted teeth, "To win."

If Chu Wanning had asked him this before their trip to Jincheng Lake, Xue Meng would have answered arrogantly and with certainty. Now all that was left behind this word was a simple, stubborn refusal to give up his pride. It wasn't that he had no self-awareness, but rather that he refused to just step aside and hand his title of "darling of the heavens" to someone else without a fight.

Having ground out these words, Xue Meng snuck a glance at Chu Wanning, his heart filled with anxiety.

Chu Wanning was looking at him without the slightest bit of any derision or doubt. He only said, simply, "Good."

Xue Meng's eyes immediately lit up, and he stumbled over his words in his excitement. "Shizun, do you think—do you think I can still… I…"

"My disciples don't give up without a fight."

"Shizun…"

"Outstanding youths from all sects participate in the Spiritual Mountain Competition. Those without holy weapons will naturally be no match for you, but even if your opponent does wield one, there's no need for you to be afraid. A holy weapon isn't the sort of thing one can easily master in a short period of time. Although your blade, Longcheng, is slightly lesser in comparison, it is nevertheless a superb, high-quality weapon of mortal craftsmanship. As long as you diligently train and practice for these next three years, winning is certainly not outside the realm of possibility for you."

It was well known that Chu-zongshi had a discerning eye and solid judgment in the realm of the martial arts. Furthermore, he wasn't the type of person to tell encouraging white lies out of sympathy. Therefore Xue Meng's spirits were lifted a great deal by these words. "Does Shizun really mean it?"

Chu Wanning narrowed his eyes. "How old are you, Xue Meng?" he asked lightly. "I don't coddle anyone over the age of five."

Xue Meng, a little embarrassed, rubbed his nose and grinned.

"Victory and defeat are not something you can control," Chu Wanning continued. "What's important is to take pride in yourself. Just do your best and don't worry overmuch about the result."

"Got it!" Xue Meng answered.

Having eased Xue Meng's worries, Chu Wanning headed toward the practice field. He approached from the end where the training dummies were located. In order to prevent disciples from accidentally injuring those who passed by while they sparred with the dummies, this area had been built a distance way. One had to walk down a long corridor and turn a corner to reach it.

Shi Mei and Mo Ran were conversing with their backs toward Chu Wanning, not too close and not too far away, just within hearing distance.

"You two..." Chu Wanning was about to call them over, but when he laid eyes on the sight before him, he suddenly stopped talking.

This Venerable One Likes You

As someone who cherished weapons, this kind of scene made Chu Wanning so outraged that he couldn't even speak. He beheld a moron.

Under a flowering tree not far away, Mo Ran had summoned Jiangui. The size of a holy weapon could be changed at will; most people liked to make their weapon larger and more impressive-looking, or at least keep it at its normal size, as Chu Wanning did. Conversely, Mo Ran had made Jiangui tiny, about the length and width of a cord for tying hair, its leaves miniscule. The dignified holy weapon looked absolutely pitiful.

Moreover, people had different innate spiritual energies. Thus, Tianwen glowed golden when Chu Wanning poured his spiritual energy into it, but Jiangui took on a scarlet hue. So, leaves aside, at present, Jiangui looked just like a red string of fate...

"Shi Mei, tie this to your hand. I want to see if Jiangui has Tianwen's power to coax the truth out of people."

"Uh...you want to test it out on me?"

Mo Ran smiled. "Yep. Cause I'm closest with you, and I know you'd never lie to me."

Shi Mei was still hesitant. "That's true, but..."

"Aiya, I won't ask anything tricky. If you don't believe me, let's pinky swear?" As Mo Ran said this, he stuck out his pinky finger.

Shi Mei didn't know whether to laugh or cry. "How old are you? Isn't this a little childish?"

"C'mon, let's pinky swear! If it's fine at eight, then it's fine at eighteen—and eighty-eight too. Nothing childish about it." Mo Ran grabbed Shi Mei's right hand and pried his pinky out with a cheeky grin. Shi Mei, caught between annoyance and laughter at this ludicrous behavior, could only go along.

Unexpectedly, instead of hooking their pinkies together, Mo Ran grinned, his eyes smiling as well. "Jiangui, time to get to work."

Jiangui zoomed faster than lightning, and in a flash it had wound itself around Shi Mei's pinky, with its other end around Mo Ran's.

The handsome young man laughed like a sly fox that had schemed its way into ascension. "Congrats, you fell for it." he said happily, framed with dimples.

"You!" Shi Mei really didn't know whether to laugh or cry. He hesitated, then said, "Let me go, come on."

"Later, later." Mo Ran grinned. "Just a couple of questions first."

Truth be told, Mo Ran had been feeling uneasy ever since that episode at Jincheng Lake—the one when he received the box Ever-Yearning, yet Shi Mei hadn't been able to open it. Even though Shi Mei had been wearing gloves at the time and hadn't directly touched the box, Mo Ran just couldn't shake his doubts. What's more, Chu Wanning had ultimately been the one to open it.

Chu Wanning... How was it possible?

So Mo Ran concluded that the box must have been broken. He wanted to use Jiangui to confirm that, just to make sure.

He was absolutely certain in his feelings for Shi Mei, but he worried that he might not have the same weight in Shi Mei's heart. As for that confession in Jincheng Lake, he couldn't be sure that he hadn't imagined it.

Shi Mei had a gentle temperament and was nice to everyone. He was totally unlike that Chu Wanning, with his sullen face day-in and day-out, like everyone else owed him something—thoroughly disagreeable.

Taxian-jun was a crude person, but when it came to his beloved, he would overthink so much that his thoughts would tie themselves up into knots.

"First off." Mo Ran's heart was filled with anxiety, but he kept grinning and feigning nonchalance. He decided to toss out a couple of easy, inconsequential questions first as padding. "What do you think of Xue Meng?"

A prickling sting on his finger, and Shi Mei fessed up. "The young master is a good person, but he's too straightforward, sometimes even intolerably tactless."

Mo Ran burst out laughing, clapping in glee. "Eh? Even you get fed up with him? Ha ha ha, understandable, he's way too annoying."

Shi Mei turned red. "Don't be so loud. What if the young master hears?"

"Okay, okay, okay." Mo Ran grinned. "But it makes me happy when you badmouth him."

Shi Mei had no response to that.

"And what do you think of Shizun?" Mo Ran continued.

"Shizun is a good person too, it's just that his temper is a little..." Shi Mei seemed like he really didn't want to critique Chu Wanning. However, he was bound by Jiangui, so even though he bit his lip for a while, he still ended up having to say, "His temper is a little short."

"Ha ha, a little short? More like ridiculously short. He gets mad every other day and won't even admit to it. He's a bigger handful than the empress herself."

Over in the corner, Chu Wanning stood silent, listening wordlessly.

"If you understand Shizun's bad temper, why did you still choose to study under him?" Mo Ran wondered aloud.

"Shizun is cold on the outside, but on the inside, he's actually kind," said Shi Mei. "I'm not as naturally gifted as others, but he never minds if I'm slow on the uptake. He said everyone deserves to learn, and since I'm no good at combat, he taught me healing instead. H-he's truly very nice to me."

Mo Ran, originally quite gleeful, grew quiet upon hearing this, the grin disappearing from his face. A while passed before he said: "When has he ever been nice to you? All he did was teach you some techniques and maybe occasionally take care of you. That's only to be expected from any master."

"That's different—"

Mo Ran grew annoyed, cheeks puffing out. "Anyway, he's not really good to you! Whatever he does for you, I can do too!"

Shi Mei stopped talking.

In the awkward silence that followed, Mo Ran slowly quelled the flames in his heart. The sight of Shi Mei looking wordlessly downward filled him with guilt, and he quietly whispered, "Sorry."

"It's all right." A short moment later, Shi Mei suddenly said, "Once, some years ago, before you came to Sisheng Peak, I was walking along a path when it suddenly started storming. At the time, I wasn't yet a disciple under Shizun. I bumped into him while running through the rain. He was holding a red oil-paper umbrella, and upon seeing my pitiful state, he offered to share it with me.

I had heard of his cold reputation, so I was terribly nervous walking by his side."

"And then?"

Shi Mei's expression was soft. "Then? Then we didn't speak a single word the whole way."

Mo Ran nodded. "He's such a stuffy person. What can anyone even say to him?"

"Yes." Shi Mei's smile was small. "Shizun doesn't talk much. But when he walked me to the door and I turned to thank him, I saw that his right shoulder was absolutely drenched. I had been walking to his left, and I hadn't been rained on at all."

Mo Ran fell silent.

"It was a small umbrella, really only big enough for a single person, and he had used most of it to cover me. I watched him walk away in the rain, and then, as soon as I got back to my room, I wrote a letter of intent asking him to accept me as a disciple."

"That's enough," Mo Ran suddenly said. "You're way too soft-hearted. If you keep on like this, I'll feel bad for you."

"A-Ran, isn't Shizun the one you should feel bad for?" Shi Mei asked softly. "He only has a small umbrella because he's always alone. No one wants to walk with him. That's why even if Shizun is a little strict with me at times, or scolds me a little much at others, I don't mind. Because I remember his drenched shoulder."

Mo Ran said nothing, the tip of his nose a little red, his heart a little forlorn. It was a hazy sort of melancholy, and he wasn't even sure for whom he felt it.

"A-Ran, let me ask you something."

"Mn, go ahead."

"Do you dislike Shizun?"

Mo Ran paused. "I..."

"Or in other words, you don't like him, do you?"

For some reason, when Shi Mei asked this, his usually gentle and serene gaze seemed somewhat sharp. Mo Ran, caught off guard, found himself suddenly speechless.

In his daze, Mo Ran neither nodded nor shook his head. A long while passed before he forced a smile onto his face. "Aiya, aren't I supposed to be the one asking questions here? I can't just let you turn it around on me like that!"

Shi Mei didn't miss the fact that Mo Ran had dodged answering, but he didn't force the issue, only smiling. "I was just wondering. Don't take it to heart."

"Mn." Mo Ran calmed his emotions and looked up through his lashes at Shi Mei's face, which was no less beautiful than the bright moon in the sky. For his third question, Mo Ran had planned to ask Shi Mei if he liked him, but this exchange had left his heart heavy. He was quiet for a bit, lips pressed together, before he abruptly said, "He's just my shizun, nothing more. Whether I like him or not is irrelevant."

When Chu Wanning heard these words from where he stood in the shadows, his eyelashes quivered slightly, like the wings of an injured butterfly. Even though deep in his heart he'd already known, hearing it confirmed made his body feel so light that it could have floated away, while his heart was so heavy that it could have sunk into the sea. He also felt a chill. Perhaps autumn had come early this year.

Mo Ran and Shi Mei were still talking in the distance. Chu Wanning closed his eyes, the mild nausea that had lately come and gone once again washing over him. Suddenly exhausted, he turned to leave.

He had only taken a few steps when the autumn wind carried Mo Ran's voice faintly toward him. Despite himself, he stopped walking.

Mo Ran was asking Shi Mei his third question. "Well, you've given me your thoughts on Xue Meng and Shizun. Do me next." He tried to play it casual, but he was very careful, almost pathetic, when he asked, "Shi Mei, what do you think about me?"

Shi Mei was quiet.

Jiangui indeed seemed to possess the same interrogation ability as Tianwen. Shi Mei refused to answer, so Jiangui's scarlet radiance grew brighter where it was wound tightly around his finger. He frowned a little. "Ow..."

"Just say something." Mo Ran's heart ached for Shi Mei, but this question had burrowed so deeply into his heart, in this life and the last, that it had practically become his personal demon, so he persisted. "What do you think of me?"

Shi Mei shook his head and closed his eyes, as if in a great deal of pain. His long lashes trembled and sweat gathered on his forehead.

Wordless, Mo Ran sighed, unable to bear hurting him like this. "Forget it..."

He was about to remove Jiangui when Shi Mei reached the limit of his endurance and, face pale, said hoarsely, "I think you're...great."

Mo Ran's eyes widened.

Shi Mei's face went from pale to red very quickly, as if vexed. He turned his eyes down, lashes lowered, and dared not look at Mo Ran.

Jiangui vanished into specks of glimmering red light, which fluttered like the petals of ravaged flowers back into Mo Ran's palm. With his head lowered, Mo Ran let out a quiet, helpless chuckle, and when he looked back up at Shi Mei, his face was warm like the first bloom of spring. There was a lazy smile in his voice, but his eyes were a little wet as he said, "I'm glad. Thank you. I think you're really great too. I already said it to you at Jincheng Lake, but since you don't remember any of it, I want to say it again. I'm really...very fond of you."

He didn't specify what kind of fond he meant, but Shi Mei still blushed all the way to his neck and couldn't find any words.

Mo Ran stared at him with deep, inky eyes that shone with a clear, bright light like an ocean filled with stars, like gentle waves in the night sky. "I want to treat you right. I want to make you happy."

Shi Mei wasn't dense, and Mo Ran's meaning was written plainly all over his expression. Shi Mei could only lower his head. Mo Ran's heart quivered, and he raised his hand to stroke Shi Mei's hair.

Before he could get close, there was a sudden flash of sharp golden light, and a lash of vine struck Mo Ran right on the face with an audible crack.

"Ah!" Stung, Mo Ran turned around in shock.

Chu Wanning stood in front of the white walls with their green eaves, pristine robes paler than snow and one hand held behind his back as he stared coldly at them. Tianwen coiled on the ground like a hissing snake, willow leaves rustling, golden light coursing along its length with the occasional spark.

"Shizun..." Shi Mei said, startled.

"Shizun," Mo Ran said, holding his face.

So what if Chu Wanning was loathed? So what if he wasn't liked? Another person might weep miserably, but would Chu Wanning *cry*? Ridiculous. Instead, he would of course deliver a beatdown.

Chu Wanning's expression was frosty. He walked over slowly, voice frozen over. "Slacking off from training to chat? Mo Weiyu, you think you're so impressive just because you claimed the last holy weapon? You think you're all-powerful now? Invincible? Aren't you just so relaxed and carefree."

"Shizun, I was just—"

Chu Wanning glared. Mo Ran shut up.

"Shi Mingjing, spar with me. Mo Weiyu." Chu Wanning paused, then said resentfully, "Go practice. If you can't hold out for at least ten moves against me later, then you'll go back and copy the book of meditation techniques three hundred times as punishment. Now get lost."

Ten moves?

Mo Ran felt like he might as well just go get started with the copying.

51

This Venerable One's Shizun... Pfft Ha Ha Ha

FOR THE NEXT THREE DAYS, Chu Wanning was even more sullen than usual, his temper even worse. Resentment was written plainly all over the Yuheng Elder's features, and a miasmic haze followed him wherever he went. The disciples scattered like prey animals at the mere sight of him. Even Xue Zhengyong dared not talk to him too much for fear of his murderous aura.

Chu Wanning didn't want to admit that he had any untoward feelings for Mo Ran, but when he had seen his two disciples rendezvous by the training dummies and act so affectionate, he had simply been unable to stop his rage from flaring and a sour feeling from flooding his chest.

He was disgusted. With others, yes, but more so with himself.

Chu Wanning and Mo Weiyu were master and disciple, nothing more. How was the matter of whom Mo Ran liked to stick to or whom he wanted to be involved with any of his business? What right did Chu Wanning have to wave around his willow vine just because he didn't like what he saw?

If he likes someone or likes being near them, what's that got to do with you? Did it inconvenience you in some way? Chu Wanning, how are you this pathetically petty?!

Anyway, backing up a thousand steps—so what if he felt

unspeakable longing for Mo Ran? He had his pride and plenty of self-restraint. Those were more than enough to keep his feelings in check, more than enough to suppress that terrifying yearning for however long it would take to suffocate it.

No one would ever know of his unsightly affections.

Nothing would remain but for the brocade pouch that held the two locks of hair.

Mo Ran would never know about Chu Wanning's feelings, just as he would never know that, at the bottom of Jincheng Lake, the one who had endured searing agony to save him hadn't been Shi Mei, but Chu Wanning himself.

But what was this feeling? Was it...jealousy? The mere thought made Chu Wanning choke.

For months after the training field incident, he tried to avoid Mo Ran as much as possible, minimizing all interactions outside of routine instructions in cultivation and training.

Time flew by, and before they knew it, it was nearly the end of the year. One day, as Chu Wanning was returning from a trip down the mountain to deal with monsters, it began to snow just as he got to the front gates.

Sisheng Peak was quickly covered in a veil of silver. Chu Wanning was no good with the cold. Tugging his robes closer for warmth, he walked briskly toward Loyalty Hall.

A hearty fire warmed the interior of the hall as firewood crackled inside the copper basin. Chu Wanning had come to report to Xue Zhengyong, but the sect leader was nowhere to be seen. Instead, he bumped into Mo Ran.

There was no one else in Loyalty Hall. This was the first time Chu Wanning had been alone with Mo Ran in many months, and he felt a little uncomfortable despite himself. What's more, this was the location where that absurd dream had taken place.

Speaking of, Chu Wanning had experienced that dream several more times since, and each time was clear and vivid. The first few times, he tried to struggle, but after a while, he grew accustomed to it and just let the Mo Ran in the dream run his mouth like a lunatic while Chu Wanning idly counted his eyelashes out of pure boredom—one, two, three...

That dream always abruptly ended at a certain critical moment. After multiple identical repetitions, Chu-zongshi decided that this cut-off must be due to his innately pure and noble disposition. Even his fantasies refrained from getting overly sordid.

Having come to this conclusion, the Yuheng Elder and his maidenly heart of fragile glass finally managed to retrieve a bit of dignity.

However, the combination of Mo Ran and Loyalty Hall filled Chu Wanning with an instinctual sense of danger.

Unfortunately, the young man in question hadn't the slightest idea about any of this. At the sight of Chu Wanning, Mo Ran's face lit up in a toothy grin. "Shizun, you're back."

Chu Wanning paused. "Mn."

"Are you looking for Uncle? My aunt's feeling a little under the weather, so he's been taking care of her. What do you need? I'll let him know."

Chu Wanning pressed his lips together and said mildly, "No need."

Then turned on his heel to leave.

Mo Ran called out to him. "Shizun, please wait."

"What is it?" Chu Wanning looked over his shoulder as he spoke and was unexpectedly met with Mo Ran's extended hand brushing against his brow.

Mo Ran brushed his brow a few more times, and said, like it was the most natural thing in the world, "Look at you—you're covered in snow."

Chu Wanning froze. At a loss for what to do, he stood paralyzed as the young man fussed, dusting the snow off his head, then took out a white handkerchief to dry his hair.

Chu Wanning was terrible with the cold. He couldn't be exposed to it or he would easily fall sick. However, this person didn't know to take care of himself. In their last life, after he had been imprisoned, he had often liked to sit in the courtyard and watch the koi fish in the pond, unheeding even when it began to snow.

As such, he constantly took ill and ran fevers. He had been even more frail after his spiritual core was destroyed. Every time he got sick, he would be bedridden for at least half a month, and bowl after bowl of medicinal decoction would have practically no effect.

And so, when Mo Ran saw Chu Wanning covered in snow, half-melted and half-frozen, he reflexively started dusting him off. Halfway through drying Chu Wanning's hair, he belatedly realized that his actions might have been a little too intimate. His head snapped up just in time to come face-to-face with a pair of inscrutable phoenix eyes.

Chu Wanning was glaring at him mutely.

Mo Ran's hands withdrew sheepishly. "Ah ha ha, this disciple overstepped his bounds. Shizun can dry himself, of course."

Chu Wanning was quite relieved when he backed off. That dream was just a dream, after all. His disciple was still the same as ever, nothing like that man in his dream who referred to himself as "this venerable one."

Chu Wanning was silent for a while before he took Mo Ran's proffered handkerchief. He doffed his cape and walked over to the fire to warm his hands, then wiped the melting snow from his hair.

"Since when did you finally learn what a boundary is?" Chu Wanning asked. Face illuminated by the warm light of the fire, he glanced sideways at Mo Ran through narrowed eyes. "Haven't you always been oblivious to such things?"

Mo Ran wisely kept his mouth shut.

Neither spoke for a moment. Chu Wanning finished drying his hair and absentmindedly tucked the handkerchief away, then shot an impassive glance at Mo Ran. "Anyway, what are you doing here?"

"It's the end of the year," Mo Ran hurried to reply. "There's a year's worth of files that need to be organized, so I'm helping—"

Chu Wanning cut him off. "I know the files need to be organized, but isn't that Shi Mingjing's job? Why are you doing it?"

Mo Ran paused. "Shizun's memory is truly quite impressive."

Chu Wanning was totally unmoved by the flattery. "Where is he?"

"He said he was a little feverish and headachey this morning." At the look in Chu Wanning's eyes, Mo Ran hurriedly continued, "Sorry, Shizun, I was the one who told him to get some rest. Please don't blame him."

This effort to cover for Shi Mei was like a sharp needle pricking at Chu Wanning, and it made his brows draw together. He was quiet for a while, then asked, "Is he okay?"

Upon realizing that Chu Wanning wasn't laying any blame, Mo Ran let out a breath of relief. "I gave him medicine and waited for him to fall asleep before leaving. He just caught a cold—should be fine in two or three days. Thank you for your concern, Shizun."

"Who said I'm concerned about you lot? I was just asking."

Mo Ran shut his mouth.

"I'll leave you to your organizing, then."

With that, Chu Wanning left.

Sisheng Peak forbade its disciples from performing each other's duties. Mo Ran had thought his shizun was definitely going to punish him, but to his surprise, Chu Wanning had let him off easy. He stood in place, dumbstruck, for quite a while, and didn't react until Chu Wanning was already a distance away.

"Shizun!" Mo Ran picked up the umbrella leaning against the door and ran after the lone figure in the snow. "Shizun, wait!"

Chu Wanning turned around. Mo Ran came to a stop in front of him, shook the snow off the umbrella, and opened it above their heads.

"The snow's really coming down. Take this umbrella with you."

Chu Wanning shot a glance at him. "No need."

Mo Ran tried to hand the umbrella over, but Chu Wanning felt only irritation and refused to accept it. In the back-and-forth struggle, the umbrella fell right as a wind picked up and was blown several feet away.

Chu Wanning stared at that umbrella planted in the snow and kept staring for quite a while. This was such a nonissue. He wanted to indifferently turn and leave, just as he always had in the past. Yet his feet refused to move.

Just like a candle will always sputter out in the end, and how even an ancient well will dry up in time, even the most tolerant person will eventually break down.

Chu Wanning turned with a sweep of his sleeve. "Mo Weiyu, would you stop messing with me?" he snapped. "I'm not Shi Mingjing. I don't need someone else to take care of me!"

A golden light gathered in his hand as he spoke, and Mo Ran reflexively took a step backward, thinking Chu Wanning was going to summon Tianwen for another whipping. Instead, the light rose into the sky like a gushing spring of gold and formed a resplendent barrier that blocked wind and snow alike.

Mo Ran stared. Oh. A barrier for blocking rain and snow...

Chu Wanning's expression was frigid, his brows even. "Do I look like I need an umbrella?"

He seemed to be truly offended; the barrier rapidly changed colors with the movement of his fingertips, from gold to red, to purple, blue, then green. The effect of the barrier changed with the color. One warded against only snow, one blocked the wind as well, and another even kept the interior of the barrier warm despite the freezing storm.

These techniques were quite powerful, and Chu Wanning normally wouldn't have wasted his spiritual energy to block the snow in this way. Such a sulkily showy display was so childish that, for a moment, Mo Ran was left utterly speechless.

"Shizun, don't be angry..."

"Who said I'm angry?!" Chu Wanning's face was pale from anger. "Get lost already!"

"Okay, okay, okay, I'm getting lost." Mo Ran glanced at the barrier. "Don't waste your energy like that, though."

"Get! Lost!"

With a wave of Chu Wanning's hand, the spiritual energy forming the barrier suddenly gathered into a strike of lightning that landed right in front of Mo Ran.

Mo Ran had just been showing him some concern out of the kindness of his heart, and for all that, he'd nearly been struck by lightning. It made him feel a bit resentful. He was about to say something, but when he looked up, he saw Chu Wanning standing in the snow, his face as pale as the drifts. The rims of his eyes were a little red.

"You..." Mo Ran said, startled.

"You and I are merely master and disciple, nothing more. There's no need for any unnecessary concern between us. So take your umbrella and get lost."

Mo Ran jerked, understanding dawning on him. "Shizun, that day at the practice field, when I was talking with Shi Mei, did you..."

Hear?

Chu Wanning said nothing. He only turned to leave.

This time Mo Ran didn't call out to him, and neither did Chu Wanning turn to look back.

A little ways away, Chu Wanning sneezed. His steps faltered, but he put his head down and walked even faster—as if he was angry, but also as if he was running away.

Mo Ran stood in the snow the entire time, lost in thought and staring numbly at Chu Wanning's back until he disappeared.

Chu Wanning fell sick as soon as he returned to the Red Lotus Pavilion.

He could use barriers to ward off rain and snow, but he never bothered to do so when it came to himself, seeing it as a waste of spiritual energy. That was why, when it rained, he used an oil-paper umbrella like any ordinary person would.

He sneezed a ton, and the headache and fever were quick to follow as well. He was used to self-medicating after all the times he had fallen ill, and he didn't even bat an eye at a little cold. So he took some medicine, washed up and changed his clothes, and burrowed into bed to sleep it off.

Maybe it was due to the chill, but the nausea that had been cropping up ever since his injury at Jincheng Lake was especially acute this night. Time passed in a haze as he slept, his entire body drenched in a cold sweat even as it burned like a furnace.

Chu Wanning didn't wake until noon the next day. Blinking his eyes blearily open, he laid there staring at nothing for a while before he slowly got out of bed to put on shoes.

He paused and stared. His boots seemed to have become quite a bit bigger overnight...

He looked more carefully and was rendered speechless. Wholly speechless. Even the Yuheng Elder's composure couldn't handle this degree of shock.

The problem wasn't that his boots had become bigger. Chu Wanning stared blankly at his hands, his legs, his bare feet, and the shoulder off of which his robe had slid.

The problem was...that he had become smaller.

52 This Venerable One Doesn't Even Get An Appearance

XUE ZHENGYONG WAS PRACTICING with his sword at the northern peak when a haitang blossom floated toward him. He uttered a curious, "eh?" and caught it while drying his sweat with a towel and muttering to himself. "Yuheng's messenger haitang? He can't even be bothered to come over to talk anymore? When did he get so lazy?"

He still took the golden orb of light from the flower's center and placed it in his ear. Out from it came the unfamiliar voice of a child. "Sect Leader, please come to the Red Lotus Pavilion at your earliest convenience..."

Xue Zhengyong didn't believe it at first, but when he stepped off from his sword in front of Chu Wanning's residence, he was perfectly dumbfounded.

A child of about five or six years stood in the pavilion by the lotus pond with a hand held behind his back, gazing at the lotuses with a dour face. Seen from the side, this person had a frosty expression and icy eyes to match. Though he was draped in Chu Wanning's robes, they were way, way too big for him. They pooled on the ground, sleeve hem and all, making him look like a fish towing a huge sweeping tail.

Xue Zhengyong stared mutely.

The child turned around, "If you laugh, I will kill myself *right here*," practically written on his face.

Xue Zhengyong didn't try very hard to hold it in before letting out a deafening howl of laughter.

The child slapped the table, livid. "What're you laughing at?! What's so funny?!"

"I am *definitely* not lau—ah ha ha ha, oh god, I can't, Yuheng, I *told* you to go to the Tanlang Elder to get that wound checked out, but you just wouldn't listen—ha ha ha ha, I can't *breathe*." Xue Zhengyong roared with laughter, holding his stomach with both hands. "I've—I've never seen a kid with such a murderous aura, ah ha ha ha ha!"

This child was none other than Chu Wanning, who had awoken to find himself shrunken. The vine that had pierced his shoulder at Jincheng Lake had seemingly been enchanted with some kind of curse that transformed those stricken into their five- or six-year-old selves. Thankfully, his spiritual power had not also diminished, or Chu Wanning felt like he really might as well have just died.

Xue Zhengyong went to fetch a set of uniforms sized for younger disciples, cackling the whole way there and back.

After changing into more fitting clothes, Chu Wanning finally looked a little less comical. He straightened out the silver-trimmed blue bracers, looked up to shoot Xue Zhengyong a glare, then said vehemently, "If you dare tell anyone, I will *end* you."

Xue Zhengyong chuckled. "I won't, I won't. But what're you gonna do about this? I don't know anything about healing, so you're gonna have to get someone to take a look, right? How about I ask the Tanlang Elder to come here?"

Chu Wanning swept his sleeves angrily—but the sleeves of the disciple uniforms were tight and form-fitting, so waving them around didn't have remotely the same effect, which left him even grumpier. "Come here and do what? Laugh at me?"

"Then how about I ask my wife to take a look?"

Chu Wanning pressed his lips together and said nothing, looking aggrieved.

"I'll take that as a yes, then?"

Chu Wanning only turned his back to him. Xue Zhengyong knew he was in a bad mood, but the sight was just too funny. He tried to hold back, but ultimately failed and once again burst into uproarious laughter.

Tianwen appeared with a whoosh as Chu Wanning glared at him out of the corner of his eyes. "I *dare* you to laugh again!"

"Okay, okay, no more laughing. I'll go call my wifey over right away, ah ha ha ha hahhh..."

Xue Zhengyong ran off and swiftly returned with a worried Madam Wang in tow. Madam Wang froze as soon as she saw Chu Wanning, and a long while passed before she finally managed to say, with disbelief, "Yuheng Elder..."

Chu Wanning did not reply.

Thankfully, unlike her husband, Madam Wang was a kind and compassionate doctor. She asked Chu Wanning some questions while looking him over, then softly said, "The elder's spiritual energy circulation is fine, and there's nothing abnormal about his body either. Nothing seems to have changed, aside from your having turned into a child."

"Does the madam know of a way to break this curse?" Chu Wanning asked.

Madam Wang shook her head. "The elder's injury was caused by an ancient willow vine; I'm afraid there is no other known incidence of this ailment, so I do not know how to treat it."

Chu Wanning lowered his lashes, stunned, and said nothing for a long while.

Madam Wang couldn't bear the sight. "Yuheng Elder," she said hurriedly, "based on what I have seen, the most likely cause of your current state is that, rather than a curse, the willow vines contained a self-healing secretion that seeped into your wounds. Otherwise, it wouldn't have taken so long to take effect. You were moreover likely only tainted by a very small amount of this secretion, and it was only able to affect your body after you overworked yourself day after day. Why don't you take care and rest up for a few days, then see if anything changes?"

Chu Wanning was silent for a while before he sighed. "There's nothing else for it. Many thanks, Madam."

"You're welcome." Madam Wang gave him another careful once-over. "With the elder's current appearance, as long as he doesn't confess, no one will be able to tell it's him."

She wasn't wrong; even Chu Wanning had forgotten what he'd looked like at this age. When he studied his reflection in the pond, he found he didn't look very much like his grown-up self at all, other than some vague similarities in facial features. Finally feeling slightly relieved, he looked up at Xue Zhengyong. "Sect Leader, I'll be going into seclusion at the Red Lotus Pavilion for a few days. Please look after my disciples."

"That's a matter of course. Xue-er is my son, Ran-er is my nephew, and Shi Mei is a disciple of Sisheng Peak. I'll certainly look after them." Xue Zhengyong grinned. "You just worry about yourself."

But three days of meditation later and Chu Wanning had yet to detect even the slightest sign that his body was returning to normal.

He couldn't help but feel even more anxious, leaving him totally unable to "take care and rest up" as Madam Wang had directed.

One evening, Chu Wanning could no longer handle his restlessness. Meditation wasn't doing anything anyway, and he figured he might as well take a stroll down the mountain to get some things off his mind.

It was after dinner and before evening classes, so Sisheng Peak's paths and corridors were full of disciples, but no one really paid him any mind. Chu Wanning strolled around for a bit, then went to the bamboo forest near the Platform of Sin and Virtue.

The elders each had their own favored practice area where they always took their disciples for cultivation and training. This bamboo forest was Chu Wanning's.

The tranquil rustling of bamboo leaves filled the air. Chu Wanning plucked a leaf and idly blew a melody with it, the crisp, serene notes soothing his agitated mind. However, it wasn't long before the sound of footsteps approached and stopped near him.

"Oi, kiddo."

Chu Wanning opened his eyes.

It was Xue Meng, long-legged and slim-waisted, standing proudly amidst the bamboo forest, Longcheng glistening in hand as he called to him. "I'm going to practice swordplay here. Go blow your leaf elsewhere."

The arch of Chu Wanning's eyebrow raised a bit. It was quite a strange feeling, having Xue Meng boss him around. He thought for a moment, then said, "I'll play my leaf and you can practice with your sword. There's plenty of space for the both of us."

"No way," said Xue Meng. "Hurry and leave. My blade could hurt you."

"You can't hurt me."

Xue Meng clicked his tongue, his patience running thin. "Don't say I didn't warn you, then. If you get injured later, it's not my problem." He unsheathed Longcheng with a powerful sound, like the hiss of a serpent emerging from the depths of a lagoon and soaring into the skies.

Instantly, Longcheng in Xue Meng's hand became a dancing shadow amidst the flying leaves, leaving a brilliant trail in its wake as light reflected off the blade. One slice rendered a leaf into ten pieces, the force of its passage plucking more leaves from the bamboo. Pierce, thrust, swipe, and slash, every motion smooth as the glide of snow upon the wind. Even a fifty-year-old cultivator would praise such an impressive display, to say nothing of a five-year-old child.

Yet even after Xue Meng had gone through ten forms, that boy was still just sitting on his rock, playing his leaf, as if there were nothing astounding nor even noteworthy unfolding in front of him.

Xue Meng, irritated, sheathed his blade and leapt down from the upper canopy of the bamboo forest, landing lightly before Chu Wanning. "Kid."

No response.

"Hey, kid, I'm talking to you."

Chu Wanning lowered the leaf and slowly opened his eyes to look expressionlessly at Xue Meng. "What is it? Did your master not teach you to be courteous when speaking to others? Don't just go, 'hey,' this, 'hey,' that. I have a name."

"Why would I care to know your name?" Xue Meng had intended to be nice about it, but after this thorny response, the remainder of his good humor vanished. "Blades don't have eyes—scoot off to the side before mine cuts off your head."

"If you can't even avoid my head, is there any point to your practice?" Chu Wanning replied with an air of indifference.

"You!" Never in all Xue Meng's life had anyone ever talked back to him like this—and to think it was coming from a beginner disciple who didn't even reach his thigh! Angry and indignant, he said, "You sure are impudent. Do you even know who I am?"

Chu Wanning glanced at him mildly. "Who are you?"

"I am the young master of Sisheng Peak." Xue Meng was about to suffocate from indignation. "How do you not know this?"

The corners of Chu Wanning's lips quirked up slightly. The smile would have looked terribly mocking on his original face, but on his current childish, adorable one, it was even more infinitely disdainful. "You're just the young master. It's not like you're the sect leader, so why would I know you?"

"Wh—wh-wh-wh-what did you say?"

"Quit putting on airs and practice with your sword." Chu Wanning lowered his long lashes and went back to playing his leaf, the melody floating leisurely in the wind, the notes rising and falling.

About to die from pure fury, Xue Meng let out a roar and actually committed to picking a fight with a little kid. But no matter how mad he was, he wasn't going to hit a child, so he could only leap up and hack ruthlessly away at the bamboo, which broke and fell in batches amidst the leaf's serene song.

Xue Meng's blade was swift and vicious; after several flashes, dozens of bamboo stalks had been carved into blunt points. If he were facing an enemy, he would've made the points razor-sharp, but this was sufficient for teaching a junior disciple a lesson.

Hundreds of pointed bamboo sticks hurtled directly toward Chu Wanning and were mere inches from hitting him. Xue Meng swooped down to move this cheeky little disciple out of the way.

He didn't actually want to hurt the kid, just scare him a bit. Unexpectedly, in the same instant he swooped, the child stopped playing and flicked the leaf between his fingertips. That tender bamboo leaf suddenly turned into hundreds of fine threads.

Instantaneously and with stunning precision, the hundreds of threads struck out toward the falling spikes.

Even the wind seemed to stop blowing.

Chu Wanning stood. Simultaneously, the hundreds of spikes surrounding him were reduced to mere powder. Perfectly obliterated.

Xue Meng stood frozen in shock, face both pale and red, unable to manage even half a word.

The little kid before his eyes looked up, silver-blue uniform fluttering, and grinned at him. "You wanna go again?"

Xue Meng gaped wordlessly.

"Your strikes are vigorous but disorderly. They're far too erratic and unsteady."

Xue Meng opened his mouth, then closed it.

Chu Wanning continued, "Start over from sparrow form. Follow my music and go through each form in time with the segments of the tune—and no faster than that."

Upon receiving such instruction from some little kid, Xue Meng's face became even more overcast. He bit his lip and didn't move. Chu Wanning didn't rush him, waiting quietly to see if Xue Meng would lay down his ego for the sake of improvement. If he would be willing to listen to a half-grown child.

A while passed before Xue Meng suddenly stomped his feet in dejection, flung his sword aside, and turned to depart.

At the sight of this fit, Chu Wanning's expression darkened a little. It was truly such a pity that Xue Meng couldn't humble himself to accept guidance...

Before he could even finish that train of thought, he saw Xue Meng pick up a branch from the ground and turn around.

"Then—then I'll use a branch," he said huffily. "Just in case I hit you."

Chu Wanning paused, then nodded with a smile. "All right."

Xue Meng plucked a bamboo leaf for him and wiped it clean before handing it over. "Here, Xiao-didi, for you."

So he was "Xiao-didi" now, not "kid"? Chu Wanning threw an amused glance at Xue Meng, accepted the leaf, and sat back down on the rock to once again begin leisurely playing.

Xue Meng had a rash personality. One maneuver included a move where the wielder leapt and turned in midair while unleashing six stabs followed by a strike. Xue Meng could never get it quite right, often stabbing over a dozen times before the strike, which led him to miss the optimum window by a long shot.

Xue Meng messed it up five, six times in a row, his brows drawing increasingly tighter as he grew more and more agitated.

In his agitation, he caught a glimpse of the child sitting on a rock, playing the bamboo leaf. Despite his tender years, he was the very image of composure, without even the slightest hint of frustration. Xue Meng couldn't stop the sense of shame that crept into him.

So he rallied his spirits and tried several more times, slowly getting a feel for the maneuver with the melody's rhythm. But he didn't get ahead of himself. He kept at it until late in the night, when the moon hung high in the sky, and he could at last perform the maneuver flawlessly.

Xue Meng wiped away the sweat on his brows. "Today was all thanks to you," he exclaimed happily. "Which elder's disciple are you, Xiao-xiongdi? You're pretty amazing. How had I not heard about you before?"

Chu Wanning was already prepared for the question. The Xuanji Elder had many disciples, so many that even he couldn't remember them all. He put the leaf aside and said with a small smile, "I am the Xuanji Elder's disciple."

Xue Meng seemed to think rather little of Xuanji. He hmphed. "Oh, the Rubbish King, huh?"

"Rubbish King?"

"Ah, pardon me." Xue Meng misunderstood the surprise in Chu Wanning's eyes. He assumed the child was upset because Xue Meng had derided his shizun, so he smiled and explained, "It's just a nickname. Your shizun accepts anyone and everyone. The rubbish part refers to those disciples of his who are totally talentless, not the Xuanji Elder himself. Don't mind it, Xiao-xiongdi."

Chu Wanning paused, then asked, "Do you guys often give the elders nicknames in private?"

53 This Venerable One's Cousin Is Certainly Not Very Smart

"WELL, OF COURSE. They all get nicknames, no one gets a pass." Xue Meng appeared to be in quite a good mood, eager to show Chu Wanning the ropes. "You look pretty young—what are you, five? You must be new to Sisheng Peak, then. Haven't gotten a chance to know everyone yet. Once you've settled in, you'll learn that the disciples have nicknames for all twenty elders."

"Oh." Chu Wanning shot him an indecipherable look. "For example?"

"Oh, man, where do I even start? But it's getting late now, and I'm kinda hungry. As thanks for all the pointers you gave me today, I'll take you for a late-night snack down the mountain and tell you over food."

Chu Wanning thought for a moment with his head lowered, then smiled and said, "Mn, okay."

Xue Meng put away Longcheng and took Chu Wanning's hand, the unwitting disciple and the downsized master strolling along the stone steps between the bamboo grove toward the main gate.

"Xiao-xiongdi, what're you called?" Xue Meng asked as they walked.

"My surname is Xia," Chu Wanning answered calmly.

"Xia what?"

"Xia Sini."[3]

Xue Meng completely failed to catch on. "That's a nice name," he said cheerfully. "Which characters do you write it with?"

Chu Wanning glanced at him sideways with the look he reserved for idiots. "Si as in 'Disciple Si,' Ni as in 'Disciple Ni.'[4] Xia Sini."

"Oooh." Xue Meng, still grinning, continued with the questions. "And how old are you? Was I right before or what? You can't be older than five."

Chu Wanning was silent, his entire face dark. Lucky for Xue Meng, he was looking at the road and not the child's face, or he really would have been in for the scare of his life. "No, the young master guessed incorrectly... I'm six this year."

"Then you're amazingly talented—though not quite as much as I was at your age, of course. Anyway, with a bit of guidance, you'll definitely grow up to be outstanding. Say, why don't you quit being Xuanji's disciple? Call me Shige, and I'll go ask my shizun to take you on. How about that?"

Chu Wanning managed, with effort, not to roll his eyes. "What did you say I should call you?"

"Shige." Xue Meng kept grinning as he bent down and flicked Chu Wanning's forehead. "This is a rare opportunity, you know."

Chu Wanning's expression was complicated.

"What, speechless from overwhelming joy?"

Chu Wanning, indeed speechless—if not from overwhelming joy—remained silent.

The two laughed and chatted as they walked—at least, Xue Meng

---

3 *"Xia Sini" is a homonym for the phrase "scare you to death."*

4 *Chinese is a highly contextual language, and many characters share pronunciations, so people often specify characters by noting a word they appear in, e.g., "昧 (mei) as in 蒙昧 (meng mei)," as demonstrated by Xue Zhengyong in Volume 1 when giving Shi Mei his courtesy name.*

thought they were laughing and chatting—when a voice suddenly came from behind them and ended this line of conversation that might have led to Xue Meng's untimely demise.

"Eh? Mengmeng, what are you doing here?"

Who else on the entirety of Sisheng Peak could have the nerve to call Xue Meng "Mengmeng"?[5]

Xue Meng was cursing before he finished turning his head. "Mo Ran, you goddamn mutt—call me that one more time, and I'll rip out your cur tongue."

Sure enough, Mo Ran stood behind them under the clear moonlight, clothes fluttering in the breeze and an easy grin on his face. He was about to throw out a retort to further tease Xue Meng when he noticed the dainty kid next to him and came to a screeching halt. "Is that..."

Xue Meng pulled Chu Wanning behind him, glowering at Mo Ran. "None of your business."

"No, no, no—don't hide him away." Mo Ran circled around and grabbed Xue Meng's hand, pulling Chu Wanning back out and crouching down to give him a careful once-over. He made a questioning noise as he muttered, "This kid looks awfully familiar."

Chu Wanning, inwardly alarmed, kept quiet.

"It feels like I've seen you somewhere before."

Chu Wanning didn't like where this was going. If he got busted here, how could he ever face anyone ever again? He took an unconscious step back and turned to run.

"Hold it!" Mo Ran grabbed Chu Wanning with a mischievous grin, then reached out and playfully swiped a finger down the child's nose. "Come, Xiao-didi," he said in a soft voice, "tell Gege your name?"

---

5 萌萌, *Mengmeng*, uses a different character from the "meng" in "Xue Meng." It basically means "super cute," or "moemoe," and is a loanword from Japanese. See glossary for definition of "moe."

The swipe gave Chu Wanning goosebumps. Awkward and self-conscious, he kept trying to back away.

Mo Ran assumed he was scared, and he laughed. "What're you hiding for? Be good and tell Gege: Is your name Xue?"

Xue Meng blinked, visibly confused.

Mo Ran pointed at Xue Meng. "Is he your papa?" he asked, smiling. "Tell the truth, and this gege will buy you candy."

"What's your problem, Mo Weiyu?!" Xue Meng exploded, his face bright red and feathers all ruffled. "Wh-wh-wh-what the hell are you thinking?! Y-you're despicable! F-f-filthy! Sh-shameless!"

For a while, Chu Wanning was also silent, but secretly he was somewhat relieved. "My surname is Xia. The Xuanji Elder's disciple, Xia Sini."

"'Scare you to death'?" Mo Ran immediately caught the meaning in the name Chu Wanning offered, and his eyes lit with amusement. "Ha ha, how interesting."

Chu Wanning said nothing.

"Seriously, what's wrong with you?!" Xue Meng said heatedly as he shoved at Mo Ran. "He's my new friend, so go away already. We're going for a late-night snack. Out of the way."

"Okay." Mo Ran moved out of the way, but then fell into step next to them, grinning and sauntering.

"What do you think you're doing?" Xue Meng snarled at him.

"I want a bite to eat too," Mo Ran said innocently. "What, am I not allowed?"

Xue Meng couldn't bring himself to reply.

Wuchang Town was a small settlement that had once been infested with all manner of ghosts and ghouls. Thanks to the establishment of Sisheng Peak nearby, over the years, it had gradually regained its peace. These days it could even be called lively.

It was late enough that the night market was open. The group walked past the many stalls lining the road and picked a gudong soup joint, taking their seats at a low wooden table in the outdoor dining area.

"Gudong soup" was made in a pot that was propped over a table-top stove, and the fire continued to burn while they ate. The broth was generally very spicy, and fresh, raw ingredients were placed on the table to be dipped into the boiling broth so they could be cooked just before eating. It was called gudong soup because of the *gudong* sound of food being tossed into the broth.

This was a famous dish in Sichuan, but Chu Wanning only ate it with clear broth free of peppers, as anything spicy made him choke. Xue Meng had been born in Sichuan, and Mo Ran had grown up around Xiangtan. In other words, both of them were used to spicy food, and they naturally assumed that "Xia Sini" could also handle it.

When they sat down to order, Xue Meng listed off a bunch of dishes without even looking at the menu and added, "With extra peppers and chili oil in the broth."

Chu Wanning suddenly tugged on his sleeve and said quietly, "I want a twin pot."

"Huh?" Xue Meng thought he had misheard.

Chu Wanning's expression was dark. "Twin pot. Half-spicy, half-mild."

Xue Meng paused for a moment, then said, "You aren't from here?"

"Mn."

"Ah." Xue Meng nodded in understanding, but there was surprise in his eyes as he glanced at Chu Wanning. "To have left your home at such a young age, that's really so... Ah, never mind." He sighed and turned to the waiter. "All right, twin pot, then."

Chu Wanning wasn't sure, but he thought he heard a hint of resistance in Xue Meng's tone.

Soon enough, he found that he indeed wasn't imagining things. Xue Meng really was reluctant to just accept this, and he fussed incessantly as they waited for their food. "Shidi, when in Sichuan, do as the Sichuan do—you gotta learn to eat spicy foods. How're you gonna get buddy-buddy with people when you go out if you don't eat spicy stuff? You don't have to know the local dialect, but spicy food is nonnegotiable. Oh yeah, where are you from, anyway?"

"Lin'an," Chu Wanning replied.

"Oh." Xue Meng mulled this over, but he knew less than nothing about that southern region. So while nibbling on the tips of his chopsticks, he asked, "Do you guys eat rabbit heads over there?"

Before Chu Wanning could respond, Mo Ran was already piping up from the side with a smile. "Of course not."

Xue Meng shot him a glare, and Chu Wanning also looked over at him.

Mo Ran had a foot up on the wooden bench and an arm propped casually on his knee as he skillfully twirled the chopsticks in his hand. He grinned at their reactions and tilted his head. "What? Why the look? They really don't eat that kind of thing."

Xue Meng turned to Chu Wanning. "Is that true?"

"Mm-hmm."

Xue Meng went back to glaring at Mo Ran, "How did you know that? You been there before?"

"Nope." Mo Ran pulled a funny face. "But Xia-xiong and our

shizun are from the same place, and don't you realize that Shizun would never eat rabbit head? When he picks cold dishes at Mengpo Hall, it's either tofu with scallions or sweet osmanthus lotus root. Look for yourself next time, if you don't believe me."

Chu Wanning listened in silence.

"Ah, I guess I never really paid attention before. I haven't had the guts to look at what's on Shizun's plate ever since that one time I saw his breakfast. Too scary." Xue Meng rubbed his chin and let his distaste show on his face. "Shizun's taste is truly beyond words. Did you know? He actually eats savory tofu pudding."[6]

Chu Wanning remained silent.

As he spoke, Xue Meng turned toward him and said, sincerely and with the utmost importance, "Xiao-shidi, definitely, absolutely, do not take after the Yuheng Elder, or no one will want to eat with you. Remember, rabbit head and spicy foods are both mandatory, and when you have tofu pudding for breakfast, do not eat it with savory sauce."

"Don't forget about the seaweed and dried shrimp," Mo Ran added.

"Right, seaweed and dried shrimp too." This was a rare instance of Xue Meng and Mo Ran uniting against a common enemy. "Absolutely unacceptable."

Chu Wanning stared at this pair of idiots, face devoid of expression. "Uh-huh."

Their dishes came in short order: fresh and crispy bamboo shoots, vividly green cabbage, tender tofu, succulent fillets of fish, thinly

---

6 *In China, regional recipes may vastly differ. For example, tofu pudding (豆花) is typically prepared in one of two ways. The savory kind, which Chu Wanning prefers, uses soy sauce, roasted seaweed, and dried shrimp. The sweet kind with which Xue Meng and Mo Ran are familiar is made with sugar. People accustomed to savory tofu pudding often find the sweet variety unpalatable and vice versa.*

sliced rolls of lamb neatly piled on a porcelain plate, meat fried to a crunchy gold and sprinkled with cumin and pepper flakes, and a jar of freshly made soy milk on the side. The little table creaked under the weight.

Food brings people together, especially a lively meal like gudong soup. A couple plates of lamb and a few cups of soy milk later, even Xue Meng and Mo Ran's strained relationship became relaxed in the thick steam, at least for the time being.

Xue Meng scoured the spicy broth with his chopsticks, "Oi, oi, where's the brain I put in here?"

"Isn't it attached to your neck?" Mo Ran laughed.

"I meant the pig brain!"

Mo Ran bit his chopstick with an impish grin. "Mm-hmm, that's the one."

"You goddamn mutt, you dare insult me—"

"Oh, hey! Your brain floated up! Time to eat!"

In a moment of excitement, Xue Meng had walked right into Mo Ran's trap. "Put that dog paw away!" he yelled. "Don't even think about stealing it—that's *my* brain!"

Chu Wanning sat on his little stool, leisurely drinking his jar of sweet soy milk while watching the brats bicker. He was in no hurry; the entire mild side of the pot was all his.

When he finished the soy milk, he licked his lips as if he wanted more. Mo Ran noticed and asked with a smile, "Does Xiao-shidi like it?"

Chu Wanning took a moment to digest the fact that he had just been called "Xiao-shidi" and internally calculated the possibility of making Mo Ran not do that again, only to arrive at the conclusion that his odds were practically zero. So he could only dryly reply, "Mn, it's not bad."

Thus Mo Ran turned toward the waiter. "Excuse me, another jar of soy milk for my shidi here."

And so Chu Wanning contentedly began drinking a second jar.

He had always loved sweets, but he'd once acquired a cavity from eating too many pastries, and the Tanlang Elder had been forced to go to quite some trouble to restore it for him. Since then, Chu Wanning had refrained from overindulging for the sake of his thin face.

Being temporarily stuck as a kid had the unexpected benefit of letting him eat all the sweets he wanted.

Mo Ran watched him eat with his cheek in his hand. "Your tastes are just like Shizun's."

Chu Wanning choked a little but managed to maintain his placid expression. After a moment, he said, "Is Shixiong talking about the Yuheng Elder?"

"Yep." Mo Ran nodded with a smile as he pushed a steamer basket toward Chu Wanning, "Try this. I think you'll like it too."

Chu Wanning picked a leaf-wrapped bun from the bamboo steamer and took a small bite. Warm steam gushed from the bun, and inside the soft, glutinous wrapper was a sweet bean-paste filling.

"Do you like it?"

Chu Wanning took another bite before nodding. "Mn."

Mo Ran smiled. "Then have some more."

As the three of them chatted while eating, Chu Wanning suddenly remembered an earlier subject. After finishing his fourth bun, he asked Xue Meng with feigned nonchalance, "By the way, young master, you mentioned earlier that every elder has a nickname. If my shizun, the Xuanji Elder, is called the Rubbish King, then what's the Yuheng Elder's nickname?"

54

This Venerable One Squabbles Over Pastries

"SHIZUN?" Xue Meng's expression immediately became more respectful. "Out of everybody on Sisheng Peak, he's the only one who doesn't have any nicknames. No one would dare joke about him."

"Bullshit, that's only because everyone knows that you like Shizun, so they just hold their tongues around you." Mo Ran rolled his eyes and pulled Chu Wanning over as he stage-whispered. "Don't listen to him, I'll tell you: out of everybody on Sisheng Peak, the Yuheng Elder has more nicknames than anyone."

"Oh? Really?" Chu Wanning lifted his eyebrows slightly, intrigued. "For example?"

"For example, one of the more courteous ones would be Bai Wuchang."[7]

"Why do they call him that?"

"Because day in and day out, he only ever wears white."

"What else is there?"

"Little napa cabbage."

"Why?"

"Because day in and day out, he only ever wears white."

"What else?"

"Big mantou."

7 *The same Bai Wuchang whom Chu Wanning was mistaken for in Volume 1.*

"Why?"

"Because day in and day out, he only ever wears white."

"What else is there?"

"Little widow."[8]

Chu Wanning stared in incredulity.

"Do you know why they call him that?" Mo Ran asked, perfectly oblivious to the flicker of murderous intent in Chu Wanning's eyes. He only continued to laugh stupidly. "Because day in and day out, he only ever wears white."

If it weren't for his self-control, Chu Wanning probably wouldn't have been able to maintain his composure. "Well? What else is there?"

"Aiyo." Mo Ran glanced at Xue Meng's expression and said in a low voice, "If I say any more, I'm afraid that my cousin here might pour the entire hotpot over my head."

Xue Meng slapped the table, gnashing his teeth. "That's ridiculous! Who allowed them to make fun of Shizun like that? What do you mean 'little napa cabbage' and 'big mantou'—not to mention 'little widow'? Are they sick of being alive?!"

"Ah," Mo Ran replied, barely able to contain his laughter. "Mad already? You haven't even heard what the female disciples call him yet. It'll give you goosebumps."

Xue Meng's eyes widened. "What do they call him?"

"Well, what else?" Mo Ran drawled lazily. "They're girls, after all. Everything out of their mouths is flowery. It's all, 'pear blossom bathed in pale moonlight,' this, 'untrodden snow of early spring,' that, or else it's, 'Sir Chu of Lin'an, purest of all lotus blossoms,' and stuff likening him to the legendary beauty Xi Shi—my god."

Chu Wanning had no words.

---

8 *In China, mourning clothes are traditionally white.*

Xue Meng had even fewer.

"Those nicknames are still fine. In comparison, look at the Tanlang Elder. He gets way worse, what with his terrible temper and mediocre looks."

Out of all the twenty elders on Sisheng Peak, the Tanlang Elder was the one with whom Chu Wanning had the worst relationship. So he asked, "What do they call him?"

"Something like 'wintertime pickles' or 'mustard greens'—because his skin is dark." Mo Ran laughed. "Mengmeng, don't make that face at me. You have your fair share of nicknames too."

Xue Meng looked like he'd just swallowed a whole egg. "What? Me too?"

"Of course," Mo Ran said, grinning.

Xue Meng cleared his throat, feigning a casual attitude. "Well, what do they call me?"

"Fanny."

"Why?"

"What do you mean, why? Isn't it obvious?" Mo Ran couldn't even make it three words in before his shoulders started to shake with laughter, until he eventually burst out cackling, slapping the table. "You're like a peacock fanning its tail feathers everywhere, ha ha ha ha ha—"

Xue Meng bound to his feet, howling in anger, "Mo Ran! I'm gonna kill you!"

By the time the three of them had eaten and drunk their fill and made their way back to Sisheng Peak, it was past midnight. Chu Wanning allowed himself to be escorted by these two dumb disciples to the quarters of the Xuanji Elder, where they parted ways. Before leaving, Xue Meng asked if they could meet again tomorrow at the bamboo forest, but Chu Wanning, not knowing when he might return to his original form, thought it best not to commit and only said that he'd come by if he had free time.

Chu Wanning waited until the two disciples had gone far enough away, and only then did he use his qinggong to fly up lightly, stepping along the edges of rooftiles to make his way back toward the Red Lotus Pavilion.

Early the next morning, Chu Wanning woke to find himself still stuck in a child's body and couldn't help but feel slightly dispirited.

Pulling a face, he stepped onto a wooden stool and glared at the person in the mirror for a long while, unable to bring himself to do so much as properly comb his hair. After some consideration, he concluded that this really couldn't go on any longer, and so he set off to find Xue Zhengyong.

"What? You saw Meng-er and Ran-er yesterday?"

"Yes. I said that I was the Xuanji Elder's disciple, and they didn't seem to doubt it," Chu Wanning said. "If Xue Meng comes asking you about me, remember to cover for me. More importantly, I've been cultivating for more than ten days, and nothing has really changed. This isn't working. I'll have to ask Tanlang to take a look after all."

"Oho, what happened to our Yuheng and his thin face, being too embarrassed to ask for help?"

Chu Wanning shot him a cold glance. However, when such a look came from a young child, it wasn't the least bit imposing. Rather, it looked like the child was pitching a fit.

Chu Wanning was quite adorable as a kid, and Xue Zhengyong couldn't resist reaching out to pat his head.

"Sect Leader," Chu Wanning said suddenly, "when my body

returns to normal, could you ask Silk-Rinse Hall to tailor a new set of Sisheng Peak robes for me? Not white."

Xue Zhengyong was entirely taken by surprise. "I thought you didn't like wearing light armor."

"Just changing my wardrobe up a little," Chu Wanning said with a dark expression as he walked away.

Although the Tanlang Elder wasn't on good terms with Chu Wanning, he had to hold himself back a little bit in the presence of their sect leader. However, though his words remained civil, his derision was evident from his gaze.

Chu Wanning raised his eyes, expressionlessly watching the Tanlang Elder. Tanlang's eyes were shining with glee, almost like fireworks were going off within them. Chu Wanning continued to stare expressionlessly.

The Tanlang Elder let go of Chu Wanning's wrist after taking his pulse. "Madam Wang's diagnosis was more or less correct."

Chu Wanning yanked his hand away and tugged his sleeve down. "Then why has there been no change even after ten days?"

"You might not have absorbed much sap from the ancient willow, but it was potent. I'm afraid that it might be quite a long time before you return to your original form."

"How long will it take?" Chu Wanning asked casually.

"Not sure, but probably about ten years."

Chu Wanning's eyes instantly widened.

The Tanlang Elder tried his best to keep a straight face, but his own eyes were brimming with glee at Chu Wanning's misfortune. "Yes, it's probably going to take another ten years before you reclaim your original form."

Chu Wanning stared at him for a while, then said darkly, "Are you kidding me?"

"Perish the thought. You *are* the Yuheng Elder, after all." Tanlang smiled. "Anyway, if you ask me, there's nothing really wrong with you. This is good, even. Your body may be smaller and your mental age slightly more immature—and only slightly, mind you—but your cultivation is intact. Why the rush to return to normal?"

Chu Wanning, ashen faced, was left unable to reply.

"However, there's no guarantee that you'll stay in this child's form for the entirety of these ten years. This variety of tree sap migrates along the same paths as your spiritual energy. If you were to refrain from using any spiritual techniques for three to five months, you would likely be able to recover your original form."

"That works too!" Xue Zhengyong's eyes lit with hope.

But Tanlang continued with a faint smile. "Hold up, Sect Leader. I'm not done explaining yet. Even if the Yuheng Elder returned to his adult form thusly, he would be unable to use too many techniques, because once his spiritual energy was depleted from overuse, the willow sap would again exert its influence and he would turn back into a child."

"Overuse? How much would count as too much?" Xue Zhengyong exclaimed.

"About that—since the sap has already spread throughout his entire body, at most, he'd only be able to use two techniques per day."

Chu Wanning spoke in a voice that was as cold and hard as steel, "The barrier to the ghost realm constantly develops breaches in need of repair, and forging automatons also requires spiritual energy. If I could only use two techniques a day, I'd be as good as useless."

"Well, that's all I've got." Tanlang's voice dripped with sarcasm.

"After all, if the mortal realm were to lose the Beidou Immortal, the sun might fail to rise on the morrow."

On the side, Xue Zhengyong fretted. "Tanlang, quit the sneering already. Your medical techniques are among the foremost in the cultivation world—please think of something. Even if Yuheng's cultivation hasn't been affected, he's still in a child's body, so his abilities simply aren't what they were. Not to mention, if the other sects hear that Yuheng was injured at Jincheng Lake, they might think to try something funny. Ten years is way too long. Could you look for some medicines or something? Some that could maybe—"

The Tanlang Elder sneered and interrupted him mid-sentence: "Sect Leader, the sap that infected the Beidou Immortal is from an ancient tree spirit, not some common poison. Do you really think that I could just come up with a cure on the spot?"

Xue Zhengyong was stunned silent.

"That's enough for now. I have to go extract medicine for pills," Tanlang said languidly. "Why don't you two see yourselves out?"

"Tanlang!"

Xue Zhengyong wanted to say more, but Chu Wanning tugged on the hem of his robes. "Sect Leader, let's go."

When they reached the door, Tanlang's voice suddenly carried to them from behind. "Chu Wanning, if you're willing to beg me properly and humbly, then who knows? I might be willing to help derive a cure. Although I've never seen someone with your condition, I might not necessarily be unable to assist. So why don't you think about it carefully?"

After a long moment, Chu Wanning looked backward. "What would count as 'properly and humbly'?"

Tanlang reclined on the couch, lazily sorting out the bundles of silver needles on the table. He raised his eyes at the sound of

Chu Wanning's voice, disdain apparent in his gaze. "When other people are at the end of their rope, they get on their knees to prostrate themselves to beg for help. We're colleagues, so I won't ask you to get down and knock your head on the floor, but if you kneel and grovel a little, I'll consider it."

Chu Wanning said nothing as he gazed indifferently at him. Only after a while did he say: "Wintertime pickles, you must be dreaming."

With that, Chu Wanning flicked his sleeves and left. The Tanlang Elder was left stunned, unable to figure out what "wintertime pickles" meant even after half a day of pondering.

The days trickled by slowly. The Yuheng Elder declared that he was going into seclusion to meditate, when he was in actuality trapped in the body of a child, unable to return to his original form. Xue Zhengyong, Madam Wang, and the Tanlang Elder had found out about it one after another, and, to prevent the secret's exposure, the Xuanji Elder was also informed.

A few months passed in the blink of an eye. The Red Lotus Pavilion's doors had been closed to visitors for quite a while, and Xue Meng and his fellow disciples worried despite themselves.

"Shizun has been in seclusion for more than seventy days now. Why hasn't he come out yet?"

"Maybe he's refining his cultivation level." Shi Mei took a sip of spiritual mountain dew from his cup and looked up at the dark, overcast skies outside the window. "Looks like it's going to snow. Soon it'll be the New Year. I wonder if Shizun will come out before then."

Mo Ran was flipping lazily through a manual of sword techniques. "Doubt it," he said in response to Shi Mei. "Didn't he send us a message with his haitang flower a couple days ago to say that it would be a while yet? I doubt he'll be out in time."

It was a day of rest on Sisheng Peak, when the disciples didn't need to practice cultivation. Mo Ran, Xue Meng, and Shi Mei had gathered to enjoy some freshly brewed tea and warmed wine. The bamboo curtains of the small pavilion in the yard were half-drawn, the heavy screens concealing its occupants, and steam wafted lightly from beneath the fringe.

There had been a new addition to their little group of late—the Xuanji Elder's disciple, Xia Sini. Ever since that day he met Xue Meng, Xue Meng had dragged the kid along to cultivate or play every couple of days, and before long, the group had become inseparable. Thus the Yuheng Elder's group of three disciples mysteriously became a group of four.

At this moment, Chu Wanning-as-Xia Sini was seated at the table eating pastries. He ate in a refined manner, but the speed at which he consumed them wasn't the least bit lacking.

Xue Meng glanced at him inadvertently and paused in surprise, doing a double take between the plate and Xia Sini. "Wow, Xiao-shidi," he said in amazement, "who'd you inherit that bottomless stomach from?"

Chu Wanning was chewing leisurely on a piece of osmanthus cake. The cake was delicious, and he didn't bother responding to Xue Meng. After all, he was fighting with somebody over the food.

Mo Ran and Chu Wanning's hands landed on the last piece of crispy lotus pastry at the same time. Their eyes shot up, and it seemed as if lightning crackled between their gazes.

"Let go," said Chu Wanning.

"Nope," Mo Ran replied.

"Hands off."

"You've already eaten eight pieces. This one's mine."

"You can have any of the others, just not the lotus pastry."

Mo Ran glared at the little fellow for a while before pulling out his trump card. "Shidi, if you eat too many sweets, you'll get cavities."

"That's fine." Chu Wanning was very calm. "I'm six, so it wouldn't be embarrassing."

Mo Ran was struck speechless.

There was a loud smack as Xue Meng's strike landed alongside his scathing complaints. "Mo Weiyu, how annoying can you get? Fighting with Shidi for food? How old are you?!"

The moment Mo Ran covered his head with an "aiyo!", Chu Wanning snatched the lotus pastry, his hands quick and face expressionless. He felt quite satisfied as he took a small bite.

"Shidi—!"

Chu Wanning ignored him, totally devoted to nibbling on his sweets.

The four disciples were busily making a ruckus when a sharp whistle pierced the skies and reverberated throughout Sisheng Peak.

Chu Wanning's expression grew solemn. "The gathering whistle?"

Xue Meng lifted the hanging curtains halfway up to look outside the window. The disciples who had been walking outside stopped in their tracks to look around with expressions of surprise.

At the sound of the gathering whistle, everyone on Sisheng Peak had to gather in the square before Loyalty Hall. As one might guess, this meant that the whistle was only blown in times of emergency. Before Chu Wanning had joined the sect, this whistle had sounded often—whenever the ghost realm barrier was breached. However, since Chu Wanning's arrival, the whistle hadn't been heard in a long, long time.

Shi Mei put down the book in his hand and got up to walk to Xue Meng's side. "How strange. What could be so urgent?"

"Don't know. No point wondering, let's go take a look first."

Only Mo Ran was silent. He pressed his lips together and his lashes fluttered downward, covering the unnatural flicker flashing through his eyes. He knew what this whistle foretold. However, the timing slightly differed from his memory of the event. He hadn't thought that it would happen so soon...

The four disciples assembled at Sisheng Peak, where the rest of the disciples arrived one after another. Before long, the entirety of Loyalty Square was filled with the sect's elders and their disciples.

Once everyone had gathered, Xue Zhengyong walked out from the tightly shut doors of Loyalty Hall to stand before the jade-banded platform railing, above flights of limestone steps. Six beautiful women followed behind him. Some looked charming while others seemed cold, but all were impossibly gorgeous. They stood against the wind wearing only thin silk robes despite the bitterly frigid weather. At a glance, their red skirts were like unto the clouds at dawn, and their eyes seemed lit with scarlet flames amidst the delicate fluttering of silken ribbons. Finally, a red dot in the shape of a flame lay between each of their eyebrows.

Xue Meng was stunned, and it wasn't only him. The expressions of just about every person in the square changed once they laid eyes on the six women.

Xue Meng stared blankly for a long time before he managed to speak, his voice trembling. "Envoys of the feathered tribe... Did—did they come from Zhuque, the land of immortals?"

55

This Venerable One Feels Uneasy

ZHUQUE MIGHT HAVE BEEN called the land of immortals, but its residents were not, in fact, immortals. Rather, they were a people of mixed blood, half-immortal and half-fae. In the cultivation world, they were the beings that most resembled immortals and were known as the "feathered tribe."

The feathered tribe had always resided at Peach Blossom Springs, which lay beyond the maze of Mount Jiuhua. They rarely ever interfered in the affairs of the mortal realm. However, as half the blood that flowed through their veins was still mortal, they weren't fully detached. Thus they often appeared in times of turmoil or disaster in the cultivation world and used their immense power to help mortals through the crisis.

When Mo Ran had raised hell and turned the world upside down in his last life, the feathered tribe had appeared in droves. In the end, their power had been unable to overcome the emperor, who had already perfected a forbidden technique. Mo Ran had hunted down and killed every last one of them, treading across ground swathed with blood and scorched feathers.

Zhuque, the land of immortals, had been burned to the ground in a single day.

It was a hellishly frenzied memory. Whenever Mo Ran recalled it, he broke out in a cold sweat, thinking himself a man possessed, endlessly cruel.

At present, he patently didn't yet have the strength to contend with the feathered tribe. In fact, due to the natural superiority of their blood, the vast majority of cultivators fell short of their power in terms of spiritual strength. Out of everyone on Sisheng Peak, only a few of the most exceptional elders could even exchange blows with one of them.

Xue Meng caught a glimpse of Mo Ran's face and got quite a scare. "What's up with you? Why's your face so pale?"

"It's nothing." Mo Ran lowered his eyelashes as he whispered, "I just ran too fast earlier."

In his prior lifetime, the arrival of the feathered tribe had marked the beginning of Shi Mei's tragedy. Mo Ran's heart jumped to his throat. He'd thought it would be a while yet before all this recurred. Why had the progression of so many events changed so drastically?

The faint winter sun hung weakly in the sky, illuminating the world in a layer of deathly white. Standing underneath it, Mo Ran found himself reaching out to take Shi Mei's hand.

Shi Mei blinked. "What's wrong?"

Mo Ran shook his head and said nothing.

At this time, Xue Zhengyong began to speak. His words didn't much differ from those he had said in their last life. "I have called everyone here today because envoys of the feathered tribe have once again arrived. Just as they did eighty years ago, they have come to the mortal realm from Peach Blossom Springs to lend aid during a foretold calamity."

A pause as he looked slowly over the disciples gathered below.

"As everyone knows, the barrier to the ghost realm was originally erected by the god Fuxi, but it has gradually weakened over these past million years and breaks every few decades. In recent years, its power has faded by the day, and despite everyone's greatest efforts—"

Xue Meng huffed under his breath. "Dad's talking some nonsense. It's obviously just the efforts of Shizun, more or less."

"Despite everyone's great efforts, the breach grows larger still, and the barrier will eventually fail, as it did decades ago. When that time comes, the boundary between the mortal and ghost realms will be broken, thousands of ghosts and spirits will flood forth, and ordinary people will suffer. In order to avert this calamity, envoys of the feathered tribe have come to the sects to select those with the most suitable spiritual energy and innate skill to go to Peach Blossom Springs, where they will cultivate in seclusion."

His words caused a commotion in the crowd. The feathered tribe was selecting people to go advance their cultivation at Peach Blossom Springs—in the land of the immortals?!

The gathered disciples went from awestruck to excited, and regardless of actual ability, each secretly nursed hopes and expectations.

Only Mo Ran wasn't the least bit enthused. Instead, his features subtly portrayed anxiety. He was typically very good at feigning appearances, so much so that other people could never tell what of him was real and what was fake, but in this moment, he couldn't remotely conceal his feelings.

This had to do with Shi Mei's survival. In the past, Shi Mei had been selected by the feathered tribe and gone to Peach Blossom Springs to cultivate. Not long after his return, the barrier suffered a large-scale breakdown, and untold hordes of ghosts climbed up from hell.

In the ensuing battle, Shi Mei fought alongside Chu Wanning, each taking one side of the array as they worked together to repair the largest breach. However, Shi Mei wasn't as strong as Chu Wanning, and when the countless ghosts saw that the mortal realm was about to be closed off, they charged toward Shi Mei in a murderous torrent as he was focusing on maintaining the balance in the barrier.

They ran him through in an instant. The demonic energy pierced his heart and soul.

And Chu Wanning didn't lift even a single finger to help—didn't even attempt to stop them. As Shi Mei fell from atop the coiled dragon pillar, Chu Wanning instead chose to use all of his remaining power to seal the rest of the barrier that Shi Mei had been unable to mend.

It had been snowing that day. Shi Mei's falling form had seemed like just another one of those innumerable small, insignificant flakes of snow.

The snow fell nonstop, covering the sky. No one cared if a given frozen crystal flake was about to melt, just like how in generation after generation, when an ordinary person met their end after the decades of their lives from birth to death, none but their close relatives cared.

In that snow, in that pandemonium, Mo Ran had held Shi Mei as his breath grew shallower and shallower, had knelt on the ground and begged Chu Wanning to please spare him a glance, to please save him.

In the end, Chu Wanning only turned away, choosing to walk into the boundless white to realize his own prestige, thus severing the bonds between master and disciple.

How laughable. The things Chu Wanning liked, the things he cared about, the things he pursued, all of it was so very laughable.

For example, Chu Wanning liked the sound of rain in the lotus pond, and he liked the melancholy verses of the poet Du Fu,[9] with his frighteningly strict adherence to form.

---

9 *Many literary critics consider Du Fu (杜甫), a Tang dynasty poet, to be one of China's greatest poets. His works were known for their mastery of classical poetic forms and furthermore touched on the sociopolitical concerns of his time, with an emphasis on compassion for the common people.*

For another, Chu Wanning cared about the sprouting of plants in the coming of spring, and the death of cicadas with the arrival of autumn; he cared about where the flames of war were lit once again, and where the common people struggled.

For yet another, Chu Wanning had always taught that it was righteous to put the people before the self.

But Mo Ran thought: Fuck the people! He didn't know or care about those people. What did it matter to him whether they lived or died?

If Chu Wanning's rain fell upon the mutterings of lost souls, if his plants were splashed with the tears of refugees, Mo Ran didn't care. His rain was everyday rain, and his plants were ordinary plants. The "common people" were just a couple of words on a piece of paper. Who the hell cared?

And so he thought Chu Wanning was despicable, a hypocrite who spouted words of duty and compassion as if his heart was big enough to hold everything under the sky. In reality, that pathetically small heart of his hadn't even had a place for his own disciple.

Afterward, Mo Ran had savagely asked Chu Wanning, *Does your heart ache? How can you live with yourself? You say to put the people before the self, but you're still alive while Shi Mei died following your commands! You're the one who got him killed, you hypocrite—you liar!*

Do you even have a heart?

When Shi Mei fell from the platform, he was calling for you. He was calling "Shizun"—did you hear him? Did you? Why didn't you save him...? Why didn't you save him?!

Chu Wanning, you have a stone for a heart.

You've...never cared about us.

You didn't care... You didn't care...

And then everything had ended up the way it did.

Chu Wanning was adored and respected by everyone in the cultivation world, practically a king in all but name, and no one spared a thought for those who had perished. Shi Mei's death was an unremarkable step under the feet of the victorious.

Chu Wanning had traded an ungifted disciple for peace and prosperity, for so-called world peace. No one would say he was wrong to do so.

Only Mo Ran saw that the brilliant crown atop his head was made of the bones of the dead. That his success had been built on Shi Mei's death.

Hatred welled from the bottom of his heart.

"Hey, young man. Hey—"

All of a sudden, there was a warm hand on Mo Ran's forehead. He started and opened his eyes as he was ripped from his pitch-black memories.

Before him was a delicate face, bright and lovely. One of the envoys of the feathered tribe had approached without his notice, and she was smiling gently at him.

"Falling into a trance with such a great opportunity right in front of you?"

"Ah, big sis, please don't mind me." Mo Ran did his best to cheer up so as to not rouse any suspicion, and he smiled back at the envoy. "I've always been given to daydreams, and I was so hoping to be selected that I got lost imagining what Peach Blossom Springs might look like. So sorry about that."

It turned out that, while Mo Ran was lost in his memories, the envoys of the feathered tribe had descended and begun selecting people. He had been so caught up in his tangled thoughts that he had been wholly unaware of the things happening around him.

The envoy smiled sweetly, then said something that Mo Ran hadn't at all expected. "Your spiritual energy is pure, and your cultivation and aptitude are both remarkable as well. If you wish to go to Peach Blossom Springs, then come along with me."

Mo Ran was stunned for a long moment before it hit him. Go to Peach Blossom Springs? In his last lifetime, only Shi Mei and Chu Wanning had been chosen, so why, in this life—

He was too shocked to speak. Luckily, being chosen by the feathered tribe was something worthy of shock and amazement, so the people nearby didn't find his reaction remotely odd and only gazed at him with envy.

The envoy brought him to Loyalty Hall, and as the initial shock subsided and Mo Ran's heart stopped hammering in his chest, his eyes began to fill with an ecstasy that no one else detected.

Things were indeed different this life.

Even though he didn't yet know if these changes were for the better or for the worse, or why exactly fate had changed at all, at least he could go to Peach Blossom Springs as well. If he also studied under the feathered tribe, then when the time came, the heavy task of repairing the barrier might not fall on Shi Mei.

Mo Ran wasn't a cultured man; even after living two lives, he still didn't understand what "putting the people before the self" really meant. What he *did* know was that Shi Mei was kinder to him than anyone else in the world, and that nothing mattered more than him—including Mo Ran's own meat sack and half a wisp of returned soul.

As long as Shi Mei lived, Mo Ran would throw everything else away.

When the envoys had finished their selection and gathered them all in front of Loyalty Hall, Mo Ran found that the lineup completely differed from the one in his last life.

Shi Mei was there, as before, but as a result of being in seclusion, Chu Wanning had missed the selection, so he wasn't amongst the chosen. In his place was the Xuanji Elder's disciple, Xia Sini.

Even more surprising was the fact that Xue Meng had also been invited. Per the words of the envoy, "The power of the Exalted Gouchen's sacred sword lingers on your person. How interesting."

From the Heaven-Piercing Tower nearby there came the deep sound of a clock reverberating throughout Sisheng Peak.

"From Sisheng Peak of the lower cultivation realm, the chosen are Xue Ziming, Mo Weiyu, Shi Mingjing, and Xia Sini, for a total of four," the head of the envoys conveyed to Xue Zhengyong, before releasing a messenger myna bird. She lifted her hand with the vividly colored bird perched atop a fingertip, then continued in a clear voice, "These four are exceptional individuals, suitable in aptitude and sincere in character. Thus concludes this report."

With that, she released the bird. The myna memorized her words and, with a flutter of its powerful wings, quickly vanished into the vast skies.

To be able to go cultivate at Peach Blossom Springs was a rare opportunity, even more so than acquiring a holy weapon, and no one would turn it down. Moreover, they would be studying techniques to ward against the breakdown of the barrier to the ghost realm, the foremost duty and obligation of all those who cultivated. No one could decline.

As for the time, it would take anywhere from a couple of months to three or even five years. The feathered tribe was not unreasonable. Seeing as it was nearly the end of the year, they instructed the chosen to stay and spend New Year's Eve at home. After that, they would return to bring the group to Peach Blossom Springs at Mount Jiuhua.

When Mo Ran thought about how he would soon be able to go with Shi Mei to Peach Blossom Springs, he couldn't be anything but overjoyed. However, it wasn't long before the joy faded. He didn't understand why, at first, until one day he passed the foot of the southern peak of Sisheng Peak and looked up to see the sealed-off Red Lotus Pavilion.

Mo Ran's steps slowed unconsciously, then came to a stop altogether. He stood there, gazing up where the mountain disappeared into the clouds.

Chu Wanning had been in seclusion for over three months.

In this life, the hatred Mo Ran held toward this person seemed to be ebbing away. Even if he reminded himself time and again to not forget the look on Chu Wanning's face when he'd abandoned Mo Ran and Shi Mei, there were times when he empathized with his shizun—when he felt confused and disconcerted.

Xia Sini was walking with him. Upon seeing the odd expression on Mo Ran's face and the way he stared at the southern peak, lost in thought, his heart skipped a beat. "What is it?"

"Xiao-shidi, do you think he'll come out before we leave?"

"He?"

"Ah." Mo Ran paused, coming back to his senses, and smiled down at Chu Wanning. Having spent quite some time together, he felt that this little shidi was clever and sensible, and he had grown very fond. "I was talking about my shizun, the Yuheng Elder."

"I see..."

Mo Ran sighed. "He's never been in seclusion for so long before," he muttered. "Could it be that the injury he received at Jincheng Lake was actually super serious?"

This was the first time in a long while that Mo Ran had brought up his shizun of his own accord. Chu Wanning already knew that it was impossible, but he still couldn't stop himself from asking, "Do you...miss him?"

56

This Venerable One Is Busy Wrapping Dumplings

UPON BEING ASKED this question, Mo Ran's face was one of bewilderment.

Do I miss him?

In spite of the deep, unforgettable resentment Mo Ran harbored from his previous life, the Chu Wanning of this life had yet to wrong him. In fact, Mo Ran's shizun had shielded him from danger over and over, and he'd furthermore been the one to get himself covered in injuries from head to toe and bruised black and blue, also for Mo Ran.

After a long time, Mo Ran finally responded, "Mn... All those times that he's been injured, it was because of me..."

When Chu Wanning heard this sentiment, he felt a twinge of warmth in his heart. However, before he could say something to Mo Ran in return, Mo Ran continued.

"He's done too much for me, and I can only hope to help him recover a little bit faster. I don't want to owe him anything."

The flicker of warmth in Chu Wanning's heart seemed to die, perfectly unmoving, frozen over. He stood still for a little while, feeling profoundly risible.

Mo Ran had already told him that their only tie was that of a master and his disciple. It was nobody's fault but his own that the slightest scrap of hope had sent him dizzy with excitement, flying like a moth into a blazing fire. If he was scorched to ashes, that was entirely on him.

Chu Wanning smiled; it was probably an ugly, dejected smile. "You're overthinking it. You are his disciple, so 'owing debts' doesn't apply. Everything he does, he does willingly."

Mo Ran's eyes turned to him. "Oh you. You're so young, but you always look so serious and talk like a grown up." He laughed brightly and patted Chu Wanning's head.

At first, having his head patted like that made Chu Wanning laugh along, but after a while, his eyes slowly filled with tears, and he looked up to the dazzlingly brilliant face in front of him. "Mo Ran," he said softly, "I don't want to play with you anymore. Let go."

Mo Ran's skull was several inches too thick. He didn't notice the change in his shidi's expression. Besides that, he had grown so used to horsing around and being rowdy with "Xia Sini" that he didn't hesitate to pinch the child's soft, baby-smooth cheeks, squishing them and tugging his lips up into a funny face. "Pfft, Xiao-shidi, what's got you mad?"

Chu Wanning stared at the child reflected in Mo Ran's eyes. The smile into which that face had been pulled was terribly ugly, making it look like an absurd, pathetic monster. "Let go."

Mo Ran obliviously continued to tease him as before. "Okay, okay, don't be mad. I won't say that you're pretending to be an adult, hm? Come here, let's make up. Call me 'Shige'?"

"Let go of me..."

"Be good, call me 'Shige,' and in a bit, I'll buy you osmanthus cake for a snack."

Chu Wanning closed his eyes, eyelashes trembling slightly, and finally spoke, his voice hoarse: "Mo Ran, I'm not kidding around. I really don't want to play with you anymore. Can you let go of me?

Let go, okay?" His slender eyebrows knitted together, and his tears didn't trickle from his eyes only because they were tightly shut. However, his voice was choked with sobs. "Mo Ran, it hurts..."

It hurt too much, holding someone in his heart like this, hidden carefully in the very depths of his thoughts. It was fine if that person didn't like him, as long as he could think about that person quietly and protect them silently. It was fine if he couldn't have that person. All of it was fine.

But that person's warmth and tenderness were bestowed upon others while the only things offered to him were barbs and thorns. So although Chu Wanning held him in his heart, whenever that person moved, his heart would start to bleed. Day after day, new wounds appeared before the old ones had a chance to heal.

It was then that Chu Wanning knew that even if he wasn't vying to capture this person's affections, every single moment that he continued to hold him in his heart would hurt him to his core. He didn't know how much longer he'd be able to bear this pain. Didn't know when it would break him completely.

Mo Ran finally noticed that something was off and frantically let go. He touched the boy's red-tinged cheeks. He had no idea what to do.

It suddenly occurred to Chu Wanning that perhaps being in the body of a child wasn't such a bad thing. At least this way he could say "it hurts" without reserve—could show a little bit of vulnerability. At least this way he could get Mo Ran to look at him with genuine concern.

This was something that he had never even dared to think before.

In the blink of an eye, it was New Year's Eve. This was the liveliest time of year on Sisheng Peak. The disciples were busy putting up red paper talismans and sweeping snowdrifts. The head chef at Mengpo Hall was busy from dawn till dusk, preparing delicacies for the end-of-year feast. On top of that, the elders devised spells and charms in their areas of expertise to add to the festivities that would welcome the New Year.

For example, the Tanlang Elder transformed a pool of fresh spring water into fragrant wine, and the Xuanji Elder released three thousand firelight mice that he'd been raising, allowing them to scatter throughout the sect and to keep watch wherever they went, bringing everyone a touch of warmth and respite from the cold. Meanwhile, the Lucun Elder enchanted the snowmen everyone had made to run around the peak and yell "Happy New Year" at anyone they ran into.

No one expected the Yuheng Elder to do anything; as a matter of fact, he was still in seclusion. He'd been gone for a long time and hadn't once been seen in public.

Xue Meng stood by the window, his face tilted upward, gazing at the petals of haitang blossoms fluttering down from the skies. "We'll be gone tomorrow," he said pensively. "It seems we won't be able to see him before we leave after all... I wonder what Shizun's doing right now?"

"He's definitely cultivating," Mo Ran said around a mouthful of apple. "Speaking of which, all the elders are supposed to put on a performance tonight. It sucks that Shizun isn't here—if he was, he'd have to perform too. I wonder what he could even do." Mo Ran laughed. "Maybe he'd put on a demonstration of 'How to Get Angry,' eh?"

Xue Meng glared at him. "How about a performance of 'Whipping Mo Weiyu to Death'?"

It was the New Year, so Mo Ran didn't feel like getting worked up over Xue Meng's harsh joke. Then he thought of something and asked, "Oh yeah, have you seen our little shidi today?"

"You mean Xia Sini?" Xue Meng asked. "I haven't seen him, but in any case, he's the Xuanji Elder's disciple. Xuanji is already being gracious enough to let him hang out with us all the time. If he stuck with us even during the New Year's festivities, his shizun might finally get upset."

Mo Ran laughed. "I guess."

The rays of the setting sun turned to evening above the Red Lotus Pavilion. Chu Wanning carefully looked over the pill he held in his hand. Xue Zhengyong was sitting across from him and pouring himself a cup of tea, since Chu Wanning hadn't invited him to have some. He also ate a crispy pastry from the plate, etiquette be damned.

Chu Wanning glared at him, but Xue Zhengyong kept chewing obliviously. "Yuheng, aren't you done looking at it yet? Tanlang can be pretty harsh with his words, but his intentions aren't remotely bad. It's not like he'd truly harm you."

"What are you saying, Sect Leader?" Chu Wanning replied lightly. "I was just thinking that since the Tanlang Elder went through the trouble to concoct a pill that will allow me to regain my adult form for a single day, why didn't he create a couple more of them? That way, I could just take one when the need arose."

"Aiya, if only it were that easy," Xue Zhengyong said. "The raw materials that go into making this medicine are rare beyond measure, and after creating three of them, Tanlang's already out of ingredients. It's not a long-term solution."

"I see," Chu Wanning said, deep in thought. "So that's how it is. Please give him my thanks."

"Ha ha." Xue Zhengyong waved his hand. "You two are actually pretty similar, you know: curt with your words, but not bad at heart."

Chu Wanning shot him a glare but didn't say anything. He poured himself a cup of tea and swallowed this medicine that would allow him to assume his original form.

Xue Zhengyong was about to eat another pastry when Chu Wanning stopped his hand.

"Huh?" the sect leader said unhappily.

"Mine," said Chu Wanning.

Xue Zhengyong blinked, at a loss.

When night fell on Sisheng Peak, the disciples filtered into Mengpo Hall, one after another. Each elder brought their disciples and sat down with them to knead dough and make dumplings. Both the snowmen and the firelight mice threaded through the throngs of people, passing them jars of salt, red pepper powder, saucers of chopped scallions, and other miscellaneous ingredients.

Every table bustled with excitement and chattering laughter. The Yuheng Elder's table was the only exception—the disciples were all there, but their master was absent.

Xue Meng looked around for a bit and sighed. "I miss Shizun."

"Didn't Shizun send us a letter a few days ago, telling us to enjoy the festivities and to work hard on our cultivation at Peach Blossom Springs?" Shi Mei replied warmly. "He said that he'll come see us as soon as he comes out of seclusion."

"He did say that, but just when will that be?" Xue Meng sighed sorrowfully, his eyes wandering listlessly past the gates. Then he suddenly sat up straight, eyes opened wide like a cat as he stared. His face paled, then colored, flushing a dizzying shade of red, and his eyes shone brightly. He was so excited that he couldn't even speak properly. "That... That's... That's..."

Mo Ran's first thought was that one of the rare spirit beasts that the Xuanji Elder raised had escaped to liven things up a bit, so he assumed Xue Meng was surprised because he was inexperienced and thus overreacting. "That's what?" he laughed. "Look at you, it's like you just saw an immortal or something. What's there to be so sur—"

Mo Ran turned around, still grinning gleefully, and casually looked up.

And couldn't finish the rest of his sentence.

Standing in the snowy dusk outside the door was Chu Wanning, dressed in white robes with a vividly red cloak. He turned elegantly to the side to put away his umbrella and shake off the dusting of snow. Then his eyelashes flicked up to reveal a pair of bright, slender phoenix eyes beneath them, and a mild glance swept over them.

By the time Mo Ran came back to his senses, this one glance had his heart beating fast and his palms covered in sweat. Even his breathing had involuntarily slowed.

The chatter in Mengpo Hall gradually quieted. Usually, whenever Chu Wanning appeared in the hall, the disciples didn't dare cause a ruckus—even more so now that he'd suddenly appeared on New Year's Eve after having been in seclusion for such a long time. The snowflakes on Chu Wanning's face seemed to make it even fairer and more beautiful, just as they made his eyebrows seem darker and more defined.

Mo Ran stood up, murmuring, "Shizun..."

Xue Meng bounded up and sprinted toward Chu Wanning like an excited kitten, yelling, "Shizun!" as he threw himself into Chu Wanning's arms.

Chu Wanning's clothes were thoroughly chilled from the bitter cold outside, but Xue Meng wore an expression like he was holding peach blossoms from early spring, or a coal fire from late summer—endlessly warm. He began to shout raucously, not stopping to take a breath: "Shizun, you've finally emerged! I thought that we wouldn't be able to see you before leaving, but you do love us after all! Shizun, Shizun...."

Shi Mei also came forward and bowed respectfully, his face beaming with delight. "Welcome back from your seclusion, Shizun."

Chu Wanning patted Xue Meng's head and nodded in Shi Mei's direction. "This master has arrived slightly late, but let's go greet the New Year together." He sat down at the feast with Xue Meng at his side and Mo Ran across from him.

With Chu Wanning's arrival—and after the initial hubbub and excitement died down—the three disciples fell into their usual habits, sitting upright and still like their shizun. Their table was weirdly silent.

Flour, ground meat, eggs, and many other types of ingredients lay on the table, along with a brand-new copper coin. Mo Ran was the one with the best cooking skills in their group, so everyone decided that he'd be the one to give instructions.

"Well, I guess I'll take charge, then," Mo Ran said, laughing. "Do you guys know how to roll dough?"

No one uttered a word.

"Okay, I'll roll out the wrappers, then. Shi Mei, you make the best wontons, and dumpling filling isn't all that different, so why don't you make the filling?"

Shi Mei hesitated for a moment before saying, "Well... There is some difference, you know. I'm afraid that I might not be able to do it properly."

"It's fine as long as it's edible, don't worry so much," Chu Wanning replied lightly.

Shi Mei smiled. "Okay, then."

"Xue Meng, you can pass the water or help roll our sleeves up or something. Just don't get in the way."

Xue Meng was speechless.

"As for Shizun." Mo Ran grinned. "Would Shizun like to sit by the side and have a nice cup of tea?"

"I'll wrap the dumplings," Chu Wanning replied coldly.

"Ah?" Mo Ran exclaimed, startled. He wondered if he'd gone violently deaf in both ears. "What did you say you want to do?"

"I said, I'll wrap the dumplings."

Mo Ran couldn't respond. He began to think that he would much rather have gone violently deaf in both ears after all.

57 This Venerable One Listens to You Play the Guqin Once Again

UNEXPECTEDLY, although Chu Wanning's dumpling-wrapping technique was clumsy, the finished product wasn't bad. The dumplings made by his long fingers were adorably round as they were lined neatly on the table.

All three disciples were dumbstruck.

"Shizun actually knows how to make dumplings..."

"Am I dreaming right now?"

Of course their hushed mutterings didn't escape Chu Wanning's ears. He pressed his lips together, eyelashes fluttering imperceptibly, and even though he was as expressionless as always, the tips of his ears turned a bit pink.

Xue Meng couldn't resist asking, "Shizun, is this your first time making dumplings?"

"Mn."

"Then how are you making them look so nice?"

"It's not so different from making automatons. You just fold a few creases, there's nothing to it."

Mo Ran watched Chu Wanning from across the wooden table, gradually becoming lost in thought. The only time he had ever seen Chu Wanning cook in his last life had been after Shi Mei's passing.

That day, Chu Wanning had gone to the kitchen and slowly made the wontons that were Shi Mei's specialty.

Before they could make it into the pot, they had been struck to the ground by a Mo Ran who had lost his senses. The snowy wontons had rolled across the floor.

Mo Ran had no recollection whatsoever as to whether those wontons had been round or flat, well-made or deformed. The only thing he remembered was the look on Chu Wanning's face, the way he had stared at Mo Ran without a word with bits of flour still on his face, looking strangely unfamiliar and somewhat uncomprehending, even a bit dumb...

Mo Ran had thought that his shizun would be angry, but in the end, Chu Wanning said nothing. He only bent over and, with his head lowered, quietly picked up the dirty wontons one by one, gathered them up, and tossed them in the trash.

Just what had been going through Chu Wanning's mind at that time? Mo Ran didn't know; he had never thought about it, never wanted to think about it, and truthfully, hadn't dared to think about it.

The dumplings were all wrapped, and the little snowmen carried them away to the kitchen to be boiled. In accordance with tradition, Chu Wanning inserted a copper coin into one of them. Whoever got it would have good luck.

It wasn't long before the snowmen brought back the cooked dumplings, complete with spicy, sour dipping sauce in the wooden tray.

"Shizun, please go ahead first," said Xue Meng.

Chu Wanning did not decline. He picked up a dumpling with his chopsticks and put it in his bowl. However, he didn't eat it and instead picked up three more to give to Xue Meng, Mo Ran, and Shi Mei. "Happy New Year," he said mildly.

The disciples were taken aback for a moment before they broke into smiles. "Happy New Year, Shizun."

As it happened, on the very first dumpling, Mo Ran bit into the copper coin with a crack. He was caught totally off guard and nearly broke a tooth.

Shi Mei laughed at the grimace on his face. "A-Ran, you'll have good luck this year."

Xue Meng said only, "Tch, lucky bastard."

Mo Ran said, teary-eyed, "Thithun, you're a li'l too goo' at pickin' dumplinth. I go' it on the ve'y firth one..."

Chu Wanning said, "Speak properly."

"I bi' my tongue."

Chu Wanning had absolutely no reply to that.

Mo Ran rubbed his cheek and took a sip of the tea Shi Mei offered before the pain finally subsided a little, and he immediately began joking around. "Ha ha, could it be that Shizun memorized which dumpling had the copper coin and deliberately gave it to me?"

"You wish," Chu Wanning said coldly, then lowered his head and started eating.

Mo Ran wasn't sure if he was seeing things, but under the warm light of the candles, Chu Wanning's face seemed a little red.

After the dumplings, a sumptuous dinner prepared by the head chef was brought out. Platefuls of meat and fish covered the entire table. Mengpo Hall grew even livelier. From the seats of honor, Xue Zhengyong and Madam Wang directed the little snowmen to deliver red packets to every group.

A little snowman bumped insistently against Chu Wanning's knee, the stones that were its eyes rolling around as it stared at him.

Chu Wanning blinked. "Hm? Even I get one?" He accepted the red packet and opened it to find several sheets of pricey gold leaf. A little lost for words, he looked up at Xue Zhengyong only to see the carefree man grinning back at him before he raised the cup of wine in his hand toward Chu Wanning in a toast.

How silly. Then again, Xue Zhengyong was really...truly... Chu Wanning stared at him for a while and, despite himself, a faint smile curved the corners of his lips. He raised his own cup toward the sect leader in return and downed it in one gulp.

Chu Wanning divided the golden leaves amongst his disciples. Three rounds of drinks later, accompanied by nonstop performances on the stage, the atmosphere at their table finally grew lively as well. This was mostly because the three brats had grown less afraid of him. As for Chu Wanning, he'd always been able to hold his alcohol.

"Shizun, Shizun, let me read your palm?" Xue Meng was the first to get tipsy. He grabbed Chu Wanning's hand and held it in front of his eyes to carefully examine. If not for the three cups of wine in his system, he never would've dared to be so bold. "Your lifeline is long but disjointed, which means your health isn't too good," Xue Meng mumbled. "You get sick easily."

Mo Ran laughed. "That's pretty accurate."

Chu Wanning shot him a glare.

"A long and slender ring finger. Shizun has good fortune with money. Three lines from a common point—the love line branches off at its tip to merge down into the wisdom line, which typically indicates a willingness to sacrifice for love..." Xue Meng stared at it blankly for a while before whipping his head up. "Is that true?"

Face ashen, Chu Wanning hissed between gritted teeth, "Xue Ziming, are you tired of being alive?"

But Xue Meng, too drunk to detect mortal danger, grinned sincerely and kept right on looking. "Ah, and the love line forms an island shape," he muttered. "Right beneath the ring finger, at that. Shizun, your taste in love is dreadful… Absolutely abysmal…"

Chu Wanning had had enough. He ripped his hand away and brushed his sleeve down to leave.

Mo Ran was about to die of laughter, doubled over holding his stomach and cackling loudly, when he suddenly caught Chu Wanning's icy, murderous gaze and forcibly swallowed his mirth. His ribs ached with the effort.

"What're you laughing about?" Chu Wanning said furiously. "What's so funny?"

He was about to storm off in a fit of pique when Xue Meng grabbed his sleeve. In the next instant, laughter disappeared from Mo Ran's face as Xue Meng pulled Chu Wanning down in a drunken daze and burrowed into his arms. His forehead pressed into the folds of his shizun's robes, and his arms wrapped around Chu Wanning's waist as he nuzzled affectionately.

"Shizun…" came the teenager's soft, velvety voice, complete with a tinge of acting cute. "Don't goooo. Come, come, have another round, heh heh."

Chu Wanning looked like he was going to choke. "Xue Ziming! Wh-what do you think you're doing? Let go!"

Right at that moment, the little snowmen from the stage suddenly clacked over. It turned out that the Tanlang Elder's sword dance performance was over, and it was now Chu Wanning's turn to put on a show.

Unfortunately, this also meant that all the eyes in the hall turned collectively toward Chu Wanning just in time to see a drunken Xue Meng clinging to the Yuheng Elder's waist and burrowing into his arms like a spoiled child. The disciples were absolutely flabbergasted. One of them even held their chopsticks upside down. All eyes staring unblinkingly at their corner.

Chu Wanning was trapped in utter silence.

For a moment, the scene was incandescently awkward. The Yuheng Elder could neither stand nor sit, locked stiffly in place by the way Xue Meng clung on him.

A long while passed in silence before two dry, forced chuckles came from Mo Ran's direction. "Come on, Xue Meng, still acting so spoiled at your age?" He reached out and tried to drag him off. "Off you get, don't cling to Shizun like that."

Xue Meng wasn't acting like a brat on purpose. In fact, if he still remembered this when the alcohol wore off, he would probably slap himself silly. At present, he was drunk beyond all reason, and Mo Ran had to pry and pull for quite a while before he finally managed to rip his cousin off of Chu Wanning.

"Sit. What number is this?"

Brows knitted, Xue Meng squinted at the single finger Mo Ran held out. "Three."

Mo Ran stared at him in incredulous silence.

Shi Mei laughed and couldn't resist teasing him. "Who am I?"

Xue Meng rolled his eyes impatiently. "You're Shi Mei, duh."

"Then who am I?" Mo Ran asked.

Xue Meng glared at him for a while. "A dog."

Mo Ran was stunned for a long moment before he roared, "Xue Ziming, I'm gonna make you eat those words!"

Suddenly, a Sisheng Peak disciple from the adjacent table—who was either naturally courageous or whose inhibitions had also been taken by alcohol—pointed at Chu Wanning and gleefully asked in a high-pitched voice, "Hey, young master, look over there. Who's that?"

Xue Meng, an authentic lightweight, could no longer even sit up. He slumped over the table, propped his cheek in one hand, and squinted at Chu Wanning long and hard.

Chu Wanning stared back in silence. Xue Meng continued to squint. Chu Wanning continued to stare. And Xue Meng continued to squint.

The deadlock lasted for a long while, but just when everyone thought that Xue Meng was about to pass out drunk, he suddenly grinned widely and tried to grab Chu Wanning's sleeve again. "Immortal-gege."

The words were clear and unmistakable. Every last one of the disciples was left utterly unable to make a sound.

"Pfft."

There was no way to tell who started laughing first, but everyone soon lost control and joined in. Even if Chu Wanning's face was dour and his fuse was short, they figured that if everyone got in on the joke, then it wasn't like he could pull out Tianwen and whip every single person in the room. And so the lively Mengpo Hall roared with laughter, everyone chiming in over meat and booze, adding to the chaos.

"Ha ha, Immortal-gege."

"The Yuheng Elder is so pretty that he really does look like an immortal."

"He really does. To tell you the truth, I secretly wrote a line of poetry about him once."

"Yeah? How'd it go?"

"The snow upon a thousand untrod mortal peaks / Would pale against an inch of white upon the immortal's robes."

"Wow, when'd you think of that?"

"Not gonna lie, it was during one of his lectures on barriers."

"That's some guts you've got there, my brave fellow. You better make sure the Yuheng Elder never finds out that you were staring at him and getting all poetically inspired during his barrier lecture, or else the immortal's gonna commit murder, and your line's gonna have to become 'The leaves upon a thousand autumn trees / Would pale against a smear of red upon the immortal's robes.'"

"So cruel!"

"Heh heh, just telling it like it is."

Chu Wanning's face spun through a roulette of colors before he finally decided to fake composure and pretend to have heard nothing at all.

He was used to being revered from a distance, but this sudden intimacy born of the festive atmosphere and the abundance of wine left him unsure of how to respond. Faced with such a situation, he genuinely didn't know how to react and could only force himself to fake a calm that he didn't feel.

Yet the bloom of pink on his ears betrayed the frozen expression on his handsome face.

Mo Ran noticed. He pressed his lips together and said nothing, but for some reason, an explosion of irritating jealousy surged through his chest.

It wasn't that he couldn't acknowledge Chu Wanning's good looks, it was only that, like everyone else, he knew well that Chu Wanning's beauty was the sharp sort, like the edge of a blade, and that when he wasn't smiling, he was cold as snow and frost, too forbidding to approach.

From his dim and narrow perspective, Chu Wanning was like a plate of savory and aromatic crispy meat that had been placed into a filthy, broken box. Mo Ran was the only person in the entire world who had opened the box and been able to taste the deliciousness inside. He'd never had to worry about someone else finding out about this delicacy and drooling over it.

But tonight, bathed in the warmth of the stove fire and tipsy from the warmed wine, so many pairs of eyes were turned toward this box that had once been of no interest to anyone.

Mo Ran suddenly felt nervous. He wanted to cover the box and chase away the people salivating over his food like he'd swat away annoying flies.

Then he remembered that, in this life, the crispy meat didn't belong to him. His hands were full of clear, translucent wontons; he had no time to chase away the wolves drooling over another meal.

To the surprise of Mo Ran and his fellows, Chu Wanning had come prepared with a New Year's performance just like the other elders: he would play the guqin.

The disciples were starry-eyed, and someone whispered, "Who would have thought that the Yuheng Elder knew how to play the guqin?"

"He's so good at it too. I nearly forgot to try the meat."

Mo Ran sat there quietly without a word. Xue Meng had fallen asleep a while ago, his breaths deep and even from where he was sprawled on the table. Mo Ran took the jar of wine by his hand and filled his own cup, drinking from it as he listened while staring at the person on stage, lost in thought.

The irritation in his chest grew worse. In his last life, Chu Wanning hadn't played anything at the New Year's Eve feast. Very few people knew how he looked when playing the guqin.

There had been a guqin made of paulownia wood in the courtyard where Mo Ran had kept Chu Wanning prisoner. One day, maybe to vent his frustrations, Chu Wanning had sat before it, closed his eyes, and played a song.

The sound of the guqin had drifted through the air, attracting birds and butterflies alike. When Mo Ran had returned, the sight that had greeted him had been that of Chu Wanning's profile in the courtyard, indescribably lofty and serene.

And just how had he treated him at that moment? Oh, right.

Mo Ran had pushed him down and fucked him next to the guqin, violated this man who was as clear and cold as the light of the moon, right there in the courtyard. Mo Ran had cared only about chasing his own pleasure. He hadn't spared a single thought for Chu Wanning's pain and discomfort. He had even disregarded the fact that it was winter, and his shizun, who couldn't handle the chill, had laid there on the ice-cold cobblestone with his robes torn off and been fucked until he couldn't take it anymore and passed out.

Afterward, he had not fully recovered even after months of careful tending.

At the time, Mo Ran had said in a chilly tone, "Chu Wanning, from now on, you're forbidden from playing the guqin in front of others. Do you have any idea? The way you look when playing is so..."

He'd pressed his lips together, but he had been unable to find the right words, so he hadn't finished the sentence.

It's so what? It was self-evidently a serene, dignified look, but for some reason, it was so alluring that it had destroyed every bit of Mo Ran's self-control.

Chu Wanning had said nothing, his lips pale and eyes closed, the set of his eyebrows stern.

Mo Ran raised a hand and hesitated for a second before touching the tightly knitted space between Chu Wanning's brows. Taxian-jun's gestures were almost gentle, but his voice was harsh and ruthless. "If you won't listen, this venerable one will chain you to the bed, and then you won't be able to do anything but sleep with him. Don't think this venerable one won't do it."

And just how had Chu Wanning responded?

Mo Ran took another sip, watching the person on the stage, and continued his melancholic recollection.

He couldn't be sure; maybe Chu Wanning had said nothing. Or maybe he had opened his eyes and icily said: "Get the hell out."

He couldn't remember anymore. Not clearly. In that life, Mo Ran had been entangled with Chu Wanning for so long that many things had become blurred at the edges.

Eventually, like a beast, he had known only one thing: that Chu Wanning was his. Even if he didn't care for Chu Wanning, he was still his to sunder and to ruin. He'd have preferred to rip Chu Wanning apart with his own hands—bite through his ribcage and tear out his organs like a beast—than allow someone else to touch him.

Mo Ran wanted Chu Wanning's blood to course with his desire, his bones to bear his curse, and his body to be filled with his passion.

Hadn't Chu Wanning always been so virtuous and untouchable? And in the end, hadn't he still had to spread his legs for the world's most wicked villain, on the bed of the most ruthless tyrant, and had his life taken by the man's fiery weapon? Mo Ran had defiled him, made him filthy inside and out, all over.

Clothes, once shredded, weren't so easy to put back on.

Mo Ran closed his eyes, knuckles white, heart hammering. Sunken deep into his memories, he could no longer hear the lively merriment of New Year's Eve festivities, nor the soothing sounds of Chu Wanning's guqin. All that remained in his mind was a callous, crazed voice, swooping back from the past and hovering like a vulture.

"Hell is too cold. Chu Wanning, I'll take you to the grave with me.

"That's right, you're a god. You're everyone's light—all of them. Xue Meng, Mei Hanxue, and all the common people are just waiting for you to shine on them. Chu-zongshi, how very saintly of you."

The voice laughed sweetly, laughed and laughed, until it suddenly became cruel, like a soul split in half. "But what about me?!" it thundered. "Have you ever shone on me?! Ever given me your warmth? All you've ever given me were these scars on my body! How very saintly of you, Chu Wanning!

"Your body is mine, and your life too. You want to be their fire, but I'll take you to the grave with me. I'll make you shine on my dead body and nothing else. I want you to rot with me.

"To live or to die, neither is your choice to make..."

Loud cheering and applause. Mo Ran's eyes flew open. His back was drenched in a cold sweat.

The performance had ended, and the disciples were clapping enthusiastically. Sitting in the crowd, Mo Ran felt his vision pulse and blur, fading in and out. He watched Chu Wanning walk slowly down the wooden steps, holding a guqin made of paulownia wood.

In that moment, for the very first time in this life, Mo Ran suddenly felt that it was all so absurd. That his past self must have been mad. Chu Wanning wasn't actually a bad guy... Why was he even...doing any of this?

Mo Ran swallowed, feeling the burn of the alcohol down his throat. But he felt at no less of a loss, exhausted and confused, until finally he fell into a drunken oblivion.

58
This Venerable One Feels a Little Hazy

As a matter of fact, Mo Ran could usually hold his liquor pretty well. It was just that on this night, in order to cover for his anxieties and fake a nonchalance he didn't feel, he downed five whole jars of pear-blossom white wine, grinning the whole time, until his consciousness grew hazy.

When he was half dragged, half carried back to his room by Shi Mei and collapsed on his bed, Mo Ran's throat moved. He wanted to call Shi Mei's name.

But habit was a frightful thing. During all those years in the past, the one by his side hadn't been the moonlight of his heart, but the mosquito blood he had grown sick of looking at. The name that came out of his mouth was that of the person he had always thought he hated.

"Chu Wanning..." It came out all muddled. "Wanning... I..."

Shi Mei hesitated, then turned to look toward Chu Wanning, who was standing by the door. Chu Wanning had carried Xue Meng back to his room, and now he walked in, a bowl of sobering soup in hand, just in time to hear Mo Ran's murmur.

After the initial surprise, Chu Wanning convinced himself that he had misheard. After all, Mo Ran had always called him "Shizun." And it was one thing for Mo Ran to call him "Chu Wanning," but to call him *"Wanning"*—

His mind tracked back to that night at the Red Lotus Pavilion, when they had slept holding one another and Mo Ran, fast asleep, had clearly called out "Wanning," then pressed a kiss to his lips, light as the touch of a dragonfly on water. Was it possible that, in Mo Ran's heart, there actually was a little bit of...

Chu Wanning smothered the thought before it could take root. He had always been straightforward and resolute, except when it came to matters of the heart, regarding which he knew well he was a dawdling coward.

"Shizun." Shi Mei's bright eyes, unmatched in elegance, looked at him with uncertainty. "You..."

"Hm?"

"No, it's nothing. Since Shizun is here to take care of A-Ran, I—I'll take my leave."

"Wait," said Chu Wanning.

"Does Shizun have any other instructions?"

"You're all leaving for Peach Blossom Springs tomorrow?"

"Mm-hmm."

There wasn't much of an expression on Chu Wanning's face. A little while passed before he spoke again. "Go get some rest. Make sure to take care of one another out there, and—" He paused. "Come back soon."

Shi Mei left.

Chu Wanning walked to the bedside, face impassive as he propped up Mo Ran and fed him the sobering soup spoonful by spoonful.

Mo Ran disliked the sour taste and coughed it all up not long after. However, he did sober up enough to open his eyes and stare, half-awake, at Chu Wanning. He mumbled, "Shizun?"

"Mn. I'm here."

"Pfft." For some reason, Mo Ran started laughing, his chuckles framed by dimples. "Immortal-gege."

Chu Wanning gave him a silent stare.

After that, Mo Ran plonked right back out, sprawled on his stomach. Worried that he might catch a cold, Chu Wanning stayed by his side, pulling his blanket back up and tucking him in now and again.

Outside the room, a number of the disciples weren't yet asleep as they stayed up to count down to the New Year. Most of them were gathered inside in groups, chattering and laughing, playing pai gow[10] or doing magic tricks.

When the hourglass hanging in front of Loyalty Hall finished trickling, signifying the changing of the year, the disciples rushed outside to set off fireworks and firecrackers. The night sky instantly filled with silvery flowers and branches of fire.

The deafening sounds outside woke Mo Ran from his hazy sleep. He cracked open an eye and pressed a hand to his throbbing temple, but the sight that greeted him was that of Chu Wanning sitting by his bedside, his handsome features composed and impassive.

"Did the noise wake you up?" Chu Wanning asked lightly when he realized that Mo Ran was up.

"Shizun..." Mo Ran woke fully, startled despite himself. Why was Chu Wanning the one watching over him? Where was Shi Mei? He hadn't said anything in his sleep that he shouldn't have, had he? Mo Ran snuck an apprehensive glance at Chu Wanning's face and only let out the breath he was holding when it seemed that nothing was out of the ordinary.

The crackling of firecrackers continued outside. The two stared awkwardly at one another for a while.

---

10 *A domino game.*

"Do you want to go see the fireworks?" asked Chu Wanning.

"Where's Shi Mei?" asked Mo Ran.

They spoke at practically the same time. It was too late to take anything back.

Mo Ran's eyes opened wide, startled, and he stared at Chu Wanning for a long while as if he didn't recognize him.

A moment passed in silence, and then Chu Wanning got up nonchalantly to leave, though he turned at the door. "Everyone's celebrating the New Year, so he's probably not asleep yet. You should go look for him."

It was only to be expected. Chu Wanning had such a terrible temper, after all. Even if he had summoned all his courage to ask Mo Ran to go watch the fireworks together, of course he had been rejected. He shouldn't have said anything. How humiliating.

Chu Wanning returned to the Red Lotus Pavilion and sat by himself beneath the haitang tree that bloomed year-round. There, alone, with a cloak draped over his shoulders, he watched the brilliant flowers blossoming across the night sky.

In the distance, the disciple quarters were warmly lit. Cheerful laughter drifted over, but none of it had anything to do with him. He should've grown used to this long ago. But for some reason, his chest was tight. Maybe it was because seeing the merriment of others made it harder to return to his own solitude.

Quietly, Chu Wanning watched the fireworks bloom—one, two—and listened to the voices of people wishing each other a happy New Year—three, five.

Leaning against the tree, he closed his eyes, feeling a bit tired.

Chu Wanning wasn't sure how much time had passed, but he suddenly felt an intrusion pass his barriers. His heart lurched, but he didn't dare open his eyes. He heard the sound of breathing, slightly winded, and familiar footsteps came to a stop not far away.

A young man's voice spoke, carrying a hint of hesitation. "Shizun."

Chu Wanning did not reply.

"I'll be leaving tomorrow."

He remained quiet.

"It's gonna be quite a while before I can come back."

Still no response.

"Actually, there's nothing going on tonight, and we have to get up early tomorrow, so I think Shi Mei probably went to bed already."

The sound of footsteps came nearer and stopped very close.

"So, if you still want to, I..."

Though Mo Ran opened his mouth, the rest of the sentence was swallowed by the bang of an especially large burst of fireworks.

Chu Wanning's eyelashes fluttered as he looked up. Backlit by the splendid river of stars in the night sky and the scattering of fire flowers like silver frost, a handsome young man stood before him, pitying and a little bashful.

Chu Wanning remained silent. He had always been prideful, and he didn't care for company born of pity. But right now, looking at Mo Ran, words of refusal suddenly wouldn't emerge. Maybe the wine had gotten to him too. Chu Wanning felt a sting in his chest, but also a warmth.

"Since you're already here, sit down with me," he said. Then he added, softly, "I will watch with you."

He gazed up at the sky with an impassive expression, but the fingers hidden in his sleeves had nervously curled. He didn't dare look closely at the person beside him, instead fixing his eyes on the fireworks above, and at the boundless night sprinkled with glittering brilliance.

"Has everyone been well these days?" Chu Wanning asked quietly.

"Mm-hmm," Mo Ran replied. "We became friends with a cute little shidi—we mentioned him in a letter to Shizun. How is Shizun's injury?"

"It's nothing. Don't blame yourself."

A firework burst in the sky, scattering resplendently.

That night, fireworks and lanterns lit the sky, firecrackers crackled nonstop, and the faint smell of smoke filled the snowy air. The two of them welcomed the New Year underneath the flowering tree. Chu Wanning was a man of few words, but Mo Ran continued to look for things to chat about until he finally grew tired and fell asleep.

Early the next morning, Mo Ran woke up, still underneath the tree, with his head in Chu Wanning's lap and a hefty but soft fur cloak covering him. It was Chu Wanning's firefox cloak, smooth and exquisitely made.

A little startled, Mo Ran looked up to see Chu Wanning leaning against the trunk of the tree, deep in slumber. His long eyelashes drooped over his cheeks, quivering slightly with each breath like butterflies in the wind.

Had they really just fallen asleep under the tree like this? How had that even happened? With Chu Wanning's obsessive-compulsive nature, he should've gone back to his room to sleep no matter how tired he was. How could he have been willing to settle for carelessly resting under a tree like this? And this fur cloak... Had Chu Wanning covered him with it?

Mo Ran sat up, his ink-black hair a little disheveled. He stared, draped in Chu Wanning's cloak, a bit mystified. He hadn't been *that* drunk last night. Although some things were a little indistinct, he could more or less remember most of it. Even running to the Red

Lotus Pavilion of his own accord to welcome the New Year with Chu Wanning had been a sober, conscious choice.

Mo Ran had obviously hated Chu Wanning, once, but when he'd heard him ask, "Do you want to go see the fireworks?" and when he had watched him turn around forlornly to leave with his head lowered... He had, in fact, felt an ache in his heart...

He'd thought, well, they wouldn't see one another again for a long time anyway, and he didn't really feel much grievance toward him in this life, and Chu Wanning was so lonely, so it was no big deal if Mo Ran kept him company till the morning, once in a while. And so he had brazenly come to join him.

When he thought back on it now, he felt like he was being really...

Chu Wanning woke up before he could finish the thought.

"Shizun," Mo Ran stammered.

"Mn." Chu Wanning rubbed his temple, his brows drawn slightly together in the haze of having just woken up. "You...haven't left yet?"

"I—I just woke up." Lately, for some reason, every time Mo Ran looked at Chu Wanning's impassive face, his silver tongue tied itself into a knot.

Mo Ran was stock-still for a moment before suddenly remembering that he was wearing Chu Wanning's cloak. He hurriedly took it off and scrambled to wrap it around his shizun instead.

While draping the cloak over his shoulders, Mo Ran noticed that although Chu Wanning wore several layers of clothing, his outfit was still a bit thin without the cloak as the outer garment, especially in all this snow. The thought made his movements even more frantic, and he ended up tying his own finger into the knot while trying to fasten the tassel cord. Mo Ran stared at his finger in bewilderment.

Chu Wanning glanced at him and reached out to untie it. "I'll do it myself."

After a long moment, Mo Ran said, "Okay." And, appended in a mumble, "Sorry."

"It's all right."

Mo Ran stood and hesitated. "Shizun, I have to go pack and eat breakfast, and then I'll be setting out."

"Mn."

"Would you like to go get breakfast together?"

Pah! The second after Mo Ran said that, he wanted to bite his tongue and die right that instant! The hell was wrong with him?! What had he done that for?!

Maybe because he saw the regret that surfaced on Mo Ran's face immediately after asking that, Chu Wanning paused, then said, "I'll pass. You go ahead."

Mo Ran was deathly afraid that he might say something even more outrageous if he stayed any longer. "I-I'm going, then..."

"All right."

After Mo Ran left, Chu Wanning sat expressionlessly under the tree for a while longer before slowly getting up with a hand on the trunk for support, but he didn't make any further movements. His legs were thoroughly numb from having served as Mo Ran's pillow all night. With all the pins and needles, he couldn't walk.

He stood there sullenly for a good while before his blood circulation returned to normal and he could finally hobble his way back inside.

Sure enough, after spending the night outside in such bitterly frigid weather, even with the haitang tree shielding them from the snow, he still ended up catching a cold.

"Achoo!" Chu Wanning sneezed, the corners of his eyes already reddening. He covered his nose with a handkerchief. Dammit... I probably...caught a cold...

The Yuheng Elder, wielder of three holy weapons and the foremost eminent zongshi who was sought after by all the sects of the cultivation world. The mere sight of Tianwen tamed the four seas, and the white of his robes bested all the colors of the world. He was such an impressive character, he could even have been said to be the strongest cultivator of the era.

Unfortunately, even the strongest person was bound to have a weakness. Chu Wanning's was that he couldn't handle the chill and easily fell ill if exposed.

Thus, when they set off from Sisheng Peak, not only had Chu-zongshi turned small again after the pill wore off, but on top of that, he was sneezing and sniffling nonstop.

And so, when the feathered tribe arrived at noon to escort them, they were met with Xue Meng, Mo Ran, and Shi Mei, who were perfectly healthy, and the pitiful little shidi "Xia Sini" who couldn't stop sneezing.

59

This Venerable One Is Only So Simple

THERE WAS NOTHING for it; even if the little shidi couldn't stop sneezing, they still had to get going. The feathered tribe led them eastward to a port on the Yangtze River. They summoned a self-navigating ferry and, with a barrier shielding the vessel, set off to sea.

That was the first night Mo Ran was able to spend time with Shi Mei on an outing without their shizun around. Strangely, he wasn't as excited as he'd thought he would be.

Xue Meng and Xia Sini had gone to bed. Mo Ran lay alone on the deck, arms folded behind his head, looking up at the starry sky. Shi Mei came out from the cabin with some dried fish they had bought from fishermen earlier and sat next to him. They nibbled idly on the snack while chatting.

"A-Ran, since we're going to Peach Blossom Springs, we might not make it to the Spiritual Mountain Competition. That doesn't matter much in my case, but you and the young master are both so strong. If you miss it, won't you regret losing your chance to make a big debut?"

Mo Ran turned his head with a smile. "It doesn't matter. Stuff like reputation and whatever, that's just words. Going to Peach Blossom Springs and learning real, useful skills to protect those important to me, that matters."

Shi Mei's gaze seemed to smile, and his voice was gentle as he said, "Shizun would be so happy if he knew you thought that way."

"What about you? Are you happy?"

"Of course I am."

Waves crashed against the wooden ferry as it rocked in the sea. Mo Ran stared at Shi Mei for a while from where he lay on his side. He wanted to tease him a bit, but he didn't know what to say. In his eyes, Shi Mei was pure and unattainable. Maybe it was because of this purity that whenever he faced Shi Mei, he found it difficult to entertain the sort of lewd thoughts he had toward Chu Wanning.

For a while, Mo Ran fell into a daze.

Shi Mei noticed that he was being stared at. He turned, tucking stray strands of hair that the sea breeze had blown behind his ear, and smiled. "What is it?"

Mo Ran flushed and angled his head away. "Nothing." He had originally planned to use this outing as a chance to confess—carefully—to Shi Mei. However, every time the words were at his lips, he couldn't open his mouth.

Confession. And after that? Mo Ran couldn't be rough or forceful with this pure, gentle person. He feared rejection, but even if his feelings *were* returned, he was afraid he wouldn't know how to behave toward Shi Mei.

After all, honestly speaking, his performance during the short time they'd spent together in their last life had been quite terrible. Other than that one moment of intimacy within the ghost mistress's illusion, he'd never even kissed Shi Mei. Moreover, after what had happened this time around, he was no longer sure if the person he'd kissed in his last life had been Shi Mei or Chu Wanning.

Shi Mei was still smiling. "You really do look like you want to say something to me, though."

It was as if they were separated by a paper window, and for an impulsive moment, Mo Ran wanted to poke through that thin layer and damn the consequences. But for some reason, a figure in white who had a face that didn't like to smile flashed through his mind—a figure who always kept to himself, who looked so lonely.

All of a sudden, it was like Mo Ran's throat had closed. He couldn't say anything else. He turned back to stare at the night sky full of stars. A while passed before he said, quietly, "Shi Mei, you're truly very important to me."

"Mn. I know. I feel the same about you."

"Do you know," Mo Ran continued, "I had a nightmare once, and in it you...you weren't there anymore. I was so sad."

Shi Mei smiled. "You're so silly sometimes."

After a long moment, Mo Ran said, "I'll definitely protect you."

"Okay, then I'll just have to thank my good shidi in advance."

Mo Ran's heart caught in his throat. He couldn't help saying, "I..."

"Was there something else you wanted to tell me?" Shi Mei asked softly. The ferry shook, and the sound of the waves seemed somehow louder. Shi Mei watched Mo Ran quietly, as if waiting for him to utter those last few words.

Mo Ran closed his eyes. "It's nothing. Why don't you go back inside and get some sleep? It's cold tonight."

Shi Mei was quiet for a moment. "What about you?"

Mo Ran could be quite dim. "I... I'm gonna watch the stars for a bit longer, feel the breeze on my face."

Shi Mei didn't move. It was a while before he smiled. "All right, then I'll go on ahead. Don't stay up too late now."

Then he turned and left.

The ferry sailed through the sea and beneath the boundless sky. The fellow lying on the vessel's deck didn't at all realize what he had just missed. He was even a bit absentminded as he tried to dig up what he really felt in the depths of his heart. He thought for a long time, but he was genuinely dim-witted. Thus even by the time the morning sun painted the eastern skies a soft white, he still hadn't figured himself out.

Mo Ran spent every waking moment with Shi Mei, and the feelings they shared were deep and sincere. Mo Ran had assumed he'd definitely want to confess to Shi Mei as soon as they were alone, that he would be unable to wait another moment. But now that this long-awaited moment had finally arrived, he found that that wasn't remotely the case. Maybe the problem was that he thought himself too awkward. If Mo Ran rashly confessed to Shi Mei right away, he'd definitely startle him. Even if Shi Mei took it in stride, it wouldn't make for a good start.

Mo Ran was more used to the hazy vagueness between them. Sometimes his heart fluttered, and he reached out to take Shi Mei's hand as if he wasn't thinking, and his chest would overflow with honey-sweet tenderness. It was such a natural feeling that he didn't quite want to destroy it, not so quickly.

It was late by the time Mo Ran went back inside the cabin, and everyone else had already gone to sleep. He lay on his sleeping mat, staring at the night outside the narrow skylight. Slowly, Chu Wanning's figure appeared before his eyes, sometimes silent, his eyes closed, sometimes wearing a severe expression.

But Mo Ran also thought about the way the man looked when he was curled up asleep, lonely and unassuming, like a haitang blossom that nobody cared for because it had bloomed too high on the branch.

The hatred he felt aside, Mo Ran's past life entanglements with Chu Wanning had in fact been more intimate than any he had shared with anyone else in the world. He had taken many of

Chu Wanning's firsts, regardless of whether the man had been willing. His first kiss, his first time cooking, his first time crying. And his first *time.*

Dammit, just thinking about it made Mo Ran's body feel hot and his blood rush downward.

In exchange, Mo Ran had given Chu Wanning some of his own firsts as well, regardless of whether his shizun had wanted them. His first apprenticeship, his first attempt to coax someone, his first gift of flowers. His first thorough disappointment.

And the first stirrings of his heart.

Yes, the first stirrings of his heart. When he'd come to Sisheng Peak, the person he'd fallen for hadn't been Shi Mei, but Chu Wanning.

That day, the white-robed young man beneath that haitang tree had been so beautiful, so focused, that after only a single glance Mo Ran decided that he wanted this man to be his master, and that no one else would do.

Just when had that changed? Just when had the one he cared for become Shi Mei, and the one he hated his shizun?

Mo Ran had thought about this a lot over the last couple of months. It had probably begun with a specific misunderstanding.

It was the first time Chu Wanning had punished him with a lashing. The fifteen-year-old boy stumbled back to his room, bruised and battered, and curled up alone on his bed, his eyes rimmed red as he choked back sobs. The wounds on his back hurt less than the cold expression on his shizun's face when he had brought Tianwen down without a shred of mercy, like he was beating a stray dog.

It was true that Mo Ran had stolen a haitang flower from the medicine garden, but he'd had no idea how precious that haitang tree was, nor how carefully Madam Wang had tended to it for the last five years before it finally bloomed.

The only thing he'd known was that, when he walked home that night, a luminous whiteness at the tip of a branch had caught his eye. The flower's petals were clear and frosty, its fragrance mild and delicate.

Mo Ran tilted his head back to admire it, thinking of his shizun. For some reason, his heart throbbed, and the tips of his fingers felt warm. Before he realized it, he had plucked the flower, carefully and with the gentlest of movements, afraid of accidentally shaking even a single drop of dew from its petals.

Through the thick curtain of his eyelashes, he gazed at the dew-laden haitang blossom under the light of the moon. In that moment, he had not yet realized just how pure the tenderness and affection he held for Chu Wanning was, nor had he known that, after that day—and for the next ten, twenty years, until his death—he would never feel it again.

Before he could give the flower to his shizun, he bumped into Xue Meng, who had come to pick medicinal herbs for his mother. In a rage, the young master dragged him to their shizun.

Chu Wanning turned from his scroll, his gaze ice-cold as he listened. He shot a glance at Mo Ran and asked if he had an explanation.

Mo Ran started to say, "I picked the flower because I wanted to give it to—"

He was still holding that haitang, specks of frost and drops of dew clinging to its freshly bloomed petals, which were icy yet indescribably beautiful.

However, Chu Wanning's gaze remained utterly cold, so cold that it chilled the molten lava in Mo Ran's chest. Mo Ran could no longer say the word "you."

This feeling was all too familiar. Before Mo Ran was brought to Sisheng Peak, he'd had to scamper between courtesans and customers as he shrank into his thin, malnourished body to appear smaller and less obstructive, and he had spent every day under that exact gaze.

A gaze of contempt. A gaze of disdain.

A shudder ran through him. Was it possible that, in truth, his shizun looked down on him?

In the face of Chu Wanning's frigid interrogation, Mo Ran felt his heart freeze over. He lowered his head, and his voice was quiet. "I…have nothing to say."

The rest was history.

Because of this mere haitang flower, Chu Wanning had lashed Mo Ran with forty strikes until all his initial fondness had shattered to pieces.

If only Mo Ran had been able to explain himself a little further, and if only Chu Wanning had asked a little more, then maybe things wouldn't have turned out the way they had. Maybe this master and disciple wouldn't have taken that first step down the road beyond redemption.

But there weren't that many what ifs.

It was at this point that Shi Mei, warm and gentle, had appeared at his side.

After returning from Chu Wanning's pavilion, Mo Ran hadn't gone to eat or even lit a lamp. He had only laid curled up on his bed.

This stiff figure curled up in the darkness was the sight that had greeted Shi Mei when he opened the door. He set the bowl of chili oil wontons in his hands gently on the table, then walked over to the bed and called out softly. "A-Ran?"

At the time, Mo Ran hadn't yet had any particular feelings for Shi Mei. He didn't even turn around, still staring at the wall with red, swollen eyes. "Get out," he said, voice hoarse.

"I brought you some—"

"I said *get out*."

"A-Ran, don't be like that."

Mulish silence.

"Shizun has a bad temper, it just takes a little getting used to. Come, get up and eat something."

Yet Mo Ran was stubborn as a donkey, immovable even if dragged by ten whole horses. "Don't want it. I'm not hungry."

"At least have a bite. If you don't eat, Shizun will get ma—"

Mo Ran shot up from bed before Shi Mei could finish the sentence. His watery eyes were angry and indignant, quivering slightly beneath his lashes. "Mad? What could he be mad about? It's my body. How is it any of his business whether I eat? He doesn't even want me as a disciple anyway. I might as well starve to death. It'd be less hassle for him. He'll be happier in the end."

Shi Mei was too stunned to respond. He hadn't expected his words to prod Mo Ran's sore spot, and for a while, he stared helplessly at the little shidi in front of him, not knowing what to say.

A long moment passed. Mo Ran pulled himself together and looked down, long hair covering half his face. After a good while, he said, "Sorry."

Shi Mei couldn't see his face, only the subdued trembling of his shoulders and the veins on the back of his tightly clenched fists.

In the end, this fifteen-year-old boy was as yet very young. Mo Ran tried to hold it in for a while, but ultimately couldn't. He buried his face in his arms, curled into himself, and bawled miserably. His voice was rough and broken, hysterical and lost, pained and grief-stricken. Body wracked with sobs, he repeated the same thing over and over.

"I only wanted to have a home… These past fifteen years, I really… I really only wanted a home… Why do you all look down on me? Why do you all look at me like that? Why, why do you all look down on me…?"

Mo Ran cried for a long time, and Shi Mei sat with him the whole while. When Mo Ran had cried himself out, Shi Mei handed him a spotless handkerchief and brought over the bowl of now cold wontons.

"Don't say silly things about starving to death anymore," he said gently. "You've come to Sisheng Peak and apprenticed under Shizun, so you are my shidi. I also lost my parents when I was young, so if you want, I'll be your family. Come now, eat something."

Mo Ran did not reply.

"I made these wontons. Even if you won't give Shizun any face, at least give me some, hm?" Shi Mei's lips curled into a small smile as he scooped up a plump, translucent wonton and held it to Mo Ran's lips. "Try one."

The rims of Mo Ran's eyes were still red. His watery gaze fixed on the youth by his bed, but he finally opened his mouth and allowed this gentle person to feed him.

Truth be told, that bowl of wontons had gone cold, and the dumplings had been soaking for so long that they were no longer as good as they could've been. But in that moment, under the candlelight, this bowl of wontons was carved deeply into his heart alongside that incomparably beautiful face with its gentle eyes. In life and in death, never would either of them be forgotten.

It probably began that night. Mo Ran's hatred for his shizun grew ever deeper, but it was also the moment when he became convinced that Shi Mei was the most important person in his life.

After all, everyone wanted warmth—especially a stray dog who had frozen in the bitter cold so many times that the mere sight of salted roads made him shiver in anticipation of snow and the coming winter.

Taxian-jun looked imposing, but he alone knew the truth about himself. He was nothing but a wandering stray. A stray who was forever searching for a place where he could curl up, a place to call "home." He spent fifteen years searching and was still unable to find it.

And so, his love and hate had become laughably straightforward. If someone gave him a beating, he would hate them. If someone gave him a bowl of soup, he would love them. He was just that simple, after all.

60
This Venerable One Discovers a Secret

BOOSTED BY THE SPELLS cast upon it, the ferry traveled quickly. By the next morning, they had reached the Port of Yangzhou. Envoys were at the harbor to receive them, with well-bred horses at the ready.

The party ate breakfast at the harbor, but since the feathered tribe didn't require sustenance, their escorts sat by the edge of the harbor with their eyes closed to rest their spirits. Dawn had only just broken, and there weren't many merchants around conducting business. Conversely, the deckhands had risen, and they gathered in threes and fives to chow down on porridge and steamed buns, as well as to peek and steal curious glances at the newcomers from time to time.

As these beefy fellows in simple laborer's garb chewed their meals, bits and pieces of their conversation fell upon Mo Ran's ears.

"Oh hey, I recognize their clothes. They're people of the lower cultivation realm."

"The lower cultivation realm is so far away, and they don't interact much with the sects from this area. So how would you know?"

"Just look at the emblem on their vambraces. Isn't it exactly the same as the one on a Holy Night Guardian?"

"You mean one of those wooden devices that repel evil?" One fellow crunched on pickles as he peered at Xue Meng's sleeve.

"Aiyoh, that's right," he exclaimed. "Who was the one who made the Holy Night Guardians again?"

"I heard it was the Yuheng Elder of Sisheng Peak."

"Who's the Yuheng Elder? Is he as powerful as our Guyueye Sect Leader Jiang?"

"Heh heh, who knows. Who's to say anything about the world of cultivators?"

The deckhands spoke in a heavy Su dialect and Mo Ran couldn't quite comprehend them, but Chu Wanning understood what these people were saying. When he heard that his invention, the Holy Night Guardian, was being successfully distributed throughout the common world, he could only feel comforted. It made him start thinking about the future. After they returned, he would work on prototypes for lighter wheelbarrows that were easier to use and thereby do more good.

Once breakfast was done, the group left with haste. Not four hours later, they reached the foot of Mount Jiuhua. It was still early in the day, and the winter sun had only just reached its zenith. Millions of threads of golden light came kissing down from it like silk. They imbued the snowy summit with a crystalline luminescence, making it glitter magnificently. Upon the slopes of the peak were hundreds of luscious ancient pines that remained evergreen. Each stood resolutely in the frost, much like a hermit cultivator with an immortal air, sleeves lowered and eyes half-lidded, deadly silent where they towered on either side of the mountain path.

It wasn't for nothing that the mortals called the summit of Mount Jiufeng the "Unmortal World."

At the foot of the mountain, the envoys of the feathered tribe whistled thrice. At the sound, a little golden sparrow with vibrantly charming feathers flew out of the white, snowy scenery and landed lightly before them. The group followed the sparrow's lead, heading west the entire way, until they came to the curtain of a turbulent, tempestuous waterfall.

"Will the xianjun please step back?"

The leader of the feathered tribe envoys stood at the fore, her hand imitating the hand of Buddha, and she silently recited a spell. Then she pursed her scarlet lips and gently blew into the wind. A shocking beam of flames appeared in midair and streaked toward the waterfall, where it divided the water curtain in half.

The women of the feathered tribe breezily turned around and smiled. "We cordially invite you to enter Peach Blossom Springs."

They followed their escorts and passed through the barrier. After crossing it, the scenery before their eyes suddenly brightened. The scene before them was vast with no end in sight, as if it was an entirely different world, one filled with pink blossoms.

Peach Blossom Springs was a sheltered land with few connections to the cultivation world. While it couldn't be compared to the real Land of Immortals, much less spoken of as its equal, it was nonetheless rich with spiritual energy. The scenery within the springs looked as if it had come out of a painting, its colors elegant and delicate.

After walking for a while, the group realized that here, the four seasons seemed to change and blend into one another in a manner wholly unlike they did in their own world.

With the women of the feathered tribe leading the way, they first passed through a wilderness where the sound of coursing rivers roared in their ears, accompanied by the cries of monkeys coming from both shores. Then they approached the outskirts of a city and saw vast farmlands of crisscrossing field paths where wheat swayed with the breeze. Finally, once they had entered the city fortress, they found immaculate and detailed buildings as far as the eye could see, with eaves both tall and grand.

The capital of Peach Blossom Springs was magnificent and beautiful, and in terms of size and amenities, it was comparable to the lively city centers of the mortal realm. The only differences lay in the spring petals and drifting snowflakes that danced together overhead, the blue birds and white cranes that took flight together in flocks, and the passing folk of the feathered tribe. These beautiful people carried themselves with ethereal grace, flowing and picturesque, and every one of them looked like an otherworldly celestial who had just stepped out of an illustration.

However, though this was a sight that the disciples had never before beheld, they had already laid eyes on the fantastic sights of Jincheng Lake, so this was no longer quite as awe-inspiring.

They came to a fork in the road and met one of the feathered tribe folk who wore a grand feathered cloak—white with gold embroidery depicting a phoenix. She stood by an ancient tree so tall it reached the skies. The flame mark on her forehead was a much richer red than that of her peers, signaling that her powers were far greater than the rest of them.

The envoys leading the way brought the group before her, then each bent one knee to the ground to bow as they greeted her. "Great Immortal Lord, the four xianjun of Sisheng Peak have come."

"Thank you for your labors. You may stand down."

"Understood."

The beautifully dressed feathered tribe woman smiled softly, and her voice was clear and stirring, like the cry of a young phoenix.

"I am called Eighteen. By the grace of the Elder Immortal of my family, I was granted the grand title of Great Immortal Lord of Peach Blossom Springs. We are most thankful that my lords have been willing to show us the courtesy of coming to train in our humble abode. Should the xianjun find their reception to be in any way inadequate during their stay here, please do forgive us, and do not be afraid to let us know."

Such beauty! And such grace when she spoke. She certainly gave a good impression.

Xue Meng didn't like it when men were better-looking than him, but he was at the age when he was beginning to become aware of the fairer sex, so naturally he didn't dislike ladies who were so beautiful that they seemed to have emerged from paintings. He smiled. "Xianzhu is too kind. But this name, 'Eighteen,' certainly is odd. Might I ask after Xianzhu's family name?"

"I have no family name," she replied, gentle and courteous. "I am only Eighteen."

Mo Ran laughed. "If you're called Eighteen, then is someone here named Seventeen?"

He'd meant it as a joke, but to his surprise, Eighteen smiled. "Xianjun is wise. Seventeen is my zizi."

Mo Ran blinked, stunned.

"We of the feathered tribe are born from the fallen feathers of the Vermillion Bird," Eighteen explained. "When our cultivation was still weak, we took the forms of the crested ibis. The first to cultivate a human form was the Elder Immortal of my family. The rest of the feathered tribe are thus named in order of when we attained human form, starting with One, Two, and so forth. I am the eighteenth, and so I am named Eighteen."

Mo Ran had absolutely no words. He had originally thought Xue Zhengyong was as bad as it got when it came to doling out names. Never had he expected to find someone who was even worse, let alone people who referred to themselves with numbers.

Then Eighteen said something that left him even more thunderstruck. "Come, let's get down to business. This is your first visit to our lands, and you aren't yet familiar with the training rules of Peach Blossom Springs. In the mortal realm, cultivation has for centuries been divided by schools and sects. In this place, things are different. We of the feathered tribe have always been very clear in our division of labor. There are those who specialize in Defense, those who specialize in Attack, and those who specialize in Healing. There are three divisions in all, and your training will thus also be conducted accordingly."

Mo Ran smiled. "That's brilliant."

Eighteen nodded toward him. "Much appreciated, Xiao-xianjun. When the cultivators from Guyueye who came here several days ago heard of this training method, they were quite displeased."

Mo Ran was mystified. "Defense is defense, Attack is attack, and Healing is healing. Isn't such a clean split a good thing? What were they unhappy about?"

"You see, there is a Duan-gongzi from Guyueye who belongs in Defense and was thus supposed to reside with the other xianjun of that division. However, his shijie belongs to Attack and will therefore need to train and live with the xianjun of the Attack Division. While I don't quite understand the affections and relationships of mortal-kind, I could tell that the gongzi was quite unwilling to be separated from his sworn sister."

"Ha ha, what's up with that—wait, hold up!" Mo Ran abruptly stopped laughing as realization dawned on him, his eyes wide. "Not only do the different divisions train separately, they have to live apart too?"

"That's right," Eighteen replied, confused. She didn't understand why his expression had so suddenly changed.

Mo Ran's entire face turned green. Was this some kind of bad joke?!

An hour later, Mo Ran—who had failed in his bargaining with Eighteen—stood dumbfounded before a bright and spacious little four-sided courtyard residence and sank into a long, deep silence.

Mo Ran, Xue Meng, and Xia Sini belonged in the Attack Division and had thus been sent to the east side of Peach Blossom Springs. The "east side" wasn't just any small allotment of land, but the region where all the xianjun who belonged in the Attack Division resided. There were more than twenty of these courtyard residences, each large enough to house four, and there were also mountains and lakes, as well as streets and markets built very much like the ones in the mortal realm. It seemed that because the feathered tribe knew their guests were going to live here for a long time, they had constructed these to alleviate homesickness.

As for Shi Mei, since he belonged in the Healing Division, he had been sent to the south side of Peach Blossom Springs. It was exceptionally far away from where Mo Ran and the others lived, and they were even divided by a barrier that could only be traversed with an access token. This meant that although Mo Ran and Shi Mei were both within Peach Blossom Springs, they would essentially have no chance to see each other outside of daily training—for which all three divisions gathered to learn the basics of the feathered tribe's cultivation method.

This wasn't even the worst of it.

Mo Ran looked up and eyed Xue Meng past his thick curtain of lashes. Xue Meng was circling the whole yard, obviously planning to pick the most comfortable residence for himself. Mo Ran could feel the veins on his forehead pop in spite of himself. Xue Meng...

That's right. Fucking hell. From today onward, he had to live in the same courtyard as Xue Meng for the entire stay! For the next long while, he would in all likelihood have to be thoroughly steeped in two of the eight great sufferings of life: separation from loved ones, and the meeting of enemies...

The feathered tribe had gone from the upper cultivation realm to the lower to find their chosen few, and by the time they reached Sisheng Peak, they had been at the end of their journey. Thus, those sent from the other sects had already settled in, and Xue Meng soon discovered that one of the residences of their little four-sided courtyard was occupied.

"Weird. I wonder who's settled here," Xue Meng mumbled as he glanced at the mattress cover being hung to dry in the yard.

"Whoever it is, it must not be someone who makes much of a fuss," Mo Ran said.

"What do you mean?"

"Let me ask you this: Which residence are you picking?"

Xue Meng's expression grew immediately guarded. "What are you planning? I've already made my choice—the one in the north that faces south is mine. If you're gonna fight me for it, then I'll—"

Xue Meng hadn't yet figured out what he was going to do before Mo Ran cut him off with a laugh. "I don't like rooms that big, so I'm not fighting you for it. But here's what I want to ask: If this residence was still empty..." He pointed at the modest abode that had already been claimed. "Would you swap with him?"

Xue Meng gazed at that simple little thatched cottage before glaring at Mo Ran. "Do you think I'm dumb? Of course I wouldn't swap."

Mo Ran laughed. "That's why I said that person isn't someone who'd make a fuss. See, when he came, all four residences in this courtyard were empty, but he didn't pick the best one, he chose that itty-bitty hovel. If this fellow isn't a fool, then he's a humble gentleman."

Xue Meng fell silent. This analysis certainly wasn't wrong, but he felt like his face had been ripped open by the hidden knife in Mo Ran's smile. If this other man was a gentleman, forgoing the best residence to pick a dilapidated hut, then didn't that make Xue Meng a stinking, vulgar, common man? A petty cheapskate?

But Mo Ran hadn't called Xue Meng out by name, so Xue-gongzi couldn't very well yell at him. However, neither could he endure this. His entire face flushed red. "Whatever the case...I'm used to living well," Xue Meng choked out resentfully, expression dark. "I can't stand for rundown accommodations, so whoever wants to be a gentleman can go right ahead. I don't care."

Having made his statement, he turned and left.

Thus the four differently styled residences of the courtyard residence were claimed by different masters.

Xue Meng chose the exquisite residence in the north, with pale walls and black shingles and a threshold lined with gold, the most luxurious abode. Mo Ran picked the stone cottage to the west, which had a peach tree planted by the entrance, its flowers at the height of their bloom. And so Chu Wanning picked the bamboo building on the east side, where the tender, gentle bamboo trees were illuminated by the setting sun to gleam with a brilliant, jade-like splendor.

And on the south side was that humble, simple thatched cottage reserved for the "gentleman" whom they had yet to meet.

Chu Wanning had not yet recovered from his cold, and his head still spun wickedly, so early on he excused himself to rest. Xue Meng stayed with him for a bit, but this little shidi didn't know how to play it up and act pitiful, nor did he want to listen to stories. Instead, he only cared to wrap himself up like a small, sticky rice ball in its leaf wrapper and sleep in muffled peace. Xue Meng sat on the edge of his bed for a bit but eventually got bored and, dusting himself off, left.

In the yard, Mo Ran had pulled out a chair and was putting his legs up, his arms pillowed behind his head as he watched the golden sun sink in the west, the blazing rays peeling leisurely away. When he saw Xue Meng emerge, he asked, "Is Xia-shidi asleep now?"

"Mn."

"Has his fever gone down?"

"If you care about him, why don't you go inside and see for yourself?"

Mo Ran laughed heartily. "The little guy probably isn't too deeply asleep yet. My clumsiness might rouse him."

Xue Meng gave him a look. "Well, at least you're aware of yourself. And here I thought you were just like Mom's cats and dogs, who only know how to idle about in the yard and be lazy."

"Ha ha, and how do you know I'm being lazy?" Mo Ran twiddled a peach blossom between his fingers and looked up with a smile. "The time I spent here sitting in the yard allowed me to discover a major, shocking secret."

Xue Meng obviously didn't want to ask, but he was nonetheless curious. After bearing with it for a good while, his face stiff, he worked up an expression of indifference and muttered, "What major secret?"

Mo Ran waved him closer and grinned. "Bring your ear closer and I'll tell you in confidence."

Though he was incredibly unwilling, after a long pause for consideration, Xue Meng lowered his gracious ear.

Mo Ran leaned in close and chuckled quietly. "Heh heh, got you. Dumb Mengmeng."

Xue Meng's eyes went round in shock, and he exploded in outrage, seizing Mo Ran's lapels. "You lied to me! How immature can you get?!"

Mo Ran laughed. "How have I lied? I did discover a secret, but I also don't want to tell you. That's all."

Xue Meng's dark brows hardened. "If I continued to believe you, then I'd truly be a fool!"

The two bickered like a bird pecking a dog and a dog snapping at a bird. Mo Ran was about to teasingly say something else to provoke his cousin even further when an unknown voice came from behind them, laced with confusion.

"Mn?" it said. "Are the two of you new trainees as well?" This man's voice was clear and crisp, smoother than that of your average youth.

Mo Ran and Xue Meng turned their heads back to see a man dressed in practical, close-fitting clothing standing there against the wind, lit by the crimson bloodred of the remnant sun.

This fellow had a striking appearance, with inky black brows and handsome, spirited features on his honey-colored face. He wore a hair crown of black jade fastened atop his head, and though he was neither towering nor burly, he carried himself with tall, upright dignity and a noble bearing. His pair of long legs were especially noteworthy; strapped as they were into those close-fitting trousers, they looked even more shapely and powerful, straight and gallant.

Mo Ran's expression instantly changed, and it felt like the blood and sins of a past lifetime were flashing before his eyes.

It was as if he was looking at a silhouette kneeling in a tempest of blood, the body's collarbones shot through with a steel chain,[11] half the face's flesh ripped away. Yet this person refused to yield, willing to die rather than surrender.

---

11 *To shoot through a martial artist with a steel chain through their collarbones was said to be the way to rip them of their abilities and subdue them.*

Mo Ran's heart trembled, like a crystal dew drop that hung from a leaf. He couldn't describe what it was he was feeling. If there was anyone whom he had respected and admired in his previous life, then the person now standing before his eyes was definitely one of them.

So the honorable gentleman who was to live with them...was actually this fellow, huh?

61 This Venerable One Is Really Great?

THE TWO BROS STOPPED BICKERING and rose to their feet at the same time. The person in front of them had an extremely dignified air.

Xue Meng stared for a moment before he finally reacted, nodding. "Mn. That's right. Who are you?"

Xue Meng had been unruly since birth, and even though Madam Wang had taught him etiquette over and over again, he'd never taken it to heart. So when he asked for other people's names, he never used honorifics, and neither did he offer his own name first. It was honestly quite rude.

However, Mo Ran knew that this wasn't someone who would stoop to Xue Meng's level. After all, this was...

"I am a disciple of Rufeng Sect, Ye Wangxi." As expected, the young man was calm and composed, and he didn't get upset. Below his dark, black brows were a pair of eyes that shone like scattered starlight, exceptionally bright and piercing. "May I inquire after your name as well?"

"Ye Wangxi?" Xue Meng frowned, muttering. "Never heard of that name before. Must not have much of a reputation."

His mutter wasn't loud, but there was no way anyone who wasn't hard of hearing could've missed that. Thus Mo Ran discreetly tugged on Xue Meng's sleeve to get him to show some restraint before masking the emotions in his own eyes and smiling lightly. "I am Mo Ran of Sisheng Peak, and the one beside me is my ill-mannered little brother, Xue Meng."

Xue Meng pulled away, throwing him a fierce glare. "Don't touch me—who's your little brother?!"

"Oh, Xue Meng, you..." Mo Ran sighed. He turned to Ye Wangxi, eyes smiling along with his lips. "My younger brother is a bit stubborn. Please don't mind him, Ye-xiong."

It wasn't that he'd suddenly decided to change his entire attitude and start being courteous about Xue Meng. Rather, it was that Ye Wangxi was an outstanding genius among his peers. Although Ye Wangxi had yet to make a name for himself, in their previous lifetime, Ye Wangxi had been second only to Chu Wanning in the entire cultivation world.

Heaven knew how greatly Mo Ran had suffered because of Ye Wangxi in his previous life. To see him after his rebirth, still sharp as a knife's edge, an upright hero pure and noble... Even if he couldn't get into Ye Wangxi's good graces, at the very least Mo Ran never again wanted to face him as an opponent.

It was already a lot having Chu Wanning beat him black and blue. If Ye Wangxi was added to the mix, how could he ever live in peace?

Ye Wangxi was a man of few words, so after a brief, polite exchange, he returned to his own residence. As soon as he left, Mo Ran's expression reverted to his annoying-as-hell, shit-eating grin. He elbowed Xue Meng. "What do you think?"

"What do I think about what?"

"That person," Mo Ran replied. "You like him? Think he's good-looking?"

Xue Meng gave him a befuddled look and scoffed. "Weirdo."

Mo Ran laughed. "The four of us are living in the same courtyard, so we'll run into each other around every corner. You should be glad that he's the one we're living with."

Xue Meng was puzzled. "The way you talk, it sounds like you know him already."

Of course Mo Ran couldn't tell him the truth, so he returned to his usual clownery. "Nope, I don't know him, but I judge people by their faces. He's good-looking, so I like him a whole lot."

"Disgusting!" Xue Meng spat.

Mo Ran laughed, waving his hand as he turned around and flipping an offensive gesture at Xue Meng behind his back. He then lazily walked back to his own little stone house and barred the door with a clunk, shutting all of Xue Meng's cursing and swearing outside.

The morning of the next day, Mo Ran got up early.

Their hosts had delayed cultivation practice for three days so they could grow accustomed to life at Peach Blossom Springs. Mo Ran freshened himself up and saw that Ye Wangxi had already left on his own and that the other two hadn't woken up yet. So he went for a solitary stroll through the streets.

Within the thin layer of morning fog, quite a few cultivators glided by with light steps, rushing to their individual cultivation grounds.

Mo Ran passed by a breakfast stall and saw a fresh pot of steam-fried buns. He thought of his little shidi, who was still sick, and walked over. "I'll take eight fried buns and one bowl of sweet congee to go, Mrs. Shopkeep."

The feathered stall owner didn't even lift her head to reply: "That will be six feathers."

Mo Ran stared blankly. "Six what?"

"Six feathers."

"So...am I supposed to go find a chicken and pluck a couple of its pinions?"

The feathered shopkeeper raised her eyes to give him a look. "No feathers and you still want food? Go away, get lost."

Caught between annoyance and amusement, Mo Ran was about to ask again when a familiar voice came from behind him. A hand wrapped in bandages reached out with six glimmering, resplendent golden feathers pinched between its fingers. "Here, Mrs. Shopkeep, I'll pay for it."

The feathered shopkeep took the feathers and, not wanting to waste any more time, turned to pack up the breakfast to go. Mo Ran turned his head to see Ye Wangxi standing by his side, tall and handsome, his presence elegant.

"Thank you very much." Mo Ran grabbed the steaming, piping hot buns and the sweet congee, and went to walk alongside Ye Wangxi. "If I hadn't run into you today, I'm afraid we might've gone hungry."

"No worries," Ye Wangxi said. "Miss Eighteen doesn't have the best memory, and she always forgets to give newcomers some feathers. I ran into you by chance, so it's no skin off my back. Don't worry about it."

"Do you need these feathers to do business in Peach Blossom Springs?"

"Yes."

"Where do the feathers come from?"

"They're plucked."

"P-plucked..." Mo Ran was slightly dumbfounded. These feathers really were plucked straight off the bodies of birds? Wouldn't the local birds end up completely bald?

Ye Wangxi glanced at his shocked face with amusement. "What are you imagining? In Peach Blossom Springs, there's a place called the Ancestral Abyss. Legend has it that it was where the Vermilion Bird ascended. The bottom of the abyss is filled with roaring flames—it's hot beyond measure and difficult to endure. Not a single inch of grass can grow there, and no beasts can survive it either."

As Mo Ran listened to this description, his mind went to the bloodred sky that he'd seen in the distance when he passed through the city outskirts the day before. "Is the abyss near the northern end of the city?"

"You are correct."

"What does that have to do with the feathers?"

"It's like this: Although no other creatures can survive in the vicinity of the Ancestral Abyss, a flock of frenzied demon owls lives within it. They make their nests with the fire, hide during the day, and come out at night. The feathered tribe uses their feathers to refine their cultivation."

"So that's how it is." Mo Ran grinned. "No wonder they want to trade goods for feathers."

"Mn. But you must be mindful. When the demon owls come out at night, their feathers turn into the ordinary sort, no different from those of other owls. Even if you catch them then, they won't be of any use. Only at daybreak every day, when the sun rises in the east, will the owl flock return to the Ancestral Abyss in the hundreds and thousands. The moment right before they enter the abyss, their feathers again turn gold, and only those have any value."

"Ha ha, isn't that basically just mandatory qinggong practice? If your skills are subpar, then you'll fall in and get barbecued. But if you don't harvest feathers, then you'll probably starve to death." Mo Ran couldn't help but click his tongue. "That's pretty rough."

"Are you perhaps not good at qinggong?" asked Ye Wangxi.

Mo Ran chuckled. "Just so-so."

"That won't do. The owls' movements are swift and violent, no slower than those of a falcon or hawk. If you don't practice diligently, then you'll go hungry after a couple of days."

"I see, I see..."

Seeing Mo Ran lost in thought, Ye Wangxi sighed. "I've acquired quite a few feathers, and for the time being I have no shortage thereof. If the three of you need some, just ask me."

Mo Ran waved his hand again, smiling. "How could we do that? Let's just count this as an initial loan of six feathers from you to me. I'm going to go eat some food, but if I can harvest some feathers tomorrow, I'll pay you back. Thanks a lot."

Mo Ran bade farewell to Ye Wangxi, then carried the congee and buns back to the courtyard.

Xue Meng's residence was empty. He'd probably woken up and gotten bored, then gone out for a stroll. So Mo Ran went to Chu Wanning's bamboo house.

Chu Wanning wasn't awake yet. Mo Ran set the congee and steam-fried buns on the table, then went to his bedside, where he lowered his head to take a look at him. All of a sudden, a familiar feeling washed over him. This little shidi's appearance as he slept... why did it seem similar to a certain someone?

Mo Ran couldn't remember who his shidi resembled. He only had a fuzzy impression of someone else who slept like this, someone who always curled up into a ball on their bed, cheeks pillowed on folded hands. Exactly who was it?

While Mo Ran was busy getting lost in his thoughts, Chu Wanning woke up.

"Mmmm..." Chu Wanning rolled over and saw the person beside his bed, at which he suddenly opened his eyes wide. "Mo Ran?"

"How many times have I told you? You should call me Shixiong."

Mo Ran ruffled his hair a bit, then felt his forehead to take his temperature. "It seems like your fever's broken. Come on, get up and eat some food."

"Eat food…" the child on the bed repeated blankly, his messy hair making his face look even cuter.

"Look at how your Shixiong cares about you—I got up early to go buy breakfast. You should eat while it's hot."

Chu Wanning got off the bed, dressed in his spotlessly white inner robes, and walked toward the dining table. On top of the dining table there were steam-fried buns with thin skins and crispy bottoms, with jade-green slivers of chopped green onion and black sesame scattered over them, all placed on a lotus leaf. Next to the buns, there was a small bowl of longan and osmanthus congee. It was soft and sticky, but simultaneously thick and rich, as well as piping hot, with clouds of steam rising from it.

The usually strong and steadfast Yuheng Elder was suddenly unsure of himself. "For me?"

"Ah?"

"Did you buy all of this…for me?"

Mo Ran was stunned for a second. "Sure did." He watched Chu Wanning, who looked hesitant and unsure. Mo Ran considered this and smiled. "Hurry and eat up before it gets cold."

Although Chu Wanning had been part of Sisheng Peak for many years and everyone respected him, almost no one ate with him due to his icy, stiff personality. They were even less likely to bring him a serving of breakfast from the dining hall. Sometimes he watched the disciples taking care of each other, and though he was unwilling to admit it, he couldn't stop his heart from being slightly jealous. And so, faced with this bowl of porridge and a couple of buns, he couldn't bring himself to actually eat them.

A long while passed in silence.

Mo Ran watched Chu Wanning sitting on the small stool, staring at the food in front of him and not moving his chopsticks, and wondered if the food might not be to his tastes. "What's wrong?" Mo Ran asked. "Is it too greasy for you?"

Chu Wanning looked back at Mo Ran mutely and shook his head. He picked up his spoon and scooped up a mouthful of congee. After he blew on it, he took a careful sip. If he were still the beautiful, frigid, and distant Chu-zongshi he usually was, eating congee in this manner would have made him seem elegant and refined, as though he was practicing restraint. In the body of a child, he just looked a little awkward and pitiful.

Mo Ran misinterpreted his hesitation. "Do you not like longans? You can pick them out and leave them by the side, then. No biggie."

"No." The little shidi's face wasn't too expressive, but when he looked toward Mo Ran again, his crow-black eyes were soft. "I like it."

"Oh... Ha ha, that's good, then. I worried that you didn't."

Chu Wanning's thick curtain of lashes swept downward. "I like it," he repeated quietly. "No one's ever taken care of me like this before." He lifted his eyes to glance at Mo Ran. When he spoke again, it was earnestly: "Thank you very much, Shixiong."

Mo Ran hadn't expected him to say something like that, and he was left feeling stunned. He wasn't a naturally kind person, and he didn't particularly like kids. He only treated Xia Sini well because his skills were unusually good for his young age, and he seemed like a junior worth befriending.

Mo Ran had only been thinking practically, but when he was met with a Chu Wanning who treated this matter so sincerely, he found himself blushing with shame. However, he also thought there was something a little odd about what his shidi had said. After waving his hand to tell Chu Wanning that he didn't require thanks, Mo Ran asked, "Has nobody ever bought you breakfast before?"

Chu Wanning nodded expressionlessly.

"Do the Xuanji Elder's disciples not know how to look after one another or something?"

"I don't hang out with them much."

"What about before you came to the sect? When you lived at your old house, did your mom and dad..." Mo Ran stopped, unable to continue that sentence.

His little shidi was quick-witted and pure as snow. What sort of parents would have the heart to leave that kind of kid on top of a mountain to cultivate, and never come back to visit him ever again? It seemed like Xia Sini had suffered the same experiences as Shi Mei and himself.

As expected, Chu Wanning said calmly: "My parents are no longer around, and I didn't have any other relatives, so there was nobody to look after me."

Mo Ran was silent for a long while before he let out a big sigh. *Originally I just wanted to be friends with this kid because one, his cultivation level is quite high, and two, he's steady and mature, unlike the typical rowdy ankle biter. Who would've thought that we came from the same background?*

When Mo Ran looked at the little shidi in front of him, he found himself thinking of his own childhood and remembering those years that had been rife with bitterness and hardships. A surge of emotion rushed through his chest and filled him with sympathy and a sense of intimacy. Suddenly, he said: "There was nobody to take care of you before, but from now on, there will be. You've already called me your Shixiong, so from here on out, I'll take care of you properly."

It seemed like Chu Wanning hadn't expected him to say this, and he was a bit surprised. After a while, his features melted slowly into a tiny smile. "You'll take care of me?"

"Mn. If you stick with me from now on, I'll teach you meditation and sword techniques."

Chu Wanning's grin widened. "You'll teach me meditation and sword techniques?"

Mo Ran misinterpreted his expression and scratched his head. "Don't make fun of me. I know that your cultivation level is already pretty good, but you're still young, and you have lots to learn. There's a lot of disciples under the Xuanji Elder, and he probably isn't able to train you individually. What's wrong with learning a bit from me? I have a holy weapon, you know."

Chu Wanning was silent for a moment. "I wasn't making fun of you," he said finally. "I…think you're great."

Chu Wanning would never have been able to say something like that before. However, ever since his body had become smaller, it seemed that his personality had grown gentler and softer as well. It was as if he had been hiding under a cloak of darkness and could finally remove his rock-hard mask.

As for Mo Ran, although he'd lived through two lifetimes, this was the first time someone had praised him like this and said, "You're great." Even though the one praising him was just a little kid, he was still at a loss as to how to respond, overwhelmed as he was by the pleasant surprise. For a while, Mo Ran could do nothing but sputter. His skin, which had always been as thick as city walls, flushed red. He repeated what had been said to him, stuttering, "I, I-I-I'm great… You really think I'm great?"

Suddenly, Mo Ran vaguely recalled that when he was young,

he had wanted to be a good person. But that small, gentle wish of his, much like all of his other little wishes—

"When I grow up, I want to ask Li-zizi from the makeup store to marry me." "When I have money, I want to eat pancake fritters every day." "If I could have just two pieces of barbecued meat for every meal, I wouldn't trade it even for immortality."

—all of it, in the end, had become nothing more than memories, blown away by the wind and scattered in the snow.

62

This Venerable One Arrives at Ancient Lin'an

THEIR TRAINING BEGAN without delay. Mo Ran liked feather-gathering most. After all, it wasn't like he'd actually expected to learn much from these losers whom he had thoroughly trounced in his last life. Even so, having the funds to indulge himself was where it was at.

Every day before the break of dawn, they went to the Ancestral Abyss to loot golden feathers. Next up was meditation in Zhurong Cave to refine cultivation by tempering their inner spiritual energy with the burning yang energy of the cave. Four hours after that was demon suppression practice with the feathered tribe. Another four hours of that, and they went to Asura Arena to engage in practice matches against one another.

Finally, in the evening before night fell, Miss Eighteen would lecture them on *The Demon Compendium* and *The Art of Exorcism* at the Stargazing Cliffs of Peach Blossom Springs.

This nightly lesson was of course Mo Ran's favorite time of day because that was the only lesson attended by cultivators from all three specialized divisions. He knew that Shi Mei wasn't great at qinggong and worried over whether he had enough to eat, so he made sure to give Shi Mei half of his harvested feathers every day. Outside of that, they hardly had a chance to interact. Instead Mo Ran spent every day with Chu Wanning, and the two gradually became inseparable.

During this span of time, they could often be seen together, day in and day out, rain or shine. Chu Wanning might be sitting on the railing of a bridge playing a tune on a leaf with Mo Ran beside him, cheek propped up in one hand, or Chu Wanning might be feeding fish by the river while Mo Ran stood to the side holding an umbrella, watching the koi fish leap, their golden scales glimmering against waters of clear jade.

When it rained at Peach Blossom Springs, Mo Ran would hold Chu Wanning's hand while they walked along a limestone footpath, its flagstones cracked from age, an oil-paper umbrella held evenly above them both. If the rainwater began to collect on the ground, Mo Ran would pick up his little shidi and carry him on his back, and the boy would cling quietly onto his shoulders as the drops of rain pitter-pattered around them.

If the close contact got to be a bit too warm and sweat started to bead on Mo Ran's forehead, the wordless shidi on his back would reach out and wipe his sweat away with a handkerchief. The handkerchief was plain white with a haitang flower sewn on a corner. Mo Ran kept thinking that it looked familiar, as if he had seen it somewhere before, but the careless thought would fly through his mind and soon be lost, like the drizzle of rain falling into a deep pond.

One day, Chu Wanning was resting in the courtyard when Mo Ran undid the boy's braid on a whim and tied his hair into a high ponytail instead. He was halfway through brushing his little shidi's hair when Ye Wangxi walked in while holding his left shoulder, expression gloomy.

Mo Ran, ever observant, raised his eyebrows slightly. "Did Ye-xiong get injured?"

"Mn." Ye Wangxi paused, then furrowed his brows. "It's nothing, just got grazed in a fight. But that guy is truly such a depraved lecher—how despicable!"

Mo Ran sputtered in disbelief before eventually managing to ask, "Did you get groped?"

"What exactly are you imagining?" Ye Wangxi asked harshly, glaring daggers.

"Ha ha ha, just kidding." Mo Ran laughed awkwardly, but he couldn't resist his own curiosity. "Who was it, though?"

"Who could it be but that flirt from Kunlun Taxue Palace?" Ye Wangxi replied.

Mo Ran let out an, "ah," at these words. *Could it be that guy?*

Recently, he'd been coming across female disciples whispering amongst themselves, saying, "Da-shixiong," this, and, "Da-shixiong," that. It was one thing for the younger ones to go on like that, but just a day ago he'd seen a forty- or fifty-year-old female cultivator in hysterics by the flower bushes as she muttered with distant eyes, "Not a single man in this world could even hope to hold a candle to Da-shixiong... If only he would look my way, or even speak to me! I'd willingly go to hell with no regrets!"

Mo Ran had lost it right then and there and erupted in laughter at the lovelorn display. He had a sneaking suspicion as to who this "Da-shixiong" might be, but Peach Blossom Springs was full of cultivators who barely even interacted with one another, so despite hearing this person mentioned time and again, he had never seen the guy. He also had at least enough shame to refrain from inserting himself into the gossip of female disciples, so he couldn't be sure.

"I was having a drink at Spirit Lake Tavern in the western market," Ye Wangxi said. "That bastard happened to be there, too, with a girl on each arm. It was depraved, but that's their choice and none of my business, so I couldn't exactly say anything."

"Makes sense," Mo Ran agreed.

"Then a female Guyueye disciple ran in, scanning the crowd with an anxious expression. She was clearly looking for someone."

Mo Ran laughed. "Let me guess, she was after that 'Da-shixiong'?"

"You've heard of this da-shixiong too?"

"Ha ha, well, I mean, if even an upstanding individual like you has heard tell of his philandering ways, how could a gossipy fellow like myself not know?"

Ye Wangxi shot him a wordless glance, then continued. "That da-shixiong is truly a piece of work. Turns out, the Guyueye girl came looking because he had exchanged tokens of affection with her some days ago, saying he would be her cultivation partner and stay by her side forever."

Mo Ran laughed again. "Yeah, that's bullshit. I bet Da-shixiong has like seventeen replicas of that 'token of affection,' one for every girl he's after. Probably spouts the same pledge of undying love word for word too."

Chu Wanning had been listening quietly, but now he glanced at Mo Ran and said, disgruntled, "Of course *you* would know."

To his surprise, Ye Wangxi took Mo Ran's side. "Mo-xiong has the right of it; that's exactly the case. That girl was a secret admirer of Da-shixiong's to begin with, so she'd taken him at his word and given him her virginity that very night."

"Aiyo!" Mo Ran hurriedly covered Chu Wanning's ears.

"What are you doing?" Chu Wanning asked, unfazed.

"Little ones can't listen to this sort of thing. It's bad for your cultivation."

Chu Wanning gave him a withering look.

The second Mo Ran was sure that Chu Wanning's ears were firmly covered, he asked, sparkles in his eyes, "And then?"

Ye Wangxi was a respectable individual; he had no idea that Mo Ran, a rascal, was consuming his recount of righteous indignation like he would some trashy romance. Thus he replied with an air of integrity, "What do you think? Da-shixiong denied it, of course. He didn't even want to give her the time of day, let alone have some words. The girl produced the sword tassel he'd given her as a token, but to her surprise, the two girls on Da-shixiong's arms each pulled out their own. They said that he gives one to every friend, and that it wasn't something reserved for a cultivation partner."

"Tsk, tsk, that's shameless all right."

"Right? I couldn't just sit and watch, so I went over to have a word with him." Ye Wangxi's expression shifted slightly, and there was a pause before he continued. "The talk went nowhere, so we ended up fighting."

Mo Ran smiled. "I see."

In actuality, he suspected that this probably wasn't the whole story. If this "Da-shixiong" was indeed the person that Mo Ran suspected, then he didn't have the sort of personality that would lead him come to blows over something like this. Ye Wangxi had likely omitted details out of embarrassment.

However, since Ye Wangxi didn't elaborate, Mo Ran didn't press the issue and changed the topic. "That da-shixiong must be pretty good in a fight, then. I can't imagine just any random person being able to land a hit on Ye-xiong."

That was evidently the wrong thing to say, as it only seemed to make Ye Wangxi even more displeased. Fury flickered like a wildfire in those dark eyes. "Pretty good? Yeah right," Ye Wangxi said with indignation. "He couldn't get any more mediocre. The women did all the fighting for him. What a good-for-nothing!"

"Ah? Ha ha ha ha ha." Mo Ran took a closer look at Ye Wangxi and found that, aside from the sword wound on his shoulder, there were a couple of bloody scratches on his cheek that had obviously come from a woman's nails. He almost fell over laughing. "Da-shixiong sure does live up to his reputation, ha ha ha ha."

Chu Wanning said nothing. He seemed to have been pondering something ever since Ye Wangxi said, "the talk went nowhere, so we ended up fighting." He waited until Ye Wangxi left to bandage his wounds in his residence before saying, "Mo Ran."

Mo Ran bopped his head. "Call me Shixiong."

After a long, dignified silence, Chu Wanning continued. "This da-shixiong, is it Mei Hanxue?"

"That's what I suspect," Mo Ran said with a grin.

Chu Wanning fell silent again, deep in thought. Then, as if suddenly coming to a realization, his eyes opened wide: "Could it be that Ye Wangxi got—"

"Shh! Quiet!" Mo Ran raised a finger to his lips in a hushing gesture, then crouched down to Chu Wanning's height, smiling. "Aren't you a little too young to be thinking about that stuff?"

"I've often heard that this Mei Hanxue person is very...unconventional. That he's done all sorts of preposterous things. To think that he'd dare have a go at a disciple of Rufeng Sect..."

Mo Ran laughed. "Ha ha ha, unconventional is one way to put it. Anyway, let's stay out of other people's business. Here, let Shixiong finish putting your hair up. I saw a pretty hair clasp while I was out on the west street earlier, and it wasn't too pricey either, so I grabbed it. Let's have you try it on."

Just as Mo Ran didn't care for Chu Wanning's taste, Chu Wanning was less than impressed with Mo Ran's. He stared silently at the overly vibrant and honestly gaudy hair clasp, which was decorated with golden orchids and butterflies. "Are you sure that's for me?"

"Yep! Little kids should wear lively colors like red and gold."

Chu Wanning continued to stare in mute horror and fascination. He sincerely didn't want it, but when he thought about it, this was the first time that Mo Ran had ever given him something. He closed his mouth and said nothing, face full of gloom as Mo Ran fastened the clasp to his ponytail. The golden orchids and butterflies glimmered garishly against his long, inky hair.

Chu Wanning lowered his lashes. Suddenly he felt that this wasn't bad. This kind of color, this kind of Mo Ran, this kind of himself. If he was in his true form, none of this would have happened.

It was as if the butterflies had come from a dream.

The clouds overhead shifted and colored as sun and moon chased one another across the sky. Half a year of training at Peach Blossom Springs flew by in the blink of an eye. Miss Eighteen had said that they would be tested at the half-year mark to gauge their progress.

"This will be your first test since coming here," Eighteen announced gracefully to the assembly. "The content of the trial will differ depending on your division, with three different disaster scenarios. Those of you in the Defense Division will enter the Domain of Blood River, those in the Healing Division will enter the Domain of Great Sorrows, and those in the Attack Division will enter the Domain of Fiends.

"Each of these three scenarios will unfold in an illusory realm that has been constructed using memories of the ghost realm invasion hundreds of years ago. You will be in no danger while within them, and you will be returned here once you have resolved the crisis therein.

"Up to two people may enter an illusory realm at a time. In other words, you may face the challenge alone or invite one other person to accompany you. As for the order of testing, that will be announced by the envoys anon."

The assembly was dismissed, and the tests began. Mo Ran didn't know how things were going over in the Defense and Healing Divisions, but at least for the Attack Division, half a dozen people had already gone through it and had all done pretty well. It seemed the trial wasn't too hard.

Ten days later, it was Mo Ran's turn.

Eighteen was in charge of the Attack Division, and she smiled as she asked, "Will Mo-xianjun be going with a partner?"

Mo Ran thought about it. "If I choose someone to go with me, would they be exempt from going through the trial again?"

"Of course."

"Then I'll bring my shidi." Mo Ran pointed at Chu Wanning. "He's still young, so I'll worry if he goes it alone."

The moon hung bright overhead as they followed Eighteen to a pitch-black cave. A thin layer of reddish-gold mist covered the entrance.

"Please listen well," said Eighteen. "The scene within the Domain of Fiends is one from the calamity two hundred years ago: the first rupture of the ghost realm barrier. Because the barrier could not be repaired in time, a mass of vengeful ghosts and malicious spirits escaped into the mortal realm and slaughtered countless living beings. This illusory realm is an emulation of the event based on the memories of a survivor from Lin'an during that time. Stepping into this cave will bring you to the battle-torn Lin'an City of two centuries ago. Slay the ghost king leading the army and the illusion will dissipate on its own."

Mo Ran glanced at Chu Wanning, then turned to smile at Eighteen. "Big sis, I'm sturdy, so it's whatever. But my shidi is only six, and swords don't have eyes. What if he gets injured?"

"There is no need to fear. The weapons inside the illusion will bring you no true harm," Eighteen explained. "Any injuries you sustain will be marked with a spiritual signifier and nothing more. However, if you are marked in a vital area representing a fatal injury, you will fail the trial."

Relieved, Mo Ran clasped his hands together and grinned. "I see. Thank you for the kind consideration."

And so, Mo Ran and Chu Wanning headed into the test without fear. The cave was pitch-black. Setting foot within it felt like missing a step; it was as if their bodies were abruptly suspended in midair. This sensation was immediately followed by a series of blurry images that flashed before their eyes. A legion of contorted faces flowed together into a river passing below them.

When their feet landed back on solid ground, they found themselves transported to ancient Lin'an, on a road at the outskirts of the city. The noon sun blazed above, and a putrid smell filled the air.

The sight of old Lin'an City of two hundred years past—plagued nightly by hordes of ghosts and accompanied by the heavy stench of rotting flesh—unfolded slowly before their eyes like a weathered scroll scorched by the flames of war.

63 This Venerable One Sees...Whom?!

THIS VERSION OF LIN'AN CITY was deeply embroiled in war. Congealing blood covered the ground as far as the eye could see, and they were surrounded by crumbled walls and ruined houses. The trees and greenery had withered away, suffocated by the heavy miasma of malicious ghosts.

Mo Ran hadn't yet collected himself before he heard some strange sounds and looked up. Not far away, fresh entrails hung from the branch of an old pagoda tree, and a dozen crows had set upon them to feast as blood and flesh dripped from them nonstop.

Underneath the tree lay the corpse of a middle-aged man; blood and organs spilled out from where his stomach had been torn open by claws. No one would ever know if he had died with his eyes open or closed, as his eyeballs had been pecked away.

Mo Ran was no stranger to such scenes. In his past life, he had once crossed the breadth of the mortal realm to put all seventy-two cities of Rufeng Sect to the sword. When he did, blood had flowed like rivers and corpses had lain strewn over the fields, amounting to a sight much like this one.

Yet for some reason he couldn't understand, even though he had reveled in the blood he had spilt in that life, and even though it had made every fiber of his being sing... Now, laying eyes on a similar scene of devastation filled him instead with a biting sympathy.

Had he been faking docility for so long that his true nature had, without his knowledge, changed?

As he pondered, he heard the sound of hooves ahead, accompanied by a cloud of dust. Anyone galloping around in such war-torn times was probably bad news.

Mo Ran yanked Chu Wanning behind himself, but there was nowhere to hide on this barren old road. A group of riders swiftly emerged from the dust cloud, some dozen in all. When they got closer, it was apparent that their horses were the opposite of sturdy—a few were so starved that their ribs protruded.

The riders were dressed in a uniform style: white attire with bright red patterns and helmets embellished with feathers in like colors, and each had donned a circlet of entwined dragons. The clothes were stained yet tidy, and the people were thin but spirited. Even more unusual was the fact that each of them carried a bow and a full quiver of arrows on their backs. In times of war, the two most valuable things were food and weapons. These were plainly not ordinary people.

Mo Ran was still trying to decide if the new arrivals were good or evil, friend or foe, when one among them—a youth of only fourteen or fifteen—cried out in horror. "Dad! *Dad!*"

The youth stumbled off his horse and fell to the muddied ground below, but he scrambled up and staggered toward the tree, where he threw himself on the mangled body of the middle-aged man, crying miserably. "Dad! Dad!"

The other riders wore expressions of pity, but they had all undoubtedly seen too much death already, so much so that they had numbed to it. While the youth held the corpse and cried in agony, no one deigned to get off their horse to offer him comfort.

One of the riders noticed Mo Ran and Chu Wanning standing

not far away. He was startled for a moment before asking in a thick Lin'an accent, "You two aren't from around here, are you?"

"Yeah..." Mo Ran answered. "We're from the Sichuan region."

"That far away?" The asker was shocked. "These days the world is full of ghosts as soon as night falls. How have you two survived thus far?"

"I can fight a bit." Mo Ran knew it would be best to reveal as little as possible, but since these people didn't seem to be malicious, he pulled Chu Wanning out to change the subject. "This is my younger brother. We were passing by and stopped to rest for a while."

Some of the riders seemed a touch taken aback by the sight of Chu Wanning. A couple turned to whisper amongst themselves.

"Something wrong?" Mo Ran asked, alarmed.

"It's nothing," said the young man at the head of the group. "But on to serious matters: you should go to the city if you want rest. There may not be any monsters around right now, but once night falls, ghosts will be crawling through the streets. Xiaoman's adoptive father came out looking for food during the day yesterday, but there was a thunderstorm, and he couldn't make it back before the sun set, so..." He sighed heavily and didn't finish.

Xiaoman was the name of the wailing youth, and the corpse under the tree was his adoptive father. Such occurrences were commonplace in these chaotic times; someone in a family would go out looking for food and be perfectly fine as they left in the morning, only to never return come nightfall.

Even knowing that these events were already two hundred years past, Mo Ran felt a tightness in his chest as he watched that youth cry so miserably that it seemed he was about to weep blood.

This was followed by a sudden unease. Had he grown soft? He'd hardly blinked when killing people in his last life.

Mo Ran grabbed Chu Wanning and bid the group farewell.

"When you get to Lin'an City, find somewhere to stay for a while," the leader said. "We're planning to relocate everyone to Putuo soon, where an abundance of spiritual energy has warded off the ghost invasion—at least for the time being. You should come with us rather than traveling with just the two of you."

"Relocate?"

"That's right." The leader's eyes sparked to life, and even his face seemed to light up. "It's all thanks to Chu-gongzi's brilliant plan. Everyone in the city, from the elderly to the infants, will get to keep their lives! But enough chatter. We still have to patrol the border before it gets dark, see if we can find any more survivors to bring back. Ai, Xiaoman, come on. We should go."

Yet Xiaoman continued to cry, clutching his father's corpse without turning around.

Mo Ran sighed and tugged at Chu Wanning's hand. "Let's go to the city first," he said quietly.

Chu Wanning nodded, but suddenly asked, "Do you think they managed it, in the end?"

The small hand in Mo Ran's felt a little cold. "Do you want the truth or a lie?"

"The truth, of course."

"The lie would be better for a little kid."

So Chu Wanning answered his own question. "They didn't."

"That's right. See, you already knew the answer. But you still had to ask, as if that would change the outcome."

Chu Wanning ignored that. "Do you know why they didn't make it out?"

"It's not like I'm some two-hundred-year-old demon. How would I know?"

Chu Wanning fell silent for a while. "Two hundred years ago," he said gloomily, "practically everyone in Lin'an City died."

Mo Ran was silent.

"Only a few escaped."

"Wait, Shidi, you're so young—how do you know so much?"

Chu Wanning shot him a glare. "The Yuheng Elder reviewed this in history lessons more than once. You decide to not pay attention in class, then turn around and ask me how I know things? How despicable."

Mo Ran was speechless. *Sure, I spaced out in class, but even my own shizun didn't scold me. What're you lecturing me for?* Then again, there was no point arguing with a kid, so he let it slide.

The pair headed toward the city, chatting along the way, and before long arrived at the city gates. The ancient city stood tall on the bank of the Qiantang River and was heavily fortified against ghosts and demons, with defensive structures lining the walls and the perimeter.

Countless corpses bearing curse marks lay piled outside the city. Such remains, if not taken care of, would reanimate at night. Cultivators had gathered outside to spread incense ash on the corpses while the sun was high in the sky and the yang energy was strong. For the bodies afflicted with especially strong curses, they performed exorcisms using talismans upon which they drew with wine-dipped cinnabar.

A pair of guards stood before spiked defensive frames by the city gates, dressed just like the riders they had met earlier, with white attire trimmed in red and twin dragon circlets, as well as bows on their arms and a full quiver of arrows on their backs.

"Halt! Identify yourselves."

Mo Ran repeated his story from earlier. The guards weren't there to refuse anyone entry, only to register new arrivals, so they were let through after putting their names down.

Before leaving, Mo Ran remembered that the riders had mentioned a "Chu-gongzi." Since the relocation was this Chu-gongzi's idea, the fellow had to be crucial to breaking the illusion.

"Sorry to bother, sir, but might I inquire about someone?" Mo Ran asked.

The guard looked at him. "Aren't you from Sichuan? You know someone here?"

Mo Ran smiled. "No, but we met some sentry gentlemen who mentioned a gongzi by the name of Chu, the one who's going to take everyone to Putuo in two days. I was wondering who this Chu-gongzi was. I know a bit of magic and wanted to see if I could help in some way."

The guard looked Mo Ran up and down and seemed to decide that he must have skill, to have been able to bring a little kid all the way here without mishap. "Chu-gongzi is the eldest son of the lord governor. The lord governor was killed a month ago when the ghost king descended, and the gongzi has led us since."

"The governor's son?" Mo Ran and Chu Wanning exchanged a glance, then Mo Ran turned to ask, "That's strange. How does the governor's son know magic?"

"What's so strange about that?!" The guard glared at Mo Ran. "Since when was there a rule that you have to be in a big sect to cultivate? That the common people can't do it?"

Mo Ran fell silent.

Sure, there were independent cultivators, but they never amounted to anything. It made Mo Ran wonder whether this amateur Chu-gongzi and his half-baked plan was what had gotten everyone in Lin'an killed.

As they followed the guard's directions toward the governor's residence, Mo Ran soon realized how wrong he was. This esteemed personage who just so happened to share a name with his shizun was inarguably no amateur.

He saw a Shangqing Barrier.

A Shangqing Barrier was a powerful variety of barrier formed of purified energy that was capable of warding off all evil. As long as this barrier stood, even thousand-year-old malicious spirits couldn't hope to pass it, much less the average ghost.

This barrier required the caster to remain within its range in order to ground the spell, and it protected a relatively small area. Even a mighty zongshi like Chu Wanning could only cover about half of Sisheng Peak with one.

Right here and now, this Chu-gongzi of two hundred years ago had erected a Shangqing Barrier that covered a radius of ten miles around the governor's residence. Although a far cry from Chu Wanning's capabilities, it was certainly far from an ordinary achievement.

Mo Ran and Chu Wanning headed toward the gates of the residence. Mo Ran intended to try his luck and have someone notify the governor gongzi that a cultivator was offering help. He wanted to see if the man would be willing to show them the courtesy of a personal meeting.

However, when they turned the corner, they were met with the unexpected sight of three long lines of people queued in front of the gates. Six female attendants, dressed like the guards, were bringing out large wooden barrels, and hundreds of emaciated people—the elderly, the infirm, women, and children—were waiting their turn to receive porridge.

Those who had received their porridge went to a haitang tree by the residence. Beneath it stood a man dressed in white, his long inky hair loosely tied back, passing out protection talismans and patiently repeating instructions. His back was to Mo Ran, so he couldn't see the man's features, but he heard the people who had received the talismans murmuring, "Many thanks for Chu-gongzi's kindness, many thanks for Chu-gongzi's kindness..." as they dispersed.

So this was the governor gongzi?

Curious, Mo Ran dragged his little shidi around to get a look at the fellow's face. Just one look, and Mo Ran's eyes were bulging out of their sockets. It was if he had been struck by lightning. W-wasn't that Chu Wanning?!

It wasn't just Mo Ran; Chu Wanning was also gobsmacked. Even though they strained to see him from their place at the end of the line, this Governor Chu-gongzi had a lean face with sword-like brows and phoenix eyes, but a gentle curve to the line of his nose—and he even wore all white, just like he did himself!

Chu Wanning was struck dumb.

Mo Ran was also struck dumb.

After a long while of being frozen stiff, Mo Ran said shakily: "Shidi, ah."

"Mn."

"Don't you feel like...this Chu-gongzi looks just like a certain somebody?"

"Like the Yuheng Elder," Chu Wanning said dryly.

Mo Ran smacked his own leg. "Right?! What's with that? Who is this? What's his relationship with Shizun?"

"Why are you asking me? How would I know?"

Mo Ran was frantic. "I thought you paid attention in class?"

"This obviously isn't the content of any class," said Chu Wanning, irked.

Then they fell silent again, scooting forward slowly with the line, both of them staring unblinkingly at the gongzi. Upon closer inspection, Chu-gongzi didn't look *exactly* like Chu Wanning. This gongzi's features were more mild and scholarly, his eyes weren't quite as long and narrow, his pupils were softer, and his gaze was much gentler.

Mo Ran stared and stared, then suddenly let out an, "eh?" and turned to look down at his little shidi. "Let me look at you."

"What do you want?" Chu Wanning turned his face away, ruffled.

At this, Mo Ran only grew more persistent, reaching out to grab his face and forcefully turn him back around. He stared for a while before finally coming to a realization and muttering, "Aiyah."

Chu Wanning forced himself to remain calm. "Wh-what is it?"

Mo Ran narrowed his eyes. "No wonder those people outside the city were muttering amongst themselves when they saw you. I just noticed, but you look kinda like Shizun too."

After a long pause, Chu Wanning hurriedly wrenched himself out of Mo Ran's grip, the tips of his ears turning red. "Nonsense."

"How come those guards noticed immediately, but it didn't occur to me for ages?"

Chu Wanning did not dignify that with a response.

In the midst of this puzzlement, the voice of a young child called out, "Papa."

64 This Venerable One Tells Shidi a Story

MO RAN LOOKED IN THE DIRECTION the voice had come from only to see its source waddling unsteadily in a little jog from the stone steps of the residence.

It was a small child, three or four years old, a bamboo pinwheel in hand as he bounced toward Chu-gongzi. He was dressed simply, with a jade pendant hanging around his neck, along with a lock of entrusted name[12] for good fortune and a protection amulet of red silk. He looked every bit like Mo Ran's little shidi, just smaller.

Mo Ran stared. Now he knew the true reason those riders had been gossiping. He couldn't help muttering, "Shidi, ah, you and Shizun are both from Lin'an, and Shizun even has the Chu name. Do you think this Chu family from two hundred years ago might be your ancestors, and that you two might be distant relatives? Seems pretty likely to me."

Chu Wanning said nothing, staring at the father and son. He'd never known his own origins, and he didn't remember much of his childhood either. Could this Chu-gongzi really be his ancestor?

He was still pondering this when Mo Ran reached the front of the line.

Chu-gongzi was about to hand Mo Ran a talisman when he looked up to see an unfamiliar face. He paused minutely before

12 *Traditional jewelry shaped like a lock and worn around the neck. Parents take their one-month-old child to cultivators or a temple to be given an "entrusted name" so that the child can receive the protection of the gods or the Buddha. The lock represents binding the child to life.*

smiling gently. "Is it your first time here?" His voice was mellow and refined, worlds apart from Chu Wanning's ice-cold severity.

"Uh... Uh, y-yeah." Being suddenly spoken to in such an open and friendly manner by someone who looked just like his shizun had Mo Ran feeling some kind of way, and he had to scramble to get his bearings.

The governor gongzi smiled. "My name is Chu Xun. May I ask for yours?"

"M-my name is Mo. M-Mo Ran."

"From where does Mo-gongzi hail?"

"R-really far away. F-from, uh, Sichuan." Chu Xun-gongzi was gentle and amiable, but Mo Ran couldn't shake the feeling that the man could see right through him.

"That is indeed quite far away," Chu Xun agreed with a smile. Then he paused, his gaze shifting down toward Chu Wanning, and surprise crossed his refined features. "And this is?"

"My name is Xia Sini." Chu Wanning supplied.

Mo Ran pulled him closer and patted him on the head, forcing a smile. "This is my little brother," he said, as he thought, *He doesn't look like me, but he sure looks like you.*

Maybe it was because battle was imminent and there were more pressing matters at hand, and therefore Chu Xun didn't have time to dwell on it. Or maybe it was because he was merely part of an illusion and didn't have the ability to really react to something that didn't originally belong in this fabricated realm. Whatever the case, he stared at Chu Wanning for a while, his brows scrunched together, then simply handed them each a talisman.

"These are difficult times, and you are our guests from afar, so please accept these talismans. If you have no other plans, then please, stay for a couple of days."

"I've heard that gongzi intends to bring the people of the city to Putuo," said Mo Ran. "What're the talismans for?"

"These are spirit-quenching talismans," Chu Xun explained. "When worn on the body, they can conceal the aura of the living."

Mo Ran understood at once. "Ah, I get it. If the aura of a living being is sealed, then any ghosts they meet won't be able to tell them apart from the dead. That way, even if we walk right past some ghosts, they'll be too confused to do anything."

Chu Xun smiled. "Precisely."

Understanding that Chu Xun-gongzi was quite busy, Mo Ran didn't want to take up more of his time with questions, so he thanked the man and pulled his little shidi along to the side.

The two of them found a spot by a wall to sit down. Mo Ran turned toward Chu Wanning to see the boy staring in a daze at the talisman. "What are you thinking about?" he asked.

"I was thinking that this is a solid plan," Chu Wanning murmured, still deep in thought. "But in that case, just what happened to prevent them from escaping in the end?"

"Is it not in the records?"

"This two-hundred-year-old disaster is covered in the most detail in *The Lin'an Records*, but even that book only spares a few lines of text to describe it."

"What does it say?"

"Lin'an was besieged, the situation therein unknown. By the time the resistance army broke through, corpses lay strewn across the roads, and the vast majority of houses were empty. Of the approximately one hundred people of the governor's residence and the seven hundred and forty common folk, none survived."

After a long moment of silence, Mo Ran said, "Nothing about how they died?"

"Nothing. Lin'an City was completely surrounded, and hardly anyone made it. The feathered tribe saved a lucky few later on, but they rarely involve themselves in mortal affairs, so they see things differently from how we do. As far as they're concerned, the truth of what happened isn't all that important, and even if they knew, they still wouldn't talk about it unless there was some particular need to do so." Chu Wanning paused. "But, since these people are setting off in two days, we'll learn what happened soon enough. In the meantime, we might as well walk around and see if we can find some clues."

The two of them tucked away their spirit-quenching talismans for safekeeping and were just getting up to leave when there was a flurry of footsteps, followed by a tug on Chu Wanning's sleeve.

"Xiao-gege."

Chu Wanning turned around. It was the little gongzi who looked just like him.

"Xiao-gege," the boy said in a small, childish voice, "Papa said you two don't have anywhere to stay, so if you don't mind, you can stay with us tonight."

"Um..."

Chu Wanning and Mo Ran looked at each other.

"Is that really okay?" Mo Ran asked. "Your papa is already so busy."

"It's okay." The little fellow grinned guilelessly. "Lots of people with nowhere to go are staying with us already. We're all living together. Papa keeps the ghosts away at night, so we don't have to be scared." He spoke with little pauses, not yet used to linking so many words together, but his open sincerity was heartwarming.

"Okay, we'll be imposing on you tonight, then," said Mo Ran. "Thank you, Xiao-didi."

"Heh heh. No worries, no worries."

Watching him bounce away, Mo Ran tugged on Chu Wanning's hand. "Hey, really, I gotta say something."

"I know what you want to say, so shut it."

"Ha ha ha, read my mind again?" Mo Ran ruffled his hair, grinning. "Once we get back to Sisheng Peak, I really gotta ask Shizun about this. Between the two of you, one looks like the dad and the other looks like the son—there's no way you guys aren't related to Governor Chu."

After a moment, Chu Wanning said, "So what? Even if we do turn out to be related, what then?"

"Eh?"

Chu Wanning looked mildly toward the father and son beneath the tree. "It's all in the past anyway," he said expressionlessly. "They're already dead."

Then he turned and walked away.

Mo Ran stood rooted in place for a while before running after him. "Oi, aren't you a little too young to be so cynical?" he muttered. "Even if they're dead, they're still your ancestors. If I were you, I'd definitely erect a shrine for them—with a statue, nine feet tall, all gold, decked out in jewelry—and burn incense for them every year. I'm counting on my ancestors for protection, you know... Hey—hey, hey, why're you walking so fast?!"

While wandering through the city, they noticed that every family was gathering straw and making straw men. When they inquired about the practice, they were told Chu Xun-gongzi had asked the citizens to do it: everyone in the city, young and old alike, had to have a matching straw man in which to insert a talisman with a drop of that person's blood. These would substitute for them as "decoy puppets."

It was the same basic idea as tossing a bunch of meat-stuffed mantou into a river as offerings to a river deity that demanded human heads. Some ghosts and deities were simply, fundamentally, not that smart. Any little trick could fool them, like that ghost mistress from Butterfly Town who'd had nothing but mud rattling around between its ears.

It seemed that Chu Xun had arranged at least two layers of precautions for his citizens. The first was the spirit-quenching talismans, so that they wouldn't be discovered by ghosts while running away. The second was these straw puppets, which would act as decoys to buy some time for their escape, so that the ghosts wouldn't immediately notice everyone in the city had vanished and become infuriated.

This only made the haze in Mo Ran and Chu Wanning's hearts heavier. How had such a carefully crafted plan end up falling through?

They returned to the governor's residence filled with misgivings. It was dark by then, and many families had brought bedding to stay the night within the Shangqing Barrier rather than returning to their homes.

The governor kept his gates open at night, with only a few guards patrolling the premises. By the time Mo Ran and Chu Wanning arrived, all the rooms of the residence were filled, with at least three or four families huddled in each. People were crowded everywhere, with hardly any room left to stand.

In the end, they could only find a corridor to rest in. There was no bedding, of course, so Mo Ran padded the ground with some straw he had requested from the guards, picked up Chu Wanning, and laid him on the makeshift pallet. "You'll have to make do with this tonight."

"Looks comfortable enough," said Chu Wanning.

"Really?" Mo Ran laughed. "I thought so too."

He flopped down next to Chu Wanning and stretched, then folded his arms behind his head and stared up at the wooden beams of the ceiling above.

"Shidi, take a look. Those bird people aren't half bad at weaving illusions, huh? They only have a survivor's memories to serve as foundation, so it's really something that the illusion is so detailed. You can even see the texture of the wood on the ceiling."

"The feathered tribe are half-immortal, after all," said Chu Wanning. "Even if they're not omnipotent, they're capable of feats beyond mortal ability."

"I guess so." Mo Ran blinked, then rolled to face Chu Wanning, propping his head up. "I can't sleep."

Chu Wanning glanced toward him and stared. "What do you want, a bedtime story?"

He was being sarcastic, but Mo Ran's face was as thick as the city walls. "Yes, please!" he laughed. "I want the one about Dongyong and the seven fairies."

Chu Wanning hadn't expected him to take the offer seriously and was taken aback for a moment before turning away in a huff. "You wish. How old are you? Aren't you embarrassed?"

Mo Ran grinned. "It's only human to want the things we can't have. That's got nothing to do with age. I never had anyone to tell me bedtime stories when I was small, and I always thought about how nice it would be to have someone like that. But that someone never showed up, and then I grew up and stopped thinking about it. Even so, deep inside, I still want it."

Chu Wanning was silent.

"You didn't have anyone to tell you bedtime stories either, did you?"

"Mm."

"Ha ha, so you don't actually know how the story of Dongyong and the seven fairies goes, right?"

"What's the point in those silly stories, anyway?" Chu Wanning asked after a long pause.

"Just admit you don't know it. Don't write it off as a silly story either, or you're gonna grow up into a boring person like my shizun and everyone will avoid you."

"Who cares if everyone avoids me?" Chu Wanning snapped. "I'm going to sleep."

With that, he lay down and closed his eyes.

Mo Ran rolled around with laughter until he rolled over next to Chu Wanning. When he gazed at his little shidi with his eyes closed, his eyelashes long and dark, looking quite adorable, he reached out to pinch his cheek. "Are you really asleep?"

"I'm really asleep."

Mo Ran laughed. "Then you keep sleeping and I'll tell you a bedtime story."

"You know one?"

"Yep, just like you know how to sleep talk."

Chu Wanning shut up.

Mo Ran lay next to him on the straw bed, their heads mere inches away. He cackled for a bit, but after a while—when he saw that his shidi was pointedly ignoring him—he stopped being quite so boisterous and instead gazed up at the ceiling, eyes still lit with mirth. Now and again, the smell of the straw wafted over them, accompanied by the quiet sounds of night.

"The story I'm about to tell you is one I made up myself. I envied those who had bedtime stories when I was young, but there was nothing for it, so every day I would tell stories to myself while lying in bed. I'll tell you my favorite one now: it's called 'Ox Eats Grass.'"

65
This Venerable One's Story Is Super Bad

HAVING SPOKEN TO THIS point, Mo Ran smiled again before he continued, "A long, long time ago, there was a small child."

Chu Wanning's eyes were closed. "Wasn't this about an ox grazing? What's with this kid?"

"Let me finish." Mo Ran grinned. "Once upon a time, there was a small child who was very poor and who didn't have a mom or a dad. He was a child laborer in the household of a landlord. He had to wash dishes, wash clothes, and wipe the floors, and he also had to take the ox out to graze. Every day, the landlord's household gave him three pieces of flatbread to eat, and the child was very happy that he could fill his stomach.

"One day, he took the ox out to graze as always. On the road, they bumped into a mad dog that bit the ox's leg. Because of this, the landlord unsurprisingly gave the boy a sound beating. After the beating, the landlord made the boy go kill the mad dog to vent his rage. If the child didn't, the landlord threatened not to give him his flatbread.

"The child was very scared and could only follow orders, so after he beat that mad dog to death, he brought it back. However, when he came home, the landlord discovered that the dog that bit his ox's leg was actually the beloved pet of the county master."

Chu Wanning opened his eyes. "And then what?"

"What else could they do? That dog was the county master's favorite, and due to its master's position, it was used to having its way and being a bully. Who could have imagined it would be beaten to death like that? If the county master were to find out, he wouldn't just let it go. The more the landlord thought about it, the angrier he became, so in the end, he didn't give the child his flatbread. He even threatened to hand the child over if the county master came looking."

"What is this mess? So unreasonable. I'm not listening to this anymore."

"Lots of things are unreasonable to begin with." Mo Ran laughed. "It's all a matter of who has more money, whose fist is tougher, and whose position is higher. The next day, the county master indeed came knocking and the child was handed over. But because he was so young, it would've been unbecoming for the county master to lock him up, so he was flogged ten times and released."

"And the child ran away after that, right?" Chu Wanning asked.

"Ha ha, he didn't run away. The kid returned to the landlord's household, recovered from his injuries, and went back to tending the ox for them. He was still getting three flatbread a day."

"Wasn't he mad?"

"As long as his stomach was full, he couldn't be mad. A sound beating is just a sound beating. After it's over, it's over. Things were peaceful for over a decade. By that point, the oxherd boy had grown up. One day, when several esteemed guests came to the landlord's house, the landlord's son—who was the same age as the oxherd—saw one of the guests had brought a particularly beautiful agate snuff bottle. He took a liking to it, so he stole it.

"The snuff bottle was an heirloom and extremely precious. The guest was quite panicked and looked all over the house for his possession. The landlord's son realized that he wouldn't be able to hide it anymore, so he stuffed the snuff bottle into the oxherd's hands and told him that if he dared to tell the truth, they would never feed him again and he would starve to death."

Having listened to this point, Chu Wanning was at a complete and utter loss for words. He found himself thinking that although Mo Ran had been lost at a young age and hadn't been able to grow up with his family at Sisheng Peak, at the very least he had grown up at a pleasure house where his mother was the madam. Even though it couldn't have been the happiest of times, it wouldn't have been miserable either. So why were all the stories he made up so gloomy and sad?

Mo Ran went on, quite enjoying himself, "The snuff bottle was soon found. The oxherd could only brace himself and take the blame so that he would continue to have food to eat, and naturally, what followed was another viciously sound beating. This time, they beat him so badly that he couldn't get out of bed for three days.

"The landlord's son got away with it all, so he secretly snuck a steamed bun stuffed with marinated pork to the oxherd. The oxherd wolfed it down and stopped resenting the landlord's son, even though he'd harmed him. He'd never tasted such a delicacy before, so as he held the bun, he kept saying, 'Thank you, thank you.'"

"I'm not listening anymore." This time, Chu Wanning was actually aggravated. "How could he stop resenting him? One steamed bun and all is forgiven? And thanking him too! What was there to thank?!"

Mo Ran blinked innocently. "No, you're not listening carefully."

"How am I not?"

"That steamed bun was stuffed with *marinated pork*," Mo Ran said with a grave air.

Chu Wanning was flabbergasted.

"Ha ha, look at your face! You don't understand, do you? Usually that kid only got his hands on a scrap or two of fatty meat on New Year's Eve. He had thought he was going to die never knowing the taste of marinated pork, so of course he'd thank whoever gave him some."

At the sight of his little shidi stumped speechless by his words, Mo Ran smiled brilliantly. "Either way, this incident passed just like that. The boy still collected his three daily flatbread, and time went on. One day..."

Chu Wanning was by now familiar with the pattern of Mo Ran's tales. The moment "one day" was uttered, nothing good could follow.

Sure enough, Mo Ran said, "One day, the landlord's son committed another crime. This time, he violated a girl at the neighboring mill, and coincidentally, the unlucky oxherd came upon the scene."

"And that child is going to take the blame again?" Chu Wanning asked.

"Aiya." Mo Ran laughed. "That's right. Congrats, congrats! You know how to tell stories now too."

A pause. Then, "I'm going to sleep."

"Nooo, I'm almost done. This is my first time telling someone a story, so grant me some face, will you?"

Chu Wanning fell into a disgruntled silence.

"This time, the oxherd *definitely* had to take the blame, because the girl, unable to take the humiliation, had committed suicide by way of bashing her head into the wall. But the oxherd wasn't dumb. He knew that whoever took the fall would have to pay for this with their life, and there was no way he was going to give his up for the sake of the landlord's son. However, when he refused, the landlord's son locked him and the dead girl inside the mill and ran off to report it to the authorities.

"This oxherd already had a troubled history. When he was young, he'd randomly beaten the county master's dog to death, then later he'd stolen a guest's snuff bottle, and this time, he'd sexually assaulted a common girl. Naturally, he could not be absolved of his crimes. No one was willing to listen to him explain himself. He was caught red-handed with all the evidence, so he was arrested."

Chu Wanning eyes went wide. "And then?"

"And then he stayed in jail for a few months. When autumn came, he was sentenced to death, to be hung at the execution platform outside the city. As he followed along the execution procession winding through the fields, he suddenly saw someone about to slaughter an ox not far in the distance. He could tell at a glance that the ox was the very same one he'd been tending since he was young. Now that it was old, it didn't have the energy to plow the fields, but it still needed to graze. However, if it only ate and performed no labor, what use was it to the landlord? It had plowed fields for them its whole life, but in the end, they were going to butcher it and eat its meat."

Even as he spoke of this cruelty, Mo Ran wasn't sad. He still smiled. "That oxherd had grown up riding on the back of that ox, and he had told it many of his secrets, had fed it hay, had hugged its neck and cried when he'd been wronged, and taken it for his only family in this world.

"So he knelt down and begged the executioner to let him go bid farewell to the ox. Of course, the executioner didn't believe there could be any such attachment between man and beast, so he thought the boy was only trying to pull a trick and didn't allow it."

"And then?"

"And then? And then that oxherd was hung to die. The ox was butchered. Hot blood flowed all over the ground, and those who gathered to watch the show dispersed. That night, the landlord's household ate beef, but the beef was old and kept getting stuck in their teeth. They ate a little, didn't like it, and dumped the rest."

Chu Wanning was once again speechless.

Mo Ran flipped over, smiling happily at him. "There, it's done. How was it?"

"Get lost," said Chu Wanning.

"Hey, the first time I made this up for myself, I cried. You're so heartless. You're not even gonna cry a little?"

"You suck at telling stories..."

Mo Ran laughed a bit and put his arm over his little shidi's shoulder to pat him on the head. "Well, that can't be helped. Your shixiong is only so talented. All right, the story's done. Let's sleep."

Chu Wanning didn't acknowledge him, but after a long time, he suddenly said, "Mo Ran."

"Call me Shixiong."

"Why is the story called 'Ox Eats Grass'?"

"Because just like people, an ox has to eat. If you want to eat, you have to do a lot of work. If one day you can't work anymore, then no one will care if you're alive or if you're dead."

Chu Wanning stopped talking again.

From the yard outside there came the muted voices of those seeking refuge, and every now and again, an ominous cry or two from ghosts and demons outside the barrier.

"Mo Ran."

"Aiya, so cheeky. Call me Shixiong."

Chu Wanning ignored him and asked, "Did that child really exist?"

"Nope." Mo Ran was quiet for a moment, then he suddenly smiled, his dimples deep and charming. He squished the little kid into his arms and said warmly, "I made it up to tease you, obviously. Be good. Go to sleep."

Yet unexpectedly, before long there was a sudden commotion in the yard.

Someone was shouting angrily, "Are you *still* trying to see the gongzi?! The gongzi is busy—who has the time to attend to your business? Toss that corpse aside! Don't you know that the ones with blue dots will rise?! Are you trying to get us all killed?"

This voice was like thunder in the middle of a dark night, and the moment the prospect of a rising corpse was mentioned, there was an uproar. In a flash, everyone who had been asleep was sitting up and looking toward the commotion.

Mo Ran shielded the little shidi behind himself and glanced over, frowning. "Hm?" he said in a low voice. "Isn't that the guy from earlier?"

The individual who was kneeling and being berated was indeed that youth named Xiaoman, whom they'd met when they arrived. He was still wearing the close-fitting clothing from earlier, but his behavior was entirely different.

It was as if his entire person had been emptied out. He could do nothing but cling tightly to the dead body of his adoptive father. The corpse's nails had grown significantly, a sure sign that a corpse would rise. When the others saw this, they all backed away.

The head steward was scolding him sharply. "Your father was my colleague—I also feel terrible that he was killed. But now what? You were the one who cried for food last night, so he went out to find food for you. You dragged your dad to his death, and now you want to drag us there too?"

Xiaoman was kneeling on the ground, his hair wholly disheveled, and his eyes were red as he sobbed. "N-no, I'm not… Dad. Daddy. Please, I beg you, let me see the gongzi. The gongzi has a way to stop my dad's corpse from rising. I want to bury him properly. Please,

I beg you all, don't...don't dismember him..." By the time he uttered the word "dismember" he was choking on his sobs. He buried his face in his palms and wiped messily at his trembling lips. "Please, I'm begging you... Let me wait until the gongzi comes back..."

"It's going to be midnight soon and the gongzi is out, so how can he possibly attend to your wishes? You know that normal corpses can still be purified, but your dad's got those blue spots and his nails have already changed. How can he hope to hold out until the gongzi gets back?"

"No... He can, Uncle Liu... I'm begging you, I'll do anything. I-I'll think of a way to repay you after. Please, I beg you, just don't touch my daddy... I beg, I...I beg you..."

The middle-aged steward let out a long sigh at his pleading, the rims of his eyes also turning red. Even so, he replied, "I can't do that for you, not when it would cost everyone else their lives as well. Guards!"

"No! Don't!"

It was too late. No one would help the boy. Everyone knew that if this corpse was left intact, then when midnight came, it would inevitably turn into a ferocious spirit.

The corpse of Xiaoman's adoptive father was forcibly dragged away to be dismembered outside. Several people held the boy back, and his bitter tears flowed furiously, sullying his whole face as bestial howls escaped his lips. In the end, he was still half pulled, half dragged away into the distance.

Once this storm had passed and after some muttered whispers, the yard returned to its peaceful quiet. However, Chu Wanning did not fall back asleep. He lowered his head pensively.

Mo Ran glanced sidelong at his little shidi. "What are you thinking about?"

"That person lost his father, then did something terribly foolish. Then, on top of that, his father's body was wrested from him. Of course he'd resent everyone. I can't be sure, but I suspect that he was the one who botched Lin'an's migration."

"I think so too," Mo Ran replied without missing a beat.

Chu Wanning shook his head. "It's too early to tell. We can't make any conclusive claims yet. Let's just keep an eye on him for now."

66

This Venerable One Sees the Heavenly Rift for the First Time

BY THE SECOND DAY, nothing unusual had happened.

Chu Xun sent guards to tally the number of straw men in the city to make sure that it matched the number of people, while the people busied themselves packing their few possessions. Just one more night and they would leave, first thing in the morning, to take refuge at Putuo in accordance with Chu Xun's plan.

Mo Ran sat by the gate of the governor's residence, watching the people come and go. He sighed. "Chu Xun's plan is watertight. Unless someone leaked the info, the average ghost wouldn't have the brains to figure out that only decoy puppets will be left in the city. Someone must have ratted them out. Shidi, what do you think?"

No response.

"Eh? Shidi?"

Mo Ran turned around. Without him noticing, his little shidi had wandered off to watch a squadron of riders getting ready, and in his place was Chu-gongzi's son, sitting with his cheeks in hand.

"Da-gege..."

Mo Ran almost jumped at his sudden appearance. "What is it?"

The little fellow pointed at an old paulownia tree nearby, in which a kite dangled from a high branch. "Mama gave it to me. It got stuck. Can't reach," he articulated with some difficulty. "Da-gege help me?"

"No prob, no prob." Mo Ran leapt nimbly to the top of the tree using qinggong, retrieved the butterfly-shaped kite, and landed steadily back on the ground, smiling as he returned it. "Here you go. Don't lose it again, okay?"

The little boy nodded.

Mo Ran watched him wandering around alone for a bit. He found himself thinking that Chu Xun probably didn't have the time to look after his son. "Where's your mom? It's a bit busy around here, so I'll take you to her."

"Mama? Mama is at the mountains in the back."

"What's she doing in the mountains?" Mo Ran asked, mystified.

"Sleeping," the kid answered in a soft voice, looking at him guilelessly. "Mama's always sleeping there. Papa takes me to see her when the flowers bloom in the spring."

"Ah," Mo Ran uttered quietly, at a loss for words.

The boy didn't mind; he was still too young to understand what death meant. He played happily with the kite in his hands for a bit, then looked up at Mo Ran and shuffled over. "Gege, thank you," he said in a whisper. "I'll give you... I have something to give you."

He dug around in his pocket as he spoke and finally produced a small half-piece of pastry wrapped in a reed leaf. No one in the city had enough to eat these days, so it was a mystery as to how the little guy had managed to save a piece of pastry. He broke it in half and handed the smaller piece to Mo Ran.

"Da-gege, for you... Shh, don't tell anyone else. I don't have any more."

Mo Ran was about to accept it when the boy suddenly changed his mind and took the smaller piece back, offering him the bigger half instead.

"It's really yummy. There's sweet bean paste inside."

This small act made Mo Ran's heart all warm and fuzzy. He was used to poor treatment and didn't quite know how to respond to charity. He reached out and took the sweet with a mumbled thanks. The boy seemed quite pleased and grinned brightly, the curve of his dark eyelashes filled with warmth and kindness.

Mo Ran couldn't bear to eat the flower cake, so he wrapped it up using a leaf from the paulownia tree and tucked it in his robes. He intended to talk further with the kid, but in the end, the boy was a little kid with a little kid's attention span. He had already bounced away into the distance.

Chu Wanning came back around that point only to see Mo Ran standing there, staring off into space. He raised an eyebrow. "What's up?"

Mo Ran watched the boy disappear and sighed. "I was just thinking, all these people... How come they all had to die?"

Night descended. Dark clouds covered the skies while occasional bolts of lightning ripped through the heavens. As the night grew deeper, a terrible gale howled amidst a torrential downpour.

Rain and its attendant yin energy enhanced the powers of ghosts and other fiends. Chu Xun gathered the survivors of Lin'an near his residence and bid them stay inside the Shangqing Barrier at all times.

Due to the rain, many of the areas that could usually be used as places of respite no longer served as such. Mo Ran kept an eye on Xiaoman, but when more and more people crowded into the governor's residence to take shelter from the rain, Xiaoman ducked out of view.

"Damn," Mo Ran muttered.

"I'll go after him," Chu Wanning said immediately. He was small, after all, and he swiftly dove into the crowd and disappeared. He returned after a while with an irate expression. "He got away."

"Outside the barrier?"

"Mn."

Mo Ran fell silent, gazing at the downpour outside and the people bustling to and fro. This was all only an illusion of events that had come to pass two hundred years ago. But he suddenly felt so wretched.

The people around them had such hope on their faces. They believed that as soon as dawn broke, Chu Xun would take them to Putuo, away from this ghost-infested hell. In the pouring rain, guards dressed in white and red put their all into making the final preparations so that they would be ready to move when the sun rose. None of them knew how little time they had left.

The night grew later still, and the noise died down as people dozed off, leaning against one another.

However, Chu Wanning and Mo Ran were wide awake. Their task was to wait for the ghost king to appear and to kill him. Since Xiaoman had already left the barrier, this night had to be the turning point.

Mo Ran turned to glance at Chu Wanning. "Why don't you get some rest? I'll wake you if anything happens."

"I'm not sleepy," said Chu Wanning.

Mo Ran stroked his hair. "Then eat something? We haven't eaten since coming here."

"I'm..." When Chu Wanning saw the pastry Mo Ran produced, the words "not hungry" were replaced by a gulp.

Mo Ran handed it over. "Here you go."

Chu Wanning accepted the sweet and broke it in half, giving the larger half back to Mo Ran and keeping the smaller portion for himself. Mo Ran stared blankly at him, face unreadable.

Chu Wanning took a bite and uttered a questioning, "Hm?" before asking, "Is this from Peach Blossom Springs? The flavor is a bit different from the ones before."

"How so?"

"It tastes of osmanthus flowers."

Mo Ran forced a smile. "Oh? Chu Xun's son gave it to me; it's probably traditional for Lin'an."

"It is indeed." Chu Wanning was opening his mouth to take another bite when he froze as if he'd suddenly realized something. All the color drained from his face. "That's not right!"

Chu Wanning shot to his feet, eyes wide and expression ghastly.

Mo Ran hadn't the slightest idea what the problem was. "What's not right?"

Chu Wanning didn't answer. Instead he walked into the courtyard and looked around in the pouring rain before picking up a sharp rock and firmly cutting into his own arm. Blood gushed out.

Mo Ran grabbed him hurriedly. "Are you crazy?"

Chu Wanning stared at the blood trickling down his arm for a moment before his head snapped up, eyes intense. "Have you still not caught on?" he said harshly. "Someone means us harm!"

Blood ran down his arm nonstop, the crimson diluted by the rain. Chu Wanning's face was pale in the deluge, his dark brows knitted tightly together and thoroughly drenched by the ceaseless downpour.

Thunder rumbled and lightning split the skies, and for an instant the harsh light turned night into day. The sudden clap of thunder jolted Mo Ran into understanding. He subconsciously took a step back. He knew what wasn't right.

Nothing in an illusion was real, however realistic it might seem. It should have been impossible for a pastry to have any taste, or for a weapon to actually cause them injury. In short, it should have been impossible for anything within the illusion to affect them.

"Someone manifested the illusion," Chu Wanning said quietly.

Manifesting an illusion, also known as "Illusion Reification," was no easy task. The ones most skilled in this technique were those of the Guyueye Sect, whose motto was: "Medicine for the people, divine physician for the heart." The latter half of the saying referred to the fact that some of them specialized in the art of manifesting illusions. Many people were unable to accept the passing of a loved one, but through Illusion Reification, the dead could once more accompany the living.

However, manifesting illusions was extremely difficult, so generally speaking, only short, individual scenes could be created, such as sharing a drink or taking a nap together. It would be only one thing at most.

This illusion, on the other hand, was extensive and continuous with a large variety of events, and moreover it had been constructed by the feathered tribe. Even Guyueye's own sect leader might not be able to manifest it all. Mo Ran immediately thought of someone else. Could it be that fake Gouchen from Jincheng Lake?

Before he could think on it further, a strange sound burst forth from the skies above. The dozing people jolted awake like startled birds, looking around with wide eyes before they finally stared up.

For a moment, it was deathly silent. Then screams erupted like an explosion of water droplets in boiling oil.

The people tried to flee in every direction, only to discover there was nowhere to go, and screams came from all sides.

There was a fracture in the sky, and an enormous, bloodred ghost eye stared unnervingly down from directly above. The eye was so close that it was practically pressed against the barrier. A harsh, garbled voice boomed forth: "Chu Xun, how very bold of you, a mere mortal daring to deceive this venerable one."

"The ghost king..." Mo Ran muttered.

There were nine kings of the ghost realm, and some were far stronger than others. The one before them now had yet to show himself, so there was no way to tell which one he was. That lone eyeball loomed in the sky, dripping with blood as it stared at the building below.

"Such arrogance. Absurd! You wish to save them, pathetic mortal? I might not have wiped out your city before, but since you wish to stand against me, I'll kill every single one of you! None shall be spared!"

With a shrill shriek, a blinding red light shot from the ghost eye, aimed directly at the barrier.

Crimson clashed with gold, and for an instant all the other colors of the world ceased to be. The force of the impact sent debris flying into the howling gale and relentless rain. The tree branches in the courtyard snapped one after another. The citizens inside the barrier grew hysterical, wailing as they huddled together.

The Shangqing Barrier withstood the first hit, but another flash of red followed immediately after and struck the same spot. The barrier held out, but a crack appeared.

"How arrogant. *Insufferable!*"

The red light struck again and again, the impacts thundering and sparks flying. When the barrier was on the verge of collapse, Chu Wanning's blood ran cold. Now that the illusion had been manifested, any attack that landed would be no different from one in the real world. If that attack were to hit them, both he and Mo Ran might die. Golden light gathered at his fingertips. This would surely blow his cover, but the situation being what it was, he had no choice.

He was about to summon Tianwen and get it over with when a resplendent bolt of light flew across the sky like an arrow and headed directly for the epicenter of the cracks in the barrier.

The crowd turned to see Chu Xun standing on a tall roof. He cradled a phoenix harp, and as his fingertips danced across its strings, they sent bolts of light sweeping forth to gather at the barrier. Each strum was as sharp and powerful as the rupturing of metal, and they instantly reinforced the Shangqing Barrier that had nearly failed.

"Gongzi is here!"

"Gongzi!"

The people below exclaimed one after another, some even crying with joy. Chu Xun held his own against the eye of the ghost king. The pair exchanged a hundred moves in an instant, and the ghost king was altogether unable to encroach past the barrier.

The cold voice rang again across the sky, even more menacingly. "Chu Xun, with your skills, you could have easily escaped by yourself. Why do you insist on meddling in affairs unrelated to you and making an enemy of the ghost realm?!"

"Your Majesty wishes harm upon my citizens. How could anything be less unrelated to me?"

"Ridiculous! We ghosts feed on the souls of the living. There is no difference between us eating souls and you eating meat! You will understand soon enough—once you're dead!"

Chu Xun didn't miss a beat, the notes of his harp never pausing. "Then we'll just have to see if Your Majesty can take this head from my shoulders."

As he spoke, the chords beneath his fingers rose to a crescendo, until a brilliant light pierced the heavens right into the bloody eye in the sky.

"Aughhh!"

The terrifying scream shook the very ground they stood on.

Fetid blood sprayed from where the eye had been burned by Chu Xun's spell, and the crimson downpour mixed with his shrill shrieks. In his anger, the ghost king unleashed a blade of light many times stronger than those before it, striking out through the sanguine rain. Chu Xun moved to block, but this attack was unlike the others, and the force of the impact forced him back several steps. The notes of his harp stuttered.

"Gongzi!"

"Crack! There's a crack! The barrier is going to break!"

"Mama! Mama—"

The crowd panicked; those with families huddled together and sobbed, while those without cowered in corners and quivered.

Chu Xun gritted his teeth, fire in his eyes, refusing to give up just like that. While he was locked in stalemate with the ghost king, lights flared to life on either side of him. He glanced to his periphery to see Mo Ran and Chu Wanning standing with him, their scarlet and golden light flowing steadily into his own, once again sealing the barrier.

A terrifying roar came from above. The ghost eye disappeared.

The three of them descended to the ground, and the sky rained rotten blood for a while longer before finally returning to clear water.

Chu Xun, face pale, bowed to Mo Ran and Chu Wanning. "Many thanks for your help."

"Don't mention it." Mo Ran waved his hands. "Go get some rest, you look terrible."

Chu Xun nodded. He had indeed burned through too much of his reserves, so Mo Ran supported him to the corridor. The people who had been in disarray only a moment ago saw that Chu-gongzi had repaired the barrier and saved them, so they gathered in gratitude, offering him water and draping clothing over his shoulders.

"Chu-gongzi," one said, "you're all drenched! Please go warm yourself by the fire."

Chu Xun thanked them one by one, but he was too exhausted to move and so could only turn down that person's invitation. Undaunted, the people carried over branches and made a bonfire beside him instead.

Things gradually quieted down, save for the crackling of the flames. Suddenly, someone asked, "Gongzi, we took so many precautions, but somehow the ghost king still saw through it all… Ai, what should we do?"

"Yeah, yeah…"

"How did they know we were going to leave? Gongzi said these ghosts couldn't tell the difference between the puppets and real people, so how did this happen? Could it be…" The man's voice faltered, and he snuck a glance at Chu Xun. He clearly wanted to say that perhaps Chu Xun had been wrong. That maybe somehow, somewhere, he'd messed up.

The white-clad guards saw that glance, and one of them swept in to rebuke the man with furrowed brows. "What are you trying to say?! It's obviously because someone couldn't keep their trap shut and leaked the plan to the ghost king!"

"Who would tattle to the ghosts though?" the person mumbled. "It's not like there's anything to be gained from that…" Then, seeing all the infuriated glares directed his way, he stopped talking, disgruntled.

A while passed in silence before someone else said, "Gongzi, that damn ghost definitely won't leave it at that. What should we do?"

Chu Xun, exhausted, didn't open his eyes, but his voice remained gentle. "We just have to hold out until dawn and then be on our way. They can do nothing in daylight."

"We have so many people—the elderly, the young, and some injured too. Can we make it to Putuo Mountain in a single day?"

"Don't worry about that," Chu Xun said softly. "Get some rest. Just focus on the journey tomorrow and I'll take care of the rest."

Chu-gongzi had always protected his citizens. When he said this, everyone listened and did as they were told. A little kid came over holding a piece of sesame candy and offered it to Chu Xun. Chu Xun opened his eyes slightly and patted his head with a smile. He was about to say something when a shouting guard ran over in a panic.

"Gongzi! Gongzi, something terrible has happened!"

"What is it?"

"The little gongzi—the little gongzi! Xiaoman—outside the City God Temple—" The guard was too shocked to finish a sentence. He stammered some more, then fell to his knees and sobbed miserably.

Chu Xun shot to his feet, what little color that lingered on his face draining away as he rushed into the rain.

67 This Venerable One's Heartfelt Anguish

THE CITY GOD TEMPLE stood at the very edge of Chu Xun's range of power. His barrier reached the stairs of the temple, but no farther.

Inside the temple, candles flickered weakly. A dozen ghosts who had cultivated corporeal forms lined either side. Between the lines was a woman in red, tied up and facing away from them, her head tilted back as she gazed up at the statue on the altar.

Next to her stood Xiaoman, his eyes downcast as he held firmly onto a young child.

"Lan-er!" Chu Xun cried out.

The child was none other than Chu Xun's son, Chu Lan. Mo Ran's heart lurched at the sight of the kid in trouble; he could still taste the pastry on his tongue. He made to go over but was blocked by Chu Wanning.

"Don't."

"Why not?!"

Chu Wanning glanced at him. "Every one of them is already two hundred years dead," he said quietly. "But this illusion has been manifested. I don't want you to get hurt."

Mo Ran fell silent. It was the truth. No matter what he did now, the dead were already gone, and there was no way to change that.

The boy wailed from outside the barrier, nearly unintelligible. "Papa! Papa, help me! Papa, please help Lan-er!"

Chu Xun's lips quivered. "What are you doing?" he yelled at Xiaoman. "I've never done you wrong. Let him go!"

Xiaoman ignored him, head lowered as if he had heard none of it. However, the hands clutching Chu Lan betrayed his inner hesitation. There was a mole between the thumb and forefinger of his left hand, and his hands trembled without stop, the veins on their backs starkly visible.

By now, everyone taking refuge at the governor's residence had arrived as well. They murmured to one another, aghast and furious at the sight within the temple.

"That's the gongzi's son..."

"How could this happen..."

In a single motion, Xiaoman cut the ropes binding the red-robed woman. She seemed to come back to her senses and turned slowly around. She was beautiful, pure as a lotus flower, her neck long and elegant—but her face was paper-pale, and her lips were tinted red as blood. The smile she directed at Chu Xun was more terrifying than it was lovely.

The low light of the candles illuminated her face. The moment Chu Xun saw her, he froze, as did the people old enough to recognize her.

There was sadness in her smile. Softly, she said, "Husband."

Mo Ran's expression was pure shock.

Chu Wanning watched on silently.

The woman was none other than Chu Xun's deceased wife.

Madam Chu looked to her side and lashed out her arm to take her son from Xiaoman. Though Xiaoman was unwilling, Madam Chu was a ghost and much stronger than he was, now that she had been freed from her bindings. She easily pulled the child from his grasp. However, the madam had died of illness before her child was even a month old, so the boy had never seen his mother. He kept crying for his father to save him.

"Be a good boy and don't cry anymore. Mama will take you to your papa."

Madam Chu hefted the child in her delicate arms and slowly walked out of the temple, down the rain-soaked stone steps, to the edge of the Shangqing Barrier. She stood facing Chu Xun, her joy mixed with sorrow.

"My husband, it's been a long time. Have...have you been well?"

Chu Xun couldn't speak. The tips of his fingers shook uncontrollably at his sides as those phoenix eyes stared at the woman behind the barrier, their rims slowly reddening.

"Lan-er has already grown so big," Madam Chu continued softly. "You've grown steadier too. A little different from the man I remember... Let me take a good look at you."

She reached out and her hand pressed against the barrier. She couldn't cross it, not while her body was that of a ghost. She could only gaze quietly across the flowing colors of the barrier at the person on the other side.

Chu Xun's eyes slid closed, wetness clinging to his lashes. He pressed his hand to hers, separated by the barrier. Then his eyes opened. The pair gazed at each other, across life and death, just as in days before.

Chu Xun choked back a sob. "My wife..."

Where the family had been separated by life and death for many years, the time they had spent together had been pitifully meager.

"The haitang tree I planted in the courtyard that year, did it take root?" she asked.

Chu Xun smiled with watery eyes. "It's grown tall and beautiful."

"I'm glad," said Madam Chu, smiling gently.

Chu Xun tried his best to keep smiling as well. "Lan-er loves that haitang tree. He's always playing under it in the spring. He likes haitang flowers, just like you, every...every year, during Qingming..."[13] Unable to keep up the act any longer, Chu Xun pressed his forehead against the barrier, tears falling without stop as his voice broke. "Every year, during Qingming, he always picks the prettiest flower to place before your grave. Wan'er, Wan'er, did you see? Every...every year, did you see?"

He was wracked with sobs by the end, every word bleeding misery, until his composure finally fell apart altogether.

Madam Chu's eyes also grew red. She was a ghost and had no tears to shed, but her miserable expression was no less unsettling to the onlookers.

For a moment, all were silent, everyone wordlessly watching the scene before them. Someone wept quietly.

Then a cold voice rang out from above. "Of course she knows. But not for long."

Mo Ran's face instantly changed. "It's the ghost king!"

Chu Wanning's expression grew dark as well. "This coward won't even show himself. Shameless!"

The ghost king's laugh sounded like nails against metal and made their blood run cold. "Lin Wan'er is one of our number now. I didn't want to hurt her, but since you're so set on opposing me and even ruined one of my eyes, I'll just have to dig out your heart to inflict a worse pain on you!"

At these words, the ghosts in the temple began chanting incantations.

---

13 清明 *Qingming, or the "Pure Brightness Festival" or "tomb-sweeping day," is a celebration to honor the dead in early April.*

"The heart is no more, let the past be erased—"

Madam Chu's eyes shot wide open and her voice shook. "My husband—Lan-er! *Take Lan-er!*"

"The heart is no more, let connections be severed—"

"Lan-er! Quickly! Go to your papa!"

Madam Chu tried to push her child across the barrier, but the thin layer of light kept him out as if he too was a ghost.

Xiaoman looked down at them from where he stood by the railing of the temple. His face, originally charming, twisted with a mixture of sorrow and glee. "It's useless. I put a ghost mark on him, as the ghost king instructed. He's just like you now—the barrier won't let him in."

Behind them, the incantation rose like a tide. "The heart is no more, let reason be shattered—"

"Husband!" Madam Chu was already panicked beyond measure, clutching her child to her breast and banging on the barrier. "Husband, take the barrier down. Take it down and let Lan-er in—you have to protect him! You have to protect him. I—I'm almost...I..."

"The heart is no more, let compassion be smothered—"

"*Husband—*!"

Madam Chu fell to her knees, her eyes wide as her whole body shook uncontrollably. Curse marks the color of blood slowly climbed up her face. "Our child—Lan-er... You promised me, you promised me that you'd take care of him... Take it down... Please, I'm begging you... Take it down... Husband!"

Chu Xun felt as if his insides were being ripped apart. Again and again, his hand lifted to dispel the barrier only to fall back down.

Outside the barrier, Chu Lan bawled loudly, staring up at him with a tear-stained face, his little hands reaching. "Papa doesn't... want Lan-er anymore? Lan-er wants Papa... Papa, hold me..."

Madam Chu held her child tightly in her arms, kissing his cheek. The pair of mother and son, one kneeling, one crying, begged Chu Xun to take down the Shangqing Barrier and let the child in.

Suddenly, someone in the crowd cried out, "Gongzi, you can't! You can't drop the barrier. You would doom the hundreds of people left in Lin'an—that's their ploy! Gongzi! You can't drop the barrier!"

"That's right, the barrier must be kept up!"

The common people's desire to live made them kneel one after another and grovel before Chu Xun, pleading.

"Gongzi, please! You can't take down the barrier or everyone will die!"

"Madam, please..." One of them knelt and bowed before Madam Chu. "Madam, please have mercy. Please be benevolent. We will be grateful to you forever, just please don't make the gongzi take down the barrier. You were always so compassionate, please, we're begging you..."

In an instant, other than the guards and a handful of others, everyone was on their knees begging and crying, their voices drowning out those of Madam Chu and her son outside the barrier.

Chu Xun felt like he was standing on the point of a needle while being stabbed by thousands upon thousands of sharp knives. Each blade grew barbs within his flesh and tore through his organs.

Before him were his wife and son, and behind him were the lives of hundreds. Thus tormented, he felt as if he had already died—as if he had been swallowed by flames and burnt to ashes.

Nevertheless, the chanting continued, even more piercing than before.

"The heart is no more, let emotion be expunged. The heart is no more, let desire be dissipated—"

More and more curse marks climbed up Madam Chu's fair neck, nearly covering her face, and they began to bleed into her eyes. She could hardly speak anymore and only stared at her husband in despair as she strained to utter: "If you… I…will…hate you… Take… take Lan-er… I hate…I…"

The curse marks oozed into her pupils. Her body shuddered as if in agony, and she squeezed her eyes shut.

"I—*hate you*!"

A wretched scream tore through the air, but by the end it turned into a bestial cry.

Madam Chu's eyes flew open. Her gentle almond-shaped eyes were stained the color of blood, and the whites of her sclera had disappeared, for there were now four pupils in each eye.

"Wan'er!" Chu Xun cried out with boundless sorrow, forgetting for a moment that the Shangqing Barrier required its caster to remain inside, wanting only to be with his wife.

Just as he was about to step out of the barrier, an arrow pierced the sky and landed firmly in his shoulder. The arm he had raised dropped back down to his side.

It was a young man of the guard, still posed with bow in hand. "Gongzi! Wake up!" he self-righteously said to Chu Xun. "You've always taught us that the righteous put the people before the self. Were those just pretty words? Will you throw away the lives of hundreds to save one person the moment your own interests are at stake?!"

"P-put that bow down," an old woman next to the young man said shakily. "How could you hurt the gongzi? Everything—everything is the gongzi's choice. Gongzi has already done his utmost. How, how could you… How could you be so ungrateful?!"

As they argued, fearful cries broke out at the fore.

Madam Chu had entirely transformed. Only a moment ago, she had held her child with such love, but now she was no different from a beast. She howled toward the sky with saliva dripping from her mouth, her teeth growing longer by the second.

In her arms, Chu Lan's voice had gone hoarse from crying, but in between sobs he still called out, "Mama..."

What answered him were Madam Chu's bloodred claws, which pierced through his throat.

All sound disappeared from the world. Droplets of blood drifted through the air like so many blossoms.

It was just like that moment years ago when Madam Chu had stood by the window holding her newborn child as she watched the petals of newly bloomed haitang flowers dancing in the courtyard. She had cradled the child gently in her arms as she sang softly. "Red haitang, yellow haitang, floating gently in the wind. Children in a land far away, missing their mom and dad."[14]

Red haitang...yellow haitang...

The hand that had caressed Chu Lan so tenderly that year tore into his skull, his limbs, his flesh.

Floating gently in the wind.

The rain came down in a deluge, blood pooling and flowing along the ground. The mother devoured her child's entrails.

Children in a land far away.

The eaves of the City God Temple towered solemnly above.

The year Chu Lan was born, his mother had knelt before this temple and clasped her warm, delicate hands in prayer. The chime of a clock had scattered the birds nearby, and in the haze of the

---

14 *Based on ancient nursery rhymes in the style of Zhuzhici (Bamboo Branch Poetry), a poetic form popular in the ancient Sichuan area.*

fragrant candles, she had bowed low to pray for her child's health and happiness, that he might live a long life free from worries...

Missing their mom and dad.

Chu Lan's heart was torn from his mangled body. Madam Chu sank her teeth into it, insatiable, blood dripping from the corners of her mouth.

"Aaaaaaaaahhhhhh!"

Chu Xun broke. He clutched his head where he had fallen to his knees and bashed his skull repeatedly against the ground. He wept, wretched and miserable, kneeling in the rain and the blood in front of his wife and son, in front of all the people of Lin'an. He knelt before the image of divinity, and he knelt in the mud underfoot.

He knelt in the depths of sin, and he knelt in the heights of virtue.

He knelt in untold gratitude, and he knelt in utmost hatred.

He hunched over in the dust, his very soul torn apart and extinguished.

Disintegrated into dust.

A long while passed before the people finally spoke in quavering voices.

"Gongzi..."

"Gongzi, condolences..."

"Gongzi's benevolence will not be forgotten..."

"Chu-gongzi is righteous. Truly a kind person! Truly a kind person..."

Someone had pulled their own child close and covered his eyes so that he wouldn't see the bloody scene. They only now let go to say to Chu Xun, "Gongzi, you saved all our lives. The madam and the little gongzi, they'll...they'll surely ascend to paradise..."

"Take your child and get lost!" someone else spat. "Why didn't you and your child go to paradise instead?!"

The parent backed timidly away.

It all seemed so distant. Chu Xun felt like he had already died. The voices sounded as if they came from across an ocean, from across a life.

In the torrential downpour, a man was covered in mud, and a thin layer of transparent light separated him from his wife and son, the dead on one side, the dying on the other.

When Mo Ran looked at this scene, he suddenly thought of his past life, in which he had wantonly slaughtered the innocent. He wondered if he had created more than one Chu Xun, more than one Chu Lan, more than one Madam Chu...

He looked down at his hands. For a split second, they seemed to be covered in blood. Then he blinked, and it was only the ice-cold rain gathering in his palms and flowing down his hands. He trembled.

In the next moment, a warm hand took his. Mo Ran snapped out of it as if he were waking from a nightmare and found his little shidi gazing up at him with concern. He looked so much like Chu Lan.

Mo Ran slowly knelt down to eye level with his shidi, like a sinner begging forgiveness from the souls of the dead, and stared at him with eyes welling from both rain and tears.

Chu Wanning said nothing, only reached up and patted him on the head. "It's already happened," he said softly. "It's all in the past."

"You're right." A while passed before Mo Ran wrangled out a sad smile. Lowering his lashes, he murmured, "It's all in the past."

However, even if it was all in the past, he had still done all those things. He hadn't killed Chu Lan, but how many people just like Chu Lan had died because of him?

The more Mo Ran thought about it, the more scared he became, and the more it hurt.

Why had he been so cruel? Why had he been so unrelenting?

68 This Venerable One Can't Bear It

CHU LAN WAS DEAD, but the illusion continued.

Dawn was still hours away; the long nightmare not yet over. The survivors returned to the governor's residence, preparing to leave for Putuo Mountain as soon as morning broke.

It was hard to believe that someone could carry on after suffering that kind of pain. Truth be told, it really did seem like all that remained of Chu Xun was a walking husk, his soul long since gone.

As Mo Ran moved through the city, he heard many people fretting. After all, Chu Xun had suffered so much. Putting aside the possibility that he would hold a grudge, in his current state, even if he was willing to lead everyone away from the city, their chances were significantly diminished.

Not everyone thought only of themselves. There weren't a lot of them, but at least a few people were genuinely sad for Chu Xun.

They all stewed in anxiety as they waited for the sky to brighten.

What arrived before the rising sun was that cold and now-familiar voice, rupturing the heavy night sky and reverberating above the barrier. This time the ghost king addressed not Chu Xun, but everyone else in Lin'an.

"The sun will soon rise. This venerable one knows you plan to leave once day breaks. But have you really thought your plan through? Putuo is a long way from here, and you'll never make it there in a single day. Once night falls, you'll have to depend on Chu Xun for safety. Do you think he'll protect you?"

"Mommy—"

A child started crying from fear at the terrifying voice, burrowing into his mother's arms. Everyone stared up at the sky.

Only Chu Xun, standing in front of the governor's residence and leaning against the haitang tree, had his eyes closed, as if he heard nothing.

"His wife and son are dead because of you. Do you really think Chu Xun will defend you? He likely has something else in mind—something to avenge his family, something to make you all wish you were dead. It's only human nature, after all... This venerable one was once human, too, you know. Sure, there are kind people, but they're only kind for their reputation. Humans are vile by nature; any so-called good person is just trying to get something in return for their deeds. Let's be honest: once forced into a corner, they won't care whether other people live or die."

The ghost king's eerie voice echoed above them.

"This venerable one said it before: I never intended to take all of your lives. In fact, the living can serve us ghosts. If you don't believe me, just look at him—"

As he spoke, a black cloud billowed toward the barrier with Xiaoman standing on top of it. Next to him was a kindly man of about forty or fifty.

"That's Xiaoman's father!" someone cried out in surprise.

"It's Xiaoman's father! Didn't he die?"

"Even though his body was dismembered—everyone saw. How could this be?!"

The ghost king continued, "As one of the nine kings of the underworld, even if this venerable one does not exert control over life and death like Emperor Yanluo, it is but a simple matter to restore the appearance of the dead. If you serve me, I will grant you the lasting company of your deceased loved ones. However, if you oppose me, you'll end up like your Chu-gongzi, watching your wife kill your child with your own eyes, powerless to do anything to stop it."

All were silent within the barrier.

"Will you really trust him? Trust that he won't take revenge for his wife and child? Do you really think he'll take you from here all the way to Putuo?"

Someone glanced toward Chu Xun, their eyes already flickering with malice.

Chu Xun finally looked up from where he stood under the flowering tree, his quiet gaze level with theirs. He honestly didn't know what to say at this point. A long while passed before he finally said, "It already is what it is. What would be the point in harming you now?"

"Ha ha ha ha ha ha ha!" The ghost king's ghastly laugh echoed from above the barrier. "Very good, very good. He *says* he won't harm you. If you believe him, then go ahead and leave with him. But if you believe me—"

His voice roared with increasing intensity, as if it might pierce their eardrums and straight into their hearts.

"If you believe *me*, you will be rewarded. I can bring back your families. All you have to do is hand over Chu Xun. You just have to... hand him over to me! I bear a grudge against *him*, not any of *you*. Hand him over, and you won't have to abandon your homes. Hand him over, and you can reunite with your families. Just hand him over, and it will all be over."

The ghost king's voice grew faint.

"I will wait at the City God Temple till sunrise."

The voice faded away.

The deadly silence slowly gave way to a rising clamor as all eyes in the crowd turned toward Chu Xun. Chu Xun looked back at them with a calm, even expression.

"What should we do?" someone started muttering helplessly.

"What should we do, my husband? I'm so afraid..."

"Mommy, I'm scared. I don't wanna get eaten!"

"The ghost king isn't wrong..." someone else said in a low voice. "These supposedly kind people always have ulterior motives. We've seen plenty of their sort before. Chu...Chu-gongzi may not have done anything yet, but look at him. Half-dead as he is, who's to say he won't do something crazy in the future?!"

"You're right," whispered someone who heard his words, in full agreement. "For all we know, he's nursing that grudge and just waiting to get us all killed! Treachery at the eleventh hour is hardly unheard of..."

A rough-looking man suddenly stood up from the crowd. "Grab him!" he yelled. "If we hand him over, we can live!"

Everyone went silent. A few moments passed before a young woman stepped forward and put herself in front of the man. "How could you be so ungrateful?" her voice was soft but determined. "Have you no dignity as a man?"

"Piss off!" The man kicked the woman to the ground and spit on her face. "You're a stupid whore who sleeps with men, no family to speak of. The hell you running your mouth for? I have to take care of both young and old—I ain't gonna let my own family go through this shit! Chu-gongzi, you're just gonna have to understand!"

With that, he made to seize Chu Xun.

He hadn't taken a step before his leg was firmly grabbed. He looked down and roared furiously, "Still getting in the way, you dumb whore? Go die by yourself if you want. How dare you try to drag everyone else down with you?!"

The woman was no less enraged. "I may be a prostitute, but at least I can tell right from wrong. If even cats and dogs know to repay kindnesses, how could we humans not?!"

"Shut the fuck up!"

The man drove his boots down on her head until her entire face was mottled with bruises. By then, the rest of the crowd had also approached and formed a circle around Chu Xun. A few in the crowd tried to stop the rest, like the woman from the brothel had tried before, but their efforts were futile, like a single leaf caught in a raging current, swallowed in no time at all.

"Gongzi! Gongzi, hurry and get out of here!" an old woman yelled shakily toward Chu Xun. "Chu-gongzi, go! Just go! Don't stay for the sake of these animals! Go!"

There was also the tender voice of a young child. "Stop fighting, Mommy, Daddy. Don't hurt the gongzi, don't hurt him—"

A maelstrom of commotion, disorder and chaos.

Chu Xun stood alone in the rain. He felt as if he was staring at a horde of ghosts who had crawled out of the very depths of hell. For a moment, he wanted to leave.

Then his gaze landed on the people, those living, breathing, crying people. He saw the young child bawling as he tried to stop his parents. He saw the young woman who had been the first to stand up for him, whose face was now bruised and swollen. He looked at the old woman shaking in the rain, and the other dozen or so people standing with their backs to him, trying their best to stop the others.

The foot that was about to leave paused. They had done nothing wrong. If he took down the barrier, these people would die too.

So, it turned out that the most disgusting thing in this world was not ghosts or demons, but those cowardly, worthless beasts who wore human skins and hid in the crowd, willing to say and to do anything in the name of their own survival. At the end of everything, they would say, "I only wanted to live. I'm pitiful and powerless—I've done nothing wrong."

Chu Xun had thought that the people he protected were helpless, good people. He was wrong. Now those beasts shed their human skins, revealing their ugly, snarling, bloodred faces... They had been so well hidden... So well hidden.

He no longer wanted to cry and bleed for those beasts in human clothing. They had been so sly, concealed so well amongst the good, kind people, their faces laughing at him, delighting in his powerlessness.

You have no choice but to save us. If you drop the barrier, we'll take the people you want to save—the people actually grateful to you—together with us to hell.

You have no choice, however much it sickens you. You chose to be virtuous. You chose to be a good person.

Since that's the choice you made, it's your duty to sacrifice yourself to save everyone else. If you refuse, then you're a swindler, a pretender, a fake, worse than a beast.

It was as if he could hear those people howling, could hear their shrill laughter:

You have no choice. You have no choice!

In that frenzied pandemonium, in the tempest of rain and wind, Chu Xun slowly lifted his head toward the heavens. Dawn was finally about to break.

The relentless downpour had washed the blood from the stone steps of the City God Temple. Chu Xun and those who had tried to protect him were tied up and walking toward the structure.

The scene was both sorrowful and laughable. The people had bound Chu Xun tightly and were smugly pleased that they had captured such a powerful person. They were completely unaware that Chu Xun could have easily turned the ropes to ash with but a single spell.

Yet he didn't. Nor did he take down the Shangqing Barrier. Enough blood had been shed in Lin'an. He didn't want any more innocent people to die purely for his own revenge.

So it was that the thin layer of light protected them all, both the thankless beasts who had turned on him and the people who stood sincerely by his side. They arrived at the temple, but the ghost king did not appear. Instead, they found a candle giving off black smoke that twisted into a dark silhouette.

"Why have you not dispelled the barrier?!" The moment the silhouette spied Chu Xun, that voice exploded with rage. "Dispel the barrier!"

"Over my dead body," Chu Xun said serenely.

The black smoke let out a shrill shriek. "Chu Xun, you must be mad! You...you lot, kill him! Or I'll take all your lives as soon as night comes!"

Daybreak. The first light of day illuminated the endless night. The ghost king, unable to maintain his form in sunlight, fled into the darkness. The candle emitting the black smoke flickered and went out.

Chu Xun pulled himself together. The City God Temple stood on high ground. From there, he could see the morning mist gently shrouding the mountains and rivers, hiding their scars from view, and for a moment, everything looked like it had in the days of old. It was a beautiful spring.

"Chu-gongzi, sorry."

"It's not that we're cruel or heartless or anything, it's just that the ghost king holds a grudge against you for ruining his eye... We have no other choice...”

“What’re you all still yammering for?! Don’t drag it out. We don’t want any surprises. I’ve got a family back there who want to live! Who’s more important, this one guy or all of us? The righteous put the people before the self—his words, not mine!”

Chu Wanning stood in the distance, looking at this person whose relation to him was unknown, his feelings complicated. A pair of hands suddenly covered his eyes.

“What are you doing?” Chu Wanning whispered.

“Not letting you watch.”

Chu Wanning paused. “Why?”

“You’ll be sad.”

Chu Wanning was quiet for a while, his eyelashes trembling against Mo Ran’s palms. “I won’t. I was the one who said it: every one of them is already two hundred years dead.”

Mo Ran sighed softly from behind. After a long pause, he said, “You little dummy. Then why are my palms wet?”

Chu Wanning didn’t know how much time passed, half an hour, two hours, or only a split second. Time blurred in the madness, the chaos.

When he opened his eyes again, the Shangqing Barrier had dissipated. Chu Xun lay in a crimson pool, surrounded by people and by ghosts—by demons wearing human skin, inhaling the scent of fresh blood.

Ecstasy and guilt. Calamity past, the rest of their lives now lay open. Agony and sin. The hearts of people were indistinguishable from those of beasts.

The air of the mortal realm smelled like death. Or perhaps this was hell. It was difficult to tell.

The crowd slowly dispersed. There was no reason to fear ghosts during the day, so they went to find food, to rest, to wait for the ghost king to return when night fell. He would inspect the body in the temple and reward them with the reunions he had promised with their deceased loved ones.

Eventually, only a dozen or so people remained in the temple, weeping in grief. The young woman from the brothel was there, as was the white-haired old woman. The young child, and his parents who had listened. A beggar, a scholar, a storyteller, the son of a once-wealthy family, a widow holding her infant son, a teacher, and a farmer. No one else.

As they wept over his body, the man lying dead in a pool of his own blood slowly opened his eyes.

"Gongzi!"

"Chu-gongzi!"

Mo Ran's heart quivered. Unable to bear it, he said: "No...this is..."

This spell was a lost art in the modern age. He hadn't expected to see it being used in an illusion.

"The Lingering Voice spell. He's dead, but he used this spell on himself before he died." Chu Wanning paused. "He still had matters yet unattended. Things he was worried about."

Sure enough, Chu Xun's eyes were blank, their pupils dilated, and his voice was flat as he spoke. "Demons and ghosts are treacherous; you must not believe their words. Without the Shangqing Barrier, they will overrun the city once night falls and slaughter at will. Please leave this place and head to Putuo."

"Gongzi..."

"I have died and will be unable to accompany you. However, I have concentrated my entire lifetime's worth of spiritual power in my spiritual core. Bring it, and the ghosts will be unable to approach you."

They wept even more sorrowfully.

Mo Ran and Chu Wanning's blood ran cold. His spiritual core. It was a crystalline formation within one's heart...

Chu Xun's body slowly lifted its hand, which had not yet gone stiff, and under the control of his spell, it grasped the knife buried in his chest to pull it out. Then—

"Gongzi!" The people around him cried out with grief, their voices twisted and hoarse, soaked with tears. "Gongzi, what are you doing?!"

With his own hands, Chu Xun ripped open the gash in his chest, dug into his flesh, and grabbed his no-longer beating heart. Slowly, inch by inch, he tore it out.

Blood dripped from the heart, which was enveloped in a golden-red flame. It was Chu Xun's spiritual core, the last flare of light from a candle that had burned out.

"Take...it..." He lifted the flaming heart and held it out in front of him. "Take it...take...it..."

Droplets of blood fell only to become so many red haitang blossoms, flaring brilliantly as they drifted downward.

"The road ahead is long and unpredictable. My life ends here, and I can do no more. Please...please take care...of...yourselves..."

As the scene unfolded before Mo Ran's eyes, he broke out in a cold sweat. He felt like thorns were digging into his back.

The scar... That scar! He had suddenly remembered that, on Chu Wanning's chest, where his heart lay—there was a scar.

That same spot on Chu Wanning was extremely sensitive. How could Mo Ran forget it? Whenever he licked that pale scar as they lay entwined in bed, Chu Wanning's usually impassive face would reveal a hint of the desire that he kept suppressed. That expression only stoked Mo Ran's own desire even higher, so he had always particularly enjoyed humiliating the person beneath him in this way.

In his past life, he had never cared about Chu Wanning's history and so had never asked how he'd acquired that scar, all the way until his death.

Now, in this life, he no longer had the right to ask.

69

This Venerable One Will Learn From You, Heh Heh

Was it a coincidence? Or...

Presently, Mo Ran couldn't just look at his shizun's chest whenever he wanted, so he could only rely on his memory of that scar's appearance. That faint, crescent-moon shape would have been left by the simple slash of a blade—not like Chu Xun's wound, which had been made by five fingers piercing flesh with force and left behind savage, bloody holes.

It wasn't the same after all.

Mo Ran let out a quiet sigh of relief as he thought it over. While Chu Xun and Chu Wanning were wholly different people in terms of personality, they shared too many points of resemblance to dismiss. From their appearances to their mutual principle of "As a cultivator, the life of the many is our priority, and the self comes last," to that long scar on their chests. So many coincidences piled on top of one another made one suspicious.

Mo Ran wasn't exactly sure *why*—perhaps it was because Chu Xun was so gentle, so different from Chu Wanning's ruthlessness, or perhaps it was because Chu Xun had a wife and a son—but if Chu Xun had reincarnated into Chu Wanning, or if he *was* Chu Wanning, Mo Ran was sure that he wouldn't be able to take it. That he would have a breakdown.

Good thing that wasn't the case.

There is no need to expand on what manner of disaster the city of Lin'an faced without Chu Xun's protection.

Of course the ghost king didn't keep his word. Once night fell, the air was thick with blood, and heaven and earth mourned in kind. The moat ran red with gore, and the howling of those still living, who had long lost their senses, echoed through the night. Zombies wandered throughout the city, picking at and devouring fresh, tender entrails, chomping down on brains.

Mo Ran took Chu Wanning to hide in a broken down little house whose master had died some time ago. Everything within it lay under a heavy layer of dust.

Mo Ran tightly shut the door and secured the surroundings. He left only a small kitchen window through which they could observe the situation in the city. From outside there came intermittent sharp wails and screams, and the ominous sounds of chewing and swallowing.

Mo Ran carried Chu Wanning to a small pile of firewood in the corner and patted his head. "According to Miss Eighteen, once we defeat the ghost king, we can leave. So stay here and be good. Don't run off anywhere."

Chu Wanning's head jerked up at this. "You're going out?"

"Not right now. I'll leave once the ghost king shows himself."

"But it's so dangerous outside. The illusion has been manifested—how will you manage on your own?"

"Well, I can't bring a kid with me to fight, can I?"

Chu Wanning shook his head. "I'm coming with you."

"Ha ha ha, Shidi is so cute! But you're still young. If you come with me, you'll drag me down. Wait till you're older, and when we run into these things again, I won't hold you back. For now, you have to listen to Shixiong."

"I won't drag you down."

"That's what they all say. Just be good and don't fuss, okay?"

Chu Wanning fell silent.

When Chu Wanning finally stopped talking, Mo Ran quietly let out a sigh of relief. He turned his gaze to the wooden window to peer outside, his expression growing serious.

Just why had the illusion meant for their training suddenly become real? His little shidi was right; someone wanted to harm him. In his previous life, there had no doubt been countless people who wanted him dead, but in this life, he had yet to cross any powerful sorts. After giving it due consideration, he could think of only one person who might want to take his life: that fake Gouchen from Jincheng Lake.

What was the real identity of that false Gouchen? If he could use the Zhenlong Chess Formation with such mastery, how come he'd never demonstrated his talents in their previous lifetime?

Could it be that Mo Ran wasn't the only person in this world who'd been reborn?

The thought gave him chills, and his eyes glinted menacingly. After rebirth, he'd wanted nothing more than to bury his past, but if someone else had been reborn, that might become quite difficult.

His brows were furrowed, but he suddenly heard Chu Wanning speak up again. "Mo Ran, I..."

"What is it?"

Chu Wanning gritted his teeth silently. After considering the pros and cons, he steeled his heart and decided he might as well be straight and tell the truth. "Listen to me: In fact, I really can help you. I'm—"

However, when Mo Ran heard, "I really can help you," he assumed his little shidi wanted to argue with him again, so he cut him off. "All right, all right, I already said I won't let you go, so I'm not letting you go. Stop trying to play tough. Listen to me."

"No, *you* listen to *me*—"

"I'm not listening," Mo Ran replied, feeling vexed. "I'm not listening, la la la."

Chu Wanning gave him a dark look.

The expression gave Mo Ran pause—maybe the attitude he was taking wasn't very nice. So he poked a finger between Chu Wanning's brows and laughed. "You're a kid! What's with all this deep, tormented suffering and refusing to listen to your seniors? Here, let me tell you something: since you call me Shixiong and we come from the same sect, when we run into peril like this, I *have* to protect you. At all costs. Do you understand?"

Chu Wanning shut his eyes and answered in a low voice, "I understand."

"Good to see you do. Then why don't you—"

"But I'm worried about you."

Mo Ran was taken aback, and for a second the finger that hung before Chu Wanning's forehead quivered. For another second, he couldn't utter a single word. He had lived for two lifetimes, but never had anyone said the words, "I'm worried about you," to him. Even in Shi Mei's moment of tenderness toward him, he had never so straightforwardly expressed his care for Mo Ran.

Mo Ran gazed with amazement at the tiny child sitting atop the pile of firewood before him, and hundreds of emotions filled his heart. After a long while, his eyes gradually softened. The finger he had used to poke Chu Wanning lifted and instead moved to ruffle his shidi's soft hair. "Don't worry. Shixiong promises you that he'll come back alive and well."

"Mo Ran, can you let me finish..."

Mo Ran grinned. "All right, what did you want to say?"

"I'm actually—"

The door crashed open with a bang.

A man with disheveled hair charged in, screaming and covered in gore, one thigh mauled to shreds. Behind him was a band of zombies, lured by the stench of blood.

The man tumbled into the room, dragging his ripped leg, and grabbed at anything he could get his hands on. He hurled the objects at the growling zombies, and as he threw, he yelled, "Fuck off! Get the hell away from me! Go away! Go the fuck away!"

Mo Ran cursed under his breath and shielded Chu Wanning with his body. A red light flashed from his hand as he summoned Jiangui. "Shidi, hide yourself," he said over his shoulder. "Don't get any closer, not under any circumstances!"

Then he attacked with vine in hand and started to slaughter the mob of corpses that had invaded the house. Although Jiangui and Tianwen were similar, Chu Wanning hadn't yet fully passed on his technique to Mo Ran, and in Mo Ran's past life, the weapon he wielded had been a blade. He thus wasn't used to supple weapons, so while at the beginning of the slaughter he held his own, it gradually became clear that he didn't quite have the finesse to match his determination.

Jiangui swung all over the place. Suddenly the voice of a child cut in, crisp and cool, "Left side. Wrap it around your wrist and strike three times, then jump in the air and swing around your back to sling it out."

Mo Ran had no time to think and just followed the instructions. The willow vine whipped the body of a zombie on the left, and with a single strike, the holy weapon broke the zombie's arm, exposing its bones. Normally no one would think it necessary to whip it twice more, but since little shidi had told him to do so, Mo Ran figured he might as well give it a try—no harm, no foul. Thus he immediately struck the zombie again twice, then jumped up and bent nimbly at the waist, flipped, and slung out the vine whip straight behind his back—

Slash!

Quite coincidentally, the next wave of corpses happened to swarm in, and Jiangui, which had accumulated three times the power, lashed out a stream of blazing fire that blasted toward them. The band of corpses was instantly lacerated by the brutal holy weapon, and every zombie lost their head. Their skulls dropped to the ground, still letting off black smoke.

Mo Ran was dumbfounded. He sent a shocked glance at the cool little shidi sitting on top of a firewood pile. *This kid... He's pretty good.*

"What next?" Mo Ran asked excitedly, newly energized.

"Next, use your left hand and pat at your right sleeve," Chu Wanning instructed him expressionlessly.

"Ooh, this action is deep and indiscernible. What move is this?"

"Nothing deep and indiscernible about it," Chu Wanning said flatly. "You were swinging too confidently earlier, and the weapon lit your sleeve on fire, that's all."

Mo Ran let out an, "ah," and looked down. Sure enough, that was the case, and he hastily patted out the fire Jiangui had started in the chaos. This guy's face sure was thick; he didn't feel remotely awkward, and he even looked up with a goofy grin. "My shidi is so amazing. I like it."

Chu Wanning softly cleared his throat and silently turned his face away to stare at the bare gray walls, his ears faintly red.

By now, only six zombies in the house could still move. Chu Wanning didn't want to look at Mo Ran any longer, so with his head still turned away, he instructed the wall: "Loosen your wrist, swing the vine toward the sky, twirl it six times to gain power, and then slash like the character 'one.'"[15]

Mo Ran followed the instructions, but when he twirled the fifth round, he suddenly wondered, "How do you 'slash like the character one'?"

"Just slash how you normally would with a sword."

"Ah, I see!" Mo Ran was enlightened and struck down with a blow. The blazing fires shone, and it was as if that soft and supple vine had blazed into an indestructible long blade, slashing through the six corpses in a single swing.

"Whoa!" This time, Mo Ran's eyes were so wide that they were practically round. "Where did you learn this? How come I feel like you're almost as familiar and practiced with the vine whip as my shizun? No, maybe you're even better. He never told me the things you taught me today."

Chu Wanning said nothing.

Mo Ran's smile widened. "Good, good, good—this is great! Now I won't have to deal with his attitude anymore because I'll learn from you. Won't that be much better?"

Chu Wanning shot him a glare. "You have a problem with the Yuheng Elder's attitude? Why don't you have a problem with my attitude?"

Mo Ran withdrew the vine whip and shut the door anew before pulling a table over to block the entrance. He laughed. "You giving me a hard time is your way of being good to me. The two of us, we've technically gone through hardships together now. Shixiong remembers how good you've been to him. From now on, I'll dote on you like my own little brother, and never mind your attitude.

---

15 *The character one is a single horizontal line: —*

Even if you were to get upset and hit me a couple times, I wouldn't get mad."

Chu Wanning's face darkened. "Who wants to be your little brother?"

Then he hopped down from that pile of firewood, unwilling to pay Mo Ran any more attention, and went to check on the injuries of the man who had barged in.

Unexpectedly, Chu Wanning took one look at him and his eyes widened a touch. "It's him?"

"Who?" Mo Ran looked over curiously too and was also stunned. "That...that Xiaoman fellow?"

The one lying in a pool of blood and groaning in tears was indeed Xiaoman. He had suffered grave injuries, and after looking him over, Chu Wanning shook his head. "Humans and ghosts were never meant to live in harmony. I imagine the ghost king stopped caring for him once he lived out his use. He really..."

"Deserved it," Mo Ran said.

Chu Wanning gave him a look.

Mo Ran laughed shortly but with a jolt, he felt a little guilty. If he were to start calling people "deserving," wasn't he himself the one who "deserved" retribution more than anyone? He changed the subject. "Oh yeah, what was it you wanted to tell me earlier? That you're actually what?"

Chu Wanning lowered his eyelashes, paused, and said softly, "I'm actually—"

Before he could finish, he felt a breeze behind his back. Chu Wanning startled and whipped around, ready to fight. However, he was in the body of a child, and his strength was far from that of a grown man. When he was seized by the throat, he couldn't struggle free.

Somehow, Xiaoman had hauled himself up from the pool of his blood in a single breath. Veins protruded from the back of his hands as he held Chu Wanning's neck in a deadly grip. The other hand twisted and locked Chu Wanning's arms in place. It was as if a wild flame burned within that filthy, unkempt face; his entire form twisted in his desperation to live, like a wax figure distorted by intense heat. His eyes were bloodshot as he croaked at Mo Ran, "Get me...out of here..."

"Let him go!"

"Get me out of here!" Xiaoman snarled furiously, his eyes practically cracking at the edges in his rage. "Or I'll kill him! Go!"

"If you want me to save you, then I'll save you. What are you doing, threatening a child? Let him go first—"

"Keep talking and I'll kill him! I've already committed so many sins—what's one more?! Are you getting me out of here or not?!"

Chu Wanning couldn't utter a sound because of the stranglehold, and his delicate little face grew red and strained. Mo Ran panicked at the sight. If he struck now, he could take Xiaoman's life. But this illusion had become reality. If Xiaoman exploded in fury before Mo Ran could move, his shidi might get terribly hurt.

"Fine, fine, fine, I'll listen to you," Mo Ran said. "Don't get riled up. Just loosen your hand a bit, and I'll—"

Before he could finish, blood splattered.

70 This Venerable One Returns

CHU WANNING WASN'T some weakling that just anyone could threaten. There was a flash of golden light—Mo Ran could've sworn he saw some kind of weapon in Xia Sini's hand, but it was gone in less than an instant—and then both of Xiaoman's hands had been sheared clean off, wrists and all.

Xiaoman screamed and stumbled backward. He had only one usable limb remaining, now that even his hands were gone.

The hands that had seized Chu Wanning dropped to the ground. Chu Wanning stood up, enraged, his expression dark as never before. His lips moved slightly, like he might say something. In the end, he seemed too angry for words and turned away, his face pale.

Mo Ran rushed over and pulled him close. "Shidi, are you okay? Are you hurt?"

In Mo Ran's arms, Chu Wanning only shook his head, too disgusted to speak.

Despite everything, the Xiaoman in front of them was merely an illusion of someone who had once lived two hundred years ago. Chu Wanning wiped the blood splatters from his face. "As you saw," he said quietly, "staying here won't be any safer for me than going out with you. I can take care of myself. I won't slow you down."

Mo Ran had heard about his little shidi's skill from Xue Meng, but he had never seen it for himself until now. It was, admittedly, quite eye-opening. "Sure, you're pretty impressive, but..."

Chu Wanning pushed harder. "I'm also familiar with all kinds of weapons, so I can give you pointers from the side."

"But..."

Chu Wanning lifted his eyes. "Won't you trust me, just this once?"

Mo Ran fell silent.

"Shixiong." Chu Wanning had meant to emphasize the sincerity of his words, but with this young, tender voice, it came out all softly adorable instead, almost like he was acting cute. When Chu Wanning heard his own voice, he was flummoxed.

Mo Ran blinked, then started rapidly scratching his head in confusion and going, "aaaah," before burying his face in both hands. A long moment passed with his face thus buried before he said, "That, um, see, I'm just worried that...you, uh..."

Two whole lives, and this was the first time a kid had called out to him so sweetly. Mo Ran felt genuinely, incredibly close to the boy at this moment, as if they were blood brothers.

When Mo Ran hated someone, he hated them to the bone, but to those he cherished, he was extremely tender. When he finished clawing at his head and finally looked back up at Chu Wanning from where he was crouched, the tips of his ears had turned red.

If only he'd really had a little brother, maybe he wouldn't have been so lonely.

Unfortunately for Mo Ran, his reaction was noticed. Chu Wanning hesitated a little, then said experimentally, in a small voice, "Shige."

"Shige" was an even more familiar form of address than "Shixiong." Mo Ran braced his forehead against a hand. He was seriously at his limit, unable to even form words.

Chu Wanning glanced knowingly at Mo Ran and mentally filed away this weak point. He figured that since he was, at present, already in a child's body, and since Mo Ran hadn't the slightest idea who he actually was, there was nothing to be embarrassed about. He opened his mouth again, and out came a soft, saccharine sweet: "Ge."

"..."

"Gege."

"........."

"Mo Ran-gege."

"Aaaaaah! Okay, okay! I'll take you, I'll take you! Stop saying that!" Mo Ran jumped to his feet, face bright red, and rubbed at the goosebumps on his arms. "All right, fine. Come along, then. You win, okay? You win. Oh my god."

Hands clasped behind his back, Chu Wanning tilted his head and smiled a tiny smile. "Let's go, then."

As he walked leisurely toward the door, he heard Mo Ran mumbling quietly behind him: "Where in the heavens did he learn that from? I nearly died from the sugar overload, holy crap..."

Chu Wanning had originally been in a dreadful state of mind after what happened with Chu Xun, but now he felt the gloom in his chest slowly lifting.

Then he heard Mo Ran ask: "Oh yeah, what *was* Shidi going to say earlier?"

Chu Wanning turned around and replied evenly, "Ah. That."

"Hm?"

"I forgot."

Mo Ran eyed him.

"If I remember it later, I'll tell Mo Ran-gege then..."

"Aaaaaaah—stop! Don't say that one! Shixiong is fine! Shixiong is enough!" Mo Ran waved his hands frantically.

Chu Wanning's eyes were like a pair of deep puddles, and the corners of his lips quirked with a hint of a smile. "If you say so, Shixiong. Anyway, I think the ghost king will show up soon. This illusion is based on the memories of survivors, and those survivors have left Lin'an by now, so it probably won't last much longer."

"That makes sense... We should be able to get out once we defeat him, right? I'm gonna find whoever it was that manifested the illusion and tried to kill us!"

Chu Wanning nodded. "Fortunately for us, judging by his battle with Chu Xun earlier, this ghost king isn't too strong. In fact, he might be the weakest of the nine kings. Although the illusion has been manifested, it seems to me that whoever did it probably thought I was an ordinary six-year-old and didn't expect me to be able to help take care of this."

Mo Ran nodded along. "Sounds about right."

Chu Wanning continued, "So rather than saying that he tried to kill us, it would be more accurate to say that I was never part of the equation. In truth, he's only after you, Shixiong."

Mo Ran nodded even more vigorously. "Checks out."

"After we get out of here, Shixiong must make sure to tell Xue Meng about this. Something is afoot in Peach Blossom Springs, and we have to be careful from here on out. Though let's not dwell on that for the time being. Shixiong, please lead the way. I won't slow you down."

Chu Wanning's prediction was spot-on. By three in the morning, the massacre in the city was winding down. A bloody rift cracked open the sky, and green smoke poured over the wreckage to solidify into the shape of a hunched-over man.

The man's eyes were bright scarlet, and his skin was ashen pale; half of his body had flesh and skin, but the other half was stark, exposed bone. He stalked through the corpse-littered city with a black banner in tow, absorbing the pain and resentment of the newly deceased as he passed.

Mo Ran studied the man's face from where they were hidden. "So that's him?" There was a hint of relief in his voice.

It was obvious to Chu Wanning why he sounded relieved, but he had no intention of revealing himself yet, and a six-year-old wouldn't know this sort of thing. So he looked up at Mo Ran with feigned cluelessness. "What do you mean?"

"You guessed right. The nine kings of the ghost realm differ in strength, and this one is indeed the weakest among them," Mo Ran said in a quiet voice as he watched the figure approach from behind a window. "We lucked out."

"What does Shixiong think of our odds?"

"Ninety percent. Always best not to be too confident, you know?"

Chu Wanning smiled a little. He of course knew that "the Skeleton King" was the weakest of the nine ghost kings, but strength was relative. Even though Mo Ran wielded the holy weapon Jiangui, at his age and with his experience, facing the Skeleton King alone would still push him a bit.

Unfortunately for the person plotting against Mo Ran, the kid by his side wasn't just some rookie from Sisheng Peak, but Chu Wanning himself.

"Help me..."

They were about to spring out the door with a surprise attack when a weak voice called out from behind them.

"Ah, he's still alive?" Mo Ran's eyes were wide as he turned to look at Xiaoman, curled up in the back.

"I don't want to die... Dad... I don't want to..."

Chu Wanning looked at the young man huddled in a rumpled heap of rags and shook his head. "In truth, this person likely died as soon as he stepped in here. He's only still alive in this illusion because we happened to be here and killed the undead that were after him. Thus some things have turned out differently."

"Ah..." Mo Ran sighed. "If he hadn't defected, do you think that maybe Chu Xun wouldn't have died two hundred years ago? That maybe Lin'an wouldn't be a pile of ruins now?"

"Maybe."

However, they both knew that no matter what they did now, the past was the past. The important thing now was to defeat the Skeleton King and escape this illusion. There was no reason to delay, so they charged out of their hiding place, killing everything in their path.

Escaping this illusion proved to possibly be even easier than they'd thought.

Mo Ran knew exactly what he had to do and immediately engaged the Skeleton King. However, as Chu Wanning watched them face off, he felt a wave of uneasiness. It wasn't because Mo Ran was struggling. To the contrary, under his guidance, Mo Ran maintained a solid upper hand. Even so, more and more Chu Wanning got the feeling that...the person behind all this had planned it all far too precisely.

That was to say, that person had carefully assessed that it would be extremely difficult for Mo Ran and one other person of average skill to escape this situation alone. Yet he also hadn't deployed anything more deadly so as not to arouse suspicions of foul play. His goal had been to make it look like Mo Ran had died in a training accident.

Who exactly was this person who plotted so meticulously against Mo Ran's life? Was it really that fake Gouchen from Jincheng Lake?

Chu Wanning observed the ferocious battle between Mo Ran and the ghost king. The longer it went on, the more Mo Ran came out on top, and as the sky slowly lightened, the ghost king's strength gradually waned. Victory was all but at hand.

Just then, in the horde of undead and demons sealed behind Mo Ran's spell, Chu Wanning saw the face of a living person.

"Who's there?!"

Standing amidst the walking corpses, this person's face was half shadowed beneath the hood of his cloak. From this distance, all Chu Wanning could see was a sharp chin, sweetly colored lips, and a gently curved nose.

A single look and Chu Wanning could tell that the man didn't belong in the illusion of two hundred years past. He hadn't assumed any kind of fighting stance and just stood there, shrouded under his hood, looking in the direction of Chu Wanning and Mo Ran. When he saw that Chu Wanning had noticed him, he smiled faintly, then lifted a hand and swept it across his neck in a "kill" gesture.

Chu Wanning cursed under his breath and lunged in an attempt to capture him.

However, the figure only smiled with the crimson lips and ivory teeth under his hood, and mouthed what looked like, "Goodbye."

Then he turned and disappeared.

"Stay right there!"

It was useless. The sky brightened, layers of fish-scale clouds painted across it.

The fight between Mo Ran and the ghost king ended with a final blow. The moment that Jiangui sheared the ghost king's head clean off, sending foul blood flying everywhere, their bodies abruptly flew up. That sunrise of old Lin'an from two hundred years ago and the ruined wreckage of that city, all of it sped away in a blur.

Thump!

When Chu Wanning hit the ground again, he found himself back in the trial cave.

Mo Ran was also there, dropped on the ground next to him and covered in blood from the fight, though mostly not his own. He was laid out on the ground, evidently still too tired to get up, only gazing at Chu Wanning with those pitch-black eyes. A few moments passed, then he lifted a hand and gently poked Chu Wanning's forehead. "We made it."

Chu Wanning made a soft sound of assent, but his expression was dark. "I saw someone in there just now."

"What?"

"It was probably the one who manifested the illusion."

Mo Ran rolled up into a sitting position, his eyes going wide. "You saw him? You saw him! Did you see who it was? What did he look like?"

Chu Wanning shook his head, brows furrowed. "He was wearing a hood, so I couldn't see clearly. Based on the figure, he's probably male, fairly young, and thin, with a pointed chin..."

He didn't voice the rest of his thoughts. He felt like that half a face had looked vaguely familiar, as if he had seen that person somewhere before, long ago. He also couldn't shake the feeling that he might be mistaken. It had only been half a face after all, and there were plenty of similar-looking people out there. He couldn't really be sure.

He was deep in thought when he felt Mo Ran pat him on the shoulder.

"Shidi."

"What is it?"

"Look over there." Mo Ran's voice was low, and a chill ran through it.

Chu Wanning looked in the direction he was pointing.

It was Eighteen. At the entrance to the trial cave, Eighteen hung from the ceiling, both eyes bulging outward, the embroidered satin shoes on her feet swaying in midair.

She was dead, and there was no wind. Judging by the angle of her body's sway, the murderer had just left.

However, the thing that turned their faces pale was the murder weapon cinched around her neck. It was a willow vine with sharp, blade-like leaves. The vine coursed with a fiery red light that crackled, erupting with sparks that fell together with the drops of blood.

Jiangui.

The thing that had strangled Eighteen and that now hung her from the ceiling of the cave was none other than the holy weapon Jiangui.

71 This Venerable One's Been Framed

FACE PALE, Mo Ran was in utter disbelief as he summoned the weapon that he'd put away only a moment ago. Jiangui answered his call, appearing in his hand in a blaze of fiery light.

When he compared the two, the weapon that had killed Eighteen was practically identical to Jiangui. It was almost like a piece of it, save for the fact that it had no hilt. Could it be that somewhere in the world, there was a second Jiangui?!

Before Mo Ran could think further, urgent footsteps approached at a rapid speed. Chu Wanning was more levelheaded than Mo Ran; he quickly assessed the situation and a chill flickered through his eyes. "Mo Ran, put Jiangui away!"

"Huh?"

Too late.

A group of people had arrived at the entrance to the cave. In that group were people from the feathered tribe and cultivators from various sects. Even Xue Meng, Ye Wangxi, and Shi Mei were there. It was as if someone had noticed that something strange was happening and called just about everyone over in a hurry.

And so, when everyone arrived one after another, the sight that greeted them was that of Eighteen, brutally murdered, the willow vine cutting into her neck. Behind her, they saw Mo Ran and a small child, markedly battered from the aftermath of a fierce battle. On top of that, Mo Ran was covered in blood and holding Jiangui in hand, his willow vine coursing with a menacing, fiery light...

No one made a sound. That is, until someone yelled, "M-murderer!"

The crowd fell into an uproar. Panic, anger, and whispered words surged into a river, the drone of voices shaking one's very bones.

"She's dead!" "Murderer!" "How vicious..." "Must be insane!" "Lunatic." Fragments of sentences were repeated over and over, until the frenzied mob looked no different from the walking corpses in the illusion. For a moment, Mo Ran almost thought that the illusion wasn't yet over—that the nightmare continued still.

It was as if the blood spilt in Lin'an two hundred years ago still covered the ground.

"No..." He took a step backward, throat dry. "It wasn't me..."

Mo Ran felt a tug on his clothes, and his step paused. Amidst the madness, he looked down and saw Chu Wanning's clear eyes. He murmured helplessly, "It wasn't me..."

Chu Wanning nodded and tried to shield Mo Ran with his own body. However, he was only a small child at present, so what could he do? As he fretted, he felt Mo Ran step forward.

More and more people joined in on the shouting. "Lock him up! The kid too! Grab them! Murderers!"

"We can't let them get away, they're too dangerous! Hurry and grab them!"

Mo Ran pulled Chu Wanning behind him, blocking him from sight, then took a moment to breathe and collect himself. "I didn't kill Miss Eighteen. Please let me explain."

The faces in the crowd looked indistinct, overlapping with a memory from his past life that he couldn't bear to recall. He strained

his eyes and caught sight of Xue Meng among the shadows in the crowd, his face filled with disbelief. Then he saw Shi Mei, eyes wide and face pale, his head shaking repeatedly.

Mo Ran closed his eyes. "I didn't kill her," he said in a low voice, "but I don't plan to run away either. At least hear me out before you lock me up?"

Even so, no one wanted to listen to him. Anger and anxiety spread through the crowd.

"Y-you've been caught red-handed," a high-pitched voice cried. "What is there to say?!"

"That's right!"

"Just toss them in the prison cave first! If it turns out they didn't do it, we can let them out then!"

"Lock them up! Lock them up!"

Xue Meng snapped out of his shocked state. He stepped out from the crowd and stood in front of those angry, twisted faces with his back to Mo Ran and raised his voice. "Everyone, please settle down. I have something to say."

"Who the hell are you?!"

"Why would we listen to you?!"

"Wait, isn't that the little phoenix?"

"Little phoenix? You mean the darling of the heavens? That Xue Meng guy?"

"That's him..."

Xue Meng's expression was terrible, nearly colorless. He took a deep breath and said, slowly, "Everyone, please listen. These two are disciples of Sisheng Peak, and I can vouch for them. Under no circumstances would they do something like murder an innocent person. So please, calm down and let them explain."

A moment of silence, then someone yelled, "Why should we

believe you? So what if they're Sisheng Peak disciples—that doesn't mean you know their true nature!"

"Exactly! There's no knowing what someone's really like, even if you're from the same sect!"

Xue Meng's expression grew darker still, his lips pressed in a thin line as his hands clenched into fists.

Behind Xue Meng, Mo Ran stood with Chu Wanning in tow. Truth be told, he was surprised that Xue Meng had come out in their defense. He hadn't exactly been close with his cousin in his past life, or rather, they had hardly been able to stand each other. Later, when he'd become the emperor of the mortal realm and burned, killed, and plundered as he liked, they had naturally ended up on opposite sides of the battlefield.

Mo Ran had never expected that Xue Meng would stand with his back to him, facing the horde and all their pointing fingers. Warmth flooded his heart. "Xue Meng, you...believe me?"

"Ugh! Yeah right, you damn mutt!" Xue Meng's face turned slightly toward him as he huffed. "Look at this mess you've gotten into! Aren't you the older one? Why do I have to clean up after you?!"

Mo Ran had no reply.

After he was done cussing out Mo Ran, Xue Meng whipped back around and started yelling at the crowd in an even fiercer tone. "What do you mean? How could I not know them? One of them is my shidi and the other is my cousin! Who knows them better? Me or you lot?"

"Xue Meng..."

"Would it kill you guys to listen to a bit of explanation? With all these people here, it's not like they're gonna grow wings and fly off if you give them a couple of minutes!"

At this time, Shi Mei also stepped forward, but his mannerisms were far too soft to be imposing, and there was fear in his voice as he said, "Everyone, I can also vouch for them. They absolutely wouldn't have hurt Miss Eighteen, so please hear them out. Thank you..."

Ye Wangxi stepped forward as well. Although he didn't vouch for them, he was much steadier than the rest of the agitated crowd. "Even if it's for a temporary detainment, they deserve the chance to explain and defend themselves. Otherwise, we might let the real killer off the hook. What if that person is among us as we speak? What then?"

At his words, the people in the crowd immediately started looking at one another with alarm in their eyes.

"Fine! We'll hear you out first!"

"We're still going to lock you up! Can't be too cautious, after all!"

"Guilty until proven innocent!"

Mo Ran let out a breath and layered thankful hands before his forehead. Then, after a moment, he actually smiled. "I never imagined that when I was surrounded on all sides, anyone would still be willing to believe in me. Okay, okay—even if I get locked up, just for you three, I won't be mad about it."

Mo Ran simply and briefly went over what had happened, from the manifestation of the illusion and the events that had transpired within it, to finding Eighteen murdered upon exit.

Unfortunately, once a Domain of Fiends scenario was overcome, a brand-new illusion was created for the next person to enter, so there was no way to validate Mo Ran's claims. It did seem like a stretch for him to have come up with such an elaborate story in mere moments, if he was making it up. So by the time he finished, more than half the people in the crowd seemed to be wavering.

A higher-up of the feathered tribe spoke quietly to her subordinate, then said, "Mo Ran, Xia Sini, although you have presented explanations, you have no evidence. For the safety of Peach Blossom Springs, we must detain you until the matter has been resolved."

Mo Ran smiled helplessly. "All right, all right. I figured it'd be like that. I won't complain too much as long as you feed me."

"Of course we shall do so." She paused. "Henceforth, everyone, please be on your guard to prevent any further accidents. Anyone who did not arrive here with due swiftness will be questioned one by one to eliminate suspicions. Furthermore, I will be informing the leaders of each sect, especially Sisheng Peak, which is most heavily involved. If possible, I would like to invite your shizun here for a chat."

At this, Mo Ran's expression instantly changed. "Shizun?!"

Chu Wanning stood quietly without a word.

"I don't want Shizun to come! Will my uncle do?"

"Issues involving a disciple shall be reported to their master. This has always been the rule in the cultivation world. Is it different at Sisheng Peak?"

"No, but..." Mo Ran scratched his head in frustration, letting out one sigh after another, but he didn't know what to say.

Issues involving a disciple shall be reported to their master—of course that made sense. However, the mere thought of Chu Wanning's indifferent face and his crisp, cold eyes... It made Mo Ran certain that if his shizun were to come, he would doubtless give Mo Ran a dressing-down first and foremost, regardless of who was in the right and who in the wrong. Mo Ran would prefer not to see him at all.

In the end, no matter what he said, there was nothing he could do. Both he and his little shidi got locked up.

The prison at Peach Blossom Springs was a cave, not very big but also not too small, and its entrance was covered by ancient brambles that only obeyed the commands of the feathered tribe. The interior never saw the light of day, but thankfully there was a firepit with enchanted flames that burned continuously.

The furnishings inside were simple: a wide, plain bed of stone padded with golden-red cushions made of woven feathers, a stone table and four stone stools, one copper mirror, and a couple sets of bowls and cups. Mo Ran and Chu Wanning were imprisoned there together.

Although judgment had yet to be passed, the one in charge of them seemed to have been close with Eighteen. As Eighteen had lost her life for no apparent reason, the feathered tribe guard took it out on them by making their lives more difficult.

On the first night, the guard deigned to deliver some food; it wasn't great or much, but there was enough to eat. However by the second day, she brought only some raw meat, vegetables, rice, flour, and salt, which she tossed casually into the cave along with a few words about not having the time to take care of their meals and how they should sort it out themselves.

"Fine, we *will* sort it out ourselves, then. It's just cooking. What's so hard about that?" Mo Ran muttered huffily where he was crouched on the ground, picking out the usable ingredients. "What does shidi want to eat?"

"Whatever."

Mo Ran sighed. "There's no dish more difficult to cook than the one called 'Whatever.' Let's see here, we have pork belly, napa cabbage... Tsk, this bird sure is stingy, it's only the outer layers of the cabbage. There's quite a bit of rice and flour, but I'm not sure how many days this is supposed to last us." He muttered while counting the ingredients, then looked up at Chu Wanning. "Do you want rice or noodles?"

Chu Wanning was resting on the bed, tummy-down. He thought about it, then said, "Noodles." A pause, then he added: "Soup noodles with spareribs."

"Ah ha ha, where am I gonna get spareribs?"

"Then whatever's fine."

Mo Ran sat cross-legged on the ground, one hand on his knee, cheek squished against the other, and thought for a bit. "There aren't many ingredients here. How about noodles with minced meat?"

"Noodles with minced meat?"

"Would you like that?"

"Sure. Is it spicy?"

Mo Ran grinned. "There isn't even a shadow of a pepper in what that bird gave us."

With dinner decided, Mo Ran set about kneading dough. Chu Wanning was short and not that strong, so he didn't bother trying to make a pretense of helping. He watched Mo Ran knead the soft, white ball from where he lay in bed, his gaze growing softer.

Chu Wanning suddenly felt that this wasn't so bad. Mo Ran didn't know who he was, so he could stay by his side, and when Mo Ran cooked, he bothered to ask what Chu Wanning wanted to eat. It really wasn't bad. He even felt a little uneasy, as if he had been given too much—as if he had stolen it all from a child named "Xia Sini."

Mo Ran finished cooking the noodles and placed the stir-fried minced meat on top. They had pitifully few seasonings, so he couldn't make anything fancy, but the noodles were pulled to a chewy consistency with just the right softness. He had also cut off the fatty part of the pork and used it to fry the meat. The meat sizzled as it was poured over the noodles, and it would no doubt be delicious once mixed in.

"Shidi, dinner's..." Mo Ran looked up to find that Chu Wanning had fallen asleep, still lying tummy-down, face turned to the side with his head pillowed on his arms. His long lashes rested against his cheeks, his expression peaceful.

"Ready..." Mo Ran finished at a mumble, then walked over to the bed and stroked Chu Wanning's smooth, inky hair.

"When I see you like this, you really do look like Shizun. I wonder what relationship you have with Shizun and the Chu family of Lin'an. Also, exactly who's after us?" Mo Ran sighed. "Wonder what Shizun's up to right now. If he knew what had happened here, would he blame me again, regardless of everything else?"

The color in Mo Ran's eyes darkened a little as he played with a strand of Chu Wanning's hair around his finger. He sighed again faintly.

"You don't know him, but anytime anything happens, he always gives me hell... He really doesn't like me at all."

However, Chu Wanning was asleep, and these words scattered weightlessly into the silence of night without an answer, just like the misunderstandings that had coiled around them for decades and decades, and across two lifetimes.

Mo Ran waited for the noodles to cool down a bit before waking Chu Wanning. "Shidi, dinner's ready."

Chu Wanning covered a yawn and blinked blearily. "Oh, dinner..."

Mo Ran carried the noodles over. He liked to cook, but he hated doing the dishes, so purely for the sake of having one less dish to wash, he had dumped the noodles directly into the pot in which he'd fried the meat.

Chu Wanning was flabbergasted by this unorthodox and uncultured way of eating, his eyes wide as he stared disbelievingly at the big pot of noodles. "How...are we supposed to eat this?"

"Together, of course." Mo Ran handed him a pair of chopsticks and was already putting his hands together with a grin. "The race to see who can scoop out more noodles is about to begin! Who's gonna get to eat more? We're about to find out."

Chu Wanning had no words.

Mo Ran laughed gleefully, his eyes smiling. Chu Wanning stared at him for a moment before saying, "It's almost like, as long as you have food, you're very..."

"Very happy, right?"

"Mn."

"Ha ha, food is the most important thing, after all!" Mo Ran cheekily scooped up a big clump of noodles for himself, slurping it all up until his cheeks puffed out. "It doesn't look great, but it's pretty tasty."

Chu Wanning's expression was dark as he stared for a long moment before he eventually said, "Don't slurp while you eat."

"Ha ha ha!" Mo Ran laughed, slapping his leg. "How is a little kid like you so much like my shizun? He also tells me to not slurp, but you know what? Once, when I was eating with him, I purposefully threw a bone in his bowl, and he got so mad! Ha ha ha ha ha—"

Chu Wanning ground his teeth. "Impudent!"

"Yeah, yeah, yeah! That was exactly his reaction, how did you know? Even the delivery was just like his! Hey, Shidi, seriously, I think you two might be distant relatives. Why don't you ask Shizun about it when he gets here? O-oi—wait, not the egg, the egg's mine—"

72 This Venerable One Stews Soup

AT NIGHT, the two of them lay on the wide stone bed. Trying to pass the time while locked up was a task in and of itself. They had already trained and eaten, and now there was nothing else to do.

Chu Wanning, calm and tranquil by nature, wasn't all that bothered, but Mo Ran paced this way and that in the constricted confines of the cave, and time only seemed to crawl even slower.

"Ahh, I'm so bored. So bored! What to do? What to do?"

"Sleep," Chu Wanning said, his eyes closed.

"But it's still so early." Mo Ran glanced at the hourglass and shook his head. "Way too early."

Chu Wanning ignored him.

Mo Ran rolled about on the bed, then scooted over and tugged at his cheeks. "Shidi."

Chu Wanning continued to ignore him.

"Shidiiii..."

Chu Wanning steadfastly continued to ignore him.

"*Shidi!*"

Chu Wanning's eyes flew open angrily. "What do you want?!"

Mo Ran took Chu Wanning's hands in his own and shamelessly swung their joined limbs back and forth. "Play with me."

"Am I the shidi here, or are you?" Chu Wanning wrenched his hands back, beyond irate. "Who's gonna fool around with you?!"

Mo Ran smiled sweetly, truly and completely shameless. "You, of course. Who else is there?"

Chu Wanning had no response.

Mo Ran took off the narrow red cord holding his hair up, tied the ends together, and wove it into a distinct pattern around his fingers.

Despite his protests, Chu Wanning sat up after all. "What is this?" he asked grumpily. "How do you play?"

"It's called cat's cradle. Mostly girls play it, not so much boys. But I grew up in a house full of girls, so I ended up learning it too."

Chu Wanning eyed him.

"It's pretty fun, actually. See, hook your finger around this string here... No, not that finger, use your pinky—yeah, like that. Then take your thumb and forefinger and hook around these two strings here..." Mo Ran instructed him slowly and patiently.

The candle flame crackled, casting its warm light on them, one big and one small, their heads lowered in concentration as they passed that loop of red string made from a hair tie back and forth, their expressions slowly softening.

Chu Wanning held segments of string taut between his fingers as he followed Mo Ran's instructions to weave a new pattern. Then he accidentally missed a loop. When the red string exchanged hands, rather than transforming into the new pattern, it returned to its original shape: a simple circle.

Chu Wanning stared at it blankly, hands held in midair and face full of incomprehension. "Why did it fall apart?" he muttered. "What happened..."

"Ha ha, you probably missed a loop again."

"Again."

"No more, no more." Mo Ran laughed. "Doing the same thing over and over gets boring, let's do something else."

"No." Now it was Chu Wanning's turn to be displeased. "One more time."

Mo Ran gaped speechlessly at him.

They spent three days in the cave. Their fourth night found Mo Ran busy preparing to cook something delicious for Chu Wanning, as usual. He had figured out a few things during these last few days together, like that his little shidi truly was from the same place as his shizun—they even had the same exact tastes in food.

Tonight's delivery from the feathered tribe guard was a hen and a couple of mushrooms. Mo Ran planned to make chicken soup with mushrooms, then add some of his handmade noodles. Altogether, it wouldn't taste too bad.

"Are we having chicken soup tonight?"

"Mm-hmm." Mo Ran glanced sideways at Chu Wanning. The kid was a genius when it came to martial arts, yet he just couldn't grasp cat's cradle. He was also stubborn to a fault, and every chance he got, he played with a hair cord trying to figure it out. Mo Ran couldn't help smiling at his mulish expression.

"Feel free to play with it while I cook," Mo Ran said with a smile. "But I'm afraid the soup's gonna finish stewing before you work it out."

Chu Wanning let out a cold hmph and paused. "Is there any ginger left?"

"Let me see... Yep, there's plenty. They gave us a bunch yesterday."

Chu Wanning made a satisfied sound. "Put some in, it gets rid of the raw meat smell."

Mo Ran stroked his chin. "Oh...and lemme guess, add some wolfberries too?"

Chu Wanning's eyes brightened. "Do we have some?"

"Pfft. Of course not. I was just thinking that your tastes really are exactly like Shizun's. He also likes ginger and wolfberries in his soup."

"You remember what he likes to eat?"

"Ha ha, yep-yep, I'm super clever." Mo Ran didn't feel like explaining. Anyway, it wasn't like he could talk about things like past lives with his little shidi, so he rolled with it. "I'm the very embodiment of The Twenty-Four Paragons of Filial Piety,[16] don't you know? It's too bad that Shizun doesn't see my heartfelt sincerity."

Mo Ran began cleaning the chicken as he talked absently, and thus he wholly missed Chu Wanning's expression. He plucked the feathers and removed the innards with a quick, practiced hand, and was about to boil the blood out when he heard his little shidi say in a quiet voice, "He isn't necessarily unaware."

"Huh?"

When Mo Ran looked up, the tips of Chu Wanning's ears reddened. He turned away and cleared his throat. "I said, the Yuheng Elder isn't necessarily unaware that you're good to him."

"Oh, that. It doesn't really matter; I'm used to it. Even though I did wish, once, that he would be like other people's masters and ask after me sometimes, or that he'd occasionally remember my preferences—like how I know what he likes to eat. That's all in the past now. When I first entered the sect, I was fooled by his pretty looks and thought he was a gentle person. Thinking back on it now is really..." Mo Ran sighed. "My esteemed shizun is so illustrious and

---

16 *The Twenty-Four Paragons of Filial Piety is a classic text of twenty-four stories of Confucian filial piety. It was written by Guo Jujing during the Yuan dynasty and was used to teach Confucian moral values.*

unapproachable, and he's busy on top of that. How could I possibly dare to hope for his attention? Ha ha, ah ha ha ha."

At first, these words made Chu Wanning a bit cross, but then he thought about them. Although he was concerned about Mo Ran in their daily life, he did indeed maintain a veneer of aloofness and distance. He hung his head wordlessly, and anger turned into consternation. After a while, he hopped off the bed and walked quietly over to Mo Ran.

"What's up?"

"You're always the one cooking. Today's meal is uncomplicated, so I'll cook for you instead."

Mo Ran blinked, then smiled. "Where'd this come from? You're too short to reach the stove—how are you gonna cook? Besides, I'm your shixiong, now that you've called me that. The least I can do is feed you."

Chu Wanning carried a stool over and climbed onto it, then stared at him stubbornly without saying a word.

Mo Ran blinked mutely. "Why are you glaring at me?"

"I can reach the stove just fine."

Mo Ran eyed him silently.

"The Yuheng Elder may not know what you like to eat, but I'm not heartless like him," Chu Wanning said expressionlessly. "Go take a break, I'll cook."

And so Chu Wanning busied himself with dinner preparations, refusing to let Mo Ran help even a little. He had an aura of menace and there was a concentrated ferocity in his eyes as he lifted the kitchen knife high into the air and brought it stiffly down on the poor chicken. Mo Ran almost couldn't bear to look.

Mo Ran tried to help, but even his little shidi's temper was exactly like his shizun's, and Chu Wanning hated getting interrupted when he was concentrating. In the end, Mo Ran could only scratch his head and wander off to go flop on the bed.

Having finally put the chicken in the pot, Chu Wanning covered it with a clay lid and was about to turn to say something when he heard a quiet voice from the cave entrance.

"A-Ran, Xia-shidi, are you there?"

As soon as Mo Ran heard this voice, he leapt off the bed as if he had been struck by lightning and dashed to the entrance. Through a gap between the brambles, the first person he saw was someone from the feathered tribe. She stood there coldly, but when Mo Ran looked around, he found Shi Mei behind her, dressed in his usual white and his face full of worry. Mo Ran was ecstatic. "Shi Mei! What...what are you doing here?"

"I have something important to tell you," Shi Mei said. "The sect leader received the report and immediately rushed to Peach Blossom Springs. He's negotiating with the feathered tribe as we speak. How have you been? Are they treating you okay?"

"I'm great. Eating well, drinking well, and lively as always." Mo Ran paused. "What about Shizun? Where is he?"

"I hear he's still in seclusion and didn't come."

"Oh..." Something flickered past Mo Ran's eyes, then he sighed. "It's fine if he didn't come..." he mumbled to himself. "It's fine."

"But the Xuanji Elder came to vouch for Xia-shidi," Shi Mei said. "Is Xia-shidi already asleep?"

"No, he's making soup. Shidi, come over here!"

Chu Wanning put down the little bamboo fan he was using to fan the flames and walked to the entrance. He looked at the two people outside, expression not the least bit surprised, and said flatly, "What is it?"

Shi Mei didn't get a chance to speak before the feathered tribe representative hmphed. "What else could it be?" she shot back. "People from Sisheng Peak came. Your master says he'll vouch for you and is meeting with our Great Immortal Lord right now."

"My master?"

"The Xuanji Elder."

"Oh." Chu Wanning paused, face totally expressionless. "Good."

The corner of the feathered tribe representative's mouth twitched. "You two can come out. Everyone is gathered at the Dewsip Pavilion waiting to hear your explanations."

Chu Wanning turned to look at the chicken soup on the stove. "I'll pass. The soup isn't done cooking yet, and I have to keep an eye on it. Mo Ran, you can speak for me."

These words made the feathered tribe representative think the child was immature and unreasonable. She smiled coldly, wanting to scare him. "You'll miss your chance to defend yourself if you don't go. And if you are deemed to be the murderer, there goes your head."

However, Chu Wanning wasn't the least bit concerned. He wore an indifferent face as he sent her a cold glance and turned to leave.

Shi Mei was about to call after him, but Mo Ran shook his head with a smile. "Let him be. I'll go."

"But the Xuanji Elder came all this way. It would be rude not to greet him..."

Before Mo Ran could say anything, Chu Wanning's voice came from afar. "Mo-shixiong, please send Shizun my regards."

Shi Mei was struck speechless. He'd spoken so quietly but the boy had still heard him. Feeling a little awkward, he cleared his throat and waited for the feathered tribe representative to open the brambles covering the cave entrance, then grabbed Mo Ran to leave.

Unexpectedly, Chu Wanning turned around and called out, "Shixiong."

Mo Ran smiled. "Did Shidi change his mind? You want to come along after all?"

Chu Wanning's little hand waved in his sleeve. "Of course not. I just wanted to remind you to come back soon, or the soup will go cold."

Mo Ran blinked, then laughed helplessly. "All right. Wait for me."

"Mn." Chu Wanning said nothing else as he watched Mo Ran walk away and disappear behind a corner. Then he turned back around to attend to the soup.

The Dewsip Pavilion wasn't far from the prison cave. On the way there, Shi Mei said offhandedly, "A-Ran, you seem to have grown even closer with Xia-shidi these days."

Mo Ran smiled. "Yeah, we went through a lot together. What, is Shi Mei jealous of a little kid?"

There was a beat of silence before Shi Mei said, "Nonsense."

"Ha ha ha, no need to worry. My favorite person is and will always be Shi Mei."

"Enough nonsense... I just feel like Xia-shidi is a little odd."

"Odd? Oh..." Mo Ran thought for a bit, then nodded, "I guess he is pretty odd."

"You think so too?"

"Yep." Mo Ran grinned. "He's such a little thing but he talks like an adult, and his power is no laughing matter either. Oh, and I haven't had a chance to tell you guys yet, but the stuff that happened in the illusion was even more bizarre. I think he might be a distant relative of our shizun, you know."

Shi Mei's eyes shifted slightly. "Why do you say that?"

"We saw someone in the illusion, the son of the Lin'an governor from two hundred years ago. His surname was also Chu, and he looked like Shizun, and his son also looked—"

Right when Mo Ran was getting to the important part, a sudden bout of loud cursing burst out in front of them. He looked up just in time to see Xue Meng striding over, face dark as a thundercloud, still cursing without stop. "Bastard! Beast! *Shameless mutt!*"

73 This Venerable One Is Confused

Having run into Mo Ran so suddenly, Xue Meng blinked. This was the first time the two had come face-to-face since Mo Ran's detention.

When Mo Ran recalled how Xue Meng had defended him in front of the crowd, he smiled at his cousin despite himself.

Xue Meng, however, was thoroughly shocked by this grin. "What?" he said contemptuously, face full of disgust. "What are you looking at?! What are you smiling about?! What's there to smile about?!"

"I'm greeting you?"

"Disgusting!"

Mo Ran blinked, stupefied.

This comeback had thoroughly killed Mo Ran's conversation starter. Shi Mei hummed pensively for a moment but didn't push for further answers either, instead turning to Xue Meng with a smile. "Young master, who's annoyed you now?"

"Who else could it be? *Who else* could it be?! Depraved! Despicable! Disgusting! Obscene!"

Mo Ran sighed. "That doesn't alliterate."

"Who cares?! You do it, then, if you're so great!"

"I'm not great, I'm uncultured," Mo Ran chuckled. "Come on, tell us. Who pissed you off?"

"I bet it was Da-shixiong again," Shi Mei said with a smile.

"Goddamn Da-shixiong! Beast! Pervert! If he sleeps around so much, how come he doesn't have an STD?! I'd happily give up ten fucking years of my life to curse him with sores on his head and pus oozing from his feet—may his nose and eyes rot off! Let's see who's still gonna think he's so hot then! That despicable, shameless, obscene—"

Mo Ran blinked, stupefied once again.

Knowing that Xue Meng was about to sink into an endless cycle, Shi Mei hastily stopped him and pointed back down the road. "Shh, look, those lady cultivators who like Da-shixiong are here."

Xue Meng jumped with a squawk, a trace of trepidation flashing across his perpetually prideful face. "Filthy degenerates," he swore under his breath. Even so, he did indeed turn and bolt, tail between his legs like a stray dog. In a last-ditch attempt to save his dignity, he snapped before leaving, "I suddenly remembered I've got something to do, so I'm heading off now!"

Mo Ran watched him scamper out of sight. "Wow," he said, amazed. "This Da-shixiong is really something, if he can scare Xue Meng that badly!"

Shi Mei held back a laugh. "It's been like this ever since Xue Meng ran into him at a restaurant the other day and got into a scuffle. I guess he's met his match."

"Amazing, amazing. I've gotta see him for myself sometime." Those were the words that left Mo Ran's lips, but inwardly he already knew more or less what was going on. If this "Da-shixiong" could make Xue Meng hide like this, he was definitely the person Mo Ran was thinking of.

Now wasn't the time to enjoy the spectacle of Xue Meng, however. Xue Zhengyong and the Xuanji Elder had arrived at the Dewsip Pavilion and were softly discussing Eighteen's murder with the master of Peach Blossom Springs, the Elder Immortal of the feathered tribe.

The Elder Immortal was practically divine. A glow of spiritual light encircled and enveloped her body, and while she looked to be a young woman of a fair, tender age, heavens knew how old she actually was.

She was explaining the case calmly to Xue Zhengyong when a personal attendant walked in and reported in a low voice, "Elder Immortal, we've brought them."

"Send them in."

Mo Ran followed Shi Mei into the warm pavilion and scanned the area. The second he saw Xue Zhengyong fanning that infamous fan while speaking to the others, he called out, "Uncle!"

"My child, my child." Xue Zhengyong looked over at the sound of Mo Ran's voice. His eyes lit, and he hastened to beckon them over. "Come, sit next to your uncle," he said, patting Mo Ran's shoulder.

"I didn't kill her..."

"Of course you didn't, of course not." Xue Zhengyong sighed again and again. "I can't imagine how this misunderstanding came about. The Elder Immortal told me everything, and I've come to help prove your innocence." He sighed yet again. "Heavens have mercy, look how downtrodden you are."

He pulled Mo Ran over, and the Elder Immortal of the feathered tribe didn't stop him, only watching them with impassive eyes.

Mo Ran also greeted the Xuanji Elder and swiftly sat down next to Xue Zhengyong. However, it struck Mo Ran as odd that Xuanji didn't immediately notice the absence of his own disciple, Xia Sini. Instead, he nodded absently at Mo Ran.

It was ultimately the Elder Immortal of the feathered tribe who said, "Eh? Where's the other child? The one named Xia."

"Ah, that's right." Only then did Xuanji seem to realize. "Where's... my disciple?"

To Mo Ran's eyes, this was an obvious lack of care for Xia Sini, and he was somewhat upset. "My shidi is still locked up. He asked me to greet you on his behalf."

"Is that so." Xuanji nodded. "Why didn't he come?"

"He's cooking," Mo Ran replied curtly.

His answer was met with stunned silence.

Once Xue Zhengyong recovered from his bewilderment, he laughed. "Is cooking more important than clearing his name?"

"What a headstrong child," Xuanji said, smiling. "I'll go check on him once the meeting is over."

"No need. We're having dinner together after this," Mo Ran said. "Interrogate me however you will, but let's get this over and done with."

Thus, Xue Zhengyong spoke, "Elder Immortal, let's continue our earlier discussion. How about this: We have an elder in our sect who is skilled in the art of refining pills.[17] Before I came, I asked him to create a number of purity pills."

"Purity pills?" The Elder Immortal was slightly taken aback, and she lightly tapped the corner of her lips with a dainty, crimson finger. "Are those the sort that can make mortals speak absolute truth?"

"That's correct."

The Elder Immortal was rather surprised. "The materials required to make these things are complex and difficult to refine, and even here in Peach Blossom Springs, it would take at least half a month to produce such a pill. I'm amazed to hear that Xianjun's sect has such a master of medicines. Why didn't you bring him along?"

---

17 *The art of "refining" in the Husky universe refers to the alchemical art of enhancing spiritual qualities of ingredients (plants, minerals, and such) into pills, elixirs, and medicines that can be used for various purposes, including enhancing cultivation, healing, and more.*

"He's antisocial and doesn't like traveling with others," Xue Zhengyong replied. "The pills are currently being refined, and they can be sent to Peach Blossom Springs by pigeon within ten days. When that time comes, I invite the Elder Immortal to verify the effectiveness of the pills, then have the young disciples take them. The truth will be revealed at that time."

The Elder Immortal contemplated this in silence for a moment, then inclined her head. "This is acceptable."

Xue Zhengyong sighed a breath of relief and smiled. "Then if that's the case, let me go bring my other disciple out of the prison cave right away."

"Hold it."

"What is it?"

"Until this affair is sorted out, both Mo Ran and Xia Sini remain under suspicion," the Elder Immortal said. "Even with the sect leader's insurance, this venerable one cannot let those two walk free."

At this, Xue Zhengyong snapped his fan shut with a smack. While a smile lingered on his face, his gaze had grown colder. "Now that's a little disingenuous, Elder Immortal."

The Elder Immortal of the feathered tribe raised her gaze and stared at him with a pair of scarlet eyes. "Is Xue-zunzhu dissatisfied with this venerable one's decision?"

"But of course. A guilty verdict has yet to be delivered to my sect's disciples. Since the Elder Immortal has the guarantee of both myself and the Xuanji Elder that we'll keep watch over them, what reason is there to keep them detained?"

"It isn't truly detention," the Elder Immortal said coolly. "They aren't mistreated, and their daily meals go uninterrupted. I've only restricted their movements. That isn't unreasonable."

Xue Zhengyong was still smiling, but that smile remained cold. "Not unreasonable? From what I hear, that prison cave never sees the light of the sun or the moon. It's where you lock up criminals who've been proven guilty. The Elder Immortal's choice to go and call it 'not unreasonable' is pure lip service."

"Xue-zunzhu," a feathered tribe guard by the side said sternly. "Please watch your tongue!"

"What, have I said something rude? I'm not humiliating or insulting your Elder Immortal, and I've said nothing but the truth. Maybe my words aren't courteous, but they're *not unreasonable*."

This response left the feathered tribe guard even more enraged. "You!"

A hand, pale as jade, reached out and stopped him. The Elder Immortal raised her head and smiled coolly at Xue Zhengyong. "Rumor from the mortal realm had it that Xue-zunzhu of Sisheng Peak was just a pretty face, with strength to spare but rather short on wits—certainly not one for wordplay. Now this venerable one sees that the rumors were rather misleading, for Xue-zunzhu is in truth quite the well-reasoned individual."

Xue Zhengyong also flashed her a smile, but there was no more mirth left in his eyes. "I'm but a vulgar man. Please don't mind me, Elder Immortal."

The Elder Immortal of the feathered tribe grinned, raised her hand, and picked a tangerine. She peeled it with great care before holding the peeled fruit out to Xue Zhengyong. "Then why don't you and I both take a step back? It will not be possible to grant your disciples the same freedoms as before, but leaving them in prison certainly isn't appropriate either. This venerable one will order Xia Sini's immediate release, and Mo Ran and Xia Sini will hence be lodged in the Campsis Pavilion, which is a place for receiving guests. The only concessions

I require: that people be sent to watch them, and that they be forbidden from taking even half a step out of the pavilion. Is this agreeable?"

Xue Zhengyong was silent for a bit. Then he raised his hand. It hovered in midair for a long moment, but eventually, he accepted the tangerine.

Campsis Pavilion might have been accommodations meant for guests, but Peach Blossom Springs didn't receive guests all that often. As such, the interior of the pavilion had been neglected for a long time. Since the Elder Immortal had permitted them to move in, Mo Ran decided to go over and clean, then return to pick up Xia Sini once everything was tidy.

Xue Zhengyong and Xuanji still had things to discuss, so under the watch of several members of the feathered tribe, Mo Ran and Shi Mei went to Campsis Pavilion first.

Campsis Pavilion was situated in the northwest area of Peach Blossom Springs. A veritable forest of flowers bloomed around it, making for a brilliant, glowing haze lit by the setting sun.

"This is a good place. It won't be so bad to stay here," Mo Ran said happily.

Shi Mei sighed. "How is this a good place? The two of you are innocent. You didn't kill anybody, yet you've been accused of doing so. Too bad Shizun couldn't come. If he had, then he could use Tianwen to interrogate you, and there wouldn't be any use for purity pills in order to reveal the truth."

"Ha ha, if only it were that straightforward. Tianwen is a holy weapon, but while it has the ability to eke out the truth, its effectiveness is entirely dependent on whether the user really intends to interrogate someone. Do you think those birds would be willing to let my shizun interrogate me? Do you think they'd believe him?"

"That's true..."

As the sun was about to set, Mo Ran set about tidying the house with Shi Mei's assistance.

It certainly was strange. Only when Mo Ran finished cleaning the pavilion and sat down to rest and drink tea did he realize that he didn't feel any secret joy in being able to spend time alone with Shi Mei. Nor was he having any flirtatious thoughts.

Mo Ran choked at the realization and almost spat out his tea.

Shi Mei jumped in surprise. "What's wrong?"

"N-nothing." Mo Ran waved his hands frantically, but internally he was swearing.

Had he been training under Chu Wanning for so long that he'd also turned into Liuxia Hui?[18] Behold: Campsis Pavilion, a desolate place with not a soul around, where the peach blossoms swayed and two single men had been left alone with only each other for company. At any point in the past, Mo Ran absolutely would've taken the opportunity to get all lovey-dovey with Shi Mei before actually getting down to business.

What was with him recently? Acting all pure and frigid, who even was he anymore?

Mo Ran scratched his head.

Shi Mei blinked.

Eyes met eyes, and Mo Ran cracked a dopey smile, his dimples precious and cute. "The peach blossoms outside are beautiful. I'll go pick a branch for you to bring with you."

"Plants are sentient—just let them bloom properly on their branches," Shi Mei said.

"Mn... You're too right. Then—then I won't pick them!"

---

18 *An ancient Chinese politician, renowned for his virtue, said to have once held a woman in his lap without the slightest impugnation on his moral character.*

They sat there in silence, and Mo Ran dug through everything he could find in his mind that could start a conversation. He soon realized that having only been able to meet up infrequently as of late, they didn't have anything worth talking about.

When he looked up, he realized that Shi Mei had a thin sheen of sweat from helping him clean. Heart twinging in sympathy, he took out a handkerchief from his robes and handed it to him. "For you to wipe yourself."

Shi Mei lowered his lashes, glancing over, and when he saw that Mo Ran was squeezing the handkerchief nervously, he could only smile. "Thank you," he gently replied.

He then took the handkerchief and lightly dabbed his forehead. The feel of the cloth was light and soft, as it had been sewn with the best of silk. After Shi Mei used it, he said, "I'll take the handkerchief back and wash it before I return it to you."

"Okey dokey," Mo Ran answered promptly. His receptiveness to whatever Shi Mei wanted was practically ingrained by this point. "If you like it, it's okay if you don't return it either."

Shi Mei laughed. "That wouldn't be right, look how well-made this handkerchief is..." He opened it, smoothing out the creases to fold it again. Yet as his slender, delicate fingers felt over the spread handkerchief, Shi Mei paused, taken aback, and let out a soft sound of surprise.

"What is it?"

Shi Mei hesitated and looked up with a smile. "A-Ran really wants to give me this handkerchief?"

"If you like it, then take it. What's mine is yours." Mo Ran was very generous.

There was laughter in the depths of Shi Mei's gaze. "Borrowing flowers from others to worship the Buddha. Aren't you afraid that Shizun will find out and whip you?"

"Huh?" This time it was Mo Ran's turn to be taken aback. "What do you mean by 'borrowing flowers to worship the Buddha'? What does Shizun have to do with this?"

"Take a look yourself." Shi Mei's tone was a little unreadable. "Such a large haitang blossom. When did Shizun give you his own handkerchief?"

74 This Venerable One's Fault

MO RAN was dumbstruck.

A long while passed before he snapped out of it, his entire face bright red as he waved his hands frantically. "No, that, uh, I dunno, this isn't mine, where did my handkerchief go? I, I-I, oh god, how am I gonna get out of this one..."

Mo Ran stared at that square of silken cloth with a haitang flower sewn on a corner, but he couldn't for the life of him remember why he even had it. He racked his brain in a panic, then suddenly smacked his head. "Ah!"

"What is it...?"

"I remembered!" Mo Ran let out a sigh of relief and took the handkerchief from Shi Mei's hands with a smile. "Sorry, this isn't mine, so I can't give it to you."

Shi Mei fell silent. *I didn't even say I wanted it to begin with.*

"It's not Shizun's either—it's not like everything with a haitang on it belongs to Shizun." Mo Ran folded the handkerchief neatly and tucked it back into his robes, beyond relieved that he hadn't accidentally taken his shizun's possession. "It's Xia-shidi's."

Shi Mei looked thoughtful. "Xia-shidi's?"

"Mm-hmm. We've been living together these last few days,

so maybe I grabbed the wrong one from the drying rack this morning or something. Ha ha, how embarrassing."

Shi Mei was silent for a moment, then he smiled gently and said, "Mm, it's no big deal." He stood. "It's getting late. We should go pick up Xia-shidi."

They left the house and headed for the cave.

They didn't get far before Shi Mei started slowing down. It wasn't too obvious at first, but then he stumbled on a rock and would have fallen if Mo Ran hadn't reacted quickly and caught him in time.

Mo Ran was shocked by Shi Mei's pallid complexion. "What's wrong?"

"It's nothing." Shi Mei took a deep breath. "I didn't eat much for lunch. Just feeling a little faint. Nothing a bit of rest won't fix."

The more he tried to gloss over it, the more Mo Ran worried. Now that he thought about it, Shi Mei wasn't great at qinggong, and everything here at Peach Blossom Springs, from food to clothes, cost feathers to purchase. Mo Ran had always made sure to give Shi Mei some feathers, but he had been locked up for a few days now, and Xue Meng was too thoughtless to take care of anyone...

The more Mo Ran thought, the more concerned he grew. "You used to skip lunch all the time back at the sect, too, but I've never seen you in such a state," he pressed. "Am I to believe this is the result of only missing one meal? Tell me the truth: When was the last time you ate?"

"I..."

Mo Ran's expression grew even darker at Shi Mei's reluctance to answer. He grabbed Shi Mei and started walking in the opposite direction.

"A-Ran, wh-where are we going?" Shi Mei fretted.

"Where the food is!" Mo Ran said sharply, but when he turned around there was only worry in his eyes. "Why didn't you take care of yourself while I was gone? You're always, always thinking about everyone else and putting others first! What about yourself? Have you ever thought about yourself?"

"A-Ran..."

Mo Ran dragged Shi Mei all the way to a tavern. Normally, Shi Mei belonged to the Healing Division and shouldn't have been in the Attack Division region without a token. However, anxiety had run high ever since the incident with Eighteen, so the feathered tribe had lifted that restriction to ease things.

"What do you want? Order whatever."

"Anything's fine." Shi Mei seemed a bit guilty. "Sorry, I wanted to come help, but I ended up getting in the way instead..."

"No need for things like 'sorry' between us." Mo Ran flicked his forehead and gentled his tone. "Go ahead and order. I'll pay for it, and then you can take your time eating."

Shi Mei looked at him. "What about you?"

"I have to go pick up Xia-shidi. There's a guard at the cave, but I'm still worried, what with the killer still being out there."

When Shi Mei realized that Mo Ran wanted to leave, his eyes seemed to darken for an instant. "Just two buns, then," he said quickly. "I'll go with you and eat on the way."

Mo Ran was going to try to talk him out of it when the bird-like chitter of feminine voices came from outside. Some dozen young female cultivators, all primped up, entered the building while giggling.

"Hey, shopkeep, I have a question," the lady at the head of the group said with a smile. "Did Da-shixiong...reserve the banquet room at this tavern tonight?"

"Indeed, indeed." The shopkeep was all smiles. It hadn't taken long for the feathered tribe to figure out that Da-shixiong liked wine and song, so every single night, they held a banquet at one tavern or another. Wherever this "Da-shixiong" went, a group of giggling ladies was sure to flock.

Sure enough, the ladies were thrilled and immediately hurried to reserve their tables. Now and again, their words drifted over to Mo Ran's ears. It was all, "Xiao-Fang, how does the painting on my eyebrows look? Do you think Da-shixiong will like it?" "It's lovely. What do you think about my eyeliner? Is it too flashy? Will it make him think I'm flighty?" and stuff like, "You're so pretty, Da-shixiong will like you for sure! Yesterday I saw him look at you quite a few times." "Aiya, stop teasing me—if only! Da-shixiong's type is definitely someone like Jiejie, refined and *so* well-read."

Mo Ran had no words. Even in such troubled times, these ladies could flutter about like this over some guy. The corner of his mouth twitched, and he turned to Shi Mei. "Buns it is, then. Let's grab and go—I'll worry if I leave you here alone in this cave of carnivorous beasts."

Shi Mei shook his head at Mo Ran's expression, his laughter light.

The tastiest thing on the menu at this tavern was their large, drool-worthy meatbuns. Mo Ran bought ten at once and gave them all to Shi Mei. When Mo Ran glanced at Shi Mei nibbling happily on the buns as they walked, he was finally able to relax a little.

No one expected the bun to do Shi Mei in.

His stomach was already weak to start with, so suddenly eating an oily bun after having had nothing in him for so long left him hurting in no time.

Now Mo Ran really couldn't leave to go pick up Xia-shidi. He carried a pale and sweaty Shi Mei back to the Campsis Pavilion in a frantic rush and laid him down on the bed he had tidied, then dashed out to ask for a physician.

After giving him some medicine and warm water, Mo Ran sat by the bed filled with self-reproach as he looked at Shi Mei's pallid face. "Does it still hurt? Here, I'll rub your tummy."

Shi Mei's voice was quiet and weak. "No need...it's okay..."

Mo Ran's large and well-defined hand had already reached over to gently knead him through the quilt. Maybe it was because the pressure was just right and it felt good, but Shi Mei didn't protest. His breaths evened out under the attentive kneading, and he fell asleep.

Mo Ran stayed until Shi Mei was sound asleep before getting ready to leave. Before he'd stood, his hand was caught.

Mo Ran's eyes, black with a tinge of purple, widened. "Shi Mei?"

"It hurts... Don't leave..." The beauty's eyes were still closed, and he seemed to be talking in his sleep.

Mo Ran stood locked in place. Shi Mei had never asked anyone for anything; he was always the one helping others without any expectation of receiving the same. Only while asleep would he plead with Mo Ran to stay in such a soft voice.

So Mo Ran sat back down, gazing fondly at the face that he yearned for day and night, while continuing to massage his stomach. Outside the lattice window, peach blossom petals drifted lazily by as the sky darkened.

By the time Mo Ran remembered that he had told his little shidi he'd be back for dinner, it was already midnight.

"Oh no!" Mo Ran jumped to his feet, smacking his head over and over, "Oh no, oh no, oh no!"

By then, Shi Mei was deeply asleep. Mo Ran dashed outside and was about to sprint to the cave when a blue light flashed in the sky and the Xuanji Elder descended from above with a child in his arms, a child who held a little clay jar.

"Xuanji Elder!"

Xuanji shot Mo Ran a reproachful glance. "What happened? Didn't you say you were going to go pick him up? If I hadn't been concerned and gone to check on him after all, Yu...ahem, my disciple would've had to wait in that cave till dawn."

"This disciple was wrong." Mo Ran lowered his head, but nonetheless lifted his eyes to look at Chu Wanning. "Shidi..."

Xuanji put Chu Wanning down. Chu Wanning, still holding that clay jar, looked calmly at Mo Ran. "Have you eaten yet?"

Mo Ran hadn't expected that to be the first thing he said, and he could only reply dumbly: "N-not yet..."

So Chu Wanning walked over and offered him the jar. "Have some," he said mildly. "It's still warm."

Mo Ran stood there motionlessly for a while. By the time he came back around, he had already pulled the little guy into a hug, along with his clay jar. "Okay, I will."

This silly kid had been worried that the soup might go cold, and he had taken off his outer robe to wrap it around the jar. His small body felt a bit chilly in Mo Ran's arms.

Mo Ran pressed their foreheads together, nuzzling him softly, and for the first time in two lives, he spoke these words and meant them: "Sorry. It was my fault."

They bid Xuanji good night and went inside the pavilion.

Chu Wanning's outer robe was now too wrinkled to wear, and Mo Ran worried that his shidi might need the warmth, so he went to the inner room to find him a blanket. Chu Wanning yawned and climbed onto a wooden bench holding the clay jar, and he was about to take out two bowls for the soup when his gaze landed on the meatbuns that Shi Mei hadn't finished. He blinked, silent.

Hopping off the bench, Chu Wanning walked over to the bedroom and looked expressionlessly at that beautiful person lying on the bed inside. He neither grew angry nor said a word, but icy tendrils seeped out of his bones, and he felt his heart, so warm only a moment ago, freeze into a solid block of ice.

When Mo Ran returned to the kitchen, Chu Wanning was sitting at the table next to the window as before, with one foot on the bench and the other dangling off, an arm propped casually on the windowsill. When he heard Mo Ran's movement, he turned his head a little and sent a glance at Mo Ran.

"Here, I found a firefox fur blanket. Bundle up, it's cold at night."

Chu Wanning didn't reply.

Mo Ran walked over and handed him the blanket, but Chu Wanning didn't take it. He only shook his head and slowly closed his eyes, as if resting.

"What's wrong? You don't like it?"

Still no reply.

"I'll go see if there's a different one, then," Mo Ran said with a smile as he ruffled Chu Wanning's hair. But when he turned to go look for another blanket, he realized that the clay jar was no longer on the table. He stared in confusion. "Where'd my soup go?"

"Who said it was yours?" Chu Wanning finally spoke, his voice wintry. "It's mine."

The corner of Mo Ran's lips twitched. He figured that the kid was throwing a tantrum. "Okey dokey. Yours, then. Where did your soup go?"

"I threw it away," Chu Wanning said flatly.

"Th-threw...?"

Chu Wanning went back to ignoring him. He hopped lightly off the bench and opened the door to leave.

"Hey—Shidi? Shidi, where are you going?" Mo Ran forgot all about the blanket—the killer was still at large, it wasn't safe out there—and hastily chased after him.

He spied the small clay jar under the peach blossom tree; it hadn't been thrown out after all. Mo Ran let out a breath. This was his own fault to start with. His little shidi had probably been trying to hold in his resentment earlier, but then been unable to hold it in any longer and let it out despite himself. And he had every right to do so.

So Mo Ran walked over and sat down next to Chu Wanning, who had seated himself under the peach blossom tree. Ignoring Mo Ran, Chu Wanning grabbed the little clay jar, opened the lid, took out a ladle bigger than his face, and tried to reach in. But the ladle wouldn't fit, and he threw it aside in a fit of anger. The ladle struck the ground with a crack and broke into pieces, and the boy sat there holding the jar in a daze.

"Just drink right out of it," Mo Ran suggested, his head turned sideways and cheek propped up. "It's just the two of us here anyway. No need to be embarrassed."

Chu Wanning did not deign to respond.

"No? I'm gonna drink it if you don't. It's the first time my shidi has made soup for me—I'm not gonna let it go to waste," Mo Ran teased as he reached for the jar with a grin.

To his surprise, Chu Wanning slapped his hand away. "Get lost."

Dumbstruck, Mo Ran blinked. This exchange left him with a bit of deja vu. Then he scooted back over with a grin on his thick face. "Shidi, I was wrong. Please don't be mad anymore. I was gonna go pick you up hours ago, but your Mingjing-shixiong suddenly fell ill so I was delayed. I didn't mean to leave you waiting."

Chu Wanning kept his head down and said nothing.

"No, really, I was so busy the whole time, and I haven't eaten yet. I'm starving." Mo Ran tugged on his sleeve pitifully. "Shidi, my kind shidi, my good shidi, please, may Shixiong have some soup?"

Chu Wanning continued to say nothing, but he eventually moved to place the jar of soup on the ground. He lifted his head a little and tilted it to the side a bit before turning away again, meaning for Mo Ran to help himself, if he wanted.

Mo Ran grinned. "Thanks, Shidi."

The little clay jar was stuffed full. A single glance and Mo Ran could tell that his shidi hadn't eaten much, leaving him the majority of the meat. It was actually mostly meat with a little bit of soup.

Mo Ran stared for a bit, eyes lit with amusement. "Are you sure this is soup?" he teased gently. "Looks more like chicken stew to me. Shidi is so generous."

Still no response.

Mo Ran stopped chattering then; after spending half the day taking care of Shi Mei, he really was starving. Besides, his shidi had worked so hard to make the soup, he couldn't possibly let the kid's good intentions go to waste. He broke off two small branches from the peach tree, smoothing them into a pair of chopsticks with a flare of spiritual energy from his fingertips, and got right down to stuffing a piece of chicken in his mouth.

"Whoa, delicious!" Mo Ran said around a mouthful of steamy chicken. "It's really good. My shidi is so capable."

In truth, it wasn't that good, and it was a bit salty too, but Mo Ran still dug in heartily to make his little shidi happy, plowing through most of the chicken in short order. The entire time, Chu Wanning sat there quietly without looking at him.

Mo Ran gulped down a big mouthful of soup—it was even saltier than the meat, so much so that it was practically bitter, but it was still bearable. He scooped up another drumstick and was about to shove it in his mouth when he froze.

"How many legs does a chicken have?" Of course there was no reply, so he answered himself: "Two."

Mo Ran looked at the drumstick held between his chopsticks, then looked at the bone from the other drumstick that he had eaten. After a long moment of silence, the idiot finally lifted his head, dazed, and asked Chu Wanning, "Shidi, were you..." He didn't have the courage to say the rest.

Were you waiting for me this whole time, and so haven't even eaten yet?

The jar of soup is all meat. Is it because you waited for me for so long that all the soup boiled off and there was only meat left, so that's all that was left to put in the jar? Only to have me think...

Only to have me think that you'd already eaten...and just left some for me... That you'd cooked it wrong and turned chicken soup into chicken stew...

Mo Ran put the clay jar down wordlessly. He had realized too late; there was hardly any meat left.

Chu Wanning finally spoke. His voice was still calm and even, with a bit of youthfulness. "You said you would be back for dinner. So I waited," he said slowly, tonelessly. "If you don't want it anymore, then at least send word so I'm not waiting like an idiot. Okay?"

"Shidi..."

Chu Wanning was still facing away, refusing to look at him. Mo Ran couldn't see his expression.

"Have someone pass me a message that you're going to go keep Shi...that you're going to go keep Mingjing-shixiong company instead. Would it have been that hard?"

Mo Ran could not reply.

"You took my jar and rambled so much before eating, but you didn't even ask if I'd eaten yet. Would that have been so hard?"

Mo Ran *had* no reply.

"Would it have been so hard to check and see how many drumsticks were in the jar first?"

That last one sounded a little funny. Even through all his remorse, Mo Ran could only smile, but his dimples froze before they had even formed.

His little shidi was crying.

Chu Wanning never would have cried over such a minor thing in his adult form. No one had realized that, although being turned into a child by the willow sap hadn't affected his mind that much, there had been some impact after all—his temperament became more childish whenever he was tired or overexerted himself. This hidden property of the sap was extremely difficult to detect, so neither Madam Wang nor the Tanlang Elder had noticed it when taking his pulse.

"I also feel hunger and sadness, I'm human too..." Even with that younger mentality in the foreground of his mind, Chu Wanning still clung to his self-restraint, fighting back sobs without a sound. But his shoulders shook uncontrollably as tears welled and fell from his reddened eyes.

All those years, the Yuheng Elder had always endured silently. No one liked him, no one kept him company, and he always feigned nonchalance as he walked through the reverent crowd, lofty and composed. Only with his mind tinged by childish thoughts could he break down and speak the truth, let out the misery that had built up within him for so long.

It wasn't that he didn't care for those around him, only that he did it quietly. Such quietude, day after day, without anyone to see or notice, was also a kind of torment.

As Mo Ran watched the minute shivering of his little shidi's shoulders, his heart clenched, and he reached out to soothe him. His hand was slapped away before it made contact. "Shidi..."

"Don't touch me." Chu Wanning always put up a strong front, regardless of his age. He firmly wiped away his tears and stood. "I'm going to bed. You can go keep your shidi company. Just stay away from me."

There was an awkward moment of silence. In Chu Wanning's indignation, he had forgotten that Shi Mei was older than Mo Ran.

Mo Ran opened his mouth to say something, but Chu Wanning had left. He disappeared into the other bedroom and the door slammed shut with a loud bang.

There were only two bedrooms in the courtyard of Campsis Pavilion. Mo Ran had been planning to let Shi Mei sleep in one while he squeezed into the other with his little shidi, but it looked like his shidi's room was out of the question, given how he was so mad he'd even locked the door.

Mo Ran didn't want to climb into bed with Shi Mei either. Not to mention, having been scolded by his little shidi, and even made him cry, Mo Ran's head was a complete mess. He wasn't in any mood to think about any kind of flirting. So he simply sat there in the courtyard in a daze, surrounded by peach blossoms in full bloom, holding the clay jar that his little shidi had brought him all the way from the cave. A long while later, he sighed and slapped himself across the face, cursing in a low voice. "You good-for-nothing."

And so Mo Ran spent the night with the earth as his bed and the sky as his blanket, lying on the ground covered in fallen peach blossom petals, staring blankly at the sky.

His little shidi... Shi Mei... Shizun... Xue Meng... The fake Gouchen from Jincheng Lake, the unknown killer... Chu Xun and his son in the illusion...

A series of hazy figures flashed through Mo Ran's mind. He vaguely felt like something was off, but the feeling was so faint that it disappeared before he really noticed.

Peach blossoms bloomed splendidly, their petals drifting gently down. Mo Ran caught a fallen blossom in his hand, holding the perished flower up against the moonlight.

He recalled the final moments of his previous life, when he had laid himself down in the coffin he had prepared ahead of time. That day, the sky had also been adrift with fallen blossoms, soundless and fragrant. Only the blossoms back then had been from a haitang tree.

Haitang...

The person he liked, in this life and the last, was Shi Mei. But for some reason, moments before death, he had chosen to bury himself under the haitang tree in front of the Heaven-Piercing Tower, where he had first met Chu Wanning.

Many of the things Mo Ran had done in his past life now frightened him to think about. The more time passed since his rebirth, the less he understood why he had been so cruel. Slaughtering entire cities, oppressing the weak, killing his master... Even forcing Chu Wanning to do things like that with him...

Mo Ran tossed the peach blossom away and laid his hand across his forehead, then slowly closed his eyes. The words his little shidi had said earlier, "I also feel hunger and sadness, I'm human too," circled in his mind. The one who had said it had been his little shidi, but for an instant, Mo Ran saw the silhouette of another person.

A person dressed in snow-white robes.

Then he blinked and the white robes became red wedding robes that dragged on the ground. It was just the way they had looked on that man during the cermony in the ghost mistress's illusion.

"I'm human too..."

I also feel sorrow and pain. Mo Ran... I also feel pain.

A suffocating pressure suddenly filled Mo Ran's heart, as if something was trying to burst out. A sheen of cold sweat covered his forehead. He squeezed his eyes shut, drawing labored breaths, and murmured, "I'm sorry..."

He didn't know to whom he was apologizing—to his little shidi, or to that person in wedding robes...

Inside his bedroom, Shi Mei sat up.

Padding quietly over to the window without turning on the light, he looked through the gap in the shutters. He gazed from afar at Mo Ran, lying amongst the fallen petals with an arm wrapped around that clay jar, his own eyes dark and his thoughts unknowable.

Early the next morning, Mo Ran wrinkled his nose where he lay in the flowers and grass, inhaled a deep breath of the fresh air, and stretched lazily before getting up.

He only got halfway through the stretch when a shriek shattered the peace at Campsis Pavilion.

"Aaaah!"

Mo Ran's eyes flew open as he rolled to his feet. The sight before him made his blood run cold, and all he could do was stare in shock.

Each and every one of the fifteen feathered tribe elites assigned to guard Campsis Pavilion had been murdered overnight, and in the exact same manner as Eighteen: a willow vine glowing brightly scarlet was wrapped around each of their necks—Jiangui!

All of them dangled amidst the grove of peach trees in full bloom, their crimson sleeves drifting in the breeze and long skirts reaching to the ground. Their bodies swayed in time with the wind like so many preserved flowers, eerie yet uncannily beautiful.

The one who had screamed was a low-ranking member of the feathered tribe who had come to deliver breakfast. She trembled in fright, the bamboo basket she'd held now lying on the ground, congee and pastries spilled everywhere.

She trembled even more violently upon seeing Mo Ran standing in the courtyard and reached behind her for something.

Mo Ran stepped forward without thinking. "No wait, it's not what—"

It was too late. She had activated the Seal of Imminent Crisis tattooed on her lower back. The seal functioned as an urgent summons to the feathered tribe, and in an instant, the people of the feathered tribe across Peach Blossom Springs sprouted fiery wings and descended upon Campsis Pavilion.

They were stunned by the sight that greeted them.

"A-Jie!"

"Jie—!"

After the initial shocked silence, they erupted in screams and wails. The commotion drew cultivators as well. In an instant, shock and suspicion, anger and grief surrounded Campsis Pavilion.

"Mo Ran! What defense could you possibly have at this point?!"

"Murderer! Lunatic!"

The gathered people of the feathered tribe were beyond furious as they screamed and cried. "He has to pay with his life! Kill him! *Kill him!*"

It would have been a struggle for Mo Ran to defend himself even if he had a hundred mouths to argue, and he only had the one. "If I really was the killer, and I could kill all of them this easily, then why would I stay? To wait to get caught?"

"You shut up!" spat a feathered tribe member with flame-red hair and a tear-stained face. "Y-you've already gone this far, and you still, you still dare to..."

"If you're not the killer, then why was everyone but you killed?" someone else snarled.

"That's right!"

"Deceitful and treacherous!"

"Even if you aren't the killer, he's absolutely related to you! Why else would he not kill you?! Huh?!"

"Blood for blood!"

Mo Ran was so mad that he wanted to laugh. He had slaughtered with wanton abandon in his past life and hardly anyone had ever dared to say something like "blood for blood" to him. Yet now, when he wasn't actually the killer, he was being accused to the high heavens. This world was truly... He closed his eyes for a moment and was about to say something when a crimson light shot through the sky.

The Elder Immortal of the feathered tribe descended lightly from a cloud and coldly scanned her surroundings, her expression exceedingly dark. "Mo Weiyu."

"Elder Immortal."

The Elder Immortal stared him down for a while, then walked over to one of the corpses and lifted the bloodstained willow vine wrapped around its neck. "Where is your weapon? Take it out and show me."

Mo Ran was silent.

"Are you refusing?"

Mo Ran let out a sigh. His weapon was Jiangui. A large number of people had already seen it during training, and a bunch more had seen it at the site of Eighteen's murder. If he were to take it out now, it would be compared with the willow vines around the necks of the murdered guards, and doubtless it would be used to implicate him. But if he refused, it would look like he had a guilty conscience.

A scarlet blaze appeared with a whoosh in his palm as Jiangui took form, coursing with a fiery, crackling flare. "Feel free to look, Elder Immortal."

75 This Venerable One Is Illiterate, Deal With It

THE GATHERED CROWD gawked at Jiangui, then looked at the blazing red willow vines wrapped around the necks of the murdered and grew even more agitated.

"You did it! Just like when you killed Eighteen!"

"How could you be so cruel?"

"Kill him!"

The clamor hurt the Elder Immortal's head. With a hand pressed against her temples, she said coldly, "Mo Weiyu, I will ask you one last time: Did you or did you not kill them?"

"I did not."

"Very well." The Elder Immortal nodded.

Mo Ran let out a breath, thinking she was going to let him go. He was about to express his gratitude for her wisdom and righteousness when she lifted a hand in a gesture of indifference.

"This person has committed myriad transgressions and refuses to admit to his crimes," she said in an icy tone. "Seize him."

When Shi Mei came outside after washing up and getting dressed, he saw Mo Ran being restrained with magic by over a dozen high-level members of the feathered tribe while another tied his wrists with immortal-binding rope.

"What are you doing?!" All color drained out of Shi Mei's face as he hurried to Mo Ran's side. "What happened?"

No one replied, but the corpses swaying eerily between the peach blossoms were answer enough. Shi Mei drew in a sharp breath and took a step back, bumping into Mo Ran's chest. "A-Ran..."

"Don't panic, calm down." Mo Ran kept his eyes on the Elder Immortal while whispering to Shi Mei. "Go get Uncle and the Xuanji Elder."

With the situation being what it was, the feathered tribe might not be open to reason. If they decided to rip him apart no matter what he said, he had zero chance of winning, not with his current abilities. He needed Xue Zhengyong and Xuanji to step in as soon as possible.

Shi Mei left, and Mo Ran stood alone against those faces twisted by rage, his gaze steady as he glanced them over one by one.

"Puh!"

A gob of phlegm flew out of the crowd toward him. Mo Ran moved to dodge, but the feathered folk who had spit was too close, and it caught him anyway. He turned around slowly and came face-to-face with a pair of scarlet eyes.

"You killed so many people and you dare to call for help? I'm going to put you down right now!"

With that, a fiery blaze gathered in the feathered tribe folk's palm and hurtled directly toward Mo Ran.

Mo Ran stepped back and to the side. The scorching fire singed his bangs as it shot past and crashed into the peach tree behind him, snapping the sturdy trunk in half.

Thud. The peach tree fell over, flowers scattering across the ground like snow in the wind.

Mo Ran looked at the tree on the ground, then turned to the attacker. "I already said: I didn't kill them. The purity pills will be ready in ten days. If you want revenge, you could at least wait till then."

"Ten days? You'll have murdered everyone here by then!" his attacker roared furiously and lunged at Mo Ran. "Give me back my zizi!"

Mo Ran dodged the attack once again, and his eyes landed on the Elder Immortal looking on from the side. She had no intention whatsoever of stopping this. Mo Ran felt a flare of rage and raised his voice in a bellow, "Hey! You old bird! Get a grip on your people!"

No response.

"Fucker." Mo Ran cursed under his breath when she still refused to budge. "Pretending to be deaf-mute at this juncture. You wanna watch me get burned to death or something? If I'd known you shitty birds couldn't even tell right from wrong, I wouldn't have come to this shithole to start with! Who wants to get incriminated like this for no reason?!"

The Elder Immortal's expression twitched slightly, and there was a fierce thwap as she lifted her sleeve in a sweeping flourish—that landed right on Mo Ran's face.

The feathered tribe looked like humans, but their way of thinking was quite alien. In the cultivation world, not even the head of a small martial hall—much less the leader of an entire tribe—would jump to conclusions without definitive proof. But in the end, the feathered tribe was half-beast, and their blood ran thick with their bestial nature.

The color of the Elder Immortal's hair changed from black to bright scarlet, and what looked like steam rolled from every strand. Her eyes opened wide in a glare as she said darkly, "Who is your master? Who taught such an uncouth disciple?! Watch your mouth!"

At her words, the rest of the feathered tribe began to shriek, one after another, and closed in on Mo Ran with murder written in their crimson eyes.

Whoosh!

An arrow of flame pierced through the sky, flying directly toward Mo Ran's heart.

Mo Ran dared not dismiss the threat, and sparks coursed through Jiangui as he dodged while brandishing the willow vine. The shot was only a feint, and when he turned to block, one of the feathered tribe bereaved rushed his back with sword drawn.

Arrow at the fore, sword at the rear—there was no way out. These half-beasts meant to kill him right here. Mo Ran steeled himself, called to mind how Chu Wanning had wielded Tianwen before, and raised his hand with a flick of his wrist.

Jiangui was flung into the air then abruptly pulled taut, the bloodred willow vine whirling into a blur and creating a massive vortex. The leaves on the vine instantly turned knife sharp as the maelstrom pulled in everything in his vicinity, even the air itself, and shredded it all to pieces.

It was one of Chu Wanning's ultimate techniques: "Wind!"

With his vine as the eye of the storm, everything surrounding Mo Ran was pulled in by powerful spiritual energy—swallowed by the vortex, ground into dust, and swept away by the wind until nothing remained.

"Ahhh!" The attacker screamed. Her arrow had been pulverized by Jiangui, and her longsword was lost in the storm as well, too close to rescue.

Clang!

There came the sharp sound of metal breaking, and before anyone could react, she had also been pulled to the edge of the bloodred storm as she shrieked, “Let me go! You lunatic! You fucking lunatic!”

The Elder Immortal was infuriated by the sight of her own people endangered. Her red robes fluttered as she rose into the air. A brilliantly red crystal of high purity appeared in her hand, and her sleeves billowed as she channeled spiritual energy into it. A frenzied gale roared to life, sweeping clouds along and flattening grass and trees alike.

The image of a fire phoenix blazed into being behind her. Her eyes were a deep, unsettling red, and that originally beautiful face twisted. “Bastard,” she hissed. “Still not standing down?”

“You’ve called out your phoenix. If I stopped now, wouldn’t that just be asking for death?” As Mo Ran spoke, the phoenix cast a massive shadow over him, its fiery reflection dancing across his face. “You stop first, then I will!”

“You—”

The Elder Immortal rose even higher into the air.

“Have—”

Her bloodred eyes stared Mo Ran down as she spit out each syllable.

“No right—to make demands—of me!”

An explosive sound came from above, then the phoenix dove toward Mo Ran with a screech.

Bang!

Another deafening sound, louder than the last, like the awakening of an ancient dragon from its thousand years of slumber as it smashed through stone and earth to burst forth from the depths of the ground.

The phoenix was met by a golden light, and the force of the impact sent shock waves through the air. The weaker members of the feathered tribe shrieked as the gales bashed into them. Some even spat blood as they were thrown dozens of feet away.

The tempest swept through Campsis Pavilion, instantly obliterating trees and buildings until they were leveled to the ground.

When the dust settled, a slender, familiar figure was in the air in front of Mo Ran, shielding him.

"Sh-Shizun...?!"

Robes white as snow, sleeves billowing in the wind. When he heard Mo Ran's call, his face turned slightly, his expression as cool and composed as ever, and his phoenix eyes swept over Mo Ran where he knelt on the ground. Chu Wanning's voice was cold and deep, like clear water from the well on a hot summer's day. "Are you injured?"

Mo Ran was too stunned to react. His eyes were wide, and his mouth opened in shock as he gaped wordlessly.

Chu Wanning looked him up and down and detected no obvious injuries, so he turned back to the Elder Immortal. "Weren't you asking who his master was a moment ago?" He released his terrifyingly potent spiritual energy and slowly descended to the ground, where he said, simply and sharply, with not a single superfluous word, "Chu Wanning of Sisheng Peak. Show me your best move."

"Wh-what?"

Chu Wanning frowned. It looked like these bird people didn't understand etiquette. That was fine by him. He was out of patience. "I said, I am his master." A pause. "And I don't remember giving you permission to hurt my disciple."

The Elder Immortal might have been called an immortal, but this was only on account of her noble bloodline—she was far from an actual immortal. In their exchange moments ago, Chu Wanning had shattered her phoenix and Tianwen had slashed her arm. She wore a sour expression as she held her limb, black blood seeping from between her fingers. "H-how dare you—a mere mortal! Who let you into Peach Blossom Springs?! How did you even get in here?!" She was almost crazed. "You conceited—"

Slash!

Tianwen appeared as summoned and lashed straight across her face, splitting the corner of her lips and spilling blood.

"Yes? Go on," Chu Wanning said with a cold smile as he smoothed down his sleeve, which had fallen slightly askew while he brandished Tianwen. Then he grabbed Mo Ran by the collar and dragged him upright with one hand, eyes never once leaving the Elder Immortal. "You were saying? I'm a conceited what?"

"H-h-how dare you, you—"

"Why wouldn't I dare?" Chu Wanning gazed at her, unimpressed. "What ought I be afraid of?" He paused, then pulled Mo Ran closer. "Listen up: This person is mine. I'm taking him."

Mo Ran hadn't even recovered from his shock at Chu Wanning's sudden god-like descent before he was smashed into smithereens by the words, "This person is mine."

"Sh...Shizun..."

"Shut your trap." Chu Wanning's face was as impassive as ever, but Mo Ran could clearly see the anger simmering in his eyes. "All you ever do is bring me trouble. Can't do anything right."

This scold was punctuated by a slap to the back of his head. Then Chu Wanning took off into the air with Mo Ran in tow, and he was dozens of feet away in a single leap. By the time Mo Ran realized what was happening, they were at the barren outskirts of Peach Blossom Springs.

"Shizun! My shidi is still back there—"

Chu Wanning glanced at him and let out a cold hmph at the panic on his face. "Shidi? The one named Xia?"

"Yes, he's still at Campsis Pavilion. I have to go save him—"

Chu Wanning lifted a hand to interrupt. "I already sent him to Xuanji with a spell. There's no need to worry."

Mo Ran finally let out the breath he was holding and lifted his eyes to look at Chu Wanning. "Shizun, why...are you here?"

Chu Wanning had been woken by the commotion outside his room, and when he saw that the situation was dire, he'd quickly taken one of Tanlang's pills to temporarily regain his adult form. He couldn't explain that to Mo Ran right now, so he only said, icy as ever, "Why can't I be here?" Then he lifted a hand and manifested a golden haitang on the tip of his finger.

"Withered blooms outside the wistful tower / Night and spring breeze down the Qiantang River." Chu Wanning lowered his lashes and blew gently on the flower bud, which instantly bloomed with a flourish of resplendent light. He flicked his slender fingertip and gave it a quiet command: "Seek."

The haitang flower drifted away with the wind and disappeared into the forest.

"Shizun, what spell was that?" Mo Ran asked curiously.

"Flower Toss."

"Huh?"

"Flower Toss." Chu Wanning's expression was totally serious, without the slightest hint of humor. "It didn't have a name, but since you asked, I've given it one."

Mo Ran's mouth hung open. This guy could not possibly be this lazy.

"The sect leader already told me what happened." Chu Wanning gazed in the direction where the haitang had gone, voice deep and cold as always, like jade in the flow of a stream. "The person responsible for these events is likely also responsible for the incident at

Jincheng Lake. I'm afraid that the Zhenlong Chess Formation has been performed here at Peach Blossom Springs as well."

Mo Ran was startled. "How could that be?"

He'd excelled at the Zhenlong Chess Formation in his previous lifetime, and when Eighteen was killed, he had checked for signs of its use. This forbidden technique was always accompanied by the stench of blood—once unleashed, murder was inevitable. So, one only had to look for intense yet seemingly unfounded resentful energy to determine whether the Zhenlong Chess Formation had been deployed in the vicinity. If this mysterious person had indeed used that forbidden technique again, he would have had to pull it off perfectly. Otherwise, Mo Ran would have been able to detect it.

There was a tinge of suspicion in the look Chu Wanning threw him, and Mo Ran hurried to explain himself. "I mean...they're all half-immortal at Peach Blossom Springs. How could they miss a forbidden technique being used here?"

Chu Wanning shook his head. "This person had already proved themselves capable of controlling the ancient spirit beasts of Jincheng Lake. Although spirit beasts can't hope to compare to holy beasts in terms of strength, they are equipollent to demi-immortals. As he was able to control Jincheng Lake, he is very likely doing the same at Peach Blossom Springs right now."

"I see..."

"Mn."

Mo Ran lifted his head, the bashful grin on his face framed with dimples. "Shizun, what does equipollent mean?"

Chu Wanning gave him a look.

76 This Venerable One Meets That Guy Again

Chu Wanning had never been the kindly teacher type, and neither was Mo Ran a five-year-old at his first lesson. A hammy question like this didn't warrant a response, so Chu Wanning, lashes lowered, ignored it.

The haitang flower that he had sent off with a speed-boosting wind spell quickly scouted the entirety of Peach Blossom Springs. Mere moments later, a golden amulet drifted down from the sky into his hand.

"The Ancestral Abyss?"

They went to the Ancestral Abyss every day to pluck feathers from the frenzied owls that roosted there. The feathered tribe said that the bottom of the abyss was filled with roaring flames, and that anyone who slipped and fell there—other than the demon owls, who had lived there since ancient times—would be melted into nothingness.

Chu Wanning cast a concealment barrier on himself and Mo Ran to avoid detection by the feathered tribe. When they arrived at the Ancestral Abyss, they looked down. There was an eerie red light and no bottom to be seen, but thousands of owls were perched along the walls of the steep cliffs. The birds were asleep, their heads tucked into their wings, and they were packed so densely that from this distance, they looked like countless dots on the cliffside.

According to Chu Wanning's hypothesis, if the Zhenlong Chess Formation had indeed been cast within the abyss, then all this talk of "fierce flames" and "being burned until not even ashes remained" was likely a fabrication.

"How can we be sure that the fire down there isn't actually dangerous?" Mo Ran stared at the uncanny light below as he murmured. "Looks real enough to me."

"Throw something in first."

"I'll go grab a rabbit."

"No need." Chu Wanning leapt up with a flutter of his pristine robes and disappeared into the forest of peach trees nearby. A moment later, he fluttered back like an immortal exiled from the ninth heaven, a branch of peach blossoms in hand.

Mo Ran understood. Peach blossoms were even more fragile than rabbits, so if the peach blossoms could handle the supposed "fierce flames," then there could be no doubt that the fire posed no danger to people.

Chu Wanning ran a finger lightly down the branch as he mouthed a spell, covering it with a soft layer of translucent blue light. He pointed toward the abyss and said, "Go on."

The peach blossom floated gently down. One foot, two feet, ten feet, a hundred.

Though the branch was too far away to see, the spell Chu Wanning had cast allowed him to sense the condition of the flowers. He waited with eyes closed for a good while before opening them. "The flowers are fine. Let's go."

If Chu Wanning was certain, there was no need to say anything else. Mo Ran leapt into the Ancestral Abyss alongside him. Both of them were proficient in martial arts, and they nimbly arrived at the bottom with ease.

When Mo Ran laid eyes on the scene below, a shiver ran down his spine even though he had mentally prepared himself.

He now knew the nature of the eerie red light.

Thousands of crosses stood at the bottom of the abyss. To every one was bound a member of the feathered tribe, entirely naked and drenched in blood. Within each of their mouths was stuffed a lingchi[19] fruit, and these were what emitted that piercing red light. From above, the collective blaze of these thousands of fruits had easily been mistaken for flames burning deep within the abyss.

Chu Wanning's face was terrible. Well-learned as he was, he recognized this red fruit as a forbidden object—the very mention of it would make any person in the cultivation world pale.

Placing this fruit into the mouth of a person on the verge of death extended their last moment into three hundred and sixty-five days. In other words, the victim would be denied release and instead be forced to suffer an excruciatingly slow death. The instant cessation of their heart would be stretched into an unending torment, thus the name: "lingchi."

As Mo Ran stared at the throngs of feathered tribe folk living in death, dense as a forest, he murmured: "Soul-Locking Array."

If an individual were to use still-living humans as pillars in this array, they could confine resentful energy within their victims and thereby prevent that energy from leaking out. They could even conceal the energy of thousands of souls trapped within a Zhenlong Chess Formation. No wonder Mo Ran hadn't sensed the slightest bit of resentful energy, which would have indicated the presence of the technique.

---

19 凌迟, *lingchi, also known as "slow slicing" or "death by a thousand cuts" is a form of punishment in which pieces of a person are sliced away until they die.*

Mo Ran could only shudder. Was the fake Gouchen from Jincheng Lake truly the person who had orchestrated the events at Peach Blossom Springs?

Everything they'd seen at Jincheng Lake had seemed like the work of someone who only knew the fundamental basics of the Zhenlong Chess Formation—just enough to control the creatures of the lake. This time, while the feathered tribe of Peach Blossom Springs had been a bit dumb and emotionally stunted, they had been nigh indiscernibly different from their original selves. They had even been capable of using the unique magic of the feathered tribe. It was clear that the perpetrator's grasp of the forbidden technique was now at least comfortably adept. Could the fake Gouchen truly have become this proficient so quickly?

Chu Wanning walked into the center of the Soul-Locking Array, where stood a crystal pillar.

A member of the feathered tribe was bound to this pillar as well, only she was dead. The lingchi fruit in her mouth had long since withered, and her body was in the beginning stages of decomposition. However, her identity was made clear by the yellow robes she wore, which were embroidered in golden thread with a phoenix, as well as by the star-shaped mark between her brows.

"This is..."

Mo Ran startled. "That's the real Elder Immortal!"

"Correct." Chu Wanning looked at the forest of human pillars, stretching out as far as the eye could see. "So many of the feathered tribe were captured to use in the Soul-Locking Array," he said quietly. "At least eight hundred, if not a thousand. The Elder Immortal certainly wouldn't have tolerated this were she still alive. I thought it was odd earlier, when I exchanged blows with her outside the pavilion, that she didn't even seem to be as strong as the ghost mistress of

Butterfly Town. If I'm not wrong...it seems that the feathered tribe of Peach Blossom Springs has been exterminated, and all those we met were merely walking corpses under the control of Zhenlong Chess Formation."

Mo Ran stared in shock. Sure enough, Chu Wanning had come to the same conclusion that he had. As soon as Mo Ran recovered from his shock, he turned to leave, but Chu Wanning blocked his path with a wave of his sleeve.

"Where are you going?" Chu Wanning asked.

"I have to go tell Uncle and the others. If this is the case, then this place is terribly dangerous."

"Don't be too hasty." Chu Wanning shook his head. "Right now, we're out in the open, but the enemy is hidden in the shadows. There are many cultivators at Peach Blossom Springs, and we don't know who's pulling the strings. Acting rashly might make things worse."

"Heh heh. Long time no see. Chu-zongshi is still so cautious."

A small giggle came from above them, but the effect of the sound was no different from that of thunder striking the depths of the Ancestral Abyss. Their heads snapped up as blood drained from their faces, only to see a mangled child of the feathered tribe sitting on a branch sticking out from the cliffside, kicking his legs. The dead child tilted his head, a pair of eyeballs soaked in bloody tears rolling around in their sockets, and grinned brightly at them.

"Zhenlong Chess Formation!" Mo Ran said, startled.

Chu Wanning cursed under his breath. "Another white chess piece."

"Eh heh heh, that's right, another white chess piece." The child clapped gleefully. Terrifyingly. "What, did you think I would come here personally? I'm not dumb."

"So you are that fake Gouchen from Jincheng Lake!" Mo Ran said. "What do you want, you madman?"

"Heh heh, who do you think you are? Some no-name sproutling still stumbling over foundations—you aren't fit to speak to me. Tell your master to do the asking himself."

"You—"

Chu Wanning's slender fingers emerged from his wide sleeve with a sweep to hold back Mo Ran, who was so pissed that smoke practically rose from his head. With a lift of his eyelashes, Chu Wanning looked up and asked coldly, "What are you trying to accomplish?"

The child continued to kick his legs. He was noticeably already dead, but under the control of the forbidden technique, he moved nonstop, making all kinds of gestures like a puppet on a string. "Oh, nothing much, really."

Chu Wanning's voice dropped several degrees in temperature. "Then why do you keep coming after my disciple?"

"I'm not planning anything too important. I just so happen to need your little disciple's spiritual core to do it," the child said, beaming. "He has only himself to blame for having such a fine core. It's even better than yours, and by far. I noticed back at Jincheng Lake that he's a superb spiritual essence of wood. If not for that, I might have been more interested in you, Chu-zongshi."

Mo Ran was about to gag—the child spoke in a young voice, but greasily, and with such an adult tone. "If I'm ever so goddamn unlucky as to get caught by you, I'll immediately self-destruct my fucking core," he snapped. "So don't even think about touching me!"

"It's not like I want to touch you," the child continued in that infuriatingly honey-sweet tone. "I'm only chasing you around because I have to. All men love beauties, and your shizun is much prettier than you. I'd rather touch him."

"You!" Mo Ran bristled. "Some ugly thing like you, hiding behind white chess pieces all day long, too afraid to show your ugly mug—you think you have any right to touch my shizun?"

The child rolled his eyes at Mo Ran, as if tired of acknowledging his existence. He returned his attention to Chu Wanning. "Chu-zongshi, back at Jincheng Lake, I advised you to leave things alone, but you wouldn't listen. I'm so very hurt, you know."

"Now that this matter has come to my attention, even if you stopped hounding Mo Ran, I would still intend to get to the bottom of things."

"Pfft, I knew you'd say that." The child was quiet for a moment, then grinned again. "Why are you righteous zongshi types all so stubborn?" He paused again. "Fine, since Chu-zongshi won't leave well enough alone, we'll have to wait and see. I wanted to figure out which was stronger anyway: your Tianwen, or my forbidden techniques."

Chu Wanning's brows furrowed. "Must you slaughter so many innocents to further your ends?" he asked darkly.

"The people of the world are like the oranges from Huainan."[20]

"What do you mean?"

"Sour." The child started giggling. "Super sour. All these worthless people are sour. I hate them, I want to crush them—step on them."

Mo Ran was at a loss for words.

Chu Wanning's voice filled with killing intent. "You truly are irredeemable."

"Zongshi deems me irredeemable, but I think Zongshi is just as incurable. Our justice differs at the root. Why sweat the small stuff?" The child tilted his head to and fro. "Just think of our little spat as a game of chess. You won the match at Jincheng Lake. As for this

---

20 *Huainan is a famously unsuitable place to grow oranges.*

one here at Peach Blossom Springs, since Zongshi has found the Ancestral Abyss and seen my white chess piece—and I've run out of tricks by which to acquire your little disciple—let's just say you won this one too."

He paused, then his eyes crinkled with a smile. In so doing, he squeezed more blood from them. "You better watch out. You may have protected him this time, but I wonder if you can protect him his whole life?"

Chu Wanning did not reply.

"As for the secret down here, I suggest you keep it to yourselves," the child said, holding a red and gold feather between his fingers.

"Is that one of the golden feathers used as currency here?" Mo Ran asked, alarmed.

"That's right." The child smiled. "These feathers have circulated everywhere by this point. If the two of you keep quiet and leave of your own volition, then nothing will happen. But if you don't behave and try to expose me... These feathers are imbued with the resentful energy of the feathered tribe. They won't kill those cultivators, but they would dissipate the better part of their cultivation."

"You planned this from the start?!" Mo Ran said with anger in his voice.

"Well, of course," the child said, incredulous. "Do you think everyone is a dumb brute like you?"

Mo Ran fell silent.

He was so! Pissed! Off! He was willing to admit that he was rather straightforward about the way he did things, and that he didn't know much about schemes and strategies. However, being so overtly called out by this little bastard made him really want to summon Jiangui and give him what for—to teach him what it meant to be a real dumb brute.

"Chu-zongshi, I'm sure you know what's best for everyone involved. Even if the others learned the truth, if their cultivation were greatly damaged, I'm afraid they wouldn't thank you for your integrity."

"As I'm sure you heard earlier, when you were eavesdropping, I wasn't planning to alarm them to begin with," Chu Wanning said coldly. "For the time being."

"For the time being? Ha ha, so Zongshi was planning to tell them later, then. Although there'd be no point in doing that either." The child beamed. "Once these people leave, I'll destroy Peach Blossom Springs, just like I did Jincheng Lake. Good luck getting anyone to believe you with no evidence."

Chu Wanning's gaze was icy. "I'm impressed that you have the nerve to call Mo Ran a dumb brute when you conduct yourself thus."

Chu Wanning's derision washed right over the child. He got up and twirled in place a couple times, at which point a flame flared to life at his feet and slowly burned through his flesh and bones. "Why don't you save that for when you catch me? Chu-zongshi, out of respect for your character, I'll remind you one last time: stay out of this. If you still refuse to listen, then we...will certainly meet again..."

The flames exploded and roared into the sky.

The feathered tribe child who had been used as a puppet was burned into nothingness. A translucent white chess piece fell from the sky, spun a couple times on the ground, and stilled.

For a while, there was nothing but silence.

Mo Ran knew the perpetrator wasn't spouting empty threats, but he also didn't want to take this sitting down. So at length, he asked, "Shizun, are we really going to leave like this? Do you have any other ideas?"

"Best not take any chances for now. Let's depart Peach Blossom Springs first." Chu Wanning's expression was dark as well. "If he went to the trouble of erecting a Soul-Locking Array to prevent anyone from noticing his use of the Zhenlong Chess Formation, he still wants to keep things under wraps—at least for now. I will send word to the sect leader to take Xue Meng and Shi Mei and leave as soon as possible, without alarming the enemy. As for you…"

Chu Wanning paused. "Both times, he was after you. This time around, he planned to frame you with the hopes of isolating you from help. There's no need for you to do anything further with regard to this matter; the sect leader will step in and take care of it."

"What should I do, then?" Mo Ran asked. "It wouldn't be right to make others take care of my mess while I sit on my hands and do nothing."

"What are you trying to prove at this juncture? It's obvious what that man is after. The tree spirit at Jincheng Lake fell, so he's looking for a replacement. You are a spiritual essence of wood, suitable for his purposes, but if he can't get to you, then he'll go for the next best thing and look for some other substitute." Chu Wanning paused again. "And once he finds that something, it will be another massacre. He must be stopped."

"That's not wrong, but Shizun, it's not like spiritual essences are all that easy to find. If he wants to find a substitute, he'll have to…" Mo Ran suddenly stopped talking and lifted his head. He stared at Chu Wanning for a while. "If that little bastard wants to find other spiritual essences, he'll have to check sect by sect. Even so, cultivators don't expose their spiritual roots for any old reason. They only do so when choosing a new weapon or a refinement crystal, in order to check their compatibility. So the simplest way to test for a spiritual essence would be to sell weapons and spiritual stones. Which means, if we keep watch on the weapon markets near the sects in the coming days, we'll have a pretty good chance of sniffing the bastard out."

After Mo Ran had said all this, he realized Chu Wanning was looking at him thoughtfully, and he couldn't help but second-guess himself. "Uh...I guess?"

"It's a good guess," Chu Wanning said slowly. A moment later, he got the feeling that Mo Ran was a little too informed, and his eyes narrowed in suspicion. "Mo Ran. Is there something you're not telling me?"

"Wh-what could I possibly have to hide from Shizun?" Mo Ran said, but the hairs on his back stood on end, and he felt as if Chu Wanning's eyes, clear as glass, were staring right through his reborn body and directly at the soul cowering within.

A moment passed in silence, and Chu Wanning thankfully didn't press the subject. Lowering his eyelashes, he said, "Starting now, you will come with me to covertly investigate the major sects. For the time being, we will not be returning to Sisheng Peak."

77 This Venerable One Feels Very Awkward

CHU WANNING AND MO RAN left Peach Blossom Springs and traveled all over the map, searching for information regarding when markets opened at the various sects. After several days of hasty travel, they finally decided to stay a night at an inn in a small town.

They'd hardly rested since leaving Peach Blossom Springs, so Mo Ran had retired to his own room a while ago. Chu Wanning sat at a table, lit a candle, and contemplated the porcelain bottle in his hand under warm yellow light.

Inside the white jade porcelain bottle were thirty or so golden pills. It was fortunate that the Xuanji Elder had brought this bottle with him when he came. If not for that, Chu Wanning didn't know what identity he would have had to assume with Mo Ran.

"This is new medicine from Tanlang. There's about thirty in there," Xuanji had told Chu Wanning back at the cave. "He did some research in the ancient archives and changed some ingredients, so one pill will allow you to regain your adult form for seven days. Here, these will last you a while."

"Send Tanlang my thanks."

"There's no need for thanks." Xuanji smiled with a wave of his hand. "Tanlang puts on a stern face, but he's very curious about your condition. Oh, right, he also said to let you know that this medicine isn't too stable. Intense emotions might diminish its effectiveness, so be careful about that."

Chu Wanning was caught up thinking through Xuanji's words when he heard a knock at the door. He quickly tucked the porcelain bottle away and extinguished the incense in the burner. "Come in."

Mo Ran had just gotten out of the bath, so he walked into Chu Wanning's room wearing only a thin bathrobe while wiping his long hair, which was dark as black jade.

Chu Wanning cleared his throat, thankful that his face remained neutral before eventually saying, "What is it?"

"My room is no good. I don't like it. Shizun, can I sleep on your floor tonight?"

Mo Ran was being awfully vague, and Chu Wanning wasn't that gullible, so he obviously sensed that something was up. "What don't you like about it?"

"I-it's just...just no good." Mo Ran snuck a glance at Chu Wanning before mumbling, "The sound insulation is terrible."

Chu Wanning furrowed his brows, too noble and chaste by nature to catch his meaning. Without another word, he pulled on his outer robe and walked barefoot to Mo Ran's room. Mo Ran couldn't have stopped him if he tried, and so could only follow after.

"It's a little spare, but not so much as to be intolerable." Chu Wanning stood in the room and looked around, a tinge of chiding in his voice. "When did you get so spoiled?"

Then a series of crashing sounds came from the room next door, like something heavy had fallen to the floor.

Mo Ran couldn't bear to listen to anymore, so before things got even worse, he reached out and tugged the corner of Chu Wanning's sleeve. "Shizun," he pleaded, "let's leave already."

Chu Wanning's brows furrowed. "Really, what's the matter with you? Just what do you find so objectionable?"

Mo Ran opened his mouth, but before he could get his words together, coquettish giggles drifted over through the wall.

"Chang-gongzi is sooo naughty, always bullying me—nnh, n-no, wait...*ah*!"

"Heh heh, babe, this peony on your chest is so pretty. Let me take a whiff, see if it smells nice too."

The walls were so thin that they could hear even the rustling of clothes on the other side. The rough pants of the man and the sweet moans of the woman mingled together into something truly harrowing to the ears.

Incredibly, Chu Wanning didn't understand what was happening at first. It wasn't until a few moments later that he put two and two together, and his pretty eyes flew wide open while the color of his face changed rapidly from white to red to blue, then finally settled on ashen as he cursed, "Shameless!" and stormed out of the room with a sweep of his sleeve.

"Pfft."

Mo Ran failed to hold it in and started chuckling quietly behind him. Luckily, Chu Wanning was so flustered that even his arms were swinging out of sync as he walked stiffly away, so he didn't notice Mo Ran laughing at him.

Only after getting back to his room and downing a whole cup of tea did Chu Wanning finally regain some semblance of composure. He nodded toward Mo Ran. "Such obscene speech is indeed detrimental to one's cultivation. You may stay here tonight."

"Oh." Truth be told, when Chu Wanning had suddenly appeared at Peach Blossom Springs and done everything in his power to protect Mo Ran without doubting him in the slightest, Mo Ran had been beside himself with shock and happiness in equal measure. Now that things had settled down, he couldn't help feeling giddy. At this moment, under the candlelight, his shizun's habitually impassive face somehow seemed a lot cuter. Sitting cross-legged on the floor with his chin propped up, Mo Ran's eyes lit with his smile as he stared at Chu Wanning.

"What are you looking at?"

"I haven't seen Shizun for so long—I just wanna take an extra look." The youth's tone carried his smile, and his gaze was warm and bright. Now that Mo Ran studied him, Chu Wanning...really did look quite like Xia-shidi.

Chu Wanning glared. "Instead of looking at me, go dry your hair. How are you going to sleep with it dripping like that?"

"I forgot the towel in my room." Mo Ran grinned. "Shizun, do it for me?"

Chu Wanning eyed him.

For a period of time, Xue Meng had been injured and unable to lift his arm, and whenever he washed his hair, his shizun had dried it for him. Chu Wanning had always done it very quickly by regulating his spiritual energy to warm the towel and evaporate the water.

Chu Wanning looked at Mo Ran and his perfectly functional limbs, then hmphed coldly. "You're neither sick nor injured. Why would I do it for you?"

Still, he waved him over.

The candle cast warm light on Mo Ran's incomparably handsome face. It had already been almost a year since his rebirth, and he was reaching that age when growth spurts occurred. Without really noticing it, he had gotten quite a bit taller these past few months. At present, when he sat on the bed, he was nearly the same height as Chu Wanning.

This height made it a little difficult for Chu Wanning to wipe his hair, so Mo Ran leaned back on his arms and shifted his body lower. Standing at the side of the bed, Chu Wanning rubbed his long hair dry with an exasperated expression. Mo Ran yawned contentedly, closing his eyes to enjoy this rare moment of peace. Outside the window, a frog croaked now and again.

"Shizun."

"Mn."

"Did you know? The feathered tribe's illusion sent me back to Lin'an two hundred years ago, and I met someone named Chu Xun."

The rubbing didn't even pause. "How would I know that?"

Mo Ran rubbed his nose with a grin. "He looked like you."

A long pause. Then, "There are plenty of similar-looking people out there. Nothing strange about that."

"No, really," Mo Ran said, all serious. "You were practically cast from the same mold. Shizun, do you think he might be your ancestor?"

"It's possible," Chu Wanning replied mildly. "But with something from two hundred years ago, who can say?"

"He had a son who looked like Xia-shidi," Mo Ran continued. "I feel like all this is a bit too much to be coincidence. Shizun, is Xia-shidi perhaps a lost relative of yours?"

"I don't have any relatives."

"That's why I said, 'lost'..." Mo Ran mumbled. He was so close to Chu Wanning that he could detect the light, soothing fragrance of haitang.

It smelled so *good*. Whether in their previous lifetime or this one, Chu Wanning's scent always seemed to soothe him. In his past life, whenever he returned from a bloodbath, he had always needed to bury his face in the crook of his shizun's neck just to breathe again.

Whether he wanted to admit it or not, he was already hopelessly addicted to Chu Wanning's scent. He closed his eyes and slowly relaxed into the familiar peace, mind drifting in the flow of time.

In his last lifetime, he would on occasion return to the empty Wushan Palace after another slaughter, soaked head to toe in rain. He had clearly committed countless sins, but he was nothing more than a drenched stray with no home to speak of.

At such times, he would sit and wrap his arms around Chu Wanning's waist, bury his face against his abdomen, and have his shizun stroke his hair over and over again. It was the only way to calm the madness within.

Those bygone dreams were things of the past—of another life. But with his eyes closed, they seemed like only yesterday.

Chu Wanning noticed that the chatterbox had stopped talking and lowered his lashes to glance down at him. In the dim light of the candle, Mo Ran's face was relaxed, at peace.

Although his face still had a touch of the soft tenderness of youth, his features had matured with striking definition, like a natural handsomeness blooming through haze that still carried the deadly freshness and vitality of the young.

Chu Wanning's hand wavered for a split second, and his heart seemed to beat a little faster. He had no idea what compelled him to say in a soft voice, "Mo Ran."

"Mm..." Mo Ran absentmindedly mumbled a reply. Then, as if exhausted, he leaned closer and pressed his face against Chu Wanning's waist, just like he once had in his past life.

Chu Wanning was struck speechless.

Thump. Thump. Thump.

His heartbeat was rapid in his chest, like war drums on a battlefield. The reverberations made him dizzy.

Chu Wanning pressed his lips together. Not knowing what else to do, he could only continue to wipe Mo Ran's hair, steaming away the last droplets of water.

A long while passed in this fashion, until he set the towel down, brushed aside some stray strands of hair from Mo Ran's forehead in passing, and said in a low voice, "All done. You can go to sleep now."

Mo Ran opened his eyes, black with a tinge of purple and still a bit dazed. After a few moments, they gradually became clearer.

When he finally broke out of his daze and noticed that he had gone so far as to give in to habit and lean into Chu Wanning's waist—and even more unexpectedly, that he hadn't in fact been shoved off—Mo Ran was startled, to say the least. His eyes opened wide in stupefied astonishment, making him look just like a dumb dog.

Chu Wanning had at first still felt a bit uneasy, but he couldn't stop himself from smiling at that look on Mo Ran's face.

As Mo Ran realized that he was actually smiling—however lightly, it was definitely a smile—his eyes became even rounder. He sat up straight, hair a bit of a mess, and suddenly said with utmost seriousness, "Shizun, you have a scent. It smells really nice."

Chu Wanning was once again struck speechless.

Mo Ran paused, then suddenly furrowed his brows, as if trying hard to remember something. When he did manage to remember it, consternation crept into his expression. "Huh, that's strange," he mumbled. "Doesn't...Xia-shidi also smell like that?"

Chu Wanning's expression went instantly rigid. He flung the towel onto Mo Ran's head before he could react and physically tossed him off the bed. "I'm tired now," he said coldly. "Get the hell off and go to sleep."

Mo Ran landed stupidly on his back, caught completely off guard. He lay on the floor in a daze for quite a while before sitting up and rubbing his nose, not mad at all, and obediently got up to make his bed on the floor.

78

This Venerable One's Shizun Has a Nightmare

CHU WANNING AND MO RAN spent the night in the same room. Mo Ran heedlessly fell asleep on the floor in no time. Conversely, Chu Wanning's thoughts were restless and erratic, and he tossed and turned for a long while before he finally dozed off into fitful slumber.

His eyes were closed, and he could hear the howling of wind by his ears.

Chu Wanning opened his eyes to find himself kneeling in the snow.

A dream? Then why did this moment feel so real, as if he had, at some point, actually lived through it?

It was the middle of winter. The sky was dark and gray and heavy with clouds that covered the land and stretched to the distant horizon. The snow had piled up past his ankles, freezing the very ground itself, and even the thick cloak draped across his shoulders couldn't stave off the bite of winter.

Looking down, he saw a sky-blue cloak lined with fur, sewn with intricate patterns in silver thread. It looked somehow familiar, but between one moment and the next, that feeling slipped away.

Chu Wanning tried to get up, unsure of why he was having this manner of harrowing dream. But it was as if his body was not his own; he continued to kneel motionless on the ground. Even when

snow covered his shoulders and specks of ice stuck to his eyelashes, his body still showed no intention of moving.

The quavering voice of an elderly person came from behind him. "Chu-zongshi, it's getting dark. His Imperial Majesty surely won't see you today—let's go back."

The Chu Wanning in the dream didn't turn around even as footsteps approached, crunching through the snow, and an umbrella appeared above him.

Chu Wanning heard himself say, "Thank you, Liu-gong. You're getting on in age, so please head back to the pavilion. I'll be all right here."

"Zongshi..."

The elderly voice seemed to want to continue, but Chu Wanning said, "Go on."

The feeble voice sighed, and heavy steps walked a few paces away. Then they turned back around, and the umbrella reappeared over his head. "This old one will keep Zongshi company."

Chu Wanning felt his eyes close in the dream, and nothing else was said.

It all seemed so strange, this ridiculous dream of his. The words they uttered were absurd, incomprehensible. What was all this "His Imperial Majesty" and "Liu-gong" nonsense? These inner palace phrases had no place in the cultivation world Chu Wanning knew.

He tried to take in the scenery of the dream through the lowered lashes of this body. The place looked like Sisheng Peak, but some things were different.

The structures were more or less the same, but they were much more lavishly decorated. The corridors surrounding the courtyard were draped with pale violet veils dotted with embroidered stars, and bells carved into the shape of pearl-holding dragons dangled from the roofs. Clear, crisp jingles danced faintly through the air whenever a gust of wind blew past.

He was kneeling facing the main hall, in front of which a row of guards were stationed, wearing uniforms that he had never seen before. He wondered which sect they were from.

The sky gradually darkened, and a line of palace maids, their hair done up in a traditional style, filed out from a side door to light the standing lamps on either side of the palace gate with fair, slender hands. Each lamp was as tall as a person, with nine layers each, including forty-nine haitang-shaped lamps hanging from slender copper branches. Candles at the center of the haitangs glowed brightly, their light scattering on the ground like the starry sky from above, and illuminated the front of the palace with a dazzling radiance.

Finished with her task, the head maid shot Chu Wanning a glare. "It's freezing out here tonight," she said, malice in her voice as she smirked coldly. "Who are you putting on that pitiful act for? His Imperial Majesty and the empress are currently delighting in their revelries. You can kneel there for as long as you like; no one will care."

How impudent!

All Chu Wanning's life, no one had ever dared to speak to him like that. He opened his mouth angrily, but although the voice that came out was his own, the words spoken were not. "I do not mean to interrupt his leisure, but I truly have important matters to discuss. Please inform him."

"Who do you think you are? Why should I play messenger for you?" The head maid sneered. "His Majesty and the empress are quite enjoying themselves. Who would dare disturb them? If you really want to see His Majesty, you can stay right there. Maybe he'll spare you a glance in the morning, hmph."

The old servant behind Chu Wanning couldn't take it anymore, and he spoke up in his wavering voice, "Yes, His Majesty favors your mistress, but shouldn't you still consider to whom you speak? Take at least some care with your words."

"To whom I'm speaking? Who here at Sisheng Peak doesn't know that His Majesty hates him more than anyone? What need is there to be respectful toward him?! Bold of a senile old fool to lecture me!" The head maid's eyes were wide with rage as she called, "Guards!"

"What do you mean to do?!" The feeble old man, back hunched from age, stepped forward to shield Chu Wanning behind himself.

"Extinguish the fire basins," the palace maid said coyly as she glared at him.

"Right away!"

The guards immediately went to the basins in the courtyard and put out the fires burning within.

Chu Wanning thought to himself that while the maid had a sharp tongue, she wasn't dumb. With the temperature this painfully cold, she had no need to argue with them or directly do anything. She only had to put out the fire and the courtyard would be as an icy cavern, too cold for even the hardiest individual to tolerate.

The night grew deeper, and music and song drifted without cease from the warmly lit palace.

Chu Wanning was still kneeling. His legs had gone numb long ago.

"Zongshi...go back..." The old servant sounded like he was about to sob. "Please go back—your body can't take this. You know how His Majesty is. If you fall sick, he probably won't even send a physician. You have to take care of yourself."

"This ruined body is hardly worth anything," Chu Wanning said softly. "If I can only stop him from attacking Kunlun Taxue Palace, I'm willing to die."

"Zongshi! Wh-why go to such lengths..."

The Chu Wanning in the dream was already greatly weakened. He coughed a few times, but his eyes were clear and bright. "Everything that he is today, all of it was my fault. I..."

He couldn't finish speaking before he was overtaken by an alarmingly violent coughing fit. Chu Wanning covered his mouth with his sleeve, tasting iron in his throat. When he pulled his hand away, it was covered in blood, crimson against the snow-white world.

"Chu-zongshi!"

"I..."

Chu Wanning still wanted to say something, but black washed over his vision and he collapsed into the snow, unable to hold on any longer.

There was a confused racket by his ear, a sudden chaos. It also seemed very far away, as if separated by layers of fog, oceans apart, and he could barely hear the commotion around him.

Hazily, he heard the old servant yelling in a panic, but he could only catch a few scattered words.

"Your Imperial Majesty! Your Majesty, please... Chu-zongshi, he can't hold on much longer. Please grant him an audience! This old one will gladly die—"

The disturbance grew and spread. Footsteps came from all around, lights turned on.

The melody of instruments and the sweet voices of songstresses came to an abrupt halt. The palace gates seemed to be flung open, and there was a gust of warm, fragrant air from inside. Chu Wanning felt himself being picked up and brought into the warmth of the palace hall. A large hand touched his forehead, then flinched away as if stung.

A low, familiar voice bellowed dangerously: "Why was this venerable one not informed?"

No one answered.

The man was infuriated, and there was a loud crashing sound of something heavy being smashed. He continued to roar, voice booming like thunder inside the hall. "Are you trying to defy me? He is the master of the Red Lotus Pavilion, this venerable one's shizun! And not a single one of you came to notify this venerable one that he was kneeling outside? Why was this venerable one not informed?!"

Someone fell to their knees with a thud, quivering all over. It was the head palace maid who had been flouncing about earlier. "This lowly one deserves death. This lowly one saw that Your Majesty and the empress were in good spirits and dared not disturb you..."

The man paced briskly back and forth a few times, but rather than subsiding, his anger only worsened. His black robes, trimmed with gold, billowed across the floor like a dark cloud before finally stilling, and when he spoke again, his voice was twisted. "His constitution is poor; he can't take the cold. That you made him wait in the snow without informing me, and even...even put out the fire in the courtyard..."

His voice shook with rage, and he drew in a deep breath before continuing. The words he spoke next weren't loud, but his tone carried a murderous aura that chilled those present to the bone.

"You wanted to kill him."

The maid went pale from fright, her head banging repeatedly against the ground until her entire forehead was blue and purple, voice pitching higher through her trembling lips. "No! No! This lowly one wouldn't dare! Your Majesty! Please have mercy, Your Majesty!"

"Take her to the Platform of Sin and Virtue for execution."

"Your Majesty! Your Majesty—"

The shrill voice scratched along the inside of his ears like bloodred nails as the dreamscape began to shake and fall apart amidst her terrified shrieking. The scene scattered and disintegrated like the drift of snowflakes.

"Do you have any idea how much effort it took this venerable one to drag him back from the gates of death? Aside from this venerable one, no one is allowed to harm so much as a hair on his head..."

That hoarse voice was perfectly calm, but that very calmness framed the frightening madness beneath.

Chu Wanning felt that person come closer and stop in front of him. A hand gripped his jaw.

Blearily, he opened his eyes, trying to get a look at him. Under the bright, dazzling lights, he saw a blurry face with strong, pitch-black brows, a straight nose, and eyes dark like the blackest satin, with a faint tinge of purple in the light of the candle.

"Mo Ran...?"

"Shizun!"

Suddenly, a voice called to him in sharp definition.

Chu Wanning's eyes flew open. He was still lying in the room at the inn, it was still dark outside, and a lone candle flickered on the table.

Mo Ran was sitting at the edge of the bed with one hand pressed against Chu Wanning's forehead and the other braced on the bed, looking at him worriedly.

"What did I..." Chu Wanning felt all out of sorts. That dream had been far too real, and for a while, he couldn't quite break out of his daze.

"You had a nightmare. You were shaking so much," Mo Ran said as he tucked his blanket around him. "You looked like you were freezing. I was worried you might be running a fever, but thankfully not."

Chu Wanning uttered a quiet, "oh," and turned to look out of the slightly opened window. The sky was yet dark outside, the night yet deep. "It was snowing in my dream," he murmured, then said no more. He sat up, burying his face in one hand and taking a moment to steady himself before exhaling slowly. "Must've been overtired."

"I'll go make some ginger tea for you." Mo Ran gazed worriedly at the paleness of his face. "Shizun, you look terrible."

Chu Wanning did not respond.

Faced with this lack of reply, Mo Ran sighed and, without really thinking, instinctively pressed his own forehead against Chu Wanning's cold, sweat-drenched brow. "If you don't say anything, I'll take that as a, 'yes.'"

Startled by the sudden closeness, Chu Wanning reflexively leaned backward a little. "Mn."

Mo Ran, also not quite awake, offhandedly stroked Chu Wanning's hair like he had in his past life. Then he pulled on his outer robe and went downstairs to borrow the kitchen. A little while later, he returned with a wooden tray.

Mo Ran wasn't heartless. Chu Wanning had rushed to Peach Blossom Springs to save him and had also gone to great lengths to protect him. No matter how much resentment he'd harbored toward this person before, for the time being, he was grateful.

The tray bore a pot of steaming ginger tea and a small jar of brown sugar. Mo Ran knew that while Chu Wanning didn't like things with overly strong flavors, he was quite fond of sweet foods.

Besides the ginger tea, he had also brought a mantou from the kitchen, which he had sliced into thin pieces, soaked in fresh milk, then fried until crispy, before finishing them off with a sprinkling of powdered sugar to make for a plate of simple light snacks.

Color gradually returned to Chu Wanning's face as he held a cup of ginger tea in both hands and sipped slowly from it. He picked up a piece of the sweet, crispy mantou between porcelain-white fingertips and contemplated it for a while. "What's this?"

"I just threw something together. It doesn't have a name yet." Mo Ran scratched his head. "Try it, Shizun. It's sweet."

Chu Wanning disliked fried foods, thinking them greasy, but on hearing the word "sweet," he held one to his lips and hesitantly took a small bite. "Mm..."

"Is it good?" Mo Ran asked experimentally.

Chu Wanning glanced at him and said nothing, but he picked up another piece to eat with the ginger tea.

The pot of tea and plateful of snacks quickly disappeared, and in this warmth, the remnants of the nightmare also dissipated like smoke. Chu Wanning yawned and lay down once more. "I'm going back to sleep."

"Hang on." Mo Ran lifted his hand to wipe the corner of Chu Wanning's lips. "You got some crumbs there."

Chu Wanning did not reply. That open smile on Mo Ran's face made his ears feel a little warm despite himself. He turned his face away with a soft sound of assent and paid him no more heed.

Mo Ran collected the dishes and went downstairs to return them. When he came back, he saw Chu Wanning lying on his side, facing the wall, perhaps already asleep. He walked up and quietly put down the curtain, at which point Chu Wanning spoke. "It's cold at night. Don't sleep on the floor anymore."

"Then..."

Chu Wanning, with his long eyelashes lowered, truly wanted

Mo Ran to stay. However, the words, "Sleep up here," wouldn't come out, even as the tips of his ears kept getting warmer and warmer.

He cared for Mo Ran and so didn't want him to sleep on the floor, but he also liked him and didn't want him to leave.

Chu Wanning's face was terribly thin, and he knew all too well that even if he did manage to get out the words, he would surely be rejected. Then both his veneer and dignity would be forfeit. Even thinking about it made him feel pathetic. Things had been so much easier as Xia Sini. Little ones were allowed to be a bit willful.

Yet Mo Ran had been good to him today. He'd even remembered that Chu Wanning liked a lot of brown sugar in his ginger tea. Was it acceptable for him to think that, maybe, Mo Ran did actually care for him a little bit?

The thought made Chu Wanning's chest warm, and in a hot-headed moment, he blurted out: "Come sleep up here."

"I'll go see if they're done yet, and if so, I'll return to my own room."

Chu Wanning and Mo Ran spoke at practically the same time. Mo Ran didn't fully process his shizun's words until after he had finished speaking himself. His eyes widened slightly when he did.

"Sounds good," Chu Wanning concurred instantly, as if rushing to cover up what he had said. "Go on."

"Shizun, you..."

"I'm tired. You can leave."

"All right... Rest well, Shizun."

Mo Ran left, the door creaking open and then shut.

In the darkness, Chu Wanning opened his eyes. His heart raced in his chest, and his palms were covered with sweat, humiliated by his loss of self-control. He really had been alone for too long, if he could mistake a tiny sliver of kindness and care from someone for sincere tenderness. Like an idiot.

Irritated, he turned over and buried his face in his pillow, where he sank into a bottomless pit of self-loathing. He was well aware that Mo Ran liked Shi Mingjing and that there was nothing between himself and Mo Ran but for the polite distance of master and disciple. And yet…

The person from his dream appeared unbidden in his mind.

The same exact face, only older. The way he had looked at Chu Wanning with a surly expression and eyes too deep to read.

With a creak, the door opened again.

Chu Wanning froze, his entire back going stiff like a bow stretched taut.

Someone came over to his bed. There was a moment of silence, then he felt that person sit at the edge, bringing with him the light scent of freshly laundered clothes. "Shizun, are you asleep?"

No response.

So Mo Ran continued, voice even like he was discussing the weather. "They're still at it." He chuckled softly and lay down next to Chu Wanning with his head propped up on one arm, gaze sweeping over his shizun's back as it very obviously and visibly tensed several degrees further. "Is Shizun's offer from earlier still open?"

Chu Wanning did not reply.

"Shizun sure likes to ignore people. If Shizun doesn't say anything, I'll take it as a 'yes,' again."

"Hmph."

Mo Ran's eyes lit with pleasure, purple-black and flickering with amusement at the cold hmph that came from the other side of the bed. If doting on Shi Mei was his habit, then teasing his shizun was a game he never tired of.

He never could figure out just what it was that he felt toward Chu Wanning. All he knew was that this person made his heart itch, made him want to bare his fangs and bite him until he started either crying or laughing—although either was, for the most part, wishful thinking.

But whenever that face, ever cool and impassive, showed the slightest bit of emotion because of Mo Ran, he found himself becoming fervently excited.

"Shizun."

"Mn."

"Nothing, just felt like saying it."

Chu Wanning didn't bother replying.

"Shizun."

"If you have something to say, out with it. If not, shut up."

"Ha ha ha." Mo Ran laughed, then suddenly thought of something and asked, half-joking and half-serious, "I was thinking that Xia-shidi and Shizun really are incredibly alike. Shizun, is he your son?"

A long, long silence.

Chu Wanning had endured far too much emotional turmoil for one night, and he was in a sulky mood. Suddenly getting made fun of like this, he couldn't help feeling irritated.

"Pfft, I was just messing with Shizun, don't mind—"

"Yes," Chu Wanning answered coolly. "He's my son."

Mo Ran was still grinning. "Oh, that's what I figured. So he's your son—wait! Son?!" Mo Ran's eyes flew wide as if he'd been struck by lightning, his mouth hanging open in disbelief. "*S-s-s-s-son?!*"

"Mn." Chu Wanning rolled over and pinned Mo Ran with a deadpan gaze, his face thoroughly serious and without the slightest hint of jest.

Chu Wanning had blundered too much tonight and feared that his facade might not hold. If Mo Ran wanted to make this joke, he might as well take the chance to muddy the waters. Chu Wanning would do whatever it took to ensure that Mo Ran didn't realize that he liked him.

As Chu Wanning thought this, he calmly picked up the pieces of his dignity that he had dropped and said with all seriousness, "Xia Sini is my illegitimate child. Even he doesn't know this. As of right now, this is a secret known to the heavens, the earth, you, and me. If a third person were ever to find out, I would utterly end you."

Mo Ran was struck absolutely, completely, totally dumb.

79
This Venerable One's Shizun Is an Actor

If Mo Ran hadn't known Chu Wanning like the back of his own hand, he feared he might have been taken in by his serious demeanor and believed that nonsense.

Xia Sini was Chu Wanning's son? Yeah right, like he was dumb enough to fall for that!

However, it wasn't like he could brush off his shizun. So in the days that followed, he simply played along, putting on a show with things like, "Oh heavens," "So that's how it is," "I can't believe Shizun is actually a playboy," and other such.

Mo Ran had to admit that it was an interesting time, even though he had no idea what Chu Wanning was up to. Thus Mo Ran made a sport of it, poking playfully at Chu Wanning every so often.

One time, as they stopped at a teahouse for a snack, Mo Ran called out, cheek in hand, eyes bright and round. "Shizun, Shizun."

Chu Wanning swallowed his tea before lifting his lashes to look evenly at him. "Mn?"

"Why won't you acknowledge Xia-shidi as your child?"

"It's not that I *won't* acknowledge him, it just isn't the right time," Chu Wanning replied.

"Then when will it be the right time?"

"That will depend on him."

Chu Wanning had such an air of profundity that Mo Ran's ribs hurt from holding in his laughter, even as he forced himself to put on his best pitying face. "Poor Xia-shidi."

Another time, as they were traveling side by side on horseback, Mo Ran reached up and snapped a willow branch while passing by. He was fresh out of distractions and bored out of his mind, so he fussed at Chu Wanning again.

"Shizun, Shizun."

"What is it?"

"Can I ask you something?" Mo Ran was all smiles. "About Shiniang...what kind of person is she? Is she pretty?"

Chu Wanning choked, then hastily cleared his throat to cover for himself. "She's all right."

"Eh? Just 'all right'?" Mo Ran said, shocked. "I was so sure that someone who could catch Shizun's eye had to be devastatingly beautiful."

Chu Wanning did not bother to reply.

Mo Ran steered his black horse closer to Chu Wanning's white one and asked slyly, "Is Shizun still keeping in touch with Shiniang?"

"How would I do that?" Chu Wanning threw him a chilly look and said darkly, "Your shiniang is dead."

They'd barely started, and he was already offing his own wife? Mo Ran almost choked on his own spit. "D-dead? How did she die?"

"Birth complications," Chu Wanning said expressionlessly.

That so? Pfft ha ha ha ha ha. If the situation had been any different, Mo Ran probably would've fallen off his horse from laughing too hard.

Of course Mo Ran couldn't let such an amusing subject go. The next day, he washed a pouchful of fresh, plump cherries before setting off to entice Chu Wanning into talking some more on the way.

"Shizun, can I know who Shiniang was? What was her name?"

Chu Wanning picked a cherry and ate it with no discernible reaction. "She's already passed," he said indifferently. "What's the use in knowing her name?"

Mo Ran didn't miss a beat. "The sect leader has always taught us to be filial. Even if Shiniang is no longer with us, I, as a disciple, should still remember her name and go pay my respects every winter solstice and Qingming."

Chu Wanning kept eating his cherries. "No need," he replied evenly. "Your shiniang was not the worldly sort, and she also disliked the smell of incense."

Mo Ran pursed his lips, rolling his eyes. *It's obvious that you couldn't make up a backstory for Shiniang on the fly. Can't believe you'd say she never cared for these things with such a serious face.*

Outwardly, he kept smiling. "If Shiniang was so refined, she must have been a cultivator too."

Chu Wanning paused, then picked another cherry between snow-white fingertips and ate it at his leisure before answering, "Correct."

Mo Ran blinked curiously. "Which sect was she from?"

Chu Wanning estimated Xia Sini's age and quickly calculated in his head that he would've still been at Linyi at the time, so he said evenly: "Rufeng Sect."

"Oh..." Mo Ran's eyebrows went up slightly. He had to give Chu Wanning props for that. Rufeng Sect had always favored male disciples. Although their female disciples received the same education, they were never given the same opportunities to stand out and make a name for themselves. In fact, they never even left their names when they went on missions, so even though the female cultivators of Rufeng Sect were no less accomplished, the rest of the world only knew them as "the female cultivators of Rufeng Sect." No one knew their individual names. Thus Chu Wanning could make up whatever he felt like and there would be absolutely no way to verify.

Mo Ran wasn't one to surrender. He perked back up and persisted. "Then when did Shizun and Shiniang meet? *How* did you two meet?"

"Er..." Chu Wanning hesitated, not quite up to the task of inventing all that on the spot. When his gaze fell on Mo Ran's bright, sparkly eyes, he suddenly realized that he didn't have to answer this question. He pressed his lips together and, with a sweep of his sleeve, said sharply, "What are you doing, prying into this master's personal matters?"

With that, he urged his horse on, white robes disappearing into the distance and leaving Mo Ran in the dust.

Chu Wanning and Mo Ran roamed for a couple weeks, visiting the markets at numerous smaller sects and checking every stall that sold weapons and spiritual stones, but they found absolutely nothing of note.

One particular day, after Chu Wanning finished exchanging notes with Xue Zhengyong via haitang message, he and Mo Ran set off from the inn and headed toward the market at Guyueye to continue their investigation.

Guyueye was the foremost medicinal sect of the world, as well as the sect from which Xue Meng's mother, Madam Wang, hailed.

The sect was built on an island named Rainbell Isle. It wasn't an actual island, but rather the back of an enormous tortoise that was thousands upon thousands of years old and bound to the founder of the sect by blood pact. The tortoise carried the entire sect on its back as it traveled the oceans, and it nourished the flora of the isle with its unique spiritual energy.

The disciples of Guyueye had always been enigmatic and removed from the rest of the world. The sect rarely ever interacted with outsiders; only on the first and fifteenth day of each month would the tortoise dock at Yangzhou Port so that other sects could board and purchase medicines, while merchants could peddle their weapons, spiritual stones, and other wares that weren't usually found on the island itself.

Yet the most famous attraction on Rainbell Isle wasn't Guyueye, but Xuanyuan Pavilion. The pavilion was a subsidiary trading post of Guyueye, and it was well-known throughout the cultivation world.

This pavilion opened its doors twice per month to auction off goods like Guyueye's top-grade medicines and rare treasures from various sellers. The merchandise often toed the line of permissibility in terms of the cultivation world's taboos, but no one was so bored as to make an enemy of Guyueye. After all, most of the medicines circulating in the world originated at this sect. All things considered, Guyueye was no less powerful than the leading Rufeng Sect.

"Put your hood up. Too many eyes here," Chu Wanning quietly reminded Mo Ran while tugging the hood of his own cloak lower. More and more people were arriving at Rainbell Isle.

Xuanyuan Pavilion's auction house kept lavish private rooms for each of the great sects as a show of respect. However, since shady deals were made and stolen goods exchanged hands in this establishment, cultivators generally kept their identities hidden so as to not attract any undue attention or fatal misfortune.

Mo Ran and Chu Wanning stepped into Xuanyuan Pavilion. The interior was split into three floors, and the center of the first floor was occupied by a platform of white jade. The platform was shaped like a nine-petaled lotus flower, and it was enshrouded by nine layers of impenetrable defensive barriers. This was where the merchandise would be displayed during the auction.

Several hundred rows of redwood benches extended in the four cardinal directions around the white jade platform. These were the standard seats.

The second floor held private booths, each with a large window made of golden cedar and a curtain of silver moon silk that allowed those within to clearly see out of it, but blocked sight from the outside-in. These booths protected the privacy of the guests, but they were expensive: nine thousand gold for two hours.

Chu Wanning disliked crowding among others, so he took out the gold pieces Xue Zhengyong had sent and didn't hesitate.

The servants of Xuanyuan Pavilion who attended the guests had made death pacts with the master of the pavilion, and thus would never divulge the personal information of any guest. Even so, Chu Wanning remained wary. He booked the booth with the best view and had the servant bring two pots of snowy fragrance tea, eight pieces each of fresh and candied fruit, four pastries, and four sweets, and then sent the servant away.

Once he was alone with Mo Ran in the room, Chu Wanning finally lowered his hood as he stood by the window, looking down at the masses of people below.

"According to the sect leader, Xuanyuan will be auctioning off a weapon named Guilai."[21]

"Guilai?" Mo Ran shook his head. "Never heard of it."

"It's a holy weapon."

Mo Ran started. "A holy weapon? But didn't Jincheng Lake—"

"Indeed. Supposedly this Guilai was found in a nameless grave in

21 To return.

the Wanshen Mountains. Its master probably didn't have any heirs to pass it to, and so he had it buried with him."

"I see..."

A holy weapon took only one master: the one who named it. Upon their death, it would accept their heirs. Even if someone else were to get their hands on the weapon, they would be unable to draw out even a tiny fraction of its true power. As far as Mo Ran was concerned, there wasn't much point in buying a weapon like that.

"It's true that a holy weapon that doesn't acknowledge its wielder as its master won't display its true power," Chu Wanning said, having seen through his thoughts. "Even then, it will be many times stronger than a normal weapon. These people will definitely go all out."

Mo Ran grasped the situation. "I understand Shizun's meaning now. Most people go their whole lives without even seeing a holy weapon. Since this 'Guilai' was found in a nameless grave, and an ages-old one at that, everyone here will very likely extend their spiritual energy to test it on the off-chance they happen to be a descendant of its original master. There's no harm in trying, after all."

"Precisely."

"Holy weapons are rarely even seen, but one without a master just so happens to pop up for sale right at this juncture?" Mo Ran continued contemplatively. "No matter how you look at it, this has to be the work of that fake Gouchen. He's bringing out a high-quality counterfeit to bait everyone into exposing their spiritual energy so he can see if anyone here has the spiritual essence he's looking for."

Chu Wanning sat down in a cushioned chair, poured himself a cup of snowy fragrance tea, and leisurely drank it. Then he looked at the swarm of people below and said in a quiet voice: "It's exactly as you say. Regardless of whether the holy weapon is real or whether it's part of the fake Gouchen's scheme, it can't hurt to check."

At that moment, there was a ruckus down below.

Chu Wanning and Mo Ran peered downward and were both caught off guard by what they saw.

Xuanyuan Pavilion's golden gates stood wide open, and two rows of blue-robed young men with their hair done up in jade crowns were striding with their faces exposed through the crowd of cloaked cultivators, whose own faces were hidden under hoods. The one in the lead was slender and handsome, and he didn't bother with any form of concealment even as he strolled right into the black market.

"Ye Wangxi?" Mo Ran uttered, surprised.

This Venerable One's Ex-Wife... Is Here

THE INDIVIDUAL who had just arrived was indeed the modest gentleman with whom Mo Ran had shared a residence at Peach Blossom Springs: Ye Wangxi.

Today he had come donned in the colors of Rufeng Sect, his blue cloak embroidered in silver with a crane. His hair was fastened with a deep, vivid blue ribbon, and hanging at his waist was a silver incense bell filigreed with a pattern of a rare beast carrying a pearl in its mouth. Perhaps it was because he wasn't wearing armor, but his usual aura of valiant heroism carried a trace of a refined, elegant air.

Xuanyuan Pavilion's chief steward approached and greeted Ye Wangxi, eyes lowered and head inclined. "Ye-xianjun."

Ye Wangxi nodded. "I've come in my yifu's name to bid for an item. Would it please the chief steward to lead us to the upper floors?"

"The pavilion master anticipated Xianjun's presence, and a booth has been reserved for Rufeng Sect. Allow me to lead my lord there straightaway."

Ye Wangxi then led the group of ten or so Rufeng Sect disciples upstairs, leaving behind an entire hall of hooded figures who whispered amongst themselves.

"Have Rufeng's people also come today?"

"Who's that xianjun? How come we've never seen him before?"

Obviously there's a reason *none of you have seen him before,* Mo Ran thought, but he found himself curious too. He watched Ye Wangxi's back disappear around the corner before he turned to Chu Wanning. "Shizun, you've stayed with Rufeng Sect before. Do you know this Ye-xianjun?"

"No." Chu Wanning's brows knitted slightly. "Although for some reason he looks rather familiar..." He paused for a moment and closed his eyes to think, but he shook his head. "I can't quite put my finger on it."

Mo Ran scratched his head. "This Ye-xianjun stayed in the same residence as I did back at Peach Blossom Springs. Ability-wise, he isn't bad. If he's been sent to bid on behalf of Rufeng Sect, I imagine his status within the sect can't be low either. Shizun really doesn't know him?"

"There are seventy-two cities within Rufeng Sect; its people are spread far and wide. Furthermore, I don't like to run around and can't be bothered to pry into internal affairs, so it's not strange that I wouldn't know him."

As they spoke, the booth reserved for Rufeng Sect on the third floor lit up with a bright yellow glow. No doubt the lights had been lit for Ye Wangxi and company, who had entered and settled in their seats. The highest level of Xuanyuan Pavilion was specially reserved for the great sects, so it was seldom used. Thus the crowd looked up to see, thinking it a rare event.

The instant Rufeng Sect arrived, anticipation for the auction had increased a few notches. After a quarter of an hour, the white jade lotus platform at the center of the hall began to glow, and a vibrant length of brilliant red satin unrolled from the ceiling of Xuanyuan Pavilion. A dainty young girl of eleven or twelve, barefoot and dressed in delicate, snow-white silk, spun through the air holding onto the satin banner. She landed light and dainty on the ice-cold lotus platform.

"Honored Xianjun, thank you for waiting. I am the Second Pavilion Master of Xuanyuan Pavilion." The pretty little girl smiled. "You have come from all across the four seas, and we are honored by your presence. Naturally, Xuanyuan Pavilion will, as always, express our gratitude by putting the rarest and best of items on display."

Mo Ran's excellent hearing picked up murmurs from the crowd below.

"The Second Pavilion Master of Xuanyuan Pavilion is just a little girl, still wet behind the ears?"

"Aiyoh, buddy, you really don't know anything, do you? Do you know how old this 'little girl' is?"

"Ten? Fifteen? She can't be more than twenty at most."

"Heh. Stunned, are you? She's over a hundred now. You should call her Great Granny, not 'little girl.'"

"What?! Liu-xiong, you're pulling my leg! How can that little thing be a hundred?!"

"This is Guyueye, the number one medical sect in the world. How could anything be impossible? It's just some medicine of everlasting youth or whatever."

"Whoa..."

This was doubtless the awestruck man's first time at the pavilion. After that conversation, he excitedly craned his neck, his hands clutching his money pouch. He was obviously impatient to see what manner of miraculous medicine and sacred items Xuanyuan Pavilion would produce for the auction.

The Second Pavilion Master didn't disappoint either. With a snap of her fingers, a gap cracked open at the center of the jade lotus platform, and a small stand shaped like the seedpod of a lotus flower slowly rose. Upon it rested five silk brocade boxes the size of one's palm, and each box was open wide, revealing the medicinal pills within and their pearlescent sheen.

Someone burst out laughing. "Aren't those just infatuation pills? What's so rare about those?"

"That's right! Even if you don't start out with rare treasures, at least make it something better than basic infatuation pills!"

The Second Pavilion Master wasn't at all irritated by the crowd's gripes. Instead she smiled with delight in her eyes and said in a clear, bright voice: "You certainly have good eyes, everyone. These are indeed infatuation pills. As you all know, while these pills are difficult to refine, they aren't remotely exotic. And of course, Xuanyuan Pavilion would *never* offer ordinary items merely to placate our customers."

As she spoke, she picked up one of the brocade boxes and, holding it in her palm, snapped the box shut.

Though the crowd was seated at varying distances from the stage, an enchanted mirror had been placed in front of each individual; it allowed them to view the treasures in detail. Only then did the crowd notice the serpentine emblem on the cover of the box.

Someone gasped. "Hanlin the Sage?!"

The Second Pavilion Master smiled. "That's right. Each of these five pills came from the refinery cauldron of the elder of my sect: Hanlin the Sage. Ordinary infatuation pills can confound the heart and cause whomever takes one to become obsessed with whomever gave it to them, but the effect lasts for a mere half a year, and the antidote is very easy to produce. However, these five pills..." Her delicate, tender fingertips held the brocade box as she continued solemnly. "*These* are guaranteed to work for ten years, and they have no antidote."

"What?"

"My heavens, how is that possible?"

"Hanlin the Sage is frightening..."

The Second Pavilion Master waited until the commotion died down somewhat before she smiled again. "In order to differentiate these from ordinary infatuation pills, Hanlin the Sage has named them 'Love Pills.' Purchase only one of these pills, dissolve it in water, and convince your object of desire to drink it. Then, for the duration of ten years, we guarantee they will remain obsessed with you without ever wavering."

"Is there really no cure after one takes the pill?" a female cultivator called from down below. "If I lose interest in him before the ten years are up, wouldn't I be stuck with him crawling all over me?"

The crowd chuckled and laughed, and the Second Pavilion Master smiled politely. "My lady has only pointed out a true thing. This is why Xuanyuan Pavilion will take this chance to remind everyone that the Love Pill has no known cure. Until the ten years are up, nothing will be able to break the bond they create. Outside of a case of tormented, unrequited love, we cannot recommend delivering the pill to another party."

With that conclusion, the bidding began, and the price started to rise. Mo Ran noticed that it was mostly female cultivators screaming to fight for bids, and he couldn't help but click his tongue. "This is unbelievably scary."

"Indeed. To earn sentiments thusly would truly be beyond tasteless."

This response made Mo Ran turn to glance at Chu Wanning. "Shizun, you'll have to watch out," he said, smiling. "You're awfully good-looking. What if there are female cultivators from Sisheng Peak here and they buy one of the pills, then secretly drop it in your water to make you fall in love with them? Better be careful you don't fall for that, since you're a married man and all."

Chu Wanning couldn't respond. Mo Ran was undoubtedly saying such things to mock him, and his instinct was to be angry. However, never in his life had he ever heard Mo Ran call him good-looking, and he couldn't find it in himself to be upset. His lips pressed into a cool and distant line and, turning his head away, he refused to acknowledge his disciple.

"If they're resorting to using pills like these, they must be desperately in love," Mo Ran mumbled. When he saw how fast those five boxes were purchased, he sighed and shook his head. "How pitiful."

Chu Wanning stared at that snow-white wall for a moment, then replied calmly, "If they truly loved the object of their affection, how could they have the heart to use a pill like these? You're still young. There are some things you don't understand."

I'm still young? Mo Ran turned his head, dimples deepening with his smile. "I don't understand, but Shizun does? Is Shizun going to tell me about Shiniang?"

"Begone."

"Ha ha ha ha ha ha."

In the midst of their banter, the second item had been presented on the platform.

"Tapir Fragrance Dew," the Second Pavilion Master announced crisply. "Also from the kiln of Hanlin the Sage. This is the newest medicinal dew refined by Hanlin. The first generation of disciples of Guyueye have tried it, and it works like magic."

Cultivator A was somewhat learned. "Typing Fragrance Dew?"

Cultivator B was a little hungry. "Tapas Fragrance Dew?"

Cultivator C was perverted. "Tupping Fragrance Dew?"

Chu Wanning gave it a ponder, then raised his gaze to those five porcelain bottles. The thick curtain of his lashes trembled fractionally. "Tapir Fragrance Dew...from the Dream-Consuming Tapir?"

The Second Pavilion Master had no intention of losing the audience's interest. The instant she realized that the crowd was confused, she explained with a smile: "The reason this is called Tapir Fragrance Dew is because the formula requires blood taken from the quick of Dream-Consuming Tapir claws. A single drop in a cup of tea will guarantee good dreams, every single night, for a week. This might not mean much to ordinary cultivators, but after the influence of certain cultivation methods and spells, some xianjun experience relentless nightmares and have difficulty finding peaceful slumber. If the problem persists, it can lead to qi deviation, in which case this Tapir Fragrance Dew would be the absolute best remedy."

When Chu Wanning heard this, he was reminded of that realistic dream he'd experienced. Though it hadn't been a nightmare, it had indeed made him feel rather unsettled...

The Second Pavilion Master pushed this product with all she had. "Besides all that, the Tapir Fragrance Dew also has the ability to regulate spiritual energy and aid in one's cultivation."

Chu Wanning was still deep in thought and remained unmoved.

"Moreover, if one has children training at home, the Tapir Fragrance Dew would be extremely beneficial for them. Hanlin the Sage had the foresight to expect that elders and teachers might purchase the dew for their young trainees, so he specially made the five bottles of Tapir Fragrance Dew in five different flavors. The red bottle is lychee, the yellow bottle is orange, the white bottle is milk candy, the purple bottle is grape, and the black bottle is mulberry. Furthermore, with but one sip, the taste will remain on one's lips and tongue for an entire day—it's quite lovely."

Just as she finished, a silver stick was dropped from a dignitary booth on the second floor.

The second and third floors were much farther away from the platform, and it was thus inconvenient to yell to bid, so bidders up there wrote their offer on a silver stick before tossing it down. A spell had been cast on those silver sticks that made them float to the Pavilion Master without error.

The Second Pavilion Master caught the stick that drifted toward her and gave it a glance, only to be stunned.

At the same time, within the dignitary booth, Chu Wanning casually laid down the brush he had just used and leisurely took a sip of tea. Mo Ran watched from the side, and his lips twitched.

The voice of the Second Pavilion Master rang from below. "From the Tian dignitary booth on the second floor: five-hundred-thousand gold. Do I hear any other offers?"

When these words were spoken, the crowd was abuzz. The Tapir Fragrance Dew was good, sure, but it obviously wasn't as popular as the Love Pill. The five boxes of Love Pills had gone for three hundred thousand gold altogether, so an offer of five hundred thousand gold for these five bottles of dew was already considerably high.

"Probably an offer from the parents of some little gongzi," someone grumbled.

"Must be for some rich little gongzi's training."

Meanwhile, some cultivators in the crowd had suffered enough of qi deviations. One steeled himself and said, "I'll take all five. I offer five-hundred-and-fifty-thousand gold."

"The Tapir Fragrance Dew, now going for five hundred and fifty thousand. Do I hear—"

Before the Second Pavilion Master could finish, another silver stick floated errantly through the air, again tossed from the Tian dignitary booth on the second floor. She glanced at it and her eyes unconsciously widened.

"I apologize, everyone. I misunderstood the initial offer, and I will rectify my error now. What the customer on the second floor actually meant was that he is offering five hundred thousand *per bottle*, for a total of two million and five hundred thousand..."

Only a fool would fight Chu Wanning at that price point. As Mo Ran watched those five bottles of Tapir Fragrance Dews being delivered into the room, he felt like his soul was leaving his body.

Chu Wanning had spent two-and-a-half million... On sweets...

Sensing Mo Ran's incredulous look, Chu Wanning asked indifferently, "What is it?"

"Ah ha ha, nothing. I just didn't think Shizun was partial to stuff like this."

"Why would I care for childish things?" Chu Wanning replied placidly. "I bought them for Xia Sini."

Mo Ran had no words. What an act! His brows twitched. *Let's see how much longer you can keep this up.*

The auctioned items continued to be presented one by one, and while everything that came afterward was also a unique spiritual medicine or treasure, they held no value for either Mo Ran or Chu Wanning. They sipped tea as they waited for the holy weapon Guilai to appear.

Mo Ran leaned by the window, his black clothes wrapped tightly around his thin waist, emphasizing the broadness of his shoulders and the length of his legs. He glanced down at the lively event below, then looked up to gaze at the reserved Rufeng booth upstairs.

"Come to think of it, Shizun, how did Uncle settle the affair at Peach Blossom Springs? You never gave me the details."

"It isn't really settled. We can't call attention to the affair lest we alert the enemy. Even though the sect leader knows the truth, he can't make much of a fuss. However, he did entirely sever ties with the feathered tribe and brought both Shi Mei and Xue Meng back to Sisheng Peak. Moreover, our fight was rather intense, and disciples of several sects bore witness to it. Some began to harbor doubts about Peach Blossom Springs and thus departed. I imagine this Ye Wangxi was one of them." Chu Wanning finished an orange osmanthus cake and reached for a second. "The sect leader told the rest of the world that you caused some trouble and are therefore confined to Sisheng Peak for reflection. That should cover your tracks for a while at least."

Mo Ran scratched his head. "Sounds like quite the mess. I've really troubled Uncle..."

As he was mumbling, the Second Pavilion Master of the Xuanyuan Pavilion, still standing upon the nine-petaled lotus platform, used an amplification spell to clear her throat. Her voice, sonorous and pleasant as the sound of tinkling jade, echoed throughout every nook and cranny: "The next auction item is a rare treasure of the highest grade, extremely difficult to come by. It has ranked among the top ten items in our auction guide for the past three years."

With those few words, silence fell. After a moment, it was like a spoonful of clear water had splashed into a pot of boiling oil. The audience erupted with murmurs as they whispered to each other, and nearly every eye glinted with interest.

Just what manner of treasure could rank among the top ten items auctioned at Xuanyuan Pavilion in the past three years? Never mind actually buying something like that, for many people, even catching a glimpse of it with their own eyes would be extremely good luck in itself. The buyers became more and more excited, and the air grew so tense that it was almost tangible.

The people below strained their necks to look, and those in the booths also lifted the blinds. All eyes were on the lotus platform.

"Is it the holy weapon Guilai?" Mo Ran wondered in a soft voice.

Chu Wanning didn't reply.

As the gap at the center of the platform cracked open once more, the clear voice of the Second Pavilion Master of Xuanyuan Pavilion echoed. "Presenting the next treasured item: a Butterfly-Boned Beauty Feast."

"What?!" Mo Ran was stunned, his hands gripping the windowsill. "It's not a holy weapon?!"

Chu Wanning hadn't expected this either. He abruptly rose to his feet, coming to Mo Ran's side to look down with him.

A stone divan slowly rose from the open center of the lotus platform. Eight iron chains, each as thick as a wrist, crisscrossed the divan to hold down a living creature that struggled unceasingly upon it. However, that living creature was fully covered beneath a drape, and it was hard to see what it was at first glance.

That didn't dampen the boiling excitement below in the slightest. A "Butterfly-Boned Beauty Feast," no matter its class or appearance, was an object in itself renowned throughout the world.

According to legend, during the primordial era, when the heavens and the earth had yet to be separated, demons had lived alongside humans on the cultivation continent. At that time, there had lived a clan of demons called the Butterfly-Boned Clan. While their martial prowess had been wanting, their bodies had contained an immense amount of spiritual energy. To consume the blood and flesh of one of the Butterfly-Boned Clan, or to engage in intercourse with them, could greatly enhance a human's cultivation. Those without spiritual roots could instantly establish a foundation, and those who had roots could directly achieve the power of a zongshi.

That was why, after the demons were defeated, the Butterfly-Boned Clan had been hunted to extinction. They were all either captured to be bed slaves or directly killed and eaten.

In the present day, the full-blooded Butterfly-Boned Clan had long since been eradicated from the world. However, within the vast sea of humanity, there were individuals in whose veins the blood of the Butterfly-Boned Clan yet ran. The flesh and blood of the majority of these individuals had no effects whatsoever, and they were indistinguishable from that of any other cultivator. However, a very small number of descendants manifested the traits of their ancestral bloodline. The flesh and blood of such individuals, although not as potent as that of their primordial ancestors, could still greatly enhance a cultivator's ability.

These people were called Butterfly-Boned Beauty Feasts, and this "feast" had two meanings: a feast in bed, or a feast of the flesh. In other words, they could be taken to bed or eaten alive. Whether it was the former or the latter depended entirely on the buyer.

In the cultivation world, someone descended from the Butterfly-Boned Clan who manifested ancestral traits wasn't seen as "human." Even though they were no different from ordinary people, out of collective self-interest, the cultivation world had deemed them "merchandise." Thus, although horrible, the act of selling a Butterfly-Boned Beauty Feast did not violate any taboos.

However, Chu Wanning, righteous zongshi that he was, had an ugly look on his face.

"This Butterfly-Boned Beauty Feast was not obtained by Guyueye. Rather, this sale is on consignment, and thus Xuanyuan Pavilion will take an additional thirty percent of the agreed transaction payment as commission. Honored Xianjun, please take this into account when bidding and make an offer within your means."

Once the Second Pavilion Master had spoken, she snapped her fingers, and with the signal, the wool blanket covering the divan fell.

Silence abruptly blanketed the pavilion.

Everyone was staring at the body chained to the stone divan with such rapt attention that within the vast Xuanyuan Pavilion, one could almost hear breath and heartbeats.

On the divan was a delicate young girl with snowy fair skin. Long locks like silk draped across her nearly naked body, and she was wrapped in only a translucent silk tulle. Her supple, smooth bare body trembled like frozen fresh snow or dampened jade, and she glowed gently under the light.

Eight iron chains firmly restrained her delicate body and clanged with her struggling. This only served to more easily arouse the savage desires of the men in the crowd. Even experienced philanderers would admit without hesitation that this girl was a rare beauty.

"A supreme treasure of the highest grade: a female Butterfly-Boned Beauty Feast at her ripening age." The Second Pavilion Master smiled, then approached to release one of the chains. Before the girl could fight back, her hand was caught as fast as lightning and raised to the air. "Hanlin the Sage has marked her with a dot of chastity cinnabar. As everyone can see, she is still a virgin."

A snow-white cloth was bound around the girl's mouth, muffling her pitiful cries. Large beads of tears rolled down from the corners of her eyes; those golden tears confirmed her identity as a descendant of the Butterfly-Boned Clan who had maintained ancestral traits.

Some sucked in their breaths, some swallowed hungrily. This revelation had turned the atmosphere of Xuanyuan Pavilion from that of an establishment filled with cultivators into that of a house squeezed to the brim with starving wolves, whose drool dripped from the corner of their mouths as they greedily eyed their prey.

A sharp crack resounded.

Chu Wanning's cool gaze withdrew and landed on Mo Ran. Mo Ran's face was pale, his nails digging into the wood. He had broken a corner of the windowsill with his grip.

"What's wrong?"

"No... It's nothing." Mo Ran inhaled deeply before he managed to calm himself and shook his head at Chu Wanning. "I just think selling live humans like this is...incredibly disgusting."

He wasn't telling the truth. His eyes quietly returned to the form of that Butterfly-Boned Beauty Feast.

This woman was none other than the number one beauty of the cultivation world, the woman whom he had taken as his wife after he'd named himself emperor in his previous life: Song Qiutong.

81 This Venerable One's Bugui!

MEANWHILE, in Rufeng Sect's private room on the third floor, Ye Wangxi stood tall and elegant by the intricately carved ornamental wooden railing, eyebrows drawn tightly together and lips pressed into a thin line.

"Ye-gongzi, Elder Xu sent us here for that holy weapon. If you bid on the Butterfly-Boned Beauty Feast as well, I'm afraid we won't have enough left..."

"It's fine. I'll use my own funds."

The attendants realized that Ye Wangxi had already made up his mind, so they exchanged a couple of furtive glances but said nothing else.

"The starting bid is ten million gold," the Second Pavilion Master of Xuanyuan Pavilion announced in her precise tones. "Ladies and gentlemen, bidding is now open."

"Eleven million."

"Twelve million."

The commotion rose alongside the soaring price.

"Nineteen million!"

"I bid twenty-five million!"

When the bid shot up by six million in one go, quite a number of cultivators sighed and sat down, shaking their heads. At this time, several silver tabs floated down from the second-floor booths to the pavilion master. She collected them from the air and nimbly fanned them out in her hand, a price written on each one.

"The current highest bid..." She scanned the tabs, then announced clearly, "From the Xuan booth: thirty-five million."

"Thirty-five million?!"

The crowd sucked in a cold breath and collectively turned to look at the Xuan booth on the second floor. Lights glowed hazily from behind the gentle drifting of the silver curtains, but there was no way to see what kind of person was sitting inside.

"You could buy a whole palace on Rainbell Isle with that money."

"Whose bid was it? A little excessive, don't you think..."

"If they can throw around that kind of money, they've gotta be from one of the ten great sects. I wonder which one?"

Chu Wanning's eyes were closed. When he heard the price, he asked Mo Ran, "Did you bring enough money?"

"Absolutely not!" Meeting Song Qiutong was the last thing Mo Ran had expected to happen here, and he only snapped out of his shock when he heard Chu Wanning say this. "What does Shizun mean to do?" he asked, alarmed.

"Buy her."

Mo Ran's eyes widened as he waved his hands frantically. "No way! Don't do it, that woman will just be a burden. Where would we even put her? We'd have to rent an extra horse when we traveled and book another room at night. Nope, don't do it."

"Who said anything about bringing her along? I'll let her go after." Chu Wanning opened his eyes and held out his hand with a straight face. "Give it here."

Mo Ran clutched his money pouch. "I-I don't have any!"

"I'll repay you when we get back."

"This money is for the holy weapon!"

"Don't you already have Jiangui? What do you need another for? Hand it over!"

Mo Ran had no words. He felt a headache coming on. This Song Qiutong... When he'd met her in his past life, she had been a disciple of Rufeng Sect, and he had been razing Rufeng Sect's cities to the ground. His heart had clenched at the sight of her—she looked a little like Shi Mei—so he'd spared her life. As time went on, she had proved herself to be clever and docile, and her temperament had been rather similar to Shi Mei's as well, so he had eventually made her his empress.

That had become one of Mo Ran's greatest regrets.

Chu Wanning and that kind heart of his, concealed by his cold exterior, actually wanted to buy her. How could Mo Ran possibly allow that to happen? Forget forty million gold, he wouldn't take this woman for four coppers. As a matter of fact, even if they paid *him* forty million, he still wouldn't take her!

They were stuck in a stalemate when a tab floated down from the third floor. It was gold. A buyout tab!

The golden tab represented the highest possible bid at Xuanyuan Pavilion. No price was written upon it, for the tab itself denoted fifty million gold. Once this kind of bid was put down, no one had the means to keep competing. Hence, "buyout" tab.

For a second, the crowd was dead silent—before it exploded in an uproar.

"Rufeng Sect!"

"Rufeng Sect pulled out the buyout tab!"

Chu Wanning turned away from Mo Ran and his death grip on his money pouch to look outside. They were at just the right angle to see the first room on the third floor. Ye Wangxi didn't care for things like hiding his face. He had pulled aside the snow moon silk curtains meant for secrecy ages ago and was standing by the carved railing with his hands clasped lightly behind his back. His expression was solemn, and his handsome face betrayed nothing. He glanced down at the ruckus below, seemed somewhat aggravated, and turned to walk back into the private room.

Mo Ran let out a breath. "Shizun can rest easy," he said. "I lived with this Ye-gongzi back at Peach Blossom Springs, so I'm fairly well acquainted with him. He's a good person. He won't do anything cruel to that Butterfly-Boned Beauty Feast."

Meanwhile, inside Rufeng Sect's room on the third floor, Ye Wangxi sat down at a table covered with satin cloth that was intricately embroidered in gold and silver. There he poured himself a cup of fragrant tea. When he finished it, knocks sounded from outside the booth.

Ye Wangxi's voice was gentle and polite as he said, "Come in."

"Ye-xianjun, I've brought the Butterfly-Boned Beauty Feast for your inspection."

"Thank you. You can go."

Xuanyuan Pavilion's maid left, and for a while there was nothing in the room but silence. The Butterfly-Boned Beauty Feast knelt on the floor, hands and feet bound by spells, panic in her eyes as her whole body trembled. Her peach-blossom eyes were red at the edges from crying, and she looked truly pitiful.

Ye Wangxi glanced at her, not a shred of impropriety in that clear, principled gaze of his, and lifted a hand to dissipate the spells. "It's cold on the floor. You must be scared; have a seat and some warm tea."

The Butterfly-Boned Beauty Feast did not answer, still trembling, her beautiful eyes wide and translucent like glass. She stayed where she was, cowering on the floor—too scared to talk, much less move.

Ye Wangxi sighed and gestured for the attendants to bring her a cloak. "Please don't worry, miss. I didn't buy you for cultivation purposes. Put on the cloak, then we can talk."

"You...you..."

When Ye Wangxi saw that she still wasn't moving and was only staring pitifully up at him, he shook his head with an exasperated smile. He got down on one knee to be on eye level with her. "My name is Ye Wangxi. May I ask for yours?"

"This one's name is...Song." She gave Ye Wangxi a hesitant look through teary eyes. "Song Qiutong... Thank you, Ye-gongzi."

Downstairs, Mo Ran was deep in thought.

In his past life, Song Qiutong had been a disciple of Rufeng Sect by the time he'd met her. Ye Wangxi must have saved her from the auction house in that life too. While Butterfly-Boned Beauty Feasts generally weren't treated like ordinary people, it was a different matter if they were a disciple of a major cultivation sect.

Mo Ran sighed internally. He didn't know Ye Wangxi that well, only that he was an upright, principled person, and had been second only to Chu Wanning in terms of strength in their past life. Mo Ran had once crossed swords with him when he'd slaughtered the people of the Rufeng Sect's seventy-two cities. That fierce, imposing swordsmanship and dignified posture had left a deep impression on him.

Seventy-two cities of Rufeng Sect spread across the land, and Mo Ran had taken them all without the slightest bit of effort. And the lords of those cities, with their run-on titles and widespread tales of might and glory, each and every one of them had been as dirt under his heel.

All save for this Ye Wangxi, and only Ye Wangxi. The seven cities under his command gave Mo Ran endless trouble. Even in the end, when the cities had fallen and Ye Wangxi knelt bloodied in a field of corpses, his eyes were still clear and unrelenting.

By then, the Nangong leaders of Rufeng Sect had since fled, and multitudes of others were groveling for their lives at Mo Ran's feet. However, Ye Wangxi only knelt there with his eyes closed and brows drawn tightly together, his expression frosty.

Before killing him, Mo Ran asked, genuinely, "Will you surrender?"

"I will not."

Mo Ran smiled from where he sat on the gilded seat adorned with a dragon and phoenix, which was meant for the master of Rufeng Sect. Beneath dark lashes, his eyes swept across the throngs of people before him. Ordinary disciples aside, there were six or seven city lords and more than a dozen generals, all of them prostrating on the dusty ground and quivering.

A crow circled in the ashen grey sky above banners the color of blood, cawing.

Mo Ran lifted a nonchalant hand. "Kill them all."

Before death, Ye Wangxi said, "All the gleaming cities of Rufeng, and not one real man to be found."

Blood splattered through the air.

Mo Ran held in his arms his newest acquisition, the beautiful Song Qiutong, her loveliness unparalleled, her delicate body shivering nonstop at the hellish scene before her.

"Don't be afraid. There's a good girl. You'll be staying with this venerable one from now on." Mo Ran stroked her hair, smiling. "Come, tell me your name again? What did you do at Rufeng Sect? I forgot what you said earlier."

"This one's name is...Song Qiutong." Her voice was frightened. "I was...I was Ye Wangxi's...maid..."

Ye Wangxi's maid. That was what she had told Mo Ran.

As for how Song Qiutong, a Butterfly-Boned Beauty Feast, had been allowed to join Rufeng Sect, and how she had become Ye Wangxi's maid, Mo Ran had no idea. It was only on this day, after his rebirth and at the Xuanyuan Pavilion, that he finally realized that Ye Wangxi was the one who had paid an exorbitant sum to save her from the clutches of danger.

Hardly anyone knew that a large part of the reason for Ye Wangxi's final defeat at Mo Ran's hands had been thanks to information divulged by Song Qiutong.

The thought made Mo Ran scowl as the loathing he felt for this woman grew even deeper. He must have been out of his mind when he thought she was anything like Shi Mei.

The Second Pavilion Master's pleasant voice interrupted Mo Ran's thoughts. "The last item at this auction is a masterless holy weapon. It has been put up for auction on behalf of a third party."

There were always rumors floating around before each auction as to what kind of precious treasures would be up for sale. Thus, in contrast to the wild reaction to the Butterfly-Boned Beauty Feast earlier, the gathered crowd of cultivators actually settled down a bit, though they were still antsy.

The white jade lotus bloomed once again, and the stone platform rose slowly. Upon it lay a satin case with silver embellishments of celestial bodies and elegant landscapes.

The satin case was slim and intricately embroidered, and anyone in the know could tell with a glance that the fine needlework came from the famed embroidery house of Gusu, Xianyun Pavilion. Holy weapon aside, this case alone was worth hundreds of gold.

"This holy weapon was found at the burial mound on Jun Mountain. Its former master had passed, and we at Xuanyuan Pavilion have verified that it has yet to take a new master." The Second Pavilion Master paused before continuing. "As everyone knows, a holy weapon's name is engraved on its body. However, time has worn away the inscription on this holy weapon, and only one character remains discernible: Gui, for 'Return.'"

"Enough prattling," someone muttered. "Open the box already."

"Aiyo, let it be, you'll get used to it. Xuanyuan Pavilion always does it like this. Gotta talk it up before showing us the goods."

"I guess."

Amused by the chatter, Mo Ran turned toward Chu Wanning to quip, only to see Chu Wanning's face pale as frost, his sword-straight eyebrows tight and strained as slender fingers of cold jade pressed against his temple. Startled, he hurriedly asked, "Shizun, are you okay?"

"Suddenly… Suddenly I don't feel so good."

"Don't feel good how? Did you catch another cold?" Mo Ran scooted over and felt his forehead. "Your temperature's fine."

Chu Wanning shook his head without saying anything. He looked all out of sorts.

Unsure of what else to do, Mo Ran said, "I'll pour you some tea." He filled a cup with steaming tea, paused, then added a bit of the recently purchased Tapir Fragrance Dew.

Sage Hanlin's medicines were renowned the world over, and indeed Chu Wanning seemed to be better after drinking the tea mixed with the dew. Some color came back to his face as he returned his attention to the auction downstairs. Mo Ran tidied up the tea set and poured him another cup.

"Although there is no way to know this holy weapon's full name, since the stars have aligned to bring it back to the world, and its inscription already contains the word 'gui,' Xuanyuan Pavilion has for the time being named it 'Guilai,' 'the Returned.'"

Someone in the crowd finally lost his patience. "Pavilion Master, you've talked it up enough," he yelled. "We're already on the edge of our seats—open the box and let's have a look at that holy weapon."

The Second Pavilion Master smiled. "All things in due time, Xianjun. In accordance with the laws of the cultivation world, when the master of a holy weapon passes, the weapon shall be inherited by his blood heirs. Guilai was found at a burial mound, and we have no way to know its original master's identity. However, once the case is opened, all present are welcome to reach out with their spiritual energy to test the weapon. If it resonates with someone, that will indicate that they are of the original master's bloodline, and Guilai will naturally belong to them, free of charge."

"Ha ha ha, as if something that coincidental could ever happen."

The gathered cultivators burst out laughing.

"That's right, what are the chances?"

"Might as well try it, though. Can't hurt."

The Second Pavilion Master beamed at the crowd. "Indeed, it can't hurt to try your luck," she agreed crisply. "Now then, if I may have your attention, we will be removing the lid."

She snapped her fingers, and a pair of Guyueye disciples—both young girls of around fifteen or sixteen—approached from either side. They flew up and landed gracefully on the lotus platform, then placed their slender, jade-like hands on the satin case. Each carried an intricate crystal key that they inserted carefully into the keyholes on the case.

There were two clicks, and the case unlocked.

As Mo Ran watched the scene before him, he found himself

thinking back to when he had acquired Jiangui at Jincheng Lake. It had been clearly explained to him then that only the person he loved most in all world could unlock Ever-Yearning, but for some reason, the brocade box had opened in Chu Wanning's hands.

The audience held their breath, countless eyes staring at that narrow box from beneath hooded cloaks. The gold-embroidered lid lifted slowly as the very air strained with tension, like a bow pulled to its limit. Despite the thousands of people present, it was so quiet that one could have heard a single hair fall to the ground.

Every single person was staring unblinkingly at the ancient blade that had been revealed inside the box, aged by time. Some greedily, some curiously, some appreciatively...

Only Mo Ran's eyes flew wide the instant he saw the weapon lying there. The color drained rapidly from his face.

He had lived two lifetimes, owned two holy weapons, and crossed blades with over a dozen other wielders thereof. He had thought that he wouldn't care a whit about whatever holy weapon Xuanyuan Pavilion was selling.

He had been wrong.

"The holy weapon Guilai." The Second Pavilion Master's crisp voice shattered the silence. "A long blade, four feet in length, three inches in width. Scabbardless, with a body of pure black that does not reflect light."

Mo Ran's fingertips shook minutely as a word slipped past his lips. "Bugui..."

No Return...

Our past lies on a vermilion bridge in emerald fields

Another year gone, yet still I wait, for you do not return.[22]

---

22 *These lines are adapted from Qin Guan's "Jiangchengzi: Westside Willow Branches Adrift In Gentle Spring." The characters for "not return" are the same as those used for "Bugui."*

"Mo Ran, now that you have your own holy weapon, why have you asked me to seal its spiritual consciousness rather than give it a name?"

"To answer you, Shizun: this disciple is uncultured and has only one chance to name it. I worry that I'll pick a bad one and be stuck with it."

"A-Ran, have you still not decided on a name for your long blade? Surely you can't keep calling it, 'blade,' this and, 'blade,' that."

"It's fine, it's fine. I'm just taking my time to think about it. It's a holy weapon, after all. It deserves a super awesome name, ha ha ha."

Then Shi Mei died.

Mo Ran asked Chu Wanning to release the seal so that he could name his holy weapon "Mingjing."

However, at that time, Chu Wanning said that his spiritual energy was still corrupted from the fight with the ghost realm, and that he did not have the strength to release the sealing spell. So, he could only leave it as it was.

Later, Mo Ran and Chu Wanning finally severed ties, and Mo Ran was loath to ask him about unsealing it again. And so the bloodstained long blade remained nameless through all those years and innumerable battles. It no longer mattered. Not a soul in the world was unaware of Mo Weiyu and the hellish blade in his hand, which fed on blood and hatred.

In the end, Chu Wanning died as well.

The name-sealing spell that had laid on Mo Ran's blade for more than a decade disappeared with him.

That night, Mo Ran downed copious amounts of pear-blossom wine. A bit tipsy, he ran his hand along the ice-cold body of the blade, no longer able to tell if what he felt was ecstasy or sorrow. He flicked it and listened to its reverberations, like the sound of drums and horns on the battlefield, like a haitang chilled to the root. He lay on the roof of Wushan Palace, laughing uncontrollably, waxing from delighted to deranged.

Mo Ran didn't remember if he had shed any tears that night, only that when he woke in the morning, the long blade that had gone nameless for over a decade had been engraved with two clear-cut characters: Bugui.

For you do not return.

Never again.

But why had the weapon that had accompanied him through endless battles in his last life appeared in this world reborn? And how had it ended up at a Xuanyuan Pavilion auction?!

Before Mo Ran could think on it further, all the thousands of cultivators at the auction house released streams of spiritual energy, each rushing to commune with Bugui.

Mo Ran watched mutely.

It would be no use. Since it was Bugui, and since Mo Ran was here, under no circumstances would any other person in the world be able to command that long blade.

Did its appearance have something to do with that little bastard hiding behind the scenes? If so, then his decision to release Bugui into the world at this time meant that he knew Mo Ran and Chu Wanning were trying to track him down, and that his goal wasn't in fact to test other people's spiritual essences.

Then what *was* he trying to do?

Furthermore, was this Bugui real? Or was it merely bait, like those fakes at Jincheng Lake?

Mind filled with questions, Mo Ran reached out with a tendril of his own spiritual energy. If Bugui wasn't a fake, then it would surely resonate with him. If he wanted to avoid notice, he couldn't let the resonance be too obvious, so if he only used a little bit...

He had just released the tiniest thread of energy when a faint groan came from behind him.

"Shizun?!"

Mo Ran whipped his head around to find Chu Wanning collapsed at the table, brows locked and lips blue. His snow-white robes spread out like smoke, and his handsome face was paler than frost. He had passed out, his eyes screwed shut like some chronic illness had flared up within him.

Mo Ran had never expected something like this to happen so suddenly. He panicked, pulling back his spiritual energy and running to Chu Wanning's side to cradle him in his arms. "Shizun, what's wrong?!"

82
This Venerable One Can't Believe It

OUTSIDE THE FRAGRANCE INN of Rainbell Isle stood its willowy innkeeper, all dressed up with pearl bracelets clinking on her wrists as she leaned against the door, eating melon seeds fried in snake gall.

Whenever Xuanyuan Pavilion held an auction, most of the visitors ended up staying at her place, since she was clever on top of being pretty. A flicker of those beautiful eyes and she could easily guess what her guests desired.

It was just past noon, and the sun beamed brightly overhead. The innkeeper spit out some melon seed shells. The auction would be over in another two hours or so. The inns on Rainbell Isle were all fairly expensive, and visiting cultivators tended not to stay, so she didn't expect to make much from rentals today. That was all right. These cultivators, heroes, and whatnot still had to eat before leaving, and she fully intended to squeeze them for dinner.

She flicked some bits of fruit peel off her skirt, then turned to yell at the waiter inside. "Er Fu, wipe the tables and chairs down again, and fetch a basket of the melon seeds I fried. Put a plate on every table. Gotta get ready for our guests tonight."

"Alrighty, Boss, right away." The waiter jogged off.

Done with her sunbathing and snacking, the innkeeper grinned contentedly. She was about to head inside to supervise the work when she noticed a fast-approaching, black-and-white silhouette at the end of the road. Once it drew closer, she saw that it was a handsome cultivator dressed in black who was holding someone in his arms. Nigh instantly, he burst into her inn at full tilt and in a burning panic.

"A room—room, room, room!"

The waiter gaped. Maybe because the cultivator had appeared so suddenly and because he was acting so strangely, the waiter could only stare at him in bewilderment, mouth hanging open.

"I said, I want a room!" Mo Ran roared angrily. "What are you, deaf? Where's your boss?!"

"Aiyo, Xianjun." The voice of a young woman came from behind him, a little simpering and a lot apologetic, a voice at which it would be hard to stay mad. Mo Ran turned around and came face-to-face with the innkeeper's agreeable smile. "My apologies for the wait. He's new. I am the innkeeper. Please feel free to come to me if you need anything."

With his dark, handsome eyebrows raised, Mo Ran hurriedly repeated, "Give me a room!"

The innkeeper looked him over quickly and discreetly. The cultivator was wearing a cloak, so he was probably an attendee of the Xuanyuan auction, but the hood had fallen off in his haste, revealing a handsome face that still had a trace of tender youth. That wasn't important; what *was* important was the brocade pouch embroidered with a giant tortoise that was tied around his wrist. It was a qiankun pouch from Xuanyuan Pavilion, one they specifically gave to patrons to allow them to carry purchased goods.

The innkeeper's eyes gleamed. The cultivator had money. *Lots* of money.

Next, she glanced at the person in his arms. He was covered in a cloak and his face was turned away, so she couldn't see what he looked like. But the innkeeper's eyes were keen as a hawk's, and they swept over those snow-white robes made of high-quality silk before zeroing in on the hand peeking out from the wide opening of his sleeve.

Long and slender, porcelain-fine skin, delicate fingertips, shapely joints. A beauty.

The innkeeper understood immediately. Sure, this was a beautiful man, but it wasn't like dual cultivation between men was unheard of in the cultivation world. Nothing to write home about.

"Da Fu, open a room." The innkeeper wasted no time and asked no questions. Her orders were brisk as she snapped her fingers. "The best one we have."

Chu Wanning's sickness had come suddenly and without the slightest warning. It was a good thing they were in Guyueye territory, where good medicines and physicians were readily available.

The sage doctor's eyes were closed as he took the pulse in Chu Wanning's wrist with lightly calloused fingertips. For a long time, he didn't utter a single sound.

Mo Ran could hold it in no longer. "Doctor, how is my shizun?"

"It's not a pressing issue, but..."

Mo Ran seriously couldn't stand people who talked in circles and beat around the bush. "But what?" he pressed, eyes wide.

"But it's quite strange. Your master's cultivation is remarkable; he's at a level achieved by few in this world. Yet my careful examination has revealed that his spiritual core is exceedingly fragile, even more so than that of a fledgling cultivator still in the foundation establishment stage."

If cultivation was water, then the spiritual core was the vessel holding that water. Where one's cultivation accrued slowly over time, one's spiritual core was inborn. It was easier for someone with an innately powerful core to cultivate, but once one's cultivation reached a certain point, it would begin to bolster that core. Generally speaking, cultivation and core were interdependent and complementary. An eminent zongshi like Chu Wanning should naturally have an extremely robust core, so physicians generally didn't bother to check such a thing when taking his pulse.

Mo Ran was shocked. "How is that possible?!"

"I thought the same. However, I checked over and over, and it was the same every time."

"My shizun's spiritual core is weaker than a fledgling cultivator's? H-how could that be? There's no way! Could you please take another look? Maybe you made a mistake somewhere."

"I have always been most cautious in my practice, and I have never said anything of which I am not absolutely certain. If the young xianjun doesn't believe me, then feel free to get a second opinion. The result will be the same."

Mo Ran was stunned.

"The issue has arisen precisely because your master's spiritual core is so fragile," the doctor continued. "He appears to have recently suffered some sort of influence from a powerful weapon, one that has some sort of resonance with him yet does not belong to him. He experienced a rebound as a consequence of that resonance, then lost consciousness because his core couldn't withstand it. I will prescribe some medicinal decoctions. Have him take them and get plenty of rest; he will be fine."

Mo Ran saw the doctor off and came back to sit by Chu Wanning's bed with his cheek propped up in one hand, watching him in a daze. A weak core? How was that even possible?

However, while the old man couldn't possibly have known what had happened at Xuanyuan Pavilion, he had correctly surmised that

Chu Wanning had encountered a powerful weapon. He likely wasn't spouting nonsense.

There was also the matter of "Bugui." Mo Ran had only released a tiny bit of spiritual energy at Xuanyuan Pavilion when Chu Wanning suddenly collapsed, so he had been unable to get a chance to see if the long blade was indeed the holy weapon he had possessed in his past life. But if it was, then why had Bugui resonated with Chu Wanning? And moreover, why had it caused a rebound?

Mo Ran stared at Chu Wanning, brooding while his thoughts tied themselves into a big old knot. He didn't know how much time passed before Chu Wanning's brows scrunched up, his eyelashes quivering like he was having another nightmare.

Mo Ran reached out and gently smoothed his brow, though he had no idea what compelled him to do it. "Shizun..."

Chu Wanning did not respond.

"Shizun... Chu Wanning... I've already lived two lifetimes, but could it be that there are still things about you that I don't know?"

In short order, the innkeeper finished boiling the medicine in the inn's kitchen and came upstairs to deliver it.

Mo Ran tasted it—ridiculously bitter, as expected. Chu Wanning hated bitter things. Mo Ran sighed and called back the innkeeper, who was about to leave.

"Innkeep, do you have anything sweet?"

"Aye... We make fresh sugar candies, but today's batch is all gone. I can send someone to go buy some if Xianjun would like."

Mo Ran looked at the steaming medicine and shook his head. "Never mind, then. The medicine will be cold by then, and it has to be taken hot to be effective. Thanks, though."

"Ah, no problem. Please feel free to call on me if you need anything else." Having said that, the innkeeper tactfully left, closing the door on her way out.

Mo Ran carried the medicine over and set it down by the bed, then sat at the edge with one hand on his knee. He reached out with the other to help Chu Wanning up. "Shizun, it's time for your medicine."

Mo Ran had plenty of practice feeding Chu Wanning medicine from his last lifetime. He held Chu Wanning in one arm so that his shizun leaned against him, then scooped up a spoonful of the medicine with his other hand, blew to cool it, and slowly fed it to him.

When he thought about it now, this was the second time since his rebirth that he had taken care of Chu Wanning. He disliked this person, yet he felt such unease whenever he got sick. He really couldn't understand it.

"Bitter..." Despite being unconscious, the man in his arms could taste the medicine. Chu Wanning's eyebrows pulled together, and he turned away, refusing to drink any more.

Mo Ran was used to this behavior. Holding another spoonful, he tugged Chu Wanning back around and coaxed him patiently. "One more. You'll feel better after, here." And fed him another spoonful.

Chu Wanning coughed up half of it, brow furrowing even more. "So bitter..."

"It's sweet. The next one will be sweet, come, come."

"Nngh..."

"The next one! Promise! It's unbelievably sweet! This venerable one sent people to find the sweetest syrup in all the land!" Mo Ran was so distracted cajoling Chu Wanning into drinking the medicine that he forgot himself for a moment and absentmindedly let words from his past life fall from his mouth. "It's delicious—you'll regret it if you don't open up. Come on."

Just like that, he managed to sweet talk Chu Wanning into drinking the whole bowl. After the last spoonful, Mo Ran let out a breath and was about to get up and tidy things when there was a sudden flash of white. Before he could react, a slap landed soundly on his cheek.

"You liar, get the hell out!" Chu Wanning snapped.

Then his head drooped, and he went right back to sleep, leaving Mo Ran with his mouth hanging half-open, pitifully holding his cheek. He was about to get mad when the man in his arms groaned softly, like he was dreaming about something distressing, his face pale.

When Mo Ran saw him like this, he just couldn't be angry. He didn't have any candy, but his gaze landed on the qiankun pouch sitting at the head of the bed. Struck by a sudden idea, he took out a bottle of Tapir Fragrance Dew. Then he tapped Chu Wanning's cheek with his hand, not too gentle but not too hard, and let that count as revenge.

"Wait here a bit. I'll go make you some sweet dew water to drink."

Chu Wanning didn't respond, so Mo Ran moved to lay him back down. But when he leaned closer in the process, he heard a low exhale and a slurred mumble, "It...wronged you..."

Mo Ran froze. "What?"

Chu Wanning's eyes were tightly closed, and his eyelashes shivered unceasingly, as if he was enduring something excruciating. Blood drained from his face bit by bit. He seemed to have fallen into another dream, one that was even more frightening than the last. He shook his head minutely, an uncharacteristically sorrowful expression appearing on his habitually impassive face.

"I...it was I..."

For a split second, Mo Ran's heart stuttered erratically. A strange feeling flooded his chest, as if there was a secret right in front of him, from which he was separated by only one last layer of haze—a secret he was on the verge of unveiling. Staring fixedly at Chu Wanning, he asked quietly, "You what?"

"It was I...who wronged...you..."

Mo Ran felt suddenly disoriented. He didn't know if the dim light of the candle was making him see things, but he thought he perceived a glimmer of wetness amidst Chu Wanning's thick eyelashes.

It was I who wronged you.

The words left Chu Wanning's lips as light as mist, but they hit Mo Ran with all the force of crashing thunder.

Mo Ran abruptly shot up from the bed and went stiff. His pupils contracted into pinpoints as he stared in disbelief at the man on the bed. Instantly his expression changed, his heart pounding like a stampede of horses and hands clenching tightly into fists. In one moment, he felt the blood in his body catch fire, and in the next, it froze over.

"What did you say? Wh..." After a moment of being paralyzed in shock, Mo Ran seized Chu Wanning by the throat, his eyes flashing with danger. The guise of guileless naivety that he had worn since rebirth vanished into thin air. "Chu Wanning, what did you just say? Say it again! *Say it again!*"

It was I who wronged you. I won't blame you, in life or in death.

It was a curse that Mo Ran could never forget, a nightmare that had haunted him for two lifetimes. How many times had he closed his eyes only to hear these words sighed by his ear, though the speaker was long gone from the world?

These were words that Chu Wanning had spoken in their past life only as he lay dying. So why now would he—

Why would he—

Unless Chu Wanning had also been reborn?!

83

This Venerable One Wants You

THE LUDICROUS THOUGHT made Mo Ran see red. Reason had left him. He shook uncontrollably as his hand tightened around Chu Wanning's throat, pressing for a response with a deep-voiced roar.

If Chu Wanning said the rest of it—if he said, "in life or in death,"—then there could be no doubt... No doubt...

"Ngh!"

A stifled groan by his ear. Chu Wanning couldn't breathe. His face flushed from the lack of air as his struggles weakened.

Mo Ran stilled, madness and clarity chasing one another across his red-tinted, wide-open eyes—before he snapped out of it and hastily let go. Chu Wanning slumped heavily back onto the bed. The five stark stripes of finger-shaped bruises against his neck gradually returned Mo Ran to his senses.

He opened his mouth, wanting to say, "Shizun," but it wouldn't come out. He tried to say, "Chu Wanning," but his voice failed him there, too, until finally, hesitantly, he uttered hoarsely, "You..."

Mo Ran's throat was parched, as if it had been scorched by fire. He swallowed with difficulty while retrieving the scattered pieces of his rationality. Scenes from the days prior flashed before his eyes: In this lifetime, Chu Wanning had never behaved strangely. There was no way he could have been reborn.

Then why had he said those words? His dying words from their past life: "It was I who wronged you"? Why now, at this time?

Hadn't Chu Wanning only uttered those words to save Xue Meng? To save those sanctimonious cultivators? Weren't they empty words that he had said merely because he had no other choice?

Mo Ran had never believed—had never *wanted* to believe—that Chu Wanning would genuinely admit his wrongdoings to his face. That he would actually say something softly compassionate to him. No matter what, Chu Wanning had obviously been lying. He *obviously* detested Mo Ran. No matter what, his shizun had always looked down on him—had never treated him with sincerity.

Mo Ran didn't regret killing him at all. He didn't regret...

Mo Ran turned away, slowly closing his eyes. He didn't want to stay here a single second longer. What did it matter to him if Chu Wanning lived or died?!

He turned to leave. He wanted to leave. His feet refused to move.

It was I who wronged you.

In his memories, in the end, that cold, handsome face had looked gentle even when covered in blood. At the edge of Kunlun's Heavenly Lake, this man had lain in a pool of blood and slowly lifted a hand to poke Mo Ran's forehead. His fingers had been cold as ice, yet there had been warmth in his phoenix eyes.

Mo Ran had been sure, back then, that he was only seeing things.

I won't blame you, in life or in death, Chu Wanning had whispered, even as a trail of blood dripped slowly from his eyes.

"Mo Ran..."

The man on the bed murmured in his dream. Just two quiet syllables, and the one he called to began to tremble all over. By the time Mo Ran realized what was happening, he was standing at the bedside, one hand braced against the headboard as he leaned over Chu Wanning, staring fixedly at his pale face.

Those thin, lightly colored lips opened slightly to say again: "Mo Ran..."

Closing his eyes, Mo Ran drew his brows tightly together as his fingers dug into the cold, hard surface of the quince wood, as if he was striving to restrain something. Ultimately, he couldn't, and it came out in a raw whisper. "Chu Wanning, did you mean it? Everything that you said, did you mean it all?"

His chest hurt so terribly that it felt like it might explode. There was no way Chu Wanning had also been reborn. If he was saying these words now, it could only mean that, at this point in time, in his heart, he already felt remorse for how he'd treated Mo Ran.

Did he mean it?

Chu Wanning was only talking in his sleep, so of course he didn't answer. Even so, Mo Ran waited and wished for one.

No response. For a long while, he waited with his eyes closed, but there was only silence.

Mo Ran sighed quietly and reluctantly opened his eyes, only to be met unexpectedly by a pair of hazy, half-lidded phoenix eyes, caught between wakefulness and slumber.

He didn't know when Chu Wanning had raised his lids, but it was clear from his expression that he wasn't truly awake and aware. This was only a momentary stirring between bouts of torment. That pair of eyes the color of the night sky were vacant and glazed, as if they held eternity.

Yuheng of the Night Sky was always lightning sharp. He rarely looked so disoriented. Without his habitual keen edges, the man lying there looked unexpectedly beautiful. The corners of his eyes were tinged with a faint red as he gazed at Mo Ran, unguarded.

Mo Ran felt a violent tremor in his heart and a tightness in his throat. Voice low, he murmured, "You..."

Chu Wanning looked much too like he had when they made love in their past life. Something stirred inside Mo Ran, and for a moment he felt as if he was still at Wushan Palace and Chu Wanning was his prisoner, his personal plaything. The thought made his mouth dry and his breaths grow heavy.

I can't... I don't like him. Don't touch him anymore. The sins of a bygone life are sins of the past. In this life, we're nothing more than master and disciple.

And so Mo Ran stayed as he was, looking down at Chu Wanning with one hand braced against the headboard, preventing himself from crossing that line. His hair pooled over his shoulder from where it was tied in a ponytail, the tips brushing the pillow.

Chu Wanning lay there, fully dressed, his long hair spread loosely about him. At first, his expression was dazed and insensate, and some time passed before Mo Ran's reflection slowly appeared in his eyes. Chu Wanning hesitated. Then, as if still caught in the clutches of his nightmare, unable to discern when and where he was, he slowly reached out with a hand that for a moment paused in midair, and at last touched Mo Ran's brow.

"It was I who wronged you..." He spoke the words with an uncharacteristic gentleness, the way he had in their past life.

Something inside Mo Ran collapsed with a resonant boom. Blood boiling and head feverish, all the sense and rationality he had worked so hard to retrieve fell apart in an instant. Without thinking about any of it, he gave in to that familiar desire. He leaned down and ravenously captured those slightly parted lips with his own.

The past came crashing back in a wave, melting their surroundings away like snow and frost. Mo Ran felt as if he were back at Wushan

Palace amidst silky red satin, illuminated by the light of candles gilded with dragon and phoenix. Beneath that crimson drapery, this man was struggling and spitting curses, panting and humiliated yet unable to escape, helpless against his unyielding grasp.

"Nn..."

The noise that Chu Wanning let out between the slides of warm wetness drove Mo Ran mad. All those words about not liking him, hating him, and never touching him again, all of them vaporized into thin air.

Mo Ran felt as if he had never yet died—that the lightly quivering body beneath his still belonged to him. He wanted to kiss Chu Wanning, to hold him, to humiliate and torment him until this lofty, immaculate man was unable to take it anymore. Until he was crying and begging, fucked into oblivion.

"Chu Wanning..." Mo Ran murmured hoarsely. A wave of heat rolled through him, washing over his very soul. Even the tips of his fingers felt like they had caught flame.

Once again, he closed his lips over that cool, soft pair, which still tasted slightly of the bitter medicine. The beating of his heart was like the thunder of drums inside his chest as he kissed with abandon, mad with desire. Mo Ran knew this person through and through. Since his rebirth, he had been loath to be intimate with Chu Wanning because of the resentment he harbored toward him, but kissing him now was pure ecstasy.

It was a high so intense that it ate away at him, like the first taste of sweet dew on the tongue of a traveler dying of thirst in the desert, like being enveloped in the soft warmth of a fur coat heated over a fire in the bitter cold of a freezing night.

Mo Ran had thought that he would surely have nothing to do with Chu Wanning in this reborn life. He hadn't expected to ultimately succumb to his desires, to be driven to lose control after a mere few words, to kiss him like this.

If it were not for the fact that he couldn't get Chu Wanning's robes open—and in trying to do so was pricked by something that fell out of his shizun's robes—Mo Ran might have given in and taken Chu Wanning right then and there without any thought, consequences be damned.

Clang!

Something metallic pricked Mo Ran's finger and fell on the bed. It rolled a little before coming to a stop.

Mo Ran was far too turned on to mind the scratch. He only threw an irritated glare at the object before turning back to Chu Wanning's ridiculous robes. It was one thing when he kept his distance and didn't touch him, but now that he was on top of his shizun, the feelings from his past life came rushing back. The mere thought of how Chu Wanning's smooth, narrow waist had felt under his hands made him unbearably hot and heavy.

But Chu Wanning's silken white robes were impossible to remove, almost like they had been enchanted with some kind of spell. Mo Ran cursed under his breath and slammed his fist against the headboard before resentfully climbing off the bed to go fetch his blade. He would make short work of that thrice-wrapped belt sash.

As he sat up, he saw the fallen metallic object out of the corner of his eye. He didn't pay it any mind at first, but then a bolt of clarity flashed through his arousal-addled mind.

Mo Ran stilled. His head snapped around to take another look at that thing.

It was a golden hair clasp, vibrantly colorful and decorated with orchids and butterflies—the very same one that he had bought for Xia Sini at Peach Blossom Springs after days of saving up feathers.

He had personally pinned it to Xia Sini's ponytail to cheer up his sullen little shidi, saying, "Little kids should wear lively colors like red and gold."

Mo Ran picked up the hair clasp. He stared at it in a stupor, feeling like he had been doused with cold water. Hang on... What did this mean? Why would Chu Wanning have something that Mo Ran had given to Xia Sini?

Could it be...

A frightening thought crossed Mo Ran's mind. He turned around slowly, and his gaze, still dark with desire, landed on Chu Wanning. His shizun had passed out again. Mo Ran stared at his face, taking in those lips reddened from his kisses, and his heart skipped a few beats.

No way, absolutely not. He had to be out of his mind... Was Chu Wanning not just messing with him? Was... Was...Xia Sini seriously Chu Wanning's son?

Mo Ran shuddered at the thought. His head was about to explode!

84

This Venerable One Stole a Kiss and You Don't Even Know

When Chu Wanning woke up, it was to the sight of Mo Ran staring into the middle distance at the table with his cheek propped up in his hand. The reflection of the candle flame flickered in his pitch-black eyes, bright in his vacant gaze.

Chu Wanning thought about getting up, but there was no strength in his limbs, and he had to surrender. The patterned lilac curtains wafted. He turned onto his side, watching Mo Ran without a sound. The silly boy remained lost in thought, ignorant to the fact that his shizun was awake.

Who could blame him? Anyone who found out that their lover already had a son with some other woman would be equally shocked.

Was Xia Sini really Chu Wanning's child? How could that be...? Chu Wanning was so aloof and particular. What woman could hope to catch his eye?

Besides, if this whole thing was for real, then he must have had a kid in their past life too. But in all the years he had spent with Mo Ran in that life, Chu Wanning couldn't have been further from what one would expect of a married man, both in his daily conduct and between the sheets.

But how else was he to explain this golden butterfly hair clasp?! Mo Ran banged his head against the table in anguish, about to lose his mind from sheer confusion.

He wasn't that smart to begin with, and he had never been able to wrap his head around twisty-turny things. The more he thought, the more his head hurt, until he finally grabbed his skull and flopped onto the table with a despairing, "Ngah!" and stayed there, unmoving.

"Mo Ran, what are you doing?" asked an even, soothing voice, pleasant like the chime of scattering jade, though the undertone was slightly hoarse.

Mo Ran instantly bounced up in surprise. "Shizun, you're awake?"

"Mn." Chu Wanning coughed lightly before looking up at him. "Is this...Rainbell Isle's inn?"

"Y-yeah." Mo Ran stood and moved toward the bed, where he noticed a small tear in Chu Wanning's lower lip. His face swiftly turned red as he remembered how he had lost control in his lust-induced haze and had very nearly made a serious mistake.

"What is it?" Chu Wanning asked upon noticing his perturbation.

"Nothing, nothing." Mo Ran waved his hands and hastily changed the subject. "Anyway, Shizun suddenly fainted at Xuanyuan Pavilion, so I carri—ahem, brought you here to rest. Then I got a physician to take a look at you and prescribe some medicine, and then..."

...I heard you sleep talking, was reminded of some past affairs, couldn't stop myself, and kissed you.

Of course he couldn't say such things. Mo Ran trailed off, his gaze uncharacteristically frantic, even flustered.

When Chu Wanning heard that he had been examined by a doctor and saw the strange expression on Mo Ran's face, his heart dropped. Had Mo Ran learned of the poison that turned him into a child? His hands subconsciously tightened on the quilt as he rasped, "What did the physician say?"

"He said Shizun was affected by that holy weapon, and that's what made you faint." Mo Ran hesitated. "Shizun, your spiritual core..."

"Don't worry about it. It's just a bit weaker than average."

Mo Ran blinked. He was thinking about the scars that lay over both Chu Xun and Chu Wanning's hearts and considering the possibility of some kind of connection. However, the way Chu Wanning spoke of it, that didn't seem to be the case. He couldn't help asking, "But how? Shizun is so powerful. There's no way your spiritual core could have always been so frail. When did it happen?"

"A long time ago. I was injured once, many years in the past, and it's been that way ever since." Chu Wanning waved his hand indifferently. That wasn't what concerned him. "Did he say anything else?"

Mo Ran shook his head. "Nope."

Chu Wanning considered him in the dim haze of the candlelight. "Then why were you banging your head on the table?"

For a long moment, Mo Ran was mute. He tried and failed to hold it in, so he threw caution to the wind and produced the golden butterfly hair clasp from his sleeve. He set it in Chu Wanning's palm. "I found this."

Chu Wanning did not reply.

"On you."

The hair clasp glinted in the light as Chu Wanning's heart sank lower and lower. So he had been found out after all. He sighed quietly.

A few moments passed in silence, neither of them speaking. Finally, Chu Wanning closed his eyes, and was about to come clean when he heard Mo Ran mumble in a small voice, "Shizun, is Xia-shidi...truly your son?"

Chu Wanning was struck utterly speechless. He opened his eyes, and the blood that had been frozen in his veins began to circulate again. For a while, he didn't know what to say as he stared silently at Mo Weiyu, who stood by the bed with a complicated expression. Then, slowly, a clear verdict formed in Chu Wanning's gaze: *Moron.*

"That's right." Chu Wanning lifted a hand and calmly took back the hair clasp before Mo Ran could react. "Didn't I tell you before? Why are you asking again?"

Mo Ran buried his face in his hands. "I'm just...making sure..."

Yet despite Chu Wanning's repeated confirmations that Xia Sini was indeed his flesh and blood, Mo Ran didn't quite buy it. Shoving down his intense feelings of dismay, he decided to grill Xia Sini about it the next time he saw his little shidi. Until those two actually acknowledged their blood ties to one another, he would sooner die than believe it!

After a bit of rest, Chu Wanning recovered some strength in his limbs and moved to sit up in the bed. "My clothes..." He ran his hand over his collars and paused, frowning. "Why are they so disheveled?"

"Ahem." Mo Ran hurriedly steered the topic away, fearful that Chu Wanning might remember some fragments of his earlier behavior. "Shizun, you must be hungry, right? I heard the food at this inn's pretty good, especially the wensi tofu. Let's go down and get a bite. My treat."

Chu Wanning shot him a cold look. "What, with the money I gave you?"

He still shook out his voluminous sleeves and opened the door to go downstairs.

Rainbell Isle's cuisine was similar to Yangzhou's—light and refreshing, with a tendency toward sweetness, and very agreeable to Chu Wanning's taste.

By now, the auction was over and many of the attendees had already left. Mo Ran and Chu Wanning had also requested a private booth, so there was no longer much need to wear cloaks to conceal their identities. After they took their seats inside, a waiter came and poured them each a cup of biluochun green tea, then handed them a menu before retreating.

"Shizun can look through the menu first."

"You can order. I'm pretty content with all Jiangnan-style dishes," Chu Wanning said as he lifted the cup and took a small sip of tea. His brows furrowed as soon as the tea touched his lips, and he paused.

"What is it? Too hot?"

"It's nothing. Maybe the weather is dry; my lip is a bit cracked." Chu Wanning touched the corner of his mouth uncertainly. Weird. When had that happened?

Mo Ran lowered his head in guilty silence.

It would be a while before the food was ready, so Chu Wanning took the time to discuss the events at Xuanyuan Pavilion with Mo Ran. They had left early, so they didn't know who'd won the holy weapon in the end, but that wouldn't be too hard to ascertain if they asked around.

As they conferred, an assortment of Yangzhou dishes began to cover the table. Chu Wanning felt like they had reviewed all that they could of what they knew, so he stopped asking questions to look over the food lining the table. He paused for a moment before lifting his eyelids slightly to glance at the person across from him, whose smile was a tad nervous.

"Have you been to Jiangnan before?" Chu Wanning asked.

Mo Ran had, of course, gone to see the apricot blossoms and misty rains of Jiangnan in his previous life. However, he hadn't forgotten that he was only seventeen at present, and that he had only joined Sisheng Peak about two years ago, so he immediately shook his head. "Nope."

Chu Wanning's eyelashes lowered back down, his expression neutral as he said in a clear voice, "But you ordered all the best dishes."

Mo Ran started. Only then did he realize that he had ordered every single dish in accordance with Chu Wanning's preferences. His only thought had been to make sure Chu Wanning ate well so that he could recover his strength. He had entirely forgotten that he shouldn't be so familiar with the local cuisine.

"I worked in the kitchens of a pleasure house when I was young," he said. "So I've heard of these dishes, even if I haven't tried them."

Luckily, Chu Wanning didn't press the issue. "Let's eat."

Freshwater fare was a big part of Jiangnan cuisine, especially on Rainbell Isle, where there were baskets of crab and shrimp and strings of fish as far as the eye could see. The square beech table was naturally laden with seafood. Crispy fried eel with sauce poured over it; sweet-and-sour squirrel fish, crunchy without and tender within; steamed mantis shrimp; chrysanthemum-sauteed sea snail; and braised silver carp. It smelled heavenly.

Aside from those, the meat and vegetable dishes were just as exquisitely made and elegantly plated, as were the desserts. There were stewed crab meatballs; savory pork trotter jelly; shredded tofu simmered in chicken broth; soup dumplings; wensi tofu;[23] and more.

With his cheek in one hand, Mo Ran watched the waiter set down the last dish—osmanthus cake—and snuck a glance at Chu Wanning, wondering which dish he would go for first. He pondered for a minute and secretly placed his bet: definitely the meatballs. These were Chu Wanning's favorite Yangzhou dish, after all.

---

23 *A soup dish with thinly sliced tofu threads that melt in your mouth.*

Sure enough, as soon as the dishes were all out, Chu Wanning's chopsticks reached unhesitatingly in that direction.

Mo Ran sighed to himself. *This guy is always so predictable, be it in how he eats or what he does, it's always the—*

Plop. An adorably plump meatball landed in Mo Ran's bowl.

—same?

Mo Ran's head snapped up, surprise at this show of favor slowly crossing his face. "Sh-Shizun."

"Thanks for taking care of me these past few days."

Wait, had he heard that right? Mo Ran was astonished. Had Chu Wanning just thanked him for taking care of him?! Never once in the entirety of their last lifetime had he ever said any such thing.

Chu Wanning watched as the young man across from him slowly turned red, his eyebrows lifting higher and higher and his eyes getting rounder and rounder. A tuft of hair even curled up from his head to sway happily back and forth. Chu-zongshi didn't quite know how to react, but he had to preserve his dignity, so he took another lofty sip of tea. *Ow, my lips...*

Truth be told, during the days he'd spent by Mo Ran's side as Xia Sini, Chu Wanning had begun to feel a little guilty. When he thought about it late at night, he had to admit that his personality really was too harsh, and he had been overly stern with Mo Ran. So he told himself that, when he returned to normal, he would no longer carry on in that way—that he would do better.

When Chu Wanning had met with the Xuanji Elder at Peach Blossom Springs, he had hemmed and hawed for a good long while before finally forcing the words past his lips and asking how to be less intimidating to disciples.

Xuanji had understandably been taken aback before answering. "First, you have to actually show them that you care."

Show them that you care... Chu Wanning assumed that Mo Ran had never had these meatballs before, so he parted his lips to explain. "Stewed crab meatballs are made with finely minced, high-quality streaky pork that has been mixed with shrimp roe, crab meat, and crab roe and rolled into balls. They are then simmered in clear broth with bok choy, and finally arranged in a red clay pot for a colorful presentation."

Mo Ran was thoroughly dumbfounded. What was Chu Wanning reciting the menu for?

However, to Chu Wanning, patiently introducing new dishes to his disciple was a form of showing care, and so throughout the course of the meal, Mo Ran tried every dish in turn and got an earful of descriptions that sounded like they had come straight out of *Jiangnan Recipes*. If not for Chu Wanning's low, soothing voice, Mo Ran probably would've flipped the table and left.

"Hey, hey, did you hear yet? Linyi Rufeng Sect won the last item at the Xuanyuan Pavilion auction!"

The private booths were divided by bamboo screens, and the people in the next booth over were a bit loud. Their conversation drifted easily over to Mo Ran and Chu Wanning.

Chu Wanning abruptly stopped introducing "savory pork trotter jelly" to exchange a look with Mo Ran. They listened with rapt attention.

A rough-sounding masculine voice was speaking. "Of course I have. A holy weapon, right? Three hundred million gold, paid on the spot. Aiyo, that price—it was more gold than I've ever seen in my entire life."

"Sheesh, is that all you care about? Don't you know that Rufeng Sect also spent fifty million on a Butterfly-Boned Beauty Feast?"

"Heavens, aren't you supposed to eat those? Or dual cultivate with them? Can't believe the biggest sect in the world would use

such a reprehensible method of cultivation. And right out in the open too. How scandalous!"

"Actually, Su-xiong, cultivating through use of Beauty Feasts is perfectly reasonable. It's not in the least bit prohibited. They may look like us, but ultimately, they're not human. It's no different from eating fairy fruits to advance yourself. When you get down to it, there's nothing wrong with the practice."

"Hmph. We'll just have to agree to disagree..."

Someone else laughed lightly. "The one who bought the Beauty Feast is apparently some young disciple of Rufeng Sect who rarely shows his face—a Ye-Something-Xi. I heard he looks decent enough. Wouldn't have expected some guy like that to rely on screwing women to cultivate. If you ask me, Rufeng Sect is on its last legs."

Still another person chuckled. "What's wrong with that? Who doesn't love a beauty?"

Then their conversation turned to roundabout debates on ethics and morality—nothing worth paying attention to.

"So Rufeng Sect bought the holy weapon?" Chu Wanning repeated quietly.

"Sounds like it."

Chu Wanning seemed troubled. "That makes things more difficult. We'll have to go to Rufeng Sect to investigate further..."

Mo Ran let out an, "ah," as he remembered something and muttered, "Shizun used to be in Rufeng Sect."

"Mn."

"Don't wanna go back?"

Chu Wanning looked irritated at the mere mention of returning to them. "They may be a famed sect in the upper cultivation world," he said, brows furrowed, "but I once..."

Before he could finish, there was a sudden commotion in the main hall. Someone was yelling loudly.

"Innkeep, we'll give you five hundred gold if you get rid of these people and clear them out this instant. Our young master is reserving the whole place today."

This Venerable One Isn't Someone You Can Simply Get Rid of with a Mere Fifteen Hundred Gold

The innkeeper's apologetic voice drifted over. "Goodness, my lord is so generous. Five hundred, just like that—this humble one is flattered! But we must be courteous to all our guests if we hope to keep doing business, so we can't hustle them all out, you see. How about this: We have a spacious private room within called the Returning Fog Pavilion. It's reserved for honored guests of means like yourself. Let me show—"

She didn't get to finish before there was a loud clatter of tables and chairs being overturned.

"What's there to see?! Who the hell cares about your Rutting Fog Pavilion or Rutting Dog Pavilion? Goddamn, what kinda shitty name is that? We don't want it! Get rid of them and we'll pay you a thousand!"

"Oh, but my lord looks like such a scholarly, reasonable person. Surely he won't force such a difficult decision on this humble one, yes?" The innkeep simpered coyly, lying through her teeth without so much as batting an eye. "There are simply too many guests here already. However, if my lord dislikes Returning Fog Pavilion, I can certainly offer another room. It's a little smaller but just as elegant, and I'll throw in an entertainment package with song and dance, free of charge. How's that?"

"No! Absolutely not! Fifteen hundred! Tell 'em all to get lost!" the boorish voice bellowed. "Quit dragging your feet! Our young master will be mad if this place isn't ready when he gets here!"

"Wow..." A thousand gold was a lot to the average person, but it was a laughable amount to Mo Ran, the once-emperor of the mortal realm. Even the trinkets he had casually thrown at Song Qiutong to humor her had been priceless treasures. And so his eyes were round with amusement as he chewed idly on his chopstick, laughing to Chu Wanning in a low voice. "Shizun, Shizun, check it out. That guy thinks he can get rid of us with a mere fifteen hundred."

Chu Wanning shot him a look, then lifted the bamboo curtain to look downstairs.

There was a crowd in the main hall. They were dressed in plain clothes that concealed their sect, but every one of them had a high-quality blade glinting at their waist and a faewolf slobbering by their side. While the value of the blades was indeterminate, faewolves had a market price but were next to impossible to come by. Acquiring even one would be no small feat for a minor sect. If each of these people had a faewolf, they were clearly from a prestigious organization.

All the guests had stopped eating to stare apprehensively at the newcomers. It was so quiet inside the hall that one could have heard a pin drop.

Suddenly, a white blur flashed into the inn, bright as snow. There was a beat of silence as everyone took in what it was, then a burst of frantic clamoring as all of them scrambled away from it as the more easily spooked shrieked, "M-monster!"

It was a snow-white faewolf, as tall as three men, if not more. Its eyes were as crimson as blood, its coat as glossy as satin, and its fangs were the length of a grown man's arm, glistening coldly.

Upon that massive, vicious beast sat a handsome young man with an arrogant expression. He reclined casually, one leg over the other, and he was dressed in a set of sleek hunting gear over scarlet raiment with gold-embroidered sleeves. He also wore a silver helmet emblazoned with a lion swallowing the sun, and a lock of red tassel that hung from its crown. His weapon, a jasper bow, laid over his knees.

As soon as the showy cultivators saw him, they all dropped to one knee with hands pressed to their chests, saying in unison, "Greetings to the young master!"

"All right already." The young man waved his hand, looking irritated. "You can't even take care of a little thing like this. Greetings, my ass!"

"Pfft." Mo Ran couldn't help laughing quietly to Chu Wanning. "If they're greeting an ass, then doesn't that make him the ass?"

Chu Wanning didn't dignify that with a response.

The young man sitting stop the soft fur at the faewolf's nape looked mad indeed. "Who's in charge of this dump?"

The innkeeper was frightened, but she stepped up with forced calmness, smiling apologetically. "That would be this humble one, my lord."

"Oh." He shot her a glance. "I'm going to stay here tonight, but I'm not used to having so many people around. Have a talk with them. I'll make up for your losses."

"But my lord..."

"I know that puts you in a tough spot. Here, take this and give each table an apology on my behalf. If anyone really doesn't want to leave, let them be." The young man tossed the innkeeper a pouch, which she opened to find filled with Nine-Turn Returning Pills that glittered golden within. These pills allowed the imbiber's cultivation to grow in leaps and bounds for ten days, and a single pill cost more than two-thousand gold on the market. The innkeeper was at first shocked by this extravagant display, then discreetly breathed a sigh of relief. No cultivator would turn down something like these. With these pills, it would be perfectly acceptable to ask everyone to leave.

As the innkeeper went around the tables apologizing and offering compensation, the young man yawned before glaring down at his attendants. "All of you are so useless. Do I really have to do everything myself?"

The attendants looked at one another, after which there was a scattered response of, "Gongzi is ever brilliant and indomitable."

The guests dispersed in short order. Other than Chu Wanning and Mo Ran, who didn't care for money or cultivation pills, everyone accepted the recompense and left with zero complaints to go stay elsewhere.

"Gongzi, everyone else left, but two guests declined," the innkeeper reported. "They say that as it's already late and one of them is unwell, they don't wish to go elsewhere..."

"Never mind them, no need to hassle an invalid." The young man waved his hand, unconcerned. "As long as they don't bother me."

Chu Wanning, said invalid, listened to all this in silence.

The innkeeper beamed. "Gongzi is such a kind person," she said warmly. "It's getting late. Would Gongzi like to rest or have something to eat first?"

"I'm hungry," the young man replied. "No need for rest, just bring me a meal."

"Of course, my humble store will certainly provide Gongzi only the best. Our chef's signature dishes are crab meatballs, savory pork trotter jelly—"

"Crabby meatballs?" The young man was obviously not from the south and didn't much care for their cuisine. He blinked at the name of the dish, then waved his hand with a frown. "Pass. I can't even begin to understand these ridiculous names."

Maybe he was just some insanely rich merchant and not a cultured young master after all.

The innkeep paused for a long moment. "Then what would Gongzi like? We will do our utmost to serve."

"Easy." The young man gestured at his attendants. "Five catties of beef for each of them, ten for me, and then a catty of soju and two legs of lamb. That'll do to tide us over. One shouldn't eat too much late at night anyway."

"Wow..." Mo Ran turned to Chu Wanning, meaning to make fun of the guy's bottomless appetite. However, he found Chu Wanning staring fixedly at the young man with an indecipherable, hazy expression. "Shizun seems to know him," Mo Ran said absently.

"Mn."

Mo Ran had said it offhandedly and hadn't expected Chu Wanning to actually confirm. He tripped over his own words in surprise. "Huh? Th-then who is he?"

"The only son of Rufeng Sect's leader," Chu Wanning said softly. "Nangong Si."

Mo Ran fell silent. No wonder Chu Wanning knew him. He had once been with Linyi Rufeng Sect, after all. Of course he knew what the sect leader's son looked like. It was also no wonder that Mo Ran himself didn't know the guy, as by the time he had gone around butchering Rufeng Sect in his previous lifetime, this youth had already up and died from some illness.

At the time, he had assumed that this son of a sect leader must've been a sickly cripple, but the fellow in front of them was healthy, lively, and had ego to spare. How could a guy like this have died of illness? Some kind of sudden plague, maybe?

Downstairs, Nangong Si was happily digging in. He inhaled all ten catties of beef and both legs of lamb in no time at all and gulped down not a few bowls of wine on top of that. Mo Ran watched speechlessly from upstairs.

"Shizun, isn't Rufeng Sect all about refinement and stuff? What's up with their young master? He's got even fewer manners than our Xue Mengmeng."

Chu Wanning shoved Mo Ran's head away from where it had nosed over, even though his own face was still turned to peer at the scene downstairs. "Don't make up nicknames for your fellow disciples."

"Heh heh." Mo Ran laughed and was about to say something else when he paused, suddenly realizing something. Chu Wanning's finger was pressed against his forehead, pushing him away. In the process, his sleeve draped softly over Mo Ran's face like a wisp of mist. The sleeve was made of extremely light material, like silk or satin but not quite, and it felt both warm and cool, almost like water.

Back in their room, when he had been reeling with desire and unable to tug off Chu Wanning's robes, he'd thought the robes had just been too tightly bound. When he examined them now, Mo Ran realized that they were made of frozen mist silk from Kunlun Taxue Palace.

Kunlun Taxue Palace was the most aloof and detached sect in the upper cultivation realm. Its disciples were inducted at age five, and one year later, they were sent into secluded cultivation in the sacred land of Kunlun. There they were compelled to stay until they managed to cultivate their spiritual cores. Although spiritual cores were innate and cultivation merely awakened them, it was still a long process that often took ten to fifteen years. As others were barred from entering the sacred land during this time, the disciples' needs were a basic problem. Food was one thing, as the sacred land was adjacent to Wangmu Lake, so the Taxue Palace disciples could always go fishing for sustenance. However, it wasn't like they could weave their own clothes.

And so their sect had invented frozen mist silk. Clothes made from this silk were not only light as mist, they were also enchanted to be naturally impervious to common dust and grime. They thus didn't need washing unless they were splashed by substances like blood.

The most amazing property of this silk was its ability to morph in accordance with the wearer's body. This was absolutely necessary for the disciples of Taxue Palace, who entered the sacred land as small children at five years old, and who couldn't leave until they were young adults of fifteen or twenty. Clothes made of frozen mist silk would grow with them, so during those long years, they always had clothes that fit.

What was Chu Wanning doing, wearing robes made of this special material?

Mo Ran squinted, a spark flashing through his mind. He suddenly felt like something was off—like he had been mistaken about something from the very start. What was it?

"Excuse me, may I ask where I might find the innkeeper?"

Mo Ran's thoughts were interrupted by a confident, yet friendly and courteous voice. He looked down to see the group of Rufeng Sect disciples who had been at Xuanyuan Pavilion earlier. The one at the lead was leaning halfway inside, his crane-patterned mantle fluttering as he held the door curtain open with his sword.

Mo Ran perked up. "Aren't those Ye Wangxi's people?"

Rufeng Sect had seventy-two cities, so its disciples often didn't know one another, and Nangong Si was sitting by himself in a private booth with his back to the door. Thus the group of newcomers glanced over their fellow sect disciples inside the inn, who were dressed in plain clothes, and didn't recognize any of them.

Ye Wangxi vs. Nangong Si. This was sure to be entertaining.

"My apologies, but we've already been reserved for tonight." The innkeeper hurried over while silently cursing herself for forgetting to close up shop. "Please turn your attentions elsewhere—we're truly so sorry."

The young man at the lead looked troubled as he sighed. "What to do... We've already checked the other inns, and they're all full. There's a frail young lady with us who's in dire need of rest, so we were hoping to find somewhere for her to get a good night's sleep. Might I trouble you to ask if the one who reserved this inn would consider letting us have a few rooms?"

"That... He probably won't be willing."

The young man bowed. "Please ask anyway," he implored politely. "It's all right if he turns us down."

The innkeeper didn't get a chance to respond when one of Nangong Si's attendants at a nearby table slapped the surface and stood, outraged. "What's there to ask?! Get out—out! Don't disturb our young master while he's eating!"

"That's right! Aren't you embarrassed, taking a woman to bed while wearing Rufeng Sect's uniform, dragging your sect's name through the mud?!"

The young man hadn't expected such a misunderstanding. "Why do you slander us so?" he asked indignantly as he turned bright red. "We of Rufeng Sect have always been principled and virtuous.

Of course we wouldn't conduct ourselves with such impropriety. This young lady was kindly saved by our young master—how dare you speak such nonsense!"

"Your young master?" Nangong Si's attendant glanced toward the private booth. His own young master was still drinking wine, taking no notice of them, which he took as silent permission to chase out the interlopers. He relaxed and snickered loudly. "Everyone knows there's only one young master of Rufeng Sect. I wonder who this young master of yours is?"

A gentle, graceful voice came from outside the door. "That would be me, Ye Wangxi of Rufeng Sect."

Every head in the room turned toward the door. "Ye-gongzi—"

Ye Wangxi was dressed all in black, his handsome face taking on a delicate cast in the candlelight. He stepped inside, followed by a veiled woman with nervous eyes—Song Qiutong.

Mo Ran eyed the girl, the vein at his temple throbbing viciously at the mere sight of her. Her again. Just his luck...

Nangong Si's attendants were momentarily taken aback by Ye Wangxi's appearance. Then contempt surfaced on the faces of some of the less-composed members of their group.

Ye Wangxi was the adopted son of Rufeng Sect's chief elder, and he had once been attached to the sect's "shadow city." As implied by the name, the shadow city specialized in training the shadow guard.[24] The leader of Rufeng Sect had originally wanted Ye Wangxi to be trained as the next leader of the shadow guard. However, the nature of Ye Wangxi's cultivation had turned out to be unsuitable for the cultivation method of the shadow guard, so he had been reassigned to the main city and now acted as the sect leader's right-hand man.

---

24 *Elite guards responsible for their master's safety as well as things like assassination and spying.*

Due to his upbringing as a shadow guard, Ye Wangxi habitually kept a low profile, and very few people knew of him. However, the sect leader held him in extremely high esteem—so much so that, in recent years, there had been rumors within the sect that Ye Wangxi was actually the sect leader's bastard. Perhaps because of this, Nangong Si, the legitimate heir, was on bad terms with the other young man.

Since their young master disliked Ye Wangxi, it was only natural that his attendants shared his low opinions of him. While they were obligated to avoid offending Ye-gongzi as his juniors, they were also Nangong Si's personal attendants who directly reported to him.

So, after a long moment of awkward, frozen silence, one of the less-reserved attendants laughed coldly. "Well, Ye-gongzi, please take your leave. I'm afraid there's no place for you here."

"Gongzi, they say there's no room, so l-let's go look elsewhere." Song Qiutong tugged the hem of Ye Wangxi's clothes with slender fingers, a note of fear in her voice. "Besides, this place is so expensive. I dare not waste any more of Gongzi's money..."

Upstairs, Mo Ran rolled his eyes. It was always that weak, pitiful tone with her. She had tricked him with it in the past, and now she was manipulating Ye Wangxi the same way.

Ye Wangxi was about to speak when an enormous white shadow darted out from the inner room, headed straight for his back.

"Gongzi, watch out!" Song Qiutong cried out in alarm.

"Awoooooh! Woooooh!" Howling loudly, a snow-white faewolf lunged toward Ye Wangxi—and started excitedly running in circles around him.

No one said a word.

Ye Wangxi looked down in shock at the three-man-tall faewolf that was rolling adorably around on the floor. "Naobaijin?"

It was Nangong Si's faewolf mount, named "nao" for its eyes, the scarlet hue of carnelians; "bai" for its coat white as snow; and "jin" for the gold of its claws.

If Naobaijin was here, then so was Nangong Si. Ye Wangxi obliged the big furry head that was nudging toward him for pets while looking around.

Shff. The bamboo curtain was lifted by a hand that extended from a scarlet, gold-embroidered sleeve.

Leaning idly against the wall of the private room with his arms crossed, irritated expression half-covered by the curtain and holding a bottle of wine in hand, Nangong Si shot Ye Wangxi a glance and sneered. "Interesting. Why do you always show up wherever I go? With the way you're always trailing after me, where am I to put my face if people start gossiping about us?"

86 This Venerable One's Ex-Wife Isn't Low-Maintenance

YE WANGXI VISIBLY CHOKED at these words, but he didn't grow angry and instead took a moment to gather himself. "You've misunderstood. I'm here on the sect leader's orders to purchase something from Xuanyuan Pavilion, not to follow you."

Mo Ran and Chu Wanning exchanged a glance. The holy weapon.

Nangong Si swung the jar of wine dangling from his hand, his face darkening even further. "So Father's asking you to fetch his things now, huh? What, do I have no hands or legs that could do it for him?"

"A-Si... That's not what I meant."

"Who said you could call me that?" Nangong Si lowered his brows in a scowl, lightning crackling in his eyes. "Ye-gongzi, don't think you can be impudent with me because Father is blind enough to be friendly with you... Aren't you disgusted with yourself?"

"I call you that at the sect leader's behest. If you dislike it, you can bring it up with him." Ye Wangxi paused for a few moments. "What's the point in taking it out on me?"

"Don't you use Father against me!" Nangong Si drew in a breath and forced himself to regain his composure. There was a cold light in his dark eyes, like a silvery moon in a night sky saturated with beacon smoke.

"*Ye-gongzi*." He seemed to drag out the name. "I'm afraid that Father told you to call me A-Si because he has certain misconceptions about your position in the sect. I'd advise you to know your place. You were given an inch—don't take a mile. After all, no matter what kind of airs you put on, by birth alone, you'll never be my equal."

A hint of something dark seemed to flash across Ye Wangxi's refined features. He lowered his thick curtain of lashes. "The young master is right," he said quietly. "But I...have never once thought myself to be the young master's equal."

The change in the form of address made Nangong Si feel a bit better. He lifted the jar and downed some of its contents. The wine burned his throat, but he had always been able to hold his liquor. He stared at Ye Wangxi for a while longer, then scoffed and waved a hand. "That's what I thought. Just look at how you are now. How could you possibly—"

He caught himself before letting slip something he shouldn't in public and abruptly pressed his lips together, saying no more.

A long silence stretched out.

As for Ye Wangxi, even after being humiliated and insulted, his lashes were still lowered. No one could tell if his eyes held any anger or indignation. He gave the onlookers nothing beyond a calm, gentle face, dauntless yet reserved.

The atmosphere was uneasy in the extreme.

Nangong Si looked around uncomfortably for a bit before his gaze landed on the woman behind Ye Wangxi. As if to cover up his near blunder, he cleared his throat and tipped his chin toward her. "Someone you saved?"

"Mn."

"Where's she even from? Don't go bailing out random people."

"It's all right. She's from Xuanyuan Pavilion's auction."

Nangong Si had no interest in the auction, nor had he wasted any energy looking into it, but he was duly surprised to hear that Song Qiutong had been bought there. His initially unconcerned gaze sharpened as he stared at Song Qiutong's face for a while. "So is this thing slave-boned or a Butterfly-Boned Beauty Feast?"

In the cultivation world, only two types of people could be openly bought and sold: Butterfly-Boned Beauty Feasts and the slave-boned.

The slave-boned were those born of the union between humans and fae. People feared the inhuman nature of such crossbreeds, so once they were found out, their vital energy was destroyed and a curse was cast to place a slave mark on the bone of their shoulder blades. They were henceforth condemned to servitude.

However, the slave-boned didn't go for much and were by no means rare. They usually ended up being either servants of the larger sects or playthings of the rich and powerful. Xuanyuan Pavilion wouldn't bother auctioning some run-of-the-mill thing like that.

Sure enough, Ye Wangxi replied, "A Butterfly-Boned Beauty Feast."

Newly interested, Nangong Si walked past Ye Wangxi to look at Song Qiutong, circling around her like he was inspecting merchandise. He frowned. "What's wrong with its leg? Is it defective or something?"

"She was injured when they captured her. We applied a salve; it's healing," Ye Wangxi said. "That's why we can't walk too far and were hoping to stay here tonight."

Nangong Si said nothing, only narrowing his eyes. Then he suddenly dove to the side of Song Qiutong's neck and took a long whiff, like a feral wolf. The lecherous move frightened her so much that she paled, frozen in place while clutching her clothes like she was about to faint.

"Doesn't smell any different from normal people." Nangong Si rubbed his nose and sneezed. "Some kinda perfumed powder..." Waving his hand, he asked offhandedly, "How much?"

"Fifty million."

"Silver?"

"Gold."

Nangong Si's eyes flew wide. "Ye Wangxi, are you crazy? Do you know how many top-grade whetstones that would be? And you fucking bought a *woman* to bring back to me? What, is Rufeng Sect's money not money to you?"

"I didn't use the sect's money." Ye Wangxi paused. "And I didn't buy her for you."

"You—!" The anger that had only just subsided roared back to life. "I see how it is!" Nangong Si snarled. He glared at Song Qiutong, growing more irritated the more he looked at her. That veil straight-up pissed him off, so he ordered her, "You, take that shitty rag off your face!"

Song Qiutong, spooked, clutched tightly at Ye Wangxi's sleeve. "Ye-gongzi," she said in a pitiful voice as she shrank behind him. "I...I don't want to..."

Ye Wangxi's slender figure wasn't as tall or muscular as Nangong Si's, but there was no fear in his eyes as he tilted his head slightly to look up at the other youth. "Young master, she doesn't want to. Just let her be."

"You talk too much. You saved her, so she owes Rufeng Sect her life, and that means she has to listen to me. Take it off!"

"I saved her, yes, but the moment I did, I also set her free," Ye Wangxi said. "So please don't force her, young master."

"Who do you think you are, Ye Wangxi?!" Nangong Si punched the door frame in anger. "What do you take me for? Why the hell would I listen to you? If I tell her to take it off, then she'd damn well better take it off. I'll let you guys stay if she takes the stupid thing off—otherwise, get the fuck out!"

Ye Wangxi sighed, almost imperceptibly, before turning to Song Qiutong. "Let's leave."

This time, Nangong Si wasn't the only one to choke. Ye Wangxi had the holy weapon with him; there was no way Mo Ran and Chu Wanning could let him go.

"Go stop him," Chu Wanning said immediately.

"Okey dokey." Mo Ran had been thinking the same thing anyway, but he paused. "Shizun, where will he sleep, though?"

"He can have half of our room."

"Uh." Mo Ran looked uneasy for some reason. "That's probably not a good idea."

Chu Wanning gaze flicked slightly upward. "Why not?"

"There are some things Shizun doesn't know. It's best if we don't stay in the same room as him. Besides, he wouldn't agree to it anyway, since he's actually..."

Mo Ran was just getting to the important bit when he was interrupted by the sound of Nangong Si kicking over a table downstairs. Cups and dishes clattered to the floor, followed by a screech as he dragged over a bench and put his foot on it to bellow, "Who said you could leave?! What are you, rebelling or some shit? Get back here!"

Even Nangong Si's attendants looked on in flustered silence now.

Young master...weren't you the one who told them to get out?

However, Ye Wangxi seemed more than accustomed to Nangong Si's unreasonable temper tantrums. He pretended not to have heard anything as he tapped Song Qiutong on the shoulder and gestured at her to ignore the crazy person behind them.

"Ye Wangxi!"

Ye Wangxi did not respond.

"*Ye Wangxi!*"

Still no response.

"*Ye! Wang! Xi!*"

The vein at Ye Wangxi's temple twitched, and he looked back despite himself—only to be unexpectedly met with an oncoming wine jar hurtling directly toward him. Pupils contracting, he was about to dodge when a blur of white flashed in front of him.

"Ah!"

A delicate voice cried out in pain, startling everyone in the room, especially Ye Wangxi and Nangong Si.

Song Qiutong had blocked the hit for Ye Wangxi in the nick of time. She was bleeding profusely from where the heavy jar of red clay had struck her forehead. She touched the blood with a trembling hand as fair as jade, and tears of pain sprang from her eyes.

"Don't touch it. Let me see."

"I'm okay. As long as Gongzi didn't get injured..."

"Can't you talk without throwing things?" Ye Wangxi said in a sullen tone, shooting Nangong Si a blame-laden glare before turning to one of his attendants. "Get the jinchuang medicine."[25]

"Gongzi, we ran out," the attendant said quietly. "Should I go buy some?"

Nangong Si hadn't seen this coming either. He forced himself to remain calm, but there was a hint of guilt in his eyes. "I, I have some..." he mumbled with a stiff expression. "A-Lan, fetch my medicine bag."

Ye Wangxi, still angry, pressed his lips into a thin line and ignored Nangong Si.

---

25 *A class of anti-inflammatory pain killer that also stops bleeding.*

For a good while, Nangong Si stood there stiffly, holding the little bottle of medicine, but Ye Wangxi didn't so much as glance at him the entire time. However, Nangong Si couldn't sacrifice his pride, so he roughly shoved the bottle at Song Qiutong instead. "Here. Use it if you want, I don't care."

Song Qiutong was like a frightened little deer. She first looked shakily toward Ye Wangxi and only accepted the medicine when she saw that while he was silent, he wouldn't stop her. She then lowered her head in a bow to the person who had injured her as she said quietly, "Thank you, Nangong-gongzi."

Nangong Si hadn't expected thanks from the girl whose skull he had nearly cracked open. He was taken aback for a second before snapping out of it and waving a hand with an embarrassed cough. "No problem."

That night, Ye Wangxi's group ended up staying at the inn after all.

A multitude of candles flickered throughout the establishment like a scattering of stars in the sky.

Mo Ran sat by a window with his cheek in his hand and his thoughts wandering. It had been nearly two years since his rebirth, and numerous events had differed quite significantly from what he had seen in his last lifetime. It was strange, watching the same people do different things.

Song Qiutong, Ye Wangxi, Bugui... With the passing of time, these familiar people and objects from his past life had once again reappeared in this one. Only this time, he absolutely would not take Song Qiutong to be his wife. As for Ye Wangxi, his name would soon resound throughout the cultivation world, second to none but Chu Wanning.

And then there was Bugui. Agitation flooded Mo Ran's chest when he thought about the long blade that had accompanied him through his previous life.

"Shizun."

"Yes?"

"You've been working on that talisman for an hour already. Isn't it done yet?"

"Almost." By the dim light of the candle, Chu Wanning carefully drew the finishing strokes with a brush dipped in cinnabar to reveal a vivid, elaborate illustration of a soaring dragon.

Mo Ran shuffled over to look. "What's that?"

"Rising Dragon Array."

"What does it do?"

"It can detect all spells in an area, big or small. If our mysterious culprit intends to use the holy weapon to test for the essence of others' spiritual roots, there's sure to be some kind of trace left on the blade. This way, we'll know if the weapon's appearance was mere coincidence or part of his plan."

"Wow, neat. But then why didn't Shizun use this back at Xuanyuan Pavilion?"

"You'll understand once I awaken it."

Chu Wanning pricked his finger and brushed the blood across one of the dragon's scales. The little dragon on the paper instantly glowed golden, its eyes and tail moving nimbly.

"Are you a real dragon?" asked Chu Wanning.

A squeaky voice came from the paper. "Yep-yep, this venerable one is a real dragon."

"Prove it."

"Stupid mortal! What's there to doubt?!"

"I'll know you to be a real dragon if you can jump off this page."

"What's so hard about that?! Just give this venerable one a sec! Hah!"

There was a flash of golden light, and a mighty little dragon the size of a palm leapt out of the paper, wiggling its body and baring its fangs. It flew a circle around Chu Wanning, quite pleased with itself and making a fuss. "Ha ha ha, ha ha ha, I'm a dragon big and real, big and real," it boasted. "I know lots of secrets, lots of secrets. But I'm not gonna tell you, not gonna tell you—not, gonna, tell, you!"

Chu Wanning's eyes, clear as an icy lake, swept coldly over the little eel before he covered it under a cupped hand and turned to Mo Ran with a deadpan expression. "You see?"

"I see..."

"Let me go! You stupid mortal! You're messing up this venerable one's whiskies!"

Chu Wanning lifted his hand and curtly poked the blood-colored inverted scale at the dragon's throat. "Shut up and get to work."

87 This Venerable One Doesn't Want You to Take Any More Disciples

THE LITTLE DRAGON LEFT and returned like the wind, zooming back through the window only ten minutes later to holler, "I got it, I got it! So many magic traces in this inn, wa ha ha ha!"

"Hey li'l eel, what are you, afraid the neighbors won't hear? Yell louder." Leaning on the table, Mo Ran extended a finger and stroked the little dragon's body. Its tail swung over with a whoosh to smack his hand, but it didn't remotely hurt. Rather, it tickled—it was made of paper, after all.

"Don't touch this venerable one, you annoying pretty boy! This venerable one has yet to take a wife. Can't just let you cop a feel whenever you like!"

Mo Ran broke out into laughter. "Wait, what was that? This paper dragon wants a wife?"

"What! Puh, puh, puh! Who're you calling paper?! You damn mutt!"

"Huh, how come even you call me that? Is your surname Xue or something?"

"Xue? Hmph, idiot brat. This venerable one is the Dragon of the Candle, mighty and unmatched, splitting the heavens and cleaving the earth, day and night as I open and close mine eyes, summer and winter with each draw of mine breath! My name is Zhu Jiuyin, and don't you forget it!"

"Yeeeah, didn't get a word of that."

"Wa ya ya ya!" The little dragon turned cartwheels of anger, smashing into the candlestick with its little two-finger-wide head, which made the flame flicker and the wax sway. Mo Ran hurriedly steadied the candle, but as soon as he reached out, the little dragon bit his hand—not that it felt like much of anything, being paper and all. Mo Ran picked up Zhu Jiuyin by the tail and flung it to the side, making it splat against the collar of Chu Wanning's robes and droop glumly there.

"Chu Wanning." The little dragon lifted one of its whiskies and prodded him weakly. "That mangy mutt hit me."

Chu Wanning didn't feel like wasting his breath on this. He peeled the dragon off himself and casually slapped it onto the table. "What spells did you find?"

"Hmph, hmph. You gotta call this venerable one 'Dragon-taizi' three times first, then—"

Chu Wanning pinned it with a cold glare. "Speak."

The little dragon fell silent, but it bloated with anger at the disrespect, its whiskers pointing straight up as it glared at Chu Wanning with beady little eyes. That venerable mouth hung half-open, huffing and puffing until it heaved up a gush of ink.

Chu Wanning narrowed his eyes. "Waste any more ink and I will set you on fire." He reached for the dragon's tail as if to dangle it over the flame. "Then you'll be a real candle dragon."

"All right, all right, all right! You win! You win! I'll tell you! I'll tell you, all right? Jeez!" The little dragon spit a couple more times, sending more ink splattering while muttering not at all discreetly, "So damn mean. No wonder I never see any wife, even after all these years!"

"Eh?" Mo Ran blinked and snuck a glance at Chu Wanning, grinning cheekily. "Didn't Shizun say something about a shiniang?"

Chu Wanning ignored him, sword brows lowering as he snapped at the little dragon, "Less talking, more writing!"

"Hmph! Stinky man!"

The little dragon plopped onto the writing paper laid out on the table and used magic to gather ink in its claw. It began to scrawl messily on the page, muttering the whole time.

Alas, it couldn't simply name the spells that it had seen—there was a limit to how much information a paper brain could process, after all. It would have been too much to expect it to figure out what the spells were, based on leftover magical traces, so it could only draw out its impressions. Luckily, Chu Wanning was more than capable of discerning the original spells. He watched the little dragon scrawl away with lowered lashes and named them as it went.

The little dragon drew a waning moon.

"Soothing spell. Someone here has insomnia."

The little dragon drew the seven stars of the Big Dipper.

"Celestial bastion array. Someone has set up defenses."

The little dragon drew a rouge box.

"Radiant countenance spell..."

"Pfft." Mo Ran laughed, raising his hand. "I know this one! A simple beautification and skin care incantation that girls use at night. Probably that Butterfly-Boned Beauty Feast?"

Chu Wanning didn't comment. He seemed a bit agitated that every spell thus far had been irrelevant or inconsequential. Furrowing his brows, he tapped a slender finger against the table. "Next."

The little dragon drew a heart.

"What's this?" Mo Ran wondered.

"Heart-clearing spell," Chu Wanning said, frustrated. "It's unimportant. Someone's meditating is all. Next."

The little dragon drew a crooked dog head.

"Beast-taming spell..." Chu Wanning put a hand to his brow. "You. Pick the important spells and draw those. Skip the trivial ones for cosmetics and playing with dogs and helping people sleep and whatnot. Next."

The little dragon looked up and fumed. "Well, aren't you picky!"

"Draw!"

Fearful of getting tossed into the candle flame and really living up to its name, the wee paper beast huffily wiped its tiny claws across the paper again. This time it drew an extremely complex, mysterious-looking array.

"Looks like two circles with a cross, and then a vertical line straight down. Some kind of yin-yang divination looking thing?" Mo Ran's eyes widened, "Shizun, could this be what our guy put on the weapon?"

"No." Chu Wanning took a single glance and could already feel a headache coming on. "Voice-changing spell."

"Oh? What's it for?"

"Some people want to change their voice, either because they dislike it or out of some other necessity. This sound-changing spell lets them do that. It's not difficult." Chu Wanning paused. "However, it damages the throat if used for an extended period of time, to the point that it can become very difficult to recover one's original voice... There's something unusual about this one; I wonder who's using it."

Mo Ran only grinned. "Ah, so that's what it's for. Makes sense, then."

Chu Wanning sighed and was about to move on when he paused, eyes flickering as he realized something. He turned abruptly to

Mo Ran. "What do you mean it 'makes sense'? Do you know something?"

"What could I possibly know? I was just thinking that it's pretty normal for someone to dislike their voice. Who knows, maybe it's that Song girl. Maybe her voice is actually hoarse and grating, and she wanted to make it sound sweeter?"

Chu Wanning gave him a long look before smoothing down his sleeve. "Always thinking such nonsense." Then he turned back to the little dragon. "Next."

The little dragon drew another heart.

"Oi, didn't Shizun just tell you to skip things like heart-clearing spells?"

"Puh, what do you know, brat?" The little dragon shot him a seething glare, then smacked its tail on the paper, putting an inky blotch on the heart and proceeding to spread it around until the entire shape was colored black.

"What's this? Black-hearted spell?"

Chu Wanning grew a little awkward and was silent for a while before saying, "No. That would be an affection spell."

"What's that?"

"It's similar to the Xuanyuan Pavilion's Infatuation Pills," Chu Wanning explained. "It bewitches a person to develop feelings of love and affection toward the caster, things like that. Generally used by women."

Mo Ran's eyes widened again. "No way. Could it be that Song Qiutong..."

"How would I know about such things?" Chu Wanning seemed irate, flicking his broad sleeve. "Other people's love affairs are none of my business. Why would I care who's messing around with whom?"

"But Chu Wanning, ah, are you sure you don't care about this affection spell?" the little dragon said gleefully, tail swaying this way and that. "This one's pretty interesting, if you ask me. If you're willing to call me 'Dragon-taizi' three times, then I'll..."

Chu Wanning gazed down at it with murder in his eyes. "Shut up and draw the next one."

"Hmph! You'll regret this!"

"Are you going to draw or not?"

However, the little dragon stopped drawing, sitting down with a plop and scratching its belly with its tiny claw.

"What, out of ink?" Chu Wanning said coldly.

"Idiot. Out of spells." The little dragon rolled its eyes. "I've drawn so many already, and it's still not enough for you? There's no more, that's all there is—aside from these, this inn is perfectly clean."

Chu Wanning and Mo Ran's expressions shifted slightly.

"That's it?" asked Mo Ran.

"That's it."

"There isn't one for assessing spiritual roots?" Chu Wanning asked.

"Nope."

Master and disciple exchanged a glance, disbelief written on their faces. If this mysterious person had been using the auction to find another elemental spiritual essence, then he had to have put some kind of assessment spell on the holy weapon. Only now it appeared that no spell had been cast on the weapon at all. Were they mistaken? Did the long blade's appearance have nothing to do with the man they were hunting?

The little dragon noted their silence and soared into the air, flying around back and forth as it whined. "Oi, pay attention to this venerable one. Drawing is exhausting, you know! Where's this venerable one's round of applause?"

Chu Wanning was already irritated to begin with. When it hollered, he simply lifted a hand with a sweep of his sleeve and summoned a yellow talisman in the air. The little dragon shrieked miserably at the sight of it. "I don't wanna, I don't wanna, I don't wanna, I don't wanna!"

Nevertheless, it was sucked into the talisman and turned back into a drawing. A tap of Chu Wanning's fingertip, and the drawing itself slowly faded away. Even as the dragon disappeared, it kept narrowing its eyes in affront at Chu Wanning.

"I'll call you when you're needed," said Chu Wanning.

Tears streamed down the little dragon's face. "You only ever remember me when you need me! You're so heartless, Chu Wanning..."

"Get lost already!" Chu Wanning had at first retained civility, but at these words, his brows dipped in anger, and he folded the talisman flat in half with an unceremonious slap before tucking it back into his sleeve.

Nightfall. Chu Wanning slept on the bed and Mo Ran took the floor, both troubled with their worries.

They hadn't expected the holy weapon to be free of any spells whatsoever. Did the mysterious man have some way of gauging spiritual roots that they didn't know? Or was he not in a hurry to find a replacement with strong spiritual energy?

"Mo Ran," Chu Wanning called in the darkness.

"Hm?" Mo Ran responded reflexively.

"Let's go back to Sisheng Peak tomorrow."

Mo Ran's eyes opened. "Huh?"

"If that man would let an opportunity like the Xuanyuan auction slip past, then he probably has some other means of searching out his quarry. I'm afraid we won't find out much carrying on like this.

So let's go back to Sisheng Peak. I'll have the sect leader secretly tell the other nine great sects to check for any spiritual essences within their own sects, and to safeguard any they find. It'll be better than sitting on our hands hoping he happens to show up."

"Will that be okay? What if the guy we're after is one of the sect leaders?"

"That's very unlikely, but even if he is, it won't matter. He already knows we're after him."

"How will Shizun make all those sect leaders listen to Uncle?" Mo Ran asked, puzzled. "Tell them everything?"

"That won't be necessary. They might not believe it anyway," Chu Wanning replied mildly. "But I have my ways."

"Such as?"

"I'll take disciples."

Mo Ran jerked his head up, alarmed.

"I'll have the sect leader tell the other sects that the frequent breaches in the ghost realm barrier pose a great danger to us all," Chu Wanning said quietly. "As such, Yuheng of Sisheng Peak intends to accept up to five additional disciples to train in the use of techniques such as the Shangqing Barrier and the Shisha Barrier. The other sects have tried time and again to invite me to teach, specifically because of these barrier techniques. If I put out the word that I'm willing to impart them, they'll come. And, since I accept only those with outstanding spiritual foundation, they'll have to test all of their disciples to select the candidates, thereby fulfilling our goal."

Mo Ran didn't reply, his face going pale in the darkness. "Y-you're going to take more disciples?"

"If fate decrees it." Chu Wanning rolled over, his voice quieting as if he was getting tired. "I'll take the names of the candidates and have them practice standard barrier techniques by themselves first.

If any among them manage to persevere for three years or so, then why not?"

In the darkness, Mo Ran listened to the voice from the bed slowly drifting off. He felt like a jar of vinegar had been spilled in his chest, so sour it made his heart ache. Take on more disciples?

You only ever took three in your last life, picky as you are. How come you're not being picky now? How could you take on more disciples just like that?!

Mo Ran kept wanting to say something, but every time the words reached his lips, they never made it past.

Chu Wanning fell asleep, blissfully unaware of the sea of jealousy raging within Mo Ran.

It was cold at night. Mo Ran pulled on an outer garment and got up. He called to Chu Wanning in a low voice a couple times to ensure he was really asleep, then quietly opened the door and snuck out of the room.

The halls of the inn were still and silent. A few red silk lanterns glowed peacefully with a low light, gentle circles of orange reflecting on the wooden floor like so many ripples.

Chu Wanning might already have tested the holy weapon, but Mo Ran had yet to test *Bugui*.

A holy weapon within a hundred feet of its master could be summoned to their side with a simple spell. At Xuanyuan Pavilion, Mo Ran hadn't had a chance to check if this blade really was his weapon from his past life. How could he possibly miss this chance now?

Mo Ran's fingertip glowed with a crimson light. Lowering his eyelashes, he said in a quiet voice, "Bugui, come!"

For a few moments, there was nothing but silence. Suddenly, the muffled sound of a blade rang out from somewhere in the distance.

The sound was barely audible, but it reverberated in his ears, and his heart hammered.

Mo Ran's eyes shot open. "Bugui!"

It *was* Bugui. The long blade was struggling, crying blood, its deep roar racing to him across sanguine oceans, across lifetimes. It was as if he could *hear* Bugui weeping and wailing for him. However, it was trapped, confined by something Mo Ran knew naught of.

It could feel its master's call but could not answer. There was something missing—something that had severed their connection.

They'd once had a pact, had once seen the beautiful sights from the tallest mountains together, had once waited for death side by side in the last remaining bit of warmth in Wushan Palace. Something was forcing them apart, but still their bond remained, like a tendon linking torn flesh.

Mo Ran's eyes were red and welling with tears as he whispered, "Bugui..."

It's you. Why can't you return to my side? Who's stopping you? Who...

Creak.

The quiet sound of a door opening. In this suffocating darkness, it was as loud as crashing thunder.

88 This Venerable One Meets Another One Reborn

MO RAN'S HEAD snapped up to look in the direction the sound had come from.

A person in a floor-length, gold-patterned black cloak appeared at the end of the hall. His figure was tall and straight, and his entire body was concealed by that cloth. Even his face was shrouded behind a curtain of black silk. The only thing Mo Ran could see was a pair of eyes, but the darkness made even these difficult to clearly discern.

The person held a blade in his hand. A narrow blade, completely black, unmatched in sharpness—Bugui.

"Who are you?!"

"It doesn't matter who I am," the person said coolly. His voice sounded strangely warped, as if it had been intentionally distorted. "All you need to know is that I know who *you* are."

A chill ran through Mo Ran, but he forced himself to keep his cool. "I'm just a disciple of Sisheng Peak. So what if you know me? What's your point?"

"A disciple of Sisheng Peak? Heh, that's not wrong. But have you forgotten that you're also Taxian-jun, Emperor of the Mortal Realm, a vicious ghost who slew his teacher and spit on virtue, a soul that fled the road to the underworld?"

Mo Ran's blood grew colder with every word. He felt like he had fallen into a frozen cave.

Taxian-jun. Who had bathed all seventy-two cities of Rufeng Sect in blood. Emperor of the Mortal Realm. Who had married the most beautiful woman in the world, who had killed his teacher and family alike, who had trod on countless people to reach the top.

"You are Mo Weiyu," the person continued in an icy tone.

Mo Weiyu. Evil beyond redemption, may he die ten thousand deaths and be denied reincarnation.

Mo Weiyu, deserving of naught but to be torn to pieces at Sisheng Peak, his heart and eyes dug out—undeserving of an intact corpse!

"Who are you?!"

Mo Ran saw red. His youthful demeanor wholly vanished from his face, replaced by a ruthless, fiendish snarl as he stood off against that man at the end of the hallway. He was on the verge of lunging at the man's throat and ripping it to pieces alongside all those names he never wanted to hear again.

The man lifted a hand wrapped in black silk, and the hallway was instantly encased in layers of ice, dividing the space between them.

"You can't call this blade anymore, can you?" The man walked closer, slow and leisurely, stopping some ten paces away. "Emperor of the Mortal Realm... Or maybe it's better to call you Mo Ran? How laughable. Have you ever taken a good look at yourself as you are now?

"A heart that is no longer cold and hard as steel. You've stayed by Chu Wanning's side and even developed some genuine fondness for him...

"Rebirth, rebirth. I wonder where that person is... The one you swore to protect in your last life."

Mo Ran's expression instantly transformed. "Shi Mei?! What did you do to Shi Mei?!"

The man did not answer his question, only sneering disdainfully. "Do you know why you can't call Bugui anymore?" He slowly traced a fingertip along the black body of the blade. "It's because your soul is about to change, and your hatred about to dissipate... Your regret, as you lay dying, was that you couldn't protect your Mingjing-shixiong, and your wish was that, if there was a next life...you wouldn't fail him again."

Those piercing eyes turned on him.

"Mo Ran, have you lived up to that wish?!"

"I—"

"The ghost realm barrier is soon to rupture, and the events of the past are sure to repeat. Do you intend to watch him die again? Do you plan to beg Chu Wanning for mercy once more? You're only letting your second chance go to waste. You don't deserve to touch Bugui ever again."

"I don't need you to tell me that!" Mo Ran roared, enraged. "What happens between me and Shi Mei is no one else's business! If you know I've been reborn, then who are you? The fake Gouchen? Or some damned ghost who's been reborn like me?!"

"Heh..." The man snickered lightly. "Some damned ghost who's been reborn... Yes, I suppose I am some damned ghost who's been reborn. Or did you really think that, with the world as it is now, you were the only one the heavens graced with rebirth?"

Just who exactly was this?! Indistinct faces flashed deliriously through Mo Ran's mind, one after another.

There were the ones who had died before him in his past life: Xue Zhengyong, Madam Wang, Chu Wanning, Song Qiutong, Ye Wangxi...

There were the ones who had charged Wushan Palace just in time to see him off: Xue Meng, Mei Hanxue, the executioners from the ten great sects...

Who was this? *Who was this?!*

Just who had found out his secret and seized his weakness?! Of all his demons from a lifetime ago, which one of them had crawled out of the underworld to hound him, to force him back down the road to ruin?! Who was it?!

In the split second it took Mo Ran to think, there was a flash before his eyes, and with a flurry of robes, the man had moved to stand right in front of him. The sheer strength of this man, even after rebirth, rattled Mo Ran.

Bugui's tip was pressed to his chest. Just a bit of pressure and it would pierce through his flesh and into his heart.

"Mo Weiyu, I thought you devoted in matters of affection. Perhaps your Mingjing-shixiong doesn't enjoy the fortune of your favor. Even in your second life, you still care nothing for him."

Mo Ran gritted his teeth. "Bullshit."

"Is it, though?" The man smirked darkly. One hand closed around Mo Ran's throat, then slid slowly down to rest on his chest. "Does he truly have a place in your heart? Even the scrap of memory you used to cherish has long since worn away. Is anything left anymore?"

"As if you would know who's in my heart better than I do!" Mo Ran growled. "You've blathered on long enough. Why don't you take off that veil and show me your face already?!"

"Why the rush to see my face?" The man's voice was like smoke and his gaze like mist, both threaded with contempt. "I'll make sure you get a glimpse, right before you die."

"You die first, you—"

Mo Ran didn't finish before he suddenly felt a bone-chilling cold underfoot. He looked down to find that without his notice, the man's icy thorns had climbed up his body.

Ice spells, ice thorns... Water element... Who was it? Who from his past life had used such spells? Mo Ran had met far too many adversaries, and his head was an utter mess as he scrambled to remember them all.

Xue Meng, fire. Chu Wanning, metal and wood. Ye Wangxi, earth. Xue Zhengyong, earth.

Just who was it? Why couldn't he think of someone who had such powerful command of ice?

"You're not wrong. I'll die too. But Mo Weiyu, that won't be for a long, long time."

The ice spread rapidly over his entire body. This man's strength was truly terrifying. Mo Ran released some spiritual energy to fend off the freeze and was met with a burst of immense and oppressive force bearing down on him. The enemy before him might rival even Chu Wanning.

Water element. Who?!

For a fleeting instant, a blurry face seemed to flash through Mo Ran's mind, but before he could focus on it, his foe's hand clamped down on his neck.

Fingertips wrapped in black silk caressed his throat. There was no reflection in those dark eyes. "Your Imperial Majesty needn't concern himself with the length of my life," he said slowly. "More importantly, let me help you retrieve some basic human emotions so that you don't screw up my plans by doing everything but what you're supposed to."

"Nngh!"

There was the wet sound of something being cut into. Bugui cried out in sorrow as it pierced its former master's flesh.

"It's not deep. Just getting some of your blood to bind the seal."

True to his word, the man took only a bit of blood from Mo Ran's wound to mark him between his brows. Then he began to chant some manner of incantation.

A searing pain exploded in Mo Ran's head. "Fuck. Your. Mother!" he cursed. "The fuck did I do to you in my last life? Did I chop you into minced meat or kill all eighteen generations of your ancestors or some shit? Fucking hell! The fuck are you doing?!"

"Shh, hold still. It's just a virtue spell."

"I don't fucking care if it's a virtue spell or a vice spell—keep touching me and it's gonna be a vomit spell! Fuck off!"

"Ah, Mo Ran." The man sighed softly while drawing a seal on his brow. "How could you bear to tell me to fuck off?" He paused, then resumed chanting. "Heart lesser than water, fervor unstoppable. Heart gate...open."

Agony tore through Mo Ran's chest. "You..."

Suddenly, the ice was dispelled. Mo Ran stumbled, legs giving out as he sank slowly to his knees, face pale and colorless.

"You should thank me." For a while, the black-robed person looked down at him through lowered lashes, expression apathetic. Then he said evenly, "I've heightened the emotions in your heart, made love and hate clearer still. Surely you should be able to figure out your own feelings now. If, even after all this, you still don't understand that you must do all in your power to protect Shi Mei, up to and including giving your life, then you...are truly useless. Nothing more than an unwanted child to be tossed aside!"

So this virtue spell made love and hate more intense and clear-cut? Why would this person go to such lengths to preserve Shi Mei's life? Water element...

These were the last scattered thoughts in Mo Ran's head before his consciousness faded. He crumpled to the floor with a thud, thick curtains of lashes closing over his eyes.

The black-robed person stared dispassionately at him for a while, then slowly crouched to take his pulse. He thought for a short moment before lifting a hand to gather a brilliant blue light in his palm.

"Forget," the black-robed person intoned in a low voice. The blue light glowed brighter still, and Mo Ran's tightly locked brows slowly relaxed.

When Mo Ran woke, he would only remember going out to try to summon the holy weapon, to no avail. He would remember nothing else, nor would he know that in this world, another person had been reborn.

Meanwhile, the virtue spell, though its effects lasted for only a few days, was an excellent tool for showing the lost where their desire truly lay.

"With your emotions heightened, you might wake up to find yourself even more in love with Shi Mingjing," the black-robed man said in a cold voice. "So in love that you want nothing more than to wrench out your own heart and give it to him... See you later, Emperor Taxian-jun."

The storm blew over and the waves settled back down.

Mo Ran opened his eyes the next morning to find himself lying on the floor next to Chu Wanning's bed. He turned his head to the side. The window seemed to have been blown open by the wind sometime during the night; it was half-closed, swinging gently in the morning breeze, creaking every time it made contact with the wooden beam.

It was quiet inside the room. Mo Ran didn't have to check the bed to know that Chu Wanning was still asleep.

The sky outside the patterned window was a dull teal. The morning sky was often pale before the rising sun broke through the clouds to dust a blush on her cheeks and bathe her in warmth. Few people rose this early, so she didn't bother painting her wan, tired countenance.

The breeze from outside carried the faint scent of fresh grass and morning dew. Mo Ran lay there for a while, waiting for consciousness to come to him before sitting up—only to feel a stab of pain in his shoulder.

Weird. Why was there a rip in his clothes, and dried blood under it? He stared at it blankly for a while.

Hadn't he gone out in the night to test Bugui? He seemed to remember that it hadn't responded, so it was probably a fake after all. And then... Tsk, can't remember.

Mo Ran looked around and found a thick nail sticking out of the dark brown floor. That must've scratched him, then. Had he been so deeply asleep that he hadn't felt it? He draped an outer robe over his shoulders and looked toward the bed.

Chu Wanning lay there in peaceful repose. Mo Ran had long since grown used to him being all aloof and high-up, enjoying the best while Mo Ran had to settle for the leftovers, like making do with the floor at the foot of the bed. But for some reason, he felt extra irritable today, and he glared at his shizun's figure with an itch in his teeth.

"How come you always get the bed while I have to sleep on the floor? Sure, the saying is, 'Respect your teacher,' but doesn't it also say to, 'Love your young'?"

Mo Ran was irked. He only got more disgruntled when he remembered the nail sticking out of the floor that had cut him for no damn reason. It was still early, and he didn't want to pitifully curl up on the floor anymore, so he climbed on the bed and closed his eyes to go back to sleep.

The bed was spacious enough that he and Chu Wanning, one facing left and the other facing right, didn't have to touch. They had once slept in each other's arms; now they slept with an invisible barrier between them.

In their last lifetime, they had been skin to skin, limbs entangled, and on particularly frenzied days, Mo Ran hadn't even pulled out after making love to him.

These two, who had once been so intimate, now lay on opposite ends of the bed to sleep.

THE STORY CONTINUES IN

The Husky & His White Cat Shizun

VOLUME 3

APPENDIX

Characters, Names, and Locations

Characters

The identity of certain characters may be a spoiler; use this guide with caution on your first read of the novel.

Note on the given name translations: Chinese characters may have many different readings. Each reading here is just one out of several possible interpretations.

MAIN CHARACTERS

Mo Ran

墨燃 SURNAME MO, "INK"; GIVEN NAME RAN, "TO IGNITE"

COURTESY NAME: Weiyu (微雨 / "gentle rain")

TITLE(S):

Taxian-jun (踏仙君 / "treading on immortals")

WEAPON(S):

Bugui (不归 / "no return")

Jiangui (见鬼 / literally, "seeing ghosts"; metaphorically, "What the hell?")

SPIRITUAL ELEMENT: Wood

Orphaned at a young age, Mo Ran was found at fourteen by his uncle, Xue Zhengyong, and brought back to Sisheng Peak. Despite his late start, he has a natural talent for cultivation. In his previous lifetime, Chu Wanning's refusal to save Shi Mei as he died sent Mo Ran into a spiral of grief, hatred, and destruction. Reinventing himself as Taxian-jun, tyrannical emperor of the cultivation world, he committed many atrocities—including taking his own shizun captive—before ultimately killing himself. To Mo Ran's surprise, he woke to find himself back in his fifteen-year-old body with all the memories of his past self and the opportunity to relive his life with all new choices, which is where the story begins.

Chu Wanning

楚晚宁 SURNAME CHU; GIVEN NAME WANNING "EVENING PEACE"

TITLE(S):

Yuheng of the Night Sky (晚夜玉衡 / Wanye, "late night"; Yuheng, "Alioth, the brightest star in Ursa Major")

Beidou Immortal (北斗仙尊 Beidou "the Big Dipper," title *xianzun*, "immortal")

WEAPON(S):

Tianwen / 天问 "Heavenly Inquiry: to ask the heavens about life's enigmatic questions." The name reflects Tianwen's interrogation ability.

Jiuge / 九歌 "Nine Songs." Chu Wanning describes it as having a "chilling temperament."

SPIRITUAL ELEMENT: Wood and Metal

A powerful cultivator who specializes in barriers and is talented in mechanical engineering, as well as an elder of Sisheng Peak. Aloof, strict, and short-tempered, Chu Wanning has only three disciples to his name: Xue Meng, Shi Mei, and Mo Ran. In Mo Ran's previous lifetime, Chu Wanning stood up to Taxian-jun, obstructing his tyrannical ambitions, before he was taken captive and eventually died as a prisoner. In the present day, he is Mo Ran's shizun, as well as the target of Mo Ran's mixed feelings of fear, loathing, and lust.

Chu Wanning's titles refer to the brightest stars in the Ursa Major constellation, reflecting his stellar skills and presence. Specifically, Yuheng is Alioth, the brightest star in Ursa Major, and the Big Dipper is an asterism consisting of the seven brightest stars of the same constellation. Furthermore, Chu Wanning's weapons are named after poems in the *Verses of Chu*, a collection by Qu Yuan from the Warring States Period. The weapons' primary attacks, such as "Wind," take their names from *Shijing: Classic of Poetry*, the oldest existing collection of Chinese poetry. The collection comprises 305 works that are categorized into popular songs and ballads (风, *feng*, "wind"), courtly songs (雅, *ya*, "elegant"), or eulogies (颂, *song*, "ode").

SISHENG PEAK

Xue Meng

薛蒙 SURNAME XUE; GIVEN NAME MENG "BLIND/IGNORANT"

COURTESY NAME: Ziming (子明 / "bright/clever son")

The "darling of the heavens," Chu Wanning's first disciple, Xue Zhengyong and Madam Wang's son, and Mo Ran's cousin. Proud, haughty, and fiercely competitive, Xue Meng can at times be impulsive and rash. He often clashes with Mo Ran, especially when it comes to their shizun, whom he hugely admires.

Shi Mei

师昧 SURNAME SHI; GIVEN NAME MEI, "TO CONCEAL"

COURTESY NAME: Mingjing (明净 / "bright and clean")

EARLY NAME(S): Xue Ya (薛丫 / Surname Xue, given name Ya, "little girl")

Xue Meng's close friend, Chu Wanning's second disciple, and Mo Ran's boyhood crush. Gentle, kind, and patient, with beautiful looks to match, Shi Mei often plays peacemaker when his fellow disciples argue, which is often. Where Mo Ran and Xue Meng are more adept in combat, he specializes in the healing arts.

Xue Zhengyong

薛正雍 SURNAME XUE; GIVEN NAME ZHENGYONG, "RIGHTEOUS AND HARMONIOUS"

WEAPON: Fan that reads "Xue is Beautiful" on one side and "Others are Ugly" on the opposite.

The sect leader of Sisheng Peak, Xue Meng's father, and Mo Ran's uncle. Jovial, boisterous, and made out of 100 percent wifeguy material, Xue Zhengyong takes his duty to protect the common people of the lower cultivation realm very much to heart.

Madam Wang

王夫人

Xue Meng's mother, lady of Sisheng Peak, and Mo Ran's aunt. Timid and unassuming, she originally hails from Guyueye Sect and specializes in the healing arts.

A-Li

阿狸

Madam Wang's cat. Not pregnant, just fat.

SISHENG PEAK ELDERS

The names of Sisheng Peak's elders vary in origin. Most of their names come from the constellation Ursa Major, such as Chu Wanning's "Yuheng." Three elders take their names from the Sha Po Lang star triad used in a form of fortune-telling based on Chinese astrology.

Jielü Elder
戒律长老 JIELÜ, "DISCIPLINE"

In charge of meting out discipline.

Xuanji Elder
璇玑长老 XUANJI, "MEGREZ, THE DELTA URSAE MAJORIS STAR"

Kind and gentle; practices an easy cultivation method. Popular with the disciples.

Lucun Elder
禄存长老 LUCUN, "PHECDA, THE GAMMA URSAE MAJORIS STAR"

Beautiful and foppish. Has a habit of phrasing things in a questionable manner.

Qisha Elder
七杀长老 QISHA, "POLIS, THE POWER STAR IN SHA PO LANG"

Very done with Lucun Elder.

Pojun Elder
破军长老 POJUN, "ALKAID, THE RUINOUS STAR IN SHA PO LANG"

Forthright and spirited.

Tanlang Elder
贪狼长老 TANLANG, "DUBHE, THE FLIRTING STAR IN SHA PO LANG"

Sardonic and ungentle with his words. Skilled in the healing arts, and on pretty bad terms with Chu Wanning.

JINCHENG LAKE

Fake "Gouchen the Exalted"
勾陈上宫 GOUCHEN, "CURVED ARRAY, PART OF THE URSA MINOR CONSTELLATION"; SHANGGONG, "EXALTED")

An enigmatic figure who pretended to be the real Gouchen the Exalted, the God of Weaponry. He is in truth a corpse controlled by a white chess piece in a mysterious Zhenlong Chess Formation.

Wangyue
望月 WANGYUE, "FULL MOON"; ALTERNATIVELY, "GAZING AT THE MOON"

A huge, turquoise-black dragon who lives in Jincheng Lake. In their previous lifetime, he gave Mo Ran his sword, Bugui, in exchange for a plum blossom from the waist of the mountain.

Heart-Pluck Willow
摘心柳 ZHAIXIN LIU, "HEART-PLUCK WILLOW"

The spirit of the willow tree in Jincheng Lake, which shelters Gouchen the Exalted's arsenal of holy weapons.

PEACH BLOSSOM SPRINGS

Eighteen
十八

A member of the feathered tribe, and the eighteenth in the tribe to cultivate a human form. In charge of introductions to Peach Blossom Springs, as well as the cultivators training in the attack division.

Elder Immortal

羽民上仙 YUMIN, "FEATHERED TRIBE"; SHANGXIAN, "ELDER IMMORTAL"

The master of Peach Blossom Springs, and the first in the feathered tribe to cultivate a human form. Though she looks to be a young woman, her true age is unknown.

ILLUSORY LIN'AN

Chu Xun

楚洵 SURNAME CHU; GIVEN NAME XUN, "TRULY"

The eldest son of the lord governor of Lin'an City, who tried to lead the citizens of Lin'an to safety during the first breach in the ghost realm barrier. A strong cultivator in his own right, he is gentle, refined, and morally upright. Bears a strong resemblance to Chu Wanning.

Chu Lan

楚澜 SURNAME CHU; GIVEN NAME LAN, "TO SWELL; BILLOWING"

Chu Xun's young son, around three or four years old, who bears a strong resemblance to Chu Wanning-as-Xia Sini. A sweet-natured, generous child.

Lin Wan'er

林婉儿 SURNAME LIN; GIVEN NAME WAN'ER, "GENTLE, GRACEFUL"

Also referred to as Madam Chu. Chu Xun's wife, who passed away not long after Chu Lan's birth.

Xiaoman

小满 XIAOMAN, "THE EIGHTH OF TWENTY-FOUR SOLAR TERMS IN TRADITIONAL CHINESE LUNISOLAR CALENDARS"

A young man of Lin'an, aged fourteen or fifteen, whose adoptive father was killed during the breach in the barrier.

Skeleton King

骷髅王

One of the nine kings of the ghost realm. Referred to as "the ghost king" during the Lin'an incident until his specific identity was revealed. He bears a grudge against Chu Xun for daring to defy him.

RUFENG SECT

Ye Wangxi

叶忘昔 SURNAME YE; GIVEN NAME WANGXI, "TO FORGET THE PAST"

A disciple of Rufeng Sect who was adopted by Rufeng Sect's chief elder. Highly regarded by the sect leader of Rufeng Sect, and a competent, chivalric, and upright sort. Mo Ran noted that in their previous lifetime, Ye Wangxi was second only to Chu Wanning in the entire cultivation world.

Nangong Si

南宫驷 SURNAME NANGONG; GIVEN NAME SI, "TO RIDE, OR HORSE"

The only son of Rufeng Sect's leader, who in their previous lifetime died before Mo Ran's ascension. Brash, headstrong, and volatile in temperament. He rides on his faewolf, has a hearty appetite for meat and wine, and an antagonistic relationship with Ye Wangxi.

Naobaijin

瑙白金 NAO, "CARNELIAN"; BAI "WHITE"; JIN "GOLD"

Nangong Si's faewolf. Thrice the height of a human, with carnelian-red eyes, snow-white fur, and gold claws.

XUANYUAN PAVILION / RAINBELL ISLE

Second Pavilion Master

二阁主

A girl who looks no older than eleven or twelve, but who is in actuality over a hundred years old. As the Second Pavilion Master of Xuanyuan Pavilion, she acts as auction master for the goods being sold.

Hanlin the Sage

寒鳞圣手 HAN, "COLD"; LIN, "SCALES"; SHENGSHOU, "HIGHLY SKILLED, SAGE DOCTOR"

An elder of Guyueye Sect. Highly skilled in refining pills and medicines.

Song Qiutong

宋秋桐 SURNAME SONG; GIVEN NAME QIUTONG, "AUTUMN, TUNG TREE"

Taxian-jun's wife and empress in his previous lifetime. Bears a resemblance to Shi Mei. She hailed from Rufeng Sect before Taxian-jun burned it down, and her tombstone was engraved with the words "Grave of the Deep-Fried Empress Song." She also shares a name with a character in *Dream of the Red Chamber*.

OTHER CHARACTERS

Mei Hanxue

梅含雪 SURNAME MEI; GIVEN NAME HANXUE, "TO HOLD, SNOW"

A cultivator of Kunlun Taxue Palace who stayed with the Xue family at Sisheng Peak for a short time as a child. He is skilled in various arts, including dance and playing musical instruments, and is an appreciator of wine and song. Known as "Da-shixiong" to the lady cultivators who flock around him, as well as by less flattering epithets to others, namely Xue Meng and Ye Wangxi.

Liu-gong 刘公

An elderly servant of Taxian-jun in his previous lifetime.

Sects and Locations

THE TEN GREAT SECTS

The cultivation world is divided into the upper and lower cultivation realms. Most of the ten great sects are located within the upper cultivation realm, while Sisheng Peak is the only great sect within the lower cultivation realm.

Sisheng Peak

死生之巅 SISHENG ZHI DIAN, "THE PEAK OF LIFE AND DEATH"

A sect in the lower cultivation realm located in modern day Sichuan. It sits near the boundary between the mortal realm and the ghost realm, and was founded relatively recently by Xue Zhengyong and his brother. The uniform of Sisheng Peak is light armor in dark blue with silver trim, and members of the sect practice cultivation methods that do not require abstinence from meat or other foods. The sect's name refers to both its physical location in the mountains as well as the metaphorical extremes of life and death. Xue Zhengyong named many locations in Sisheng Peak after places and entities in the underworld because the sect is located in an area thick with ghostly yin energy, and he is furthermore not the sort to think up conventionally nice-sounding, formal names.

Heaven-Piercing Tower (通天塔)

The location where Mo Ran first met Chu Wanning as well as the location where, in his past life, he laid himself to rest.

Loyalty Hall (丹心殿)

The main hall of Sisheng Peak. Taxian-jun renamed it Wushan Palace (巫山殿) when he took over the sect.

Red Lotus Pavilion (红莲水榭)

Chu Wanning's residence. An idyllic pavilion surrounded by rare red lotuses. Some have been known to call it "Red Lotus Hell" or the "Pavilion of Broken Legs."

Platform of Sin and Virtue (善恶台)

A platform where public events in Sisheng Peak, including punishment and announcements, are carried out.

Mengpo Hall (孟婆堂)

The dining hall at Sisheng Peak. Named after the mythological old woman who distributes memory-erasing soup to souls before they are reborn.

Silk-Rinse Hall (浣纱堂)

The tailoring hall of Sisheng Peak, which creates and tailors clothing for members of the sect.

Linyi Rufeng Sect
临沂儒风门 RUFENG, "HONORING CONFUCIAN IDEALS"

A sect in the upper cultivation realm located in Linyi, a prefecture in modern day Shandong Province. Has seventy-two cities and is known for being affluent and well-respected. In Taxian-jun's lifetime, he burned them all to the ground.

Kunlun Taxue Palace

昆仑踏雪宫 TAXUE, "STEPPING SOFTLY ACROSS SNOW"

A sect in the upper cultivation realm located on the Kunlun Mountain range. Its name refers to both the physical location of the sect in the snowy Kunlun Mountain range and the ethereal grace of the cultivators within the sect.

Guyueye

孤月夜 GUYUEYE, "A LONELY MOON IN THE NIGHT SKY"

A sect in the upper cultivation realm located on Rainbell Isle. They focus on the medicinal arts. The name is a reference to the solitary and isolated nature of Guyueye—the island is a lone figure in the water, much like the reflection of the moon, cold and aloof.

Rainbell Isle (霖铃屿)

Not an actual island, but the back of an enormous ancient tortoise, which was bound to the founder of the sect by a blood pact to carry the entirety of Guyueye sect on its shell.

Xuanyuan Pavilion

A subsidiary operation of Guyueye, and a trading post well-known in the cultivation world. Xuanyuan is a name for the Yellow Emperor, a legendary Chinese historical figure and deity, who was one of the Three Sovereigns and Five Deities alongside Fuxi.

Fragrance Inn

An inn on Rainbell Isle.

PEACH BLOSSOM SPRINGS

Peach Blossom Springs
桃花源

Home of the feathered tribe, located beyond the maze of Mount Jiuhua and within the land of the immortals. *The Peach Blossom Spring* is a fable written by Chinese poet Tao Yuanming, in which the eponymous setting is an ethereal utopia where people live a peaceful, prosperous existence in harmony with nature, unaware of the outside world. In popular culture, the setting has become a symbol of an ideal world, and it has been depicted in many paintings, poems, music, and so forth.

Zhuque (朱雀)

The land of immortals. (See entry on the *Vermilion Bird* in the glossary for more details.)

Mount Jiuhua (九华山)

A mountain with a snowy summit. The path to Peach Blossom Springs begins at the foot of Mount Jiuhua. Mount Jiuhua in modern China is a site sacred to the Kṣitigarbha Bodhisattva, and is located in Anhui Province.

Ancestral Abyss (始祖深渊)

An abyss within Peach Blossom Springs, filled with roaring flames where neither flora nor fauna survive. Frenzied demon owls live within, making their nests out of the abyssal flames. They hide during the day and emerge only at night. According to legend, the abyss was where the Vermilion Bird ascended.

Dewsip Pavilion (饮露阁)
A pavilion where visitors to Peach Blossom Springs are received.

Zhurong Cave (祝融洞)
Where cultivators at Peach Blossom Springs meditate to refine their cultivation and train their inner spiritual energy against the burning yang energy of the cave. Zhurong refers to a figure in Chinese mythology who is associated with the cardinal direction of south and the element of fire.

Asura Arena (修罗场)
Where cultivators at Peach Blossom Springs go to engage in practice matches against one another.

Stargazing Cliffs (观星崖)
Where cultivators at Peach Blossom Springs attend Eighteen's evening lectures.

Spirit Lake Tavern (灵湖楼)
A tavern located in the western market of Peach Blossom Springs.

Campsis Pavilion (凌霄阁)
A residential pavilion where guests of Peach Blossom Springs are hosted.

ILLUSORY LIN'AN

Lin'an City (临安城)
The setting of an illusory realm where Mo Ran and Xia Sini undergo their trial.

Putuo (普陀)

The destination of the refugees from Lin'an during the first ghost realm barrier breach. Putuo in modern China is a location sacred to Guanyin.

Qiantang River (钱塘江)

The river by which Lin'an City is located.

City God Temple (城隍庙)

A temple dedicated to the god of the walls and moats that protect cities. Nearly every city has its own City God Temple.

OTHER

Yangzhou Port 扬州口岸

Yangzhou is a city in Jiangsu province, historically one of the wealthiest cities in China.

Wuchang Town

无常镇 WUCHANG, "THE BUDDHIST DOCTRINE OF IMPERMANENCE"

A town not far from Sisheng Peak.

House of Drunken Jade 醉玉楼

A high-class pleasure house in Xiangtan, famed for its theater, star songstress, and food. It burned down not long before the events of the current timeline.

Dawning Peak 旭映峰

A sacred mountain located in the upper cultivation realm, within the territory of Linyi Rufeng Sect. Known as the place where Gouchen the Exalted forged the Heavenly Emperor's sword, it is now a pilgrimage site for cultivators seeking holy weapons.

Dai City 岱城

A mildly prosperous city by the foot of Dawning Peak. Caters to traveling cultivators on their way to Jincheng Lake.

Jincheng Lake 金成池

A lake at the summit of Dawning Peak that remains frozen over year-round. According to legend, it was formed by a drop of Gouchen the Exalted's blood, shed as he forged the Heavenly Emperor's holy sword.

Name Guide

Courtesy Names

Courtesy names were a tradition reserved for the upper class and were typically granted at the age of twenty. While it was generally a male-exclusive tradition, there is historical precedent for women adopting courtesy names after marriage. It was furthermore considered disrespectful for peers of the same generation to address one another by their birth name, especially in formal or written communication. Instead, one's birth name was used by elders, close friends, and spouses.

This tradition is no longer practiced in modern China, but is commonly seen in wuxia and xianxia media. As such, many characters in these novels have more than one name in these stories, though the tradition is often treated malleably for the sake of storytelling. For example, in *Husky*, characters receive their courtesy names at the age of fifteen rather than twenty.

Diminutives, nicknames, and name tags

A-: Friendly diminutive. Always a prefix. Usually for monosyllabic names, or one syllable out of a two-syllable name.

DA-: A prefix meaning "eldest."

DOUBLING: Doubling a syllable of a person's name can be a nickname, i.e. "Mengmeng"; it has childish or cutesy connotations.

-ER: A word for "son" or "child." Added to a name, it expresses affection. Similar to calling someone "Little" or "Sonny." Always a suffix.

XIAO-: A diminutive meaning "little." Always a prefix.

Family

All of these terms can be used alone or with the person's name.

DI/DIDI: Younger brother or a younger male friend.

GE/GEGE: Older brother or an older male friend.

JIE/JIEJIE/ZIZI: Older sister or an older female friend; "zizi" is a regional variant of "jieije."

MEI/MEIMEI: Younger sister or a younger female friend.

Cultivation

-JUN: A term of respect, often used as a suffix after a title.

DAOZHANG/XIANJUN: Polite terms of address for cultivators, equivalent to "Mr. Cultivator." Can be used alone as a title or attached to someone's family name. Xianjun has an implication of immortality.

QIANBEI: A respectful title or suffix for someone older, more experienced, and/or more skilled in a particular discipline. Not to be used for blood relatives.

XIANZHU: "Immortal lord/leader." Used in *Husky* as a respectful title for Eighteen, the leader of Peach Blossom Springs.

ZONGSHI: A title or suffix for a person of particularly outstanding skill; largely only applied to cultivators in the story of *Husky*.

Cultivation Sects

SHIZUN: Teacher/master. For one's master in one's own sect. Gender neutral. Literal meaning is "honored/venerable master" and is a more respectful address, though Shifu is not disrespectful.

SHIXIONG/SHIGE: Older martial brother. For senior male members of one's own sect. Shige is a more familiar variant.

SHIJIE: Older martial sister. For senior female members of one's own sect.

SHIDI: Younger martial brother. For junior male members of one's own sect.

SHIMEI: Younger martial sister. For junior female members of one's own sect.

SHINIANG: Wife of shizun/shifu.

ZUNZHU: "Esteemed leader." Used to refer to the leader of a sect. Can be used on its own or appended to a family name, e.g., Xue-zunzhu.

Other

GONG/GONGGONG: A title or suffix. Can be used to refer to an elderly man, a man of high status, a grandfather, a father-in-law, or in a palace context, a eunuch.

GONGZI: Young master of an affluent household, or a polite way to address young men.

TAIZI: "Crown prince." A respectful title of address for the next in line to the throne.

YIFU: Person formally acknowledged as one's father; sometimes a "godfather."

Pronunciation Guide

Mandarin Chinese is the official state language of mainland China, and pinyin is the official system of romanization in which it is written. As Mandarin is a tonal language, pinyin uses diacritical marks (e.g., ā, á, ǎ, à) to indicate these tonal inflections. Most words use one of four tones, though some (as in "de" in the title below) are a neutral tone. Furthermore, regional variance can change the way native Chinese speakers pronounce the same word. For those reasons and more, please consider the guide below a simplified introduction to pronunciation of select character names and sounds from the world of *Husky*.

More resources are available at sevenseasdanmei.com

NAMES

Èrhā hé tā de bái māo shī zūn

Èr as in **uh**

Hā as in **har**dy

Hé as in **hurt**

Tā as in **tar**dy

De as in **di**rt

Bái as in **bye**

Māo as in **mou**th

Shī as in **shh**

Z as in **z**oom, ūn as in harp**oon**

Mò Rán

Mò as in **mo**ron

Rán as in **run**ning

Chǔ Wǎnníng

Chǔ as in **choo**se

Wǎn as in **wan**ting

Níng as in run**ning**

Xuē Méng

X as in the **s** in **s**ilk, uē as in **weh**

M as in the **m** in **m**other, é as in **uh**, **ng** as in so**ng**

Shī Mèi

Shī as in **shh**

Mèi as in **may**

GENERAL CONSONANTS

Some Mandarin Chinese consonants sound very similar, such as z/c/s and zh/ch/sh. Audio samples will provide the best opportunity to learn the difference between them.

X: somewhere between the **sh** in **sh**eep and **s** in **s**ilk

Q: a very aspirated **ch** as in **ch**arm

C: **ts** as in pan**ts**

Z: **z** as in **z**oom

S: **s** as in **s**ilk

CH: **ch** as in **ch**arm

ZH: **dg** as in do**dg**e

SH: **sh** as in **sh**ave

G: hard **g** as in **g**raphic

GENERAL VOWELS

The pronunciation of a vowel may depend on its preceding consonant. For example, the "i" in "shi" is distinct from the "i" in "di." Vowel pronunciation may also change depending on where the vowel appears in a word, for example the "i" in "shi" versus the "i" in "ting." Finally, compound vowels are often—though not always—pronounced as conjoined but separate vowels. You'll find a few of the trickier compounds below.

IU: as in **ewe**

IE: **ye** as in **yes**

UO: **war** as in **war**m

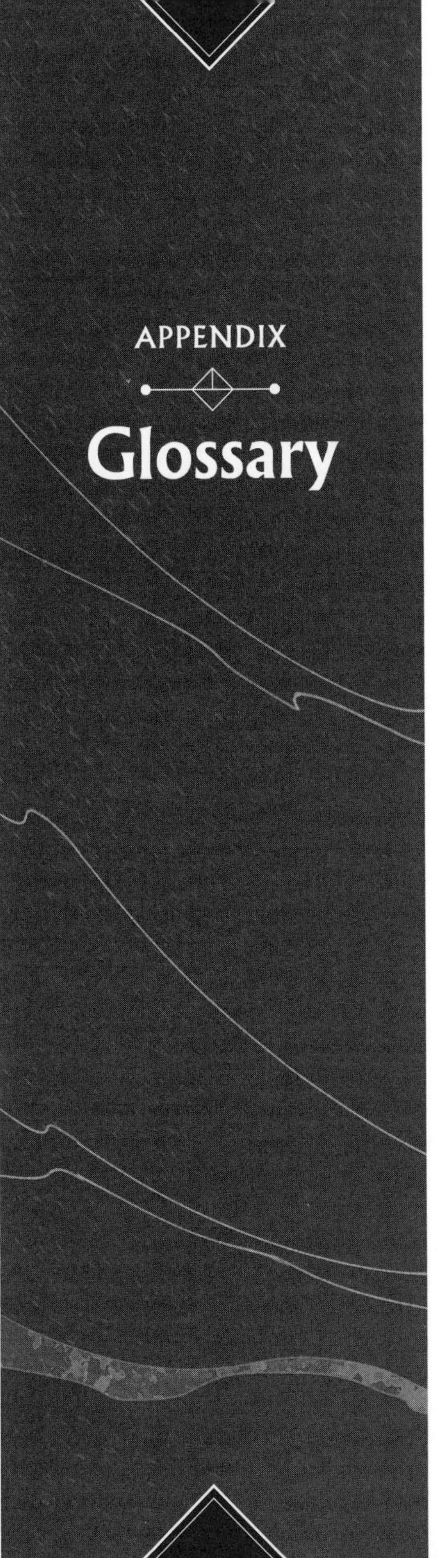

APPENDIX

Glossary

Glossary

While not required reading, this glossary is intended to offer further context for the many concepts and terms utilized throughout this novel as well as provide a starting point for learning more about the rich culture from which these stories were written.

GENRES

Danmei

Danmei (耽美 / "indulgence in beauty") is a Chinese fiction genre focused on romanticized tales of love and attraction between men. It is analogous to the BL (boys' love) genre in Japanese media and is better understood as a genre of plot than a genre of setting. For example, though many danmei novels feature wuxia or xianxia settings, others are better understood as tales of sci-fi, fantasy, or horror.

Wuxia

Wuxia (武侠 / "martial heroes") is one of the oldest Chinese literary genres and consists of tales of noble heroes fighting evil and injustice. It often follows martial artists, monks, or rogues who live apart from the ruling government, which is often seen as useless or corrupt. These societal outcasts—both voluntary and otherwise—settle disputes among themselves, adhering to their own moral codes over the law.

Characters in wuxia focus primarily on human concerns, such as political strife between factions and advancing their own personal sense of justice. True wuxia is low on magical or supernatural elements. To Western moviegoers, a well-known example is *Crouching Tiger, Hidden Dragon*.

Xianxia

Xianxia (仙侠 / "immortal heroes") is a genre related to wuxia that places more emphasis on the supernatural. Its characters often strive to become stronger, with the end goal of extending their lifespan or achieving immortality.

Xianxia heavily features Daoist themes, while cultivation and the pursuit of immortality are both genre requirements. If these are not the story's central focus, it is not xianxia. *Husky* is considered part of both the danmei and xianxia genres.

TERMINOLOGY

BARRIERS: A type of magical shield. In *Husky*, a barrier separates the mortal realm and the ghost realm, and Chu Wanning is noted to be especially skilled in creating barriers.

CLASSICAL CHINESE CHESS (WEIQI): Weiqi is the oldest known board game in human history. The board consists of a many-lined grid upon which opponents play unmarked black and white stones as game pieces to claim territory.

COLORS:

WHITE: Death, mourning, purity. Used in funerals for both deceased and the mourners.

RED: Happiness, good luck. Used for weddings.

PURPLE: Divinity and immortality; often associated with nobility, homosexuality (in the modern context), and demonkind (in the xianxia genre).

COURTESY NAMES: A courtesy name is given to an individual when they come of age. (*See Name Guide for more information.*)

CULTIVATION/CULTIVATORS: Cultivators are practitioners of spirituality and the martial arts. They seek to gain understanding of the will of the universe while also increasing personal strength and extending their lifespan.

CUT-SLEEVE: A term for a gay man. Comes from a tale about an emperor's love for, and relationship with, a male politician. The emperor was called to the morning assembly, but his lover was asleep on his robe. Rather than wake him, the emperor cut off his own sleeve.

DRAGON: Great beasts who wield power over the weather. Chinese dragons differ from their Western counterparts as they are often benevolent, bestowing blessings and granting luck. They are associated with the Heavens, the Emperor, and yang energy.

DUAL CULTIVATION: A cultivation technique involving sex between participants that is meant to improve cultivation prowess. Can also be used as a simple euphemism for sex.

EYES: Descriptions like "phoenix eyes" or "peach-blossom eyes" refer to eye shape. Phoenix eyes have an upturned sweep at their far corners, whereas peach-blossom eyes have a rounded upper lid and are often considered particularly alluring.

FACE: *Mianzi* (面子), generally translated as "face," is an important concept in Chinese society. It is a metaphor for a person's reputation and can be extended to further descriptive metaphors. For example, "having face" refers to having a good reputation and "losing face" refers to having one's reputation hurt. Meanwhile, "giving face" means deferring to someone else to help improve their reputation, while "not wanting face" implies that a person is acting so poorly/shamelessly that they clearly don't care about their reputation at all. "Thin face" refers to someone easily embarrassed or prone to offense at perceived slights. Conversely, "thick face" refers to someone not easily embarrassed and immune to insults.

FAE: Fae, *yao* (妖), refers to natural creatures, such as animals, plants, or even inanimate objects, who over time absorb spiritual energy and gain spiritual awareness to cultivate a human form. They are sometimes referred to as "demons" or "monsters," though they are not inherently evil. In *Husky*, faewolves (妖狼) are a rare and expensive breed of wolf. Similarly, the feathered tribe are beings who are half-immortal (仙) and half-fae.

THE FIVE ELEMENTS: Also known as the *wuxing* (五行 / "Five Phases") in Chinese philosophy: fire, water, wood, metal, earth. Each element corresponds to a planet: Mars, Mercury, Jupiter, Venus, and Saturn, respectively. In *Husky*, cultivators' spiritual cores correspond with one or two elements; for example, Chu Wanning's elements are metal and wood.

Fire (火 / huo)
Water (水 / shui)
Wood (木 / mu)
Metal (金 / jin)
Earth (土 / tu)

HAITANG: The *haitang* tree (海棠花), also known as crabapple or Chinese flowering apple, is endemic to China. The recurring motif for Chu Wanning is specifically the *xifu haitang* variety. In flower language, haitang symbolizes unrequited love.

INEDIA: A common ability that allows an immortal to survive without mortal food or sleep by sustaining themselves on purer forms of energy based on Daoist fasting. Depending on the setting, immortals who have achieved inedia may be unable to tolerate mortal food, or they may be able to choose to eat when desired. The cultivation taught by Sisheng Peak notably does not rely on this practice.

JADE: Jade is a culturally and spiritually important mineral in China. Its durability, beauty, and the ease with which it can be utilized for crafting decorative and functional pieces alike has made it widely beloved since ancient times. The word might evoke green jade (the mineral jadeite), but Chinese texts are often referring to white jade (the mineral nephrite), as when a person's skin is described as "the color of jade."

JIANGHU: A staple of wuxia, the jianghu (江湖, "rivers and lakes") describes an underground society of martial artists, monks, rogues, and artisans and merchants who settle disputes between themselves per their own moral codes.

LOTUS: This flower symbolizes purity of the heart and mind, as lotuses rise untainted from the muddy waters they grow in. It also signifies the holy seat of the Buddha.

MERIDIANS: The means by which qi travels through the body, like a magical bloodstream. Medical and combat techniques that focus on redirecting, manipulating, or halting qi circulation focus on targeting the meridians at specific points on the body, known as acupoints. Techniques that can manipulate or block qi prevent a cultivator from using magical techniques until the qi block is lifted.

MOE: A Japanese term referring to cuteness or vulnerability in a character that evokes a protective feeling from the reader. Originally applied largely to female characters, the term has since seen expanded use.

MYTHICAL FIGURES: Several entities from Chinese mythology make an appearance in the world of *Husky*, including:

FUXI: Emperor of the heavens, sometimes directly called Heavenly Emperor Fuxi. A figure associated with Chinese creation mythology.

VERMILION BIRD: The *Vermilion Bird* (朱雀上神) is one of four mythical beasts in Chinese constellations, representing the cardinal direction South, the element of fire, and the season of summer.

YANLUO: King of hell or the supreme judge of the underworld. His role in the underworld is to pass judgment on the dead, sending souls on to their next life depending on the karma they accrued from their last one.

PHOENIX: Fenghuang (凤凰 / "phoenix"), a legendary bird said to only appear in times of peace and to flee when a ruler is corrupt. They are heavily associated with femininity, the empress, and happy marriages.

PILLS AND ELIXIRS: Magic medicines that can heal wounds, improve cultivation, extend life, etc. In Chinese culture, these medicines are usually delivered in pill form, and the pills are created in special kilns.

PLEASURE HOUSE: Courtesans at these establishments provided entertainment of many types, ranging from song and dance to more intimate pleasures.

QI: *Qi* (气) is the energy in all living things. There is both righteous qi and evil or poisonous qi.

Cultivators strive to cultivate qi by absorbing it from the natural world and refining it within themselves to improve their cultivation base. A cultivation base refers to the amount of qi a cultivator possesses or is able to possess. In xianxia, natural locations such as caves, mountains, or other secluded places with beautiful scenery are often rich in qi, and practicing there can allow a cultivator to make rapid progress in their cultivation.

Cultivators and other qi manipulators can utilize their life force in a variety of ways, including imbuing objects with it to transform them into lethal weapons, or sending out blasts of energy to do damage. Cultivators also refine their senses beyond normal human levels. For instance, they may cast out their spiritual sense to gain total awareness of everything in a region around them or to sense potential danger.

QI CIRCULATION: The metabolic cycle of qi in the body, where it flows from the dantian to the meridians and back. This cycle purifies and refines qi, and good circulation is essential to cultivation. In xianxia, qi can be transferred from one person to another through physical contact, and it can heal someone who is wounded if the donor is trained in the art.

QI DEVIATION: A qi deviation (走火入魔 / "to catch fire and enter demonhood") occurs when one's cultivation base becomes unstable. Common causes include an unstable emotional state and/or strong negative emotions, practicing cultivation methods incorrectly, reckless use of forbidden or high-level arts, or succumbing to the influence of demons and evil spirits. When qi deviation arises from mental or emotional causes, the person is often said to have succumbed to their inner demons or "heart demons" (心魔).

Symptoms of qi deviation in fiction include panic, paranoia, sensory hallucinations, and death, whether by the qi deviation itself causing irreparable damage to the body or as a result of its symptoms—such as leaping to one's death to escape a hallucination. Common fictional treatments for qi deviation include relaxation (voluntary or forced by an external party), massage, meditation, or qi transfer from another individual.

QIANKUN POUCH: (乾坤囊/ "universe pouch") A pouch containing an extradimensional space within it, capable of holding more than the physical exterior dimensions of the pouch would suggest.

QINGGONG: Qinggong (轻功) is a cultivator's ability to move swiftly through the air as if on the wind.

RED THREAD OF FATE: The red thread imagery originates in legend and has become a Chinese symbol for fated love. An invisible red thread is said to be tied around the limb or finger of the two individuals destined to fall in love, forever linking them.

REIGNING YEARS: Chinese emperors took to naming the eras of their reign for the purpose of tracking historical records. The names often reflected political agendas or the current reality of the socioeconomic landscape.

SHIDI, SHIXIONG, SHIZUN, ETC: Chinese titles and terms used to indicate a person's role or rank in relation to the speaker. Because of the robust nature of this naming system, and a lack of nuance in translating many to English, the original titles have been maintained. *(See Name Guide for more information)*

SPIRITUAL CORE: A spiritual core (灵丹/灵核) is the foundation of a cultivator's power. It is typically formed only after ten years of hard work and study.

SPIRITUAL ROOT: In *Husky,* spiritual roots (灵根) are associated with a cultivator's innate talent and elemental affinities. Not every cultivator possesses spiritual roots.

THE THREE REALMS: Traditionally, the universe is divided into three realms: the **heavenly realm**, the **mortal realm**, and the **ghost realm**. The heavenly realm refers to the heavens and realm of the gods, where gods reside and rule; the mortal realm refers to the human world; and the ghost realm refers to the realm of the dead.

VINEGAR: To say someone is drinking vinegar or tasting vinegar means that they're having jealous or bitter feelings. Generally used for a love interest growing jealous while watching the main character receive the attention of a rival suitor.

WHITE MOONLIGHT: A romantic trope referring to a distant romantic paragon who is cherished in memory long after that person is gone. Like the moon in the sky, the memory is always present, perfect and unchanging, but like the pale light by one's bedside, it is an incorporeal shine that can only be admired, not touched. The object of admiration is out of reach, and the admiration is functionally one-way.

WILLOW TREE: Willow trees in Chinese culture have a plethora of meanings, including friendship, longing, femininity, and more. The Chinese word for willow (柳) is a homonym for the word "stay," which has led to it being featured in many poems and stories as a symbol of farewell and a reluctance to part.

YIN ENERGY AND YANG ENERGY: Yin and yang is a concept in Chinese philosophy which describes the complementary interdependence of opposite/contrary forces. It can be applied to all forms of change and differences. Yang represents the sun, masculinity, and the living, while yin represents the shadows, femininity, and the dead, including spirits and ghosts. In fiction, imbalances between yin and yang energy may do serious harm to the body or act as the driving force for malevolent spirits seeking to replenish themselves of whichever energy they lack.

ABOUT THE AUTHOR

Rou Bao Bu Chi Rou ("Meatbun Doesn't Eat Meat") was a disciple of Sisheng Peak under the Tanlang Elder and the official chronicler of daily life at Wushan Palace. Unable to deal [illegible] after Taxian-jun's suicide, Meatbun took Madam Wang's orange cat, Cai Bao ("Veggiebun"), and fled. Thereafter Meatbun traveled the world to see the sights, making ends meet by writing down all manner of secrets and little-known anecdotes of the cultivation world—which Meatbun had gathered during travel—and selling them on the street side.

NOTABLE WORKS:

"God-Knows-What Rankings"

Top of the Cultivation World Best-Sellers List for ten years straight.

"The Red Lotus Pavilion Decameron"

Banned by Sisheng Peak Sect Leader Xue and Yuheng Elder Chu Wanning; no longer available for sale.

[illegible]

No longer available for sale due to complaints filed by Yuheng Elder Chu Wanning.

[illegible]

2019 winner of the Ghost Realm's Annual Fuxi Roasting Writing Contest

Dumb

"The Husky & His White Cat Shizun"

Also being sold in another world.

...and others to come. Please look forward to them.